AN ANCIENT PROMISE

Will looked into Oonagh's eyes, then at the silent, deadly fire raging around him. Both Oonagh and Soutien had said that Mack and Aidan were in danger. What danger? And was Moira in danger, too? When he looked back down, the goblet was still there, steady in Oonagh's hand.

"It will not harm you," she said.

His head began to spin. Soutien, Oonagh, Fin Bheara—he was way out of his depth.

What danger did his brothers face?

Will took the goblet from her, startled at the cold touch of her fingers. He stared down at the clear golden liquid. It smelled sweet, like honey, but it looked like beer.

Oonagh. According to his father, she was "the most beautiful woman in two worlds, beloved wife of King Fin Bheara, to whom our family is beholden."

To whom our family is beholden.

Will took a deep breath, raised the goblet, and drank.

NOVELS BY MARCELLE DUBÉ

Mendenhall Mystery Series:
The Shoeless Kid
The Tuxedoed Man
The Weeping Woman
The Untethered Woman
The Forsaken Man
The Wronged Woman

A'lle Chronicles Series:
The A'lle Murders
The A'lle Mutation

Standalone:
Ghosts of Morocco
Identity Withheld
Jilimar
Kirwan's Son
Obeah
On Her Trail
Shelter

A Little Strangeness (collection)

KIRWAN'S SON

BY
MARCELLE DUBÉ

FALCON
RIDGE
PUBLISHING

For Emma and Isabelle
I'm pretty sure this isn't what they had in mind
when they asked for a story about fairies.

KIRWAN'S SON

Bretagne, 1717

WHEN he learned of the babe's existence, Amadan-na-Briona, eldest son of the eldest race, wildest child of the Fey, took on the countenance of the hated one and stepped sideways into the world of mortals.

As always, the transition left him momentarily disoriented. His bare feet sought the steadying comfort of grass and soil but found only stone. Then his assumed shape settled and he looked around quickly. He would retain Fin Bheara's shape for as long as his concentration held, and no longer.

Amadan had expected to find the woman asleep. Instead, she stood by the window of the dark room, her back to him, unaware of his arrival. She held the babe wrapped in a blanket and crooned softly to him as she swayed. Her white shift glowed in the moonlight.

The chamber was small and austere, with barely room for a narrow bed, a chair, and a small cradle. There were no carpets to warm the stone floor, no tapestries to ward off the night chill seeping through the window.

Amadan studied the woman's slender shape and the small bundle in her arms. Again he considered killing the child. The need to hurt Fin Bheara was a desperate thirst that the infant's death would slake.

But only temporarily, he reminded himself. And to kill a Fey babe when there were already so few... There was another way. It would take longer, but his vengeance would be that much sweeter for the wait.

Unaware of the stranger in her private quarters, Gisèle, Lady Kirwan, held her child to her breast and felt the night pressing in on her. The narrow bed stood empty and rumpled next to her, but it was the cradle upon which her gaze lingered. The abbess had hinted that hers was not the first noble child to be born at the convent.

She frowned, nose wrinkling at an unpleasant smell. Finally sensing Amadan's presence, she turned and saw him.

"You come like a lover in the dark," she said coldly, "when you have forfeited that right."

"Such treatment!" Amadan fought the impulse to revert to his own wild shape. She must not suspect that he was an impostor. "I claim the right to be here. I am the father of the child."

The woman smiled without mirth. "Another right you have forfeited. Surely you have other get strewn across the countryside—find another child to claim."

Amadan shook his head. "Nay, lady. No other get. Few babes are born to the Fey. This one is doubly precious for that."

Her anger rose fierce and hot all around her. "I care nothing for Fey problems! You seduced me with your Fey lies. Now I am exiled to a convent while my family seeks a husband for me. This child is mine, not yours."

"Lady," said Amadan gently, "already you have made plans to give the child away." Her eyes narrowed, though in anger or suspicion, he could not tell. The illusion was growing harder to maintain in the face of her scrutiny. "Let me have him. He is a halfling. He will never be happy in the world of humans."

Gisèle's chin rose sharply. "I will not have him in your world of glamours and magicks. Among humans he will be safer."

Amadan allowed the truth to weave a spell of persuasion around his words. "Lady, you know the fact of it. Among humans, he will be hated for his strangeness. Among the Fey, he will be cherished."

"Tricks," said the woman bitterly. "More words to deceive and seduce me. Leave or I shall raise the watch."

A sudden wild anger shook Amadan. He would take the child. If she resisted, he would kill her. He took a step toward her, struggling to retain the assumed shape. Sensing the danger, the woman stepped back, clutching the babe. The child woke and began to cry softly.

"One more step, my Fey lord, and I will raise a cry to heaven, a cry that will bring the Lady Oonagh to this very chamber!"

Amadan stopped, breathing hard. Oonagh. This woman did not know, could not know, of Amadan's love for Oonagh. She used the queen's name like a shield, like a threat.

It would not serve his purposes to have Oonagh discover this visit. He would have to kill the woman and take the child. He could move faster than the woman could scream.

Then another thought unfolded, stopping him. He stared unseeingly at the woman as the beauty of the inspiration revealed itself.

It was not necessary to have the child for himself. As long as the child was in the Fey world, Amadan would know where he was. And it did not matter who raised the child, as long as no one knew his birthright.

His awareness returned to the woman, startling in its intensity.

"Very well, Lady," he said softly. "Call upon Lady Oonagh. Give *her* the child. She will see to it that he is well cared for."

The woman stared at him in amazement.

"You wish me to ask your *wife* to find a home for your *son*?"

Amadan nodded. Then he stepped closer to her, so close that she pressed her back against the cold stone wall and clutched her crying child protectively.

"But know this, Lady. You *will* give the babe to the Lady Oonagh. I care not what lie you invent; however, do not tell her that the babe is yours and that I am the sire, else I will return. I will return to slay you and all those you hold dear. Do you believe me?"

Rage bloomed in her eyes, but so did fear. After a heartbeat, she nodded jerkily.

Amadan stepped away from her. So be it.

Without another look at the woman, he stepped sideways and returned to the Fey.

❧ ONE ❦

GROZNY, BOSNIA—OCTOBER 1996

THREE nights in a row, sleeping on the cold, stony ground of the Chechen rebel camp, Will dreamed of Soutien.

In his dreams, Soutien looked as wide and as wild as a hill, and his face wavered between his own and that of an animal.

Three nights in a row, Will woke with a start, heart hammering in fear, to lie in his sleeping bag, wondering why a man he had known all his life should now haunt his dreams.

On the fourth night, Will woke to find Josip standing over him.

"Come, Picture Man," said the young Chechen, grinning. "Today we fight!"

At last.

Will rolled out of his sleeping bag and stood up. The night was crisp with frost and he lost no time digging his extra socks and down vest out of his pack. "Where are we going?" He tied the sleeping bag onto his pack, and made sure his supply of film was within easy reach.

"The Russians try to reclaim Grozny," replied Josip, losing his grin. "We stop them."

A glance at the sky confirmed that morning was still hours off. The nearly full moon revealed a dozen figures moving quietly and purposefully around the camp. A small campfire filled the night air with wood smoke and the smell of coffee.

Officially, his assignment was to produce a photo essay of the Chechen rebels. For a week, he had done nothing but travel from camp to camp, take pictures of rebels looking grim, and drink bad vodka. The assignment didn't specify following the rebels into battle, but he knew from experience that the most arresting photographs would be where there was the greatest danger.

A fierce joy gripped him as he helped break camp. It started in the pit of his stomach, a humming that spread throughout his body until he felt electrified. No matter how often he felt it, it was always the same: excitement at the coming battle, followed by shame at his anticipation of it.

Was it the same for Moira, Aidan, and Mack? Of all his siblings, Moira—with her cool head and warrior instincts—was the best suited to military life. And she was too level-headed to get excited at the thought of being shot at. Not that she had ever been shot at. Of the four, only he—the only O'Rourke not in the military—had ever seen a real battlefield.

He stopped tightening the straps on his pack. He had accepted assignment after assignment in one hot spot after another. He told himself that he was working toward peace, just as Moira and the boys were, but he was uncomfortably aware of his eagerness, his willing-ness to go into battle, to be right in the thick of it.

Which was why he never carried a rifle.

As he packed, Josip told him that Russian sharpshooters were planning to infiltrate Grozny. If they succeeded, they could hold the Chechens off until the Russian tanks and troops arrived. Although Chechens held the city, they couldn't withstand an organized attack without reinforcements. The rebels were too few to fight tanks, but with help from Josip's rebel group, they could handle snipers. And if they could keep the snipers from holding key positions, the Russian troops would be unable to reclaim the city.

Will carried the camera around his neck in readiness. He stuffed his vest pockets full of spare film, made sure his waterproof notebook was in the same pocket as his pencils, and slipped his pack over his shoulders.

They finally arrived at the city's southern perimeter just as the first glow of dawn outlined Grozny's jagged skyline. They abandoned their vehicles to enter on foot, a silent swarm of grim men and women.

Will followed Josip through streets echoing in ghostly silence. Only the occasional whiff of food cooking, carried by the breeze, re-assured him that people still lived in the damaged city.

Josip jogged down the center of the streets, carrying a handheld missile launcher as easily as Will carried his camera case.

Heading for the presidential palace, they ran past homes de-stroyed by shells and fire, past still-standing houses with windows shuttered like tightly closed eyes. Will could almost smell the fear leaking though those shutters.

The sound of their footsteps bounced against the narrow canyons of the streets, and Will took to watching the roof line. Josip's inform-ants had said the snipers were coming late in the afternoon, but tips sometimes turned sour.

They reached the ruins of the presidential palace without meet-ing anyone and crawled in through a broken window, not trusting to a possibly mined doorway. The informant had warned that snipers would try to set up in the palace.

Once inside, Josip unslung the rifle from his shoulder and carried it in his free hand. With a mimed warning for silence, he led the way through the foyer.

Their passage stirred up a cloud of plaster dust, sending them both into sneezing fits that they muffled against their arms. Enough light filtered through to reveal the wreckage of what had once been an elegant building.

Will had once escorted the Canadian ambassador's daughter to a ball at the palace. Now the front doors—ten feet high, mahogany, intricately carved, and strapped with bands of etched brass—hung splintered and askew. The posts barricading them from the inside had snapped like matchsticks when a shell landed in the street ten feet from the doorway. Dust sifted through the broken windows, adding to the stifling atmosphere.

He took half a dozen shots of the doors in the early morning light, surprised by the sudden lump in his throat. How could he be sad for a pair of broken doors? They could be replaced. Nobody could replace the thousands of people who had died so far in this senseless war.

One final shot of the foyer and he turned away. Josip was already on the second floor landing. Will climbed the wide stairs, his steps echoing. The staircase had survived repeated shellings, although a coat of plaster dust and debris overlaid the fine marble and the mahogany banister. Only Josip's footsteps had disturbed the dust.

He tried not to think of the people huddling behind barricaded doors, terrified of the tanks and soldiers. Even if they wanted to escape, they couldn't. Shells had blown craters in most of the main routes out of Grozny. Those who were young enough and strong enough had already fled on foot. Only the elderly and the very young—and those who refused to leave them—remained.

The Pentax bumped against his chest, and he automatically wrapped a hand around it. His job was to take the pictures and get them out. Let the pictures goad the rest of the world into stopping this stupidity.

The atmosphere inside was hushed, as if the palace held its breath. Will shook off an irrational feeling that he and Josip were intruding on its grief.

When he reached the last landing, he discovered that it now extended the entire length of the third floor. What had been offices and meeting rooms was now one vast room whose damaged ceiling was held up by scarred cement posts. Blue sky peered at them through holes in the roof. Puddles of rainwater dotted the rubble-strewn floor.

At the far end of the room, Josip crouched by the missile launcher, loading it. Will recognized the weapon as a Cyclone. The rebels liked it because they could use it without body armor.

"Ah, Picture Man!" cried Josip, his grin startlingly white. "No one here but us turkeys!"

Will grinned back, as much in relief as in amusement at Josip's mangling of the expression. He put the Pentax to his eye, adjusted the zoom and focus, and captured Josip's smile. Then he turned and snapped a shot of the room.

The morning light seeping through the roof and the broken windows was perfect. Will moved around the room, disturbing dust and obscuring Josip's expression. Within minutes, the room had a strange, twilight quality at odds with the bright sunlight.

The young rebel finished loading the missile launcher and stood up. He swung the heavy weapon up to his shoulder, bracing himself against the recoil. He stood straight, his legs apart for balance.

Will stared at him. What was he doing? After a few seconds, Josip, without breaking his pose, glanced over at him.

"Well, Picture Man? Will I not make perfect cover for your magazine?"

Will laughed and took the picture.

As he lowered the camera, a distant growling caught his attention. The two men glanced at each other then Will looked out the ragged opening that had once been a window, past Josip's shoulder, over the rooftops. A convoy of armored trucks and tanks snaked its way down the broad, shell-pocked main avenue of Grozny.

Jesus. Will ran to the window in the south wall. More uniformed troops marched down the crater-filled main crossroads.

And in the distance but coming nearer, he heard the telltale *whup-whup* of a helicopter.

A trap.

Will snapped a shot of the approaching convoy, then turned back to Josip. The young rebel hadn't stirred.

"Let's get out of here."

Josip didn't answer, didn't move. Will took three quick steps toward the young man before noticing the sudden, eerie silence.

His scalp crawling, he reached for the young man.

"Josip?"

"He cannot hear you," said a calm voice behind him. Will whirled around and reached for the knife at his side. Something was wrong with Josip. He would have to defend them both. Then he recognized the figure standing before him.

"Soutien?" The dream flashed into his memory—Soutien strange and frightening, his shape shifting from human to animal. But this was no monster—this was Soutien, friend, business manager, caretaker for his family for as long as he could remember.

"Why are you here?"

Soutien's normally smiling face wore an unfamiliar expression. He examined Will as if he had never seen him before.

"What's wrong?" asked Will. He suddenly remembered Josip and turned back to the rebel. The young man still hadn't moved. Outside the window, the line of trucks had stopped. Will stared at the black exhaust hanging suspended in midair around each vehicle.

"Jesus Christ," he whispered. "What the hell is going on?"

"You must go to King Fin Bheara," said Soutien. "He has need of you."

"What...?" Will turned to stare at Soutien, trying to make sense of what was happening. How had Soutien tracked him down? "Fin Bheara?" What did his father's fairy tales have to do with Soutien's presence here?

"Go," repeated Soutien. "Your brothers are in danger."

And as Will watched, Soutien turned, stepped sideways, and disappeared.

Before Will could do more than gulp, the palace exhaled, Josip launched his missile, and an incoming shell landed on the roof. The explosion knocked Will against a concrete post, stunning him. By the time he shook himself into alertness, the palace was full of smoke. He found the camera still in his hand and stuffed it in its case. It took five precious minutes to dig through the rubble only to find the young Chechen with a jagged piece of wood in his throat.

"Josip!" The word barely left his lips when another high whistle announced an incoming shell. He instinctively ducked, folding his body around the Pentax and wrapping his arms over his head. Hopefully the backpack would take the brunt of any impact.

The explosion lifted him from the floor. He landed in rubble amid a rain of sharp fragments and hit his head.

He came to moments—or hours—later to the feel of a cool, soft hand on his forehead. His ears rang from the explosion and the faint smell of cordite stung his nose. He opened eyes gritty with dust, aware that there was something urgent he had to do, if he could just remember what it was.

When he could finally see again, he found a woman staring down at him. She knelt by his side, her long, golden-red hair falling like a curtain around her face. She made no effort to push it out of the way.

"You are safe." Her voice soothed his aching head. He looked closer, noticing for the first time the long, old-fashioned dress she wore and how it left her shoulders bare. It didn't look Chechen. Her green eyes smiled into his, reassuring him before he could even worry.

"Who're you?" asked Will. Even as he spoke, he remembered Josip, and then Soutien.

What the hell was going on?

"Drink," said the woman, pressing a goblet against his lips.

Will turned his head away and reached a hand to his scalp. It came away bloody. How badly was he hurt? Enough to hallucinate?

He pushed the goblet away and sat up. Only then did he realize he wasn't wearing his backpack. The destroyed room spun wildly for a moment, then righted itself.

Josip's body lay sprawled in death a few feet away. All around Will, smoke billowed and flames licked silently at the remaining walls of the palace. None of the flames touched the small pocket surrounding him and the strange woman. He sniffed. Aside from the lingering smell of cordite, the air he breathed was clean.

He turned back to her, his head starting to clear.

"Who are you?" he asked again. "What's going on?"

The woman smiled and sat back on her heels, cupping the goblet in the palms of her hands. It was made of what looked like pewter, with designs engraved in the metal. He looked up at her, noticing the creaminess of her skin, the clear green eyes, the full red mouth.

"I am Oonagh," she said, and Will's sense of reality slipped another notch. Oonagh... Oonagh had been the wife of Fin Bheara. And Soutien had told him, just before the shell hit, that Fin Bheara needed him.

"And you are William, son of Kirwan," she continued.

Son of Kirwan. Kirwan was the name of his home back in Canada, not his father. His great-great-grandfather had named their Gravenhurst, Ontario, home in honor of their distant ancestors.

"What do you want?" he demanded. He suddenly felt as if he had stepped into what he'd thought was a shallow puddle, only to find water closing over his head.

"I know you do not understand," said Oonagh softly, holding the goblet out to him again. "But I call upon the oath your ancestor made to Fin Bheara. Drink deeply and go to my lord, William, son of Kirwan. Fin Bheara needs you, as do your brothers."

Will looked into her eyes, then at the silent, deadly fire raging around him. Both Oonagh and Soutien had said Mack and Aidan were in danger. What danger? And was Moira in danger, too? When he looked back down, the goblet was still there, steady in her hand.

"It will not harm you."

His head began to spin. Soutien, Oonagh, Fin Bheara—he was way out of his depth.

What danger did his brothers face?

Will took the goblet from her, startled at the cold touch of her fingers. He stared down at the clear golden liquid. It smelled sweet, like honey, but it looked like beer.

Oonagh. According to his father, she was "the most beautiful woman in two worlds, beloved wife of King Fin Bheara, to whom our family is beholden."

To whom our family is beholden.

Will took a deep breath, raised the goblet, and drank.

Oonagh smiled and took the goblet from him. Her icy fingers traced a quick pattern on his eyelids and suddenly a great wind rushed through him, taking his breath away and knocking him flat. When he opened his eyes again, she was gone, as was the destroyed presidential palace. He lay on a green hill dotted with wildflowers under an achingly blue sky. He scrambled to his feet, surprised that he felt so good. His backpack rested by his feet, but not his camera case. He would miss the Pentax, but worse was losing the film it contained. At least he still had the small camera in his pack.

All around him, as far as he could see, spread a forest. To the south, a thin sliver of river glittered through the trees.

He turned a full circle, examining the closest trees carefully. When he spotted the blazed tree, he grinned.

"I'll be damned." Mack had been here. Will shrugged the pack onto his shoulders and set off downhill, toward the marked tree. The familiar excitement thrummed through him. As he walked, a soft voice whispered in his ear.

"Beware, son of Kirwan. See with your heart, not with your eyes."

But it might have been the wind.

❧ TWO ❧

MOIRA O'Rourke ran up the oak staircase in the center of the foyer two steps at a time, leaving melted snow in her wake. The snowstorm had delayed her return to Kirwan by three anxious hours. She hadn't even removed her parka or her boots, rushing inside as soon as she arrived.

"Mack!" She paused to listen for a moment, then swept through each room on the upper level, flinging open doors and flicking on lights. "Aidan! Mack!"

Her brothers weren't in any of the dozen rooms upstairs. She ran back down the stairs and into the kitchen. Gleaming metal appliances and marble countertops, spotless tile floor. Mildewed bread, soured milk. Nobody had been here in a while.

Sitting room, dining room, sewing room, music room—all empty.

Moira slowly returned to the foyer and, avoiding the puddles, sat down on the polished steps.

Mack and Aidan had left the same, pre-arranged message on her voice mail: "I'm going walkabout, Moira." She had no idea what had happened to make her two older brothers leave, but at least Will was safe.

Moira stifled a hysterical laugh. Will was safe, all right. He was only in war-torn Chechnya. Despite leaving messages on his home and work telephones, she'd been unable to reach him.

He would understand why she couldn't wait for him. Mack and Aidan might need her help right now—not whenever she and Will connected and got around to it.

Maybe she was already too late. She had been in the field for the last two weeks training with Military Intelligence. If she hadn't accompanied an injured soldier back to camp, she would still be in the field, unaware that her brothers were gone. Mack's voice mail had come first, dated the Sunday after she left. Then Aidan's, four days later.

Moira hid her face in her hands. She had thought Dad's stories were just that—bedtime stories his father had told him. She and her brothers had loved them, devised games based on them, pretended they had to defend the king, their friend. It had been Mack's idea to work out a signal, in case one of them was ever called away to the Fey world. But they had only been playing...

Mack's wife said that he was on exercise somewhere in Alberta. Aidan's roommate had no idea where he was. On leave, he said.

Was this a bizarre joke? She had requested permission from her commanding officer for emergency leave and driven all day and into the evening, the last part of it in a blinding snowstorm, to get here. If this was a joke, it wasn't very funny.

Standing up, she went to the Army-issue backpack she had left in the foyer. It was still damp from the trip from the carriage house, where she had left the car. Puddles had formed on the floor around it. She shrugged out of her heavy parka and hung it on the newel post. She had everything she needed in the pack. Hoisting it by one strap, she hooked it over her shoulder and walked to the doors across the foyer from the sitting room. They opened at a touch and at once the faint, expectant smell of damp soil and greenery wafted to her.

Not giving herself a chance to hesitate, she flicked on the lights and closed the doors behind her. The leather loveseat and matching club chair, the cherrywood desk and its spindly-legged chair, the faded Aubusson rug, the floor-to-ceiling bookshelves, the fireplace, all looked normal. Directly in front of her, damask curtains obscured the French doors leading to the patio. The fabric pooled onto the hardwood floor in annoying overabundance, a fashion her mother had adopted in the year before she and Dad died.

Not a plant in sight.

For the first time, Moira wondered about Soutien. He was always there to greet her whenever she returned home. Maybe he went with Mack and Aidan. Maybe she should worry about him, too.

She shook herself. Soutien was the most capable man she knew. She hoped he *was* with her brothers.

Moira strode across the carpet in her hiking boots and stood for a few moments in front of the south wall bookshelf. Her father had been a military man and his love of order carried over to alphabetizing his book collection. Within seconds, she spotted the right book.

It was too high. She shrugged off the backpack and set it on the desk chair. Then she looked around for the rolling stepladder. It was in the far corner, by the fireplace. She brought it over, climbed up its four steps, and brought down *The Vanishing People*.

Outside, the wind picked up as the storm worsened. Something banged against the south wall of the house. She noted it but didn't waste time checking it out. Then, as she was carrying the book back to the desk, the lights went out.

"Bloody hell!" She waited in vain for her eyes to adjust, but the study was as dark as a cave. She felt her way to the desk and found the shallow central drawer. Her father had always kept matches there.

She should have expected the blackout. The township hadn't gotten around to replacing the ancient power grid yet, and every heavy snowfall brought a power outage. Her father, ever prepared, had insisted on keeping candles and oil lamps in every room.

She finally found the matches and struck one. The candles were on the mantle. She brought the silver candlesticks to the desk and sat down. Only then did she notice her hands trembling.

To her surprise, a yellow, brittle slip of paper was pasted to the inside back cover of the book. She had never seen it before, even though she had pulled down the book many times over the years.

The paper was much older than the book. The spidery writing on it was so faded she could barely make it out.

As children, they had made up their own rhymes, since Dad had refused to tell them the real one.

"When the time comes," he had told them, "look in the book. It'll be there."

The wind howled, sounding like a banshee trying to break in. She slowly deciphered the words.

> *Neither friend nor foe,*
> *Yet are Kirwan and Fin Bheara linked.*
> *And should the call arise,*
> *So again shall the son of Kirwan*
> *Ride with Fin Bheara.*

Feeling foolish, she read the verse out loud three times, as her father had instructed. As she spoke the last words, she looked up, startled at the muffled sound of breaking glass. The curtains suddenly billowed out as the patio doors opened onto the study. The wind howled in, scampering around the room like a mad creature. Then a ghostly figure parted the curtains and entered, bringing with it a chilling cold.

Moira stood up, her heart banging against her ribs. She hooked an arm through her backpack strap and hauled it onto the desk in front of her. She just had time to pull out the knife in the side pocket when the candles flickered out. The room disappeared in a swirl of snow-flavored darkness.

"Hello?" said the figure uncertainly.

Before Moira could reply, the backpack tugged her off balance and she dropped to the leaf-covered ground of a forest.

***

Grace landed in a heap, too startled to cry out. Her hands broke the fall, and it took a moment to realize that they were clutching twigs and soil, not carpet.

"What...?" she said, looking up and around. Against a starry sky, a canopy of leaves fluttered in the breeze. She sat up. "This is a forest," she said wonderingly.

"Grace?" came Moira's voice in the dark. "Is that you?"

Grace looked over her shoulder. A huddled black mass suddenly rose to Moira height.

"Where are we?" asked Grace. Her fingers dug frantically through the loam, searching for the carpet beneath. "Where's your house?"

Moira dusted herself off and straightened. "I don't think we're anywhere near my house."

"What happened?" demanded Grace, rising in turn. "How did we get here?" She took a deep breath of damp, leafy forest. It smelled like a summer night. Somewhere nearby a cricket played accompaniment to a bullfrog. What had happened to the blizzard?

"Just relax," said Moira. "It won't do any good to panic."

A familiar frustration welled up in Grace, momentarily displacing the sense of unreality that threatened to overwhelm her. Moira was as patronizing as ever.

"Excuse me?" she said. "I am not panicking." Her eyes adjusted to the darkness and she made out the pale oval of Moira's face. "Although I would have every reason to." Were those wild roses she smelled? How did she end up in summer? Her feet were still cold from clambering through snow banks and her pant legs were wet from melting snow. "Just tell me where we are and how we got here."

"You should have stayed in your fabric shop," muttered Moira.

Grace clamped her teeth over a reply. All things considered, she wished she *had* stayed in her shop. She reached for the nearest tree. It was rough and barky, definitely a tree. A pine tree, by the smell of it. She looked around again now that she could see a bit more. The only light came from the stars. She couldn't hear any cars, or smell anything other than pine and—what was that? Sage? They were obviously nowhere near civilization. How did she get from Moira's house, in the middle of a blizzard, to this place?

A sudden suspicion replaced her growing anxiety. Moira didn't seem worried. Or even surprised.

"Moira Siobhan O'Rourke, what have you done?"

"You know, Grace," Moira pointed out, "nobody invited you along."

"Fine!" said Grace sharply. "Just point me to the exit and I'll leave!"

There was a long silence. Finally Moira spoke. "Why were you breaking into the house, anyway?"

For the first time, Grace thought she detected a hint of anxiety in the other woman's voice.

Grace blew out her irritation in a gusty breath. "My car broke down by your place. I was on my way to visit my folks."

"In the middle of a snowstorm?"

"It wasn't that bad when I left!"

"Well, did you have to break the window? You couldn't use the front door?"

"I tried!" protested Grace. "I rang and knocked—then all the lights went out."

Grace abruptly closed her mouth. Well, now, wasn't that a neat little bit of misdirection? Moira didn't want to answer questions, so she tried putting Grace on the defensive.

She had trudged up the road for nearly half an hour in the blizzard before finding the entrance to the O'Rourke driveway. She hadn't set out to go to Moira's house—she would rather have gone anywhere else—but houses on the country road were a quarter of a mile apart. It was Kirwan or hypothermia.

She hadn't expected anyone to be there. Since Moira's parents died, the O'Rourke children seldom made it back home.

Maybe she had fallen on her trek up that endless driveway. Maybe she had banged her head. Were hallucinations a part of freezing to death?

But if she had to hallucinate, did it have to be about Moira?

Her parka was too warm. She unbuttoned it and pushed the hood back. Her hands came away wet. The snow on the parka was melting. For a hallucination, it certainly felt real.

"Moira, this isn't funny. Where are we?"

Moira sighed. "You'll have to stay the night, anyway. Help me set up camp."

Anger struggled for a toehold against Grace's bewilderment. "You want to camp." For the first time, she noticed the backpack hanging from Moira's hand. "You came prepared? You planned to come here?" Then, something else occurred to her. "Is this some kind of military exercise?"

"Oh, for crying out loud," said Moira, "don't get your feathers in a ruffle, Gracie. Everything's under control. I'm sorry you got pulled into this, but if you hadn't broken in, you wouldn't be here now."

Grace tried to keep her tone even. "There was a blizzard, as you may recall. I didn't particularly want to see you, either." The perfume of night flowers drifted over her again, heightening the unreality of her situation.

Moira shrugged. "Lousy timing," she said. "Here, help me set this up."

Grace glanced down and saw that Moira was holding a long, narrow cylinder. "What is it?"

"A tent," said Moira.

Grace took a deep breath. "Moira, I don't want to be here. I want to go back home."

"Sorry," said Moira, pulling collapsible fiberglass poles out of the bag. "I only know how to get here. I don't know how to get back."

Damn the woman. "Could you please stop?" said Grace. "Moira!" When Moira ignored her in favor of pulling out tent parts, Grace lost patience. She pulled off her parka and flung the wet mass at the other woman.

"Hey!" came Moira's muffled voice from under the heavy coat. She pushed it aside and stood up. "Why'd you do that?"

"To get your attention," said Grace. "Stop acting like a jerk and talk to me." For the first time, she noticed Moira's stance—feet apart, knees slightly bent, arms held out in front of her—and remembered that Moira had studied several martial arts since she had joined the Army.

Then Grace realized that she was no longer the focus of Moira's attention. In the sudden silence, she heard something moving stealthily in the trees behind her.

She turned slowly, but all she saw were shadowy tree trunks. A breeze ruffled her hair, sending shivers chasing each other down her spine. An odd scent reached her and she wrinkled her nose in distaste. Pungent. After a moment, crickets picked up where they had left off. A bullfrog croaked. Another replied. Then an owl hooted and Grace understood that whatever had been out there was gone now.

She glanced back at Moira in time to see her slip something into the cargo pocket on the side of her pant leg. It gleamed dully, and with a sinking feeling, Grace recognized it as a knife.

❧ THREE ❦

LONG garlands of holly leaves and white freesias adorned the Great Hall, the perfume of the blossoms vying with the clean smell of the rush-strewn floor.

Musicians wandered through the crowd, playing fiddles and lutes. The music could barely be heard above the laughter and conversation of the assembled Fey. Soutien thought he heard the plaintive twang of a jaw harp, but didn't bother looking for the player.

He walked down the center of the hall. At the far end, past the pink-tinged marble columns, past the dozens of tables heaped with breads, fruits, cheeses, and fanciful glass bottles filled with wine, past the richly clad Fey—past all these awaited Fin Bheara.

The king sat alone on his stone throne, back straight, fierce black eyes watching Soutien's approach. The large, hooked nose seemed sharper, the mouth below it thinner. Fin Bheara wore black, not to honor his beloved queen's memory, but because he always wore black.

On a small table next to his throne rested a marble chess set, the pieces set up for play to begin.

Above, the night called down through the missing roof, cool and murmuring. The stars glowed pale against the torchlit hall.

As Soutien approached, the Fey nearest him fell silent and bowed. Soutien kept his face impassive, uncomfortable with the attention.

The Fey celebrated Oonagh's crossing with febrile gaiety, as though these were the old days and crossing over meant the end of a long, productive life. In every gaze he met, however, he found an ineffable sadness.

"Soutien," said the king. "What news?"

Soutien bowed low to his lord, observing the protocols even through the king was willing to forego them. At his back, the feast resumed, the noise level rising to cover their speech.

"My lord," he said. "They are gone."

Fin Bheara frowned. "Both of them? Where are they?"

"Here," said Soutien grimly. "Somewhere here."

The king remained silent for a moment. Then, "Amadan knows of our plan."

Soutien nodded. "Yes, my lord. It seems so."

"What of the youngest son?"

"In a war, my lord. I will continue to look for him."

"You must find Kirwan's sons, Soutien. Look for the youngest one." Then, looking away, "Do not let Amadan have them."

"I will find them, my lord." And Soutien dropped his gaze, too, unwilling to let his lord see his sorrow.

A rush of grief nearly choked him as the memory surged anew. He had tried to warn the king, tried for nearly a century. It had taken Oonagh's death for Fin Bheara to finally accept his duty.

He closed his eyes, as if that would save him from the bitter memory of that day.

The white castle and rook had Soutien's black queen pinned down. Across from him, sitting in a plain wooden chair polished smooth through centuries of use, King Fin Bheara waited silently, a satisfied smile on his lips.

Sunlight flooded in through the missing roof, warming Soutien's face and limning the king's hair in gold. Fin Bheara refused to endure a roof over his head and the study, like the Great Hall, lay open to the elements. It was Soutien's favorite room in Knockma.

With the sun warm on him and his lord happy before him, it would be so easy to believe that all was well.

"Well, lad?" Fin Bheara's voice rumbled through suppressed amusement. Like his hair, Fin Bheara's brows and beard had paled over the centuries from the fiery red of his youth to a fine, mellow copper. His heavy brows still retained their power to intimidate, especially when he frowned. Now, however, he only sat back in his chair and eyed Soutien expectantly.

With a sigh, Soutien tipped his black king over. It would take more time than he had to beat his lord at this game.

Fin Bheara's laughter boomed through the study. All of Knockma was built of stone, but only here did the ancient keep expose its gray bones. Here Fin Bheara scorned the use of tapestries and rugs; only sunlight softened the bleak strength of the room.

"A wise move, my boy," said the king, setting up the board again. Soutien studied him for a moment more, then took a deep, silent breath. Now that he had won, the king might listen to Soutien's arguments.

"My lord." His voice came out harsher than he had planned, and Fin Bheara glanced up from under a frown.

"Yes, boy?"

Soutien ignored the warning in the king's voice. "My lord, another Fey has crossed over."

Fin Bheara did not flinch, but Soutien felt each word strike his lord like a blow.

"Who?"

"Sarras."

Now Fin Bheara's eyes closed briefly. Sarras had been a friend.

"When?"

"Two days ago."

"Why was I not told?"

Because you close your ears and eyes to your people's needs, thought Soutien grimly. *Because you choose to believe that all is well when it is not. Because you have lost your way.*

"I learned of his passing today, my lord."

The king nodded and resumed setting up the board. Soutien watched in growing bewilderment. That was it? One of his last friends was dead, or at least gone from the realm of the Fey in the most permanent way open to him—and Fin Bheara played on?

"My lord," Soutien said sharply. "Is it not time?" The Fey could not survive many more losses.

"Enough, boy!" Fin Bheara's fist closed around a marble rook. "I will decide when the time is right. Are you so anxious for my death?"

The cruelty of the question took Soutien's breath away. Anxious? No, he wasn't anxious—he dreaded what the king must do. But it had to be done or the Fey would be lost. All would be lost.

Before Soutien could answer, Fin Bheara looked past him. From the way the king's gaze went unerringly to the door, Soutien knew that Oonagh had arrived.

Soutien rose from his chair and turned to greet his queen.

Oonagh stood in the doorway, her arms full of small, white wild-flowers. Although she smiled at Soutien, her gaze sought out her husband's. She did not smile at Fin Bheara—they had not smiled at each other in a century—but her face softened. The green of her gold-threaded gown picked up the hue of her eyes. Her pale hair fell in curls down her back, held away from her face by a simple gold circlet.

Soutien glanced at his lord. Although he could not seem to take his gaze from Oonagh's face, Fin Bheara's stern expression spoke of the escalating tension between husband and wife.

Oonagh approached, her slippered feet peeking beneath the embroidered hem of her gown. The scent of flowers preceded her, as if she walked in summer.

"My lord."

Soutien offered his arm but she shook her head. He stepped back, unable to keep from staring. He had never seen that particular expression on her face—sorrow and love mixed with determination.

"Have you come to badger me, too, woman?" asked Fin Bheara gruffly.

Sudden anger threatened to overwhelm Soutien. Badgering? Was that how the king thought of Soutien's appeal to save the Fey? Oonagh understood it was time to reunite the Fey and humanity before both died. Why couldn't the king? Had age so weakened his resolve? Was he so greedy for life?

Almost at once, grief swamped the anger. He couldn't ask the king to die. How could the Fey survive without Fin Bheara?

"No, my beloved husband," said Oonagh. For the first time, Soutien noticed tears in her eyes. "I will not badger you, nor again ask you to do what must be done."

Soutien took a step toward her, suddenly alarmed. Fin Bheara also rose from his seat, frowning. "What do you mean?" he demanded. He reached for her, but she put up a staying hand, spilling flowers to the floor.

"Husband," said Oonagh softly. "I cannot force you to do what is necessary. But I can no longer witness the slow death of all I hold dear."

"Oonagh." Fin Bheara stared at his wife, fear slowly blooming in his eyes. "What will you do?"

She smiled sadly at her king. "I will follow Sarras."

"No!" cried Fin Bheara, gripping her arm. More wildflowers escaped to drift to the stone floor.

Oonagh did not attempt to free herself. "I can no longer indulge you, beloved, or watch you betray yourself and the Fey. I will not be a part of it."

"I forbid it!" said Fin Bheara. He clutched both her arms and faced her, with only the flowers between them.

"This you cannot forbid me, my love," whispered Oonagh, tears spilling over. "This one thing you have no dominion over." She took a deep breath and stepped away from her husband, forcing him to release her. More wildflowers dropped from her clasp to fall at her feet.

"Soutien." She turned finally to him and placed a warm hand on his cheek. "Dearest boy." Her fingers stroked his skin.

Then she stepped back and with a swift, graceful movement, tossed the remaining wildflowers into the air. At once they burst into flight. Dozens of doves swooped and swirled, surrounding Oonagh in a flurry of white, filling the air with the sound of their beating wings. As one, they swept through the room, the great rush of air from their passage stirring Soutien's hair.

Fin Bheara stood like a stone pillar as the cloud of doves rose through the air, carrying Oonagh reverently on a bier of birds.

"My lady!" Soutien's cry of grief wrenched from his heart. But the queen was lost to them. Soutien followed with his gaze, watching helplessly as the doves disappeared into the blue sky. Finally, the dreadful silence called him back, and he looked down to see Fin Bheara kneeling amid the wildflowers on the stone floor of Knockma, his back to Soutien, his shoulders shaking.

Was it truly only days ago that they had lost her? The gauntness in the king's cheeks told Soutien it was so, as did the false revelry behind him. She was gone. His queen was gone.

And now, when it was perhaps too late, Fin Bheara finally acted. "I will send you what help I can, boy."

Soutien nodded again. They both knew the king's reach was limited, trapped as he was in Knockma. The king might be able to send help indirectly, but Soutien couldn't count on it. He would have to find Mac, Aidan, and Will on his own, before Amadan did, and bring them to Knockma.

First, he would find Will and bring him to safety.

Without another word to his lord, he left the Great Hall and its music to stand alone in the king's study. The perfume of Oonagh's wildflowers still lingered in the room. Or perhaps that was his imagination.

He closed his eyes, stilled his thoughts, and crossed the threshold, leaving behind the king's deserted chambers for his bedroom at Kirwan. He opened his eyes to darkness, the smell of the spell clinging to him. He murmured a word and the light turned on. His bedroom was exactly as he had left it, with the bed precisely made, the curtains drawn, and the door locked.

The room was on the main floor of the mansion, at the back near the kitchen. It was small and had originally been part of the servants' quarters. Soutien almost smiled. In a way, it still was.

Before he left the room, he paused to change his clothing—dark gray slacks, black woolen pullover over a white turtleneck, black calfskin boots. It would do.

The moment the door opened onto the lighted kitchen, he knew someone had been in the house. He stood quietly for a long moment, listening. A ghostly perfume teased his senses. Finally he returned to the hallway, heading for the back stairs. The lights were on everywhere upstairs. Someone had been searching.

As he came down the main stairs into the foyer, he spotted the parka hung over the newel post. He stopped, mid-step, and stared at it. A green Army parka, too small for a man.

Moira.

He ran down the last few steps and lifted the parka off the post. It was damp. Bringing it up to his face, he took a deep breath. It smelled of gasoline and wet fur and, faintly, of Moira's perfume. With an experienced eye, he examined the marble floor, noting where something had left puddles, which had then dried. Finally, he turned to the study. The doors were closed.

The scent of magic filled his nostrils as soon as he opened the doors. A drift of snow had formed on the hardwood floor in front of the open French doors and the room was freezing cold. He walked across the carpet to close the doors, absently noting the broken glass glittering in the snow on the floor like miniature icebergs. He didn't need to see the open book on the desk to know he was too late.

❧ FOUR ❦

WILL squatted on the grassy bank of the stream and examined the running water. It gurgled in eddies and whirlpools, filling the morning with song. The birch trees on either bank cast dappled shadows over the rocks lining the stream bed. He squinted into the glare and saw a long silvery shape hovering in a deeper pool. Trout. His mouth watered, but he made no move to pull the fishing line and hook from his backpack. There would be time enough for fishing once he found Mack and Aidan.

He raised his gaze past the stream to the trees beyond. On the trunk of a maple, he found what he was looking for—a blaze at a standing man's eye level. Mack had been the best among them at tracking, but he had been good at marking a trail, too. Aidan wouldn't have marked the trail. He wouldn't have expected Will to follow him.

Will stood up, the pack riding comfortably on his shoulders and hips. It was battered, having survived two Balkan wars, a Rwandan peacekeeping mission, and several armed "incidents" in Eastern Europe. His camera bag, with its professional cameras, lenses, and tape recorder, was probably buried under the rubble of the presidential palace. He rued the loss of the film, but everything else could be replaced. His pack contained everything he needed for survival in the field—compass, food, sleeping bag, knife. And his spare camera.

Boulders of different sizes dotted the stream. He could cross without getting his boots wet. Nice change. Stepping off the low bank, he tentatively set foot on the nearest boulder. When it didn't budge, he moved to the next one. The second to last one rolled as he stepped off and he jumped for the last boulder. He heard a splash behind him and automatically glanced back. Squinting in the glare of the morning sun, he made out something gray and sleek just under the surface of the water.

"Jesus Christ!"

It was a woman. She flipped over, revealing small, conical breasts. Floating on her back, she slowly rose to the surface, great round eyes staring at him. Her hair looked green under the water and drifted like a halo around her head. Will balanced on the last boulder, held there by astonishment. Had she been following him? Had she fallen in?

He crouched, holding out a hand. But the hand she lifted out of the water was tipped with claws and as her head broke the surface, her mouth split in a wide smile, revealing jagged teeth that could only be meant for tearing flesh.

Will jerked his hand back, twisted his body around and leaped for the bank. He landed awkwardly and scrambled to his feet, putting distance between himself and the creature in the stream.

When he looked back, she was sitting on the boulder he had just vacated, her naked body gleaming like a fish in the sun, laughing as she combed her claws through her hair.

As he reached for the camera in his pack, she slipped into the water, a long, silvery shape, and was gone.

***

Somewhere, very close, a cacophony of birds did its best to rouse the dead. Grace woke with a start, her hand flying to her face. She brushed an ant off her cheek and sat up, her heart pounding. Then she focused on her surroundings. One glance around the dawn-filtered forest was enough.

Oh lord. It wasn't a dream.

A bubble of panic escaped as a sob before she could contain it. She rubbed the sleep out of her eyes and ordered herself not to cry. There was a reasonable explanation. If Moira wouldn't—or couldn't—tell her, she'd find it herself.

Twenty feet away, Moira's tent huddled silently. Grace could just imagine Moira burrowing her head in the sleeping bag in an effort to escape the noise. Grace decided to give her a few more minutes. A grumpy Moira was not a cooperative Moira.

Rising stiffly, she left the heavy coat on the ground at her feet. She'd been glad of its down-filled warmth last night. Although the ground was loamy and covered in a carpet of sage, it still made for an uncomfortable bed. She stretched and twisted, trying to work the kinks out of her back.

The sky lightened to pale blue, promising a fine day. As she stretched, Grace examined her surroundings. Oaks and elms dominated, with fir and the occasional birch. Ferns and wildflowers, mostly bluebells, dotted the forest floor. Clusters of the blue flowers hung heavy and damp with dew. She had no idea if the trees concealed mountains, skyscrapers, or more trees.

She took a deep breath of clean, cool air and expelled it softly.

Now if only the birds would be quiet.

Last night's theory returned to worry at her. Had she stumbled into a military exercise? Maybe she had been knocked out and transported here during the night. Maybe they had used some new drug that left no side effects but made her lose track of time.

That didn't make sense. Why would they bring her here?

Because you were in the wrong place at the wrong time. Moira was right—she had a lousy sense of timing.

Those birds were enough to give a statue a headache. Grace finished stretching and looked around the campsite. How could Moira sleep through that noise?

Moira had pitched her tent between two fir trees. It stretched long and low, and looked even more like a lightweight blue-and-gray coffin by daylight. Grace had declined Moira's offer to share it. She'd had no intention of sleeping when she didn't know where she was, and besides, the tent was obviously designed for one. She hadn't wanted to have to struggle out of a fabric cocoon if something large and hungry stumbled across them.

Nothing had. Or if it had, she remained blissfully unaware of it.

What was it with those birds?

Annoyed, Grace walked over to an elm tree, where most of the noise was concentrated, and almost stepped on a baby bird. It was brown with grayish tufts of feathers, remnants of down. The creature looked up at her and peeped.

"Oh!" she said, suddenly understanding. She glanced up the tree and found the nest. The fledgling couldn't get back to safety.

Something zoomed by her head and Grace ducked, throwing up her hands to protect her head.

"What...?"

The mother returned for another attack and Grace shooed her away.

"Stop that!" she ordered. "I won't hurt your baby." But something else would if the baby wasn't rescued. It would be easy enough to return the fledgling to its nest, but would the mother then reject it? Hadn't she read somewhere that a mother bird would abandon her offspring if she smelled human on it?

Before climbing, she crushed sage in her mittens to disguise her human smell. Her good woolen slacks were already ruined from tramping through snow and sleeping on the ground, but the raw silk shirt had been in good shape until she got sap on it. Still, she managed to get the baby back to its nest.

Back on the ground, Grace stripped the mittens off and moved back to watch the elm for signs of activity. The mother circled the tree a few times, screaming insults at her, but eventually calmed down and dropped to the nest. After a few minutes, Grace decided that the mother didn't seem to be rejecting the fledgling.

The Greek chorus that had accompanied the mini tragedy finally settled down and Grace sighed with relief.

"You're welcome," she said.

She turned back to where she had left her coat and froze as she caught a movement out of the corner of her eye. She looked around, but saw nothing.

"Moira?" She turned in a circle, looking from tree to tree. "Is that you?"

To her surprise, she wasn't afraid. If anything was out there, it didn't carry last night's sense of danger.

A branch snapped behind her and Grace whirled to find Moira coming through the trees, carrying a small aluminum pan in front of her. A wet canteen bounced on her hip with every step and her short black hair was spiky, as if she had run wet fingers through it.

So much for her not being a morning person. She hadn't even been in the tent.

"Good morning," said Moira. "How did you sleep?"

Grace stared at her. "Fine. Was that you just now?"

Moira gave her a quizzical look. "Just now?"

"Never mind," said Grace, suddenly aware that she sounded nervous. She didn't want Moira to think she was afraid of being alone.

Moira set the pan down carefully on the ground next to the tent and opened the zippered entrance. She rummaged around, then pulled out her pack.

Her hiking boots, sturdy khaki cotton pants, and olive-green sweater with its leather-reinforced shoulders spoke of a well-prepared camper. The sweater looked like Army issue.

Grace looked down at her ruined outfit. Not exactly campout gear. Her winter boots were already getting hot and the sun hadn't even cleared the treetops. What time was it, anyway? Her parents must be frantic with worry. What about her shop? Would her clerks open up without her?

"That was unwise," commented Moira, pulling a foil package out of a side pocket.

"Excuse me?" asked Grace, disoriented.

"Keeping the food in the tent. We should have hung the pack in a tree, away from camp, just in case there are any wild animals around here."

What's this "we" stuff? thought Grace. And then, *What kind of wild animals?*

She had fallen asleep in spite of herself last night, and nothing bad had happened. It was hard to stay outraged and afraid when little birds fell out of trees and the day smelled like the morning of the world.

Yet she was in this strange place with no understanding of how she had gotten here. And her mouth tasted awful and she wanted to comb her hair, but couldn't remember where she had last seen her purse. In the car? In Moira's house?

God. What she wouldn't give for a cup of coffee.

Moira tore open the package and poured the powdery contents into the water-filled pan. Then she pulled out a canister camp stove, installed the grill, and lit the stove. Immediately, a thin blue flame sprang from the canister.

With a satisfied smile, Moira moved the pan onto the flame and crouching, plucked a fork from a different pocket of her backpack. She stirred the unappetizing mess.

"Hungry?" she asked over her shoulder. "It's dehydrated eggs— nothing to write home about, but it'll fill the belly."

Aren't you the gracious one, thought Grace uncharitably. Instead of answers, Moira offered food. Grace looked at the concoction, intensely aware of the yawning pit that used to be her stomach. Maybe it was time to change tactics.

"Sure." The confrontation could wait until after breakfast.

Grace spread her parka on the ground and took off her boots, wriggling her stockinged toes with pleasure. They ate side by side, Moira with the fork and Grace with a spoon Moira produced from the backpack. Grace ate with appetite, ignoring Moira's amusement.

"Where did you find the water?" asked Grace once the pan had been scraped clean. She leaned back on her elbows, watching the sun send streamers of light through the trees. If she tried, just a little, she could imagine she'd taken a break from her store and was on a picnic with a friend.

Grace almost sighed. Knowing Moira for almost twenty years did not make her a friend.

"Down there," said Moira, pointing down slope.

Although the trees were big—many bigger around than the full clasp of Grace's arms—they were spaced far enough apart to produce a park-like effect. She could clearly see where the slope took a sudden dip.

"In this kind of terrain, you'll usually find water in low areas," continued Moira. "There's a stream only a few hundred yards that way."

Terrain. The military-sounding word jarred Grace back to reality. Her parents were too old to go through this kind of worry. She had to get back.

Grace sat up. "So this *is* a military exercise."

Moira looked startled, as if Grace had pulled her away from her own fantasy. She sat up, too, and put on her hiking boots.

"No," she said. "It's not an exercise."

Grace waited. They might not be friends, but there was one thing she knew about Moira O'Rourke. If she waited long enough, Moira would finally tell her what she wanted to know.

Moira laced up her boots and stood.

"Time to get moving," she said. "I'll wash the pan. You take down the tent." Without a backward glance, she strode purposefully down the slope toward the stream, pan in hand.

Grace stared after her, longing to throttle the woman.

***

Moira rinsed the last of the sand out of the pan and stood up.

The stream was barely a rivulet of water, burbling over stones and forming tiny pools too small for fish. She could easily step over it and never get wet. She breathed deeply of the scent of wildflowers.

The deep breath helped steady the sudden racing of her heart. It was true. She didn't understand how, but that little rhyme had somehow gotten her here. All those years she had thought her father was playing an elaborate joke.

A frog croaked at her from a nearby rock, and a couple of bees droned in a patch of clover.

It was a perfectly beautiful summer morning. Except that it shouldn't be. She should be waking up in a tent on exercise, shivering in the winter cold, or in her bed at Kirwan. Instead of here—wherever *here* was.

Her father had always said Fin Bheara would call for them if he needed help, but no one had called for her. Maybe they had called Mack and Aidan. She suddenly wished she had waited to talk to Will. She'd feel a lot better—not to mention saner—if he were here with her.

Moira planted the handle of the frying pan in the bank to sign the spot and moved east along the rivulet, looking for signs of her brothers' passage. Mack would have left a trail. The grassy verge of the stream sprang back as she walked, barely marking her passage.

A couple of swallows swooped above the trees like young daredevils trying to impress the girls.

In spite of the open feel of it, the forest acted like a concealing wall. She couldn't tell what lay beyond the tall oaks and elms that shared space with the odd fir and cedar. Bluebells dotted the forest floor. By the stream, buttercups rioted amid the clover and willows trailed their languorous leaves. She couldn't imagine a more serene setting.

So why did she feel as if the forest had eyes?

A rhyme. An old rhyme in an old book, a rhyme which hadn't been there in all the years she and her brothers had leafed through the book. Her father had explained solemnly that when the time came, they would find what they needed in the book. If her brothers had found the rhyme, who had replaced the book in the shelves? She certainly hadn't had time to replace it before arriving here with Grace.

Grace.

Moira groaned. What could she do about Grace? She couldn't bring her along, and she couldn't leave her behind. She didn't know how to get her back home. Hell, she didn't know how to get *herself* back home.

In Girl Guides, Moira had watched Grace struggling to obtain her outdoor badges. For a girl raised in the country, Grace had been singularly inept at outdoor living.

She was just going to have to drag Grace along.

Moira walked lightly in her hiking boots, stepping over stones, avoiding clumps of buttercups. As she walked, she scanned the trees for blazes, or broken branches at eye level, anything that would indicate Mack had been there. The sun steamed the dew off the grass and flowers, releasing an intoxicating array of smells.

There was no sign of her brothers. For the first time, a small thread of panic wound its way around Moira's heart. Maybe Mack and Aidan weren't here. Maybe the rhyme had taken them somewhere else. A fine help she'd be to them then. And where was Soutien? Did he know what was going on?

After five minutes of following the stream, Moira gave up and turned around. Mack would have left a sign long before if he had come this way. She would return to the frying pan and try going west for five minutes.

But the frying pan wasn't there. Controlling a spurt of anxiety, Moira examined the ground by the stream, certain she had planted the handle right there. She found the spot where the handle had dug into the loam, but the pan was nowhere to be seen. Even if it had fallen out, the stream wasn't fast enough to have carried it off.

Then she felt it again, the same tingling in her scalp she had felt earlier. She was being watched.

"Grace?"

Only the chirping of the birds answered her. Whatever was out there, it wasn't the same creature as last night, when the entire forest seemed to hold its breath until it left.

That didn't mean it was friendly.

Out of the corner of her eye she caught sunlight flashing on something metallic. She turned quickly. Hanging from a weeping willow was her frying pan. Someone had looped the slender branch through the folding handle and left the pan to dangle in the breeze.

Dread trailed a cool finger down her spine.

She drew the hunting knife out of her pocket and unsheathed it, scanning the trees around her. Nothing. Finally she pulled the branch down, undid the loose bow, and freed the pan. Then she turned and, knife in hand, ran back toward the camp.

ɞ FIVE ᵔᵓ

WILL squatted before the remains of the campfire he had
found and switched his attention to the woods behind
him. The creature that had followed him all morning
was becoming bolder, edging ever nearer, obviously curious.

It moved in near silence. Either it didn't weigh enough to break
twigs, or it was sure-footed.

He had tried to lure it into the open with food a few times, but
it was too cautious. And with the forest growing steadily denser and
gloomier, there were many places to hide.

At least it didn't act like a predator. And its presence hadn't affected the birds. They sang and chirped all morning, a cheerful accompaniment to his steady progress. Squirrels scampered up trees
and along branches, chittering at him.

Whistling quietly, Will rose and slowly walked around the campfire. It was no more than a day old. The ashes at the bottom were
still warm. Somebody had been careful in building it, placing stones
around the perimeter to define the burning area and sprinkling soil on
top before moving on. That could be Aidan, decided Will, at least the
soil part. His stint as a fire jumper had made him wary of forest fires.

He was getting closer.

The last few days reminded Will of his youth, when he, Moira, and
his brothers would go camping by themselves. Mack, being two years

older than Aidan, five older than Will, and six older than Moira, was always the leader. Only Aidan chafed under his leadership, objecting to almost every decision. Mack would raise an eyebrow and invite Aidan to try it his way. After a while, when Aidan's methods proved ineffective, he would grudgingly accept Mack's suggestion. Which was why Mack was the youngest colonel in the Army, and Aidan was still only a lieutenant in the Air Force. Will wondered how they were getting along right now.

It was hard to sustain the level of urgency that had brought him here. He was alone in the woods on a beautiful summer day, and no one was shooting at him.

In spite of Soutien and Oonagh's warnings, he wasn't truly worried for his brothers. Mack had fifteen years of Army exercises behind him and Aidan had the quickest reflexes of all of them.

His brothers could take care of themselves.

For the first time, it occurred to him that Mack and Aidan might not have come together. And if they hadn't, they might not have caught up to each other.

They might not even be heading in the same direction.

According to Dad's stories, Fin Bheara called on the sons of Kirwan in times of need. Had they been brought here, like him, or had they come of their own free will, using the book in Father's library to get here?

Oonagh had said his brothers were in danger and that Fin Bheara needed him, but she hadn't said for what.

And how was Soutien involved? He had been with the family forever, despite his youthful appearance. He had never seemed otherworldly to Will. He'd gone drinking with the man, played chess with him, laughed at his sly humor. Soutien was family. Oonagh, at least, was part of all the stories. But Soutien...

And if Fin Bheara had called on Mack and Aidan, why not on him? Was Moira involved? Soutien and Oonagh hadn't mentioned her.

If Soutien and Oonagh had been there at all.

He examined the possibility that he might be insane the way a man examined the thickness of ice covering a river. Thick or thin, he had to cross.

Still, it was hard to believe in spectral stewards and Fey queens when the sun shone warm on his face and his stomach grumbled in anticipation of lunch.

With a sigh, Will shrugged off his pack and dropped it at the base of a large maple. Sitting down beside it, he leaned back against the rough trunk. He took a swig of water from his canteen and pulled out some beef jerky.

As he chewed, he tried to remember everything his father had told them.

"Just as Fin Bheara is bound to us, we are bound to him. If ever you have need, the rhyme in the book will take you to him. And if ever he needs our help, Fin Bheara will send for us. He will call for the sons of Kirwan and we must follow him. It is our family duty and privilege to answer his call."

It had seemed like such an adventure when his father spoke of the old legend—something fabulous, invented to thrill his children.

But he had drilled the story into them as if afraid they would forget. "It may never happen. The last time Fin Bheara called for an O'Rourke's help was eight generations ago, and Devlin O'Rourke never returned. Devlin had a young wife and babies. He had no brothers or sisters and there was no one to go with him. But you have each other. And you have me."

Had him. His parents' death in a car accident last year hit the family hard. They had no one else. No cousins, no aunts or uncles, no grandparents. Only each other. Except that Mack had Edna, of course, and after years of trying, Edna was finally pregnant. So Mack had a future family to look forward to. Moira was level-headed and dealt with the grief by throwing herself into her career. Only Aidan had spiraled out of control, drinking too much and almost losing his commission until Mack had hauled him back to Kirwan to dry out. Moira and Soutien finally penetrated Aidan's wall of grief.

Will had stayed in Afghanistan, shooting a spread for *Life* magazine. Aidan resented Will for rejecting the family tradition of military service. His pacifism baffled Aidan.

Will took a final swallow from the canteen, screwed the cap back on, and put away the rest of the jerky. Standing up, he swung the pack over one shoulder, careful not to strike the tree. His camera was in there.

A breeze played over him and he caught a whiff of his body odor. How many days since his last shower? He rubbed the bristles on his jaw and tried not to imagine his brothers' reaction when he finally caught up to them. His beard had always been an embarrassment, growing bright red in contrast to his almost black curly hair. But it was sillier to lug a shaving kit with him.

As he walked, he automatically searched for the next blaze. He found it on a hawthorn tree, then froze as he recognized the shape. It was shaped like a cross, the family's sign for danger. The skin on Will's arms prickled in alarm. Tensing, he scanned the forest around him, then looked up, searching for the danger, but saw nothing out of the ordinary.

Then he noticed the bark on the hawthorn. It was darker than the surrounding trees. It looked wet.

Again he looked up and around but could see nothing dangerous. Stepping up to the hawthorn, Will touched the trunk. His fingers came away bloody.

Before he could do more than swallow his horror, the bark on the hawthorn rearranged itself into a three-dimensional shape and a naked brown figure peeled away from the tree to land in a heap at his feet.

"Hey!" Will jumped back. What the hell kind of place was this? He glanced at the tree, but it looked normal. Its bark was no longer wet.

Almost reluctantly, he looked back at the creature at his feet. The figure was slight and rounded, curled in a fetal position. Female. As he watched, her skin paled to gray and she moaned. She glistened with blood.

She had been inside the tree. Not on a branch, not leaning against the hawthorn—she had fallen from within the tree. How was that possible?

He studied her warily for a few seconds. The photographer in him noted that she would make an arresting photograph, especially in black and white. The survivor in him warned that the only other living creature he had seen here—aside from birds and squirrels—had also been female, and she'd had claws.

But this one wasn't in any shape to hurt anyone.

"Miss?" he said finally, dropping to one knee and placing a hand on her thin shoulder. Her skin was clammy but otherwise skin-like. Maybe it was normally gray? She looked up at him with leaf-green eyes.

"What is it?" He tried to see past the blood and her curled-up position to the injury. "Let me see," he said firmly, rolling her to her back and pulling her arms away from her belly.

His breath caught in a long hiss. There were two diagonal cuts on her belly, beginning below her budding breasts, crossing above her belly button and ending on either hip. The cuts were deep and still bleeding. He examined her as gently as he could. He could see bloody ribs, but didn't think the cuts had reached her internal organs. They didn't look infected, but even if infection didn't kill her, loss of blood would.

She was just a child—how could anyone have done this to her?

He stood up, removed his backpack and dug through it for the first-aid kit. Then he stared at its meager contents. What could he use? No matter how human-like she looked, she wasn't human. There was no telling how painkillers would interact with her blood chemistry. He finally decided that antiseptic cream would probably be safe. He smeared it over her cuts, then used up most of his bandages and butterfly tape in closing her wounds.

She lay quietly while he bandaged her, staring at his face, too exhausted to even grimace. Her hair was long and snarled, and a green so deep it looked almost black. Once or twice she moaned when he was particularly clumsy, but otherwise she made no sound.

What did it mean that Mack had blazed her tree with the danger mark? Had he seen what had been done to her? Had Aidan? Will immediately rejected the thought. Neither Mack nor Aidan would ever have left an injured person. Especially not a hurt child.

When Will finished, he put away the kit and pulled out his cylinder stove.

"Let's get some broth in you," he said, hoping to ease the fear in her eyes. Did she have people here? He cut up some beef jerky into a pan and added water. While he waited for it to boil, he pulled out his sleeping bag and wrapped it around her.

She bit back a groan as he tucked it under her and he winced in sympathy. "Sorry," he said.

He stirred the broth, glancing at the tree often. She had stepped out of it. She had been in the tree, and now she wasn't.

The gray tinge to her skin was getting worse. He took turned the stove off, and stirred the broth with a spoon, trying to cool it down.

"Here," he finally said, bringing the spoon to her lips. She was too weak to sit up, so he held her head up and tried to get the liquid into her. Some of it dribbled down her cheek and he wiped it off.

After a few swallows, she turned her head away and fell asleep.

She still hadn't said a word.

While she slept, he made short exploratory forays into the woods. He hoped beyond reason to find some sign of civilization, some way of getting her to help. All he found was Mack's next blaze, a simple one this time.

He didn't dare stray from her for too long. There was no telling how quickly she might deteriorate. Not that he could do anything about it.

He returned from the last foray in mid-afternoon to find the girl's breathing shallow and her color ruddy. Her cheeks felt hot. He poured cold water from his canteen onto his bandanna and wiped her face, finally leaving the cloth on her forehead. He peered under the sleeping bag to find the flesh surrounding the cuts an angry red. The fever kept rising.

He blew out his breath, as if expelling the thought before it could form. But he had seen death too often to mistake its approach.

When she finally opened her eyes, there was no recognition in them.

"Hi," he said, squatting by her. "How do you feel?"

If she heard him, she gave no sign. Instead, her eyes began a desperate search of her surroundings. He had placed a sweater beneath her head to cushion it and now it slipped out from under as she twisted frantically. When she tried to sit up, he gently pushed her back down.

"Amadan," she said, her voice coming out as a croak. He placed the canteen against her lips and held her head while she drank. After no more than two swallows, she fell back, exhausted.

Almost at once, she turned her head, the better to continue her search. "Seabhan!" she cried, her words slurred and almost unintelligible.

The girl's distress raised goose bumps on his arms. Was she afraid of whoever had done this to her? He couldn't understand her words.

Suddenly her blood-caked hand snaked out from under the sleeping bag and fastened onto his arm. "Amadan-na-Briona..." Her voice trailed away and for the first time, she seemed to see him.

Then she fell back, unconscious. He checked the wound again. The infection had spread and a nauseating smell rose from the cuts. He had no more antibiotic cream. He tucked the sleeping bag around the girl, sat down by her side and held her hand. It was small and soft and so hot it felt like fire against his flesh. After a while, he dredged his memory and found the old lullabies his mother used to sing. The soft crooning of his voice seemed to comfort the girl.

She died three hours later. Will sat for a long time in the creeping dusk, grieving. Finally he stood up and removed the sleeping bag. He had no way of burying her.

He picked up her weightless body and placed it at the foot of the hawthorn. Her hair fell over her face, and he brushed it back. Then he stepped away.

The forest hushed and even the wind ceased. An owl hooted once, twice.

Then the tree's trunk spread itself out like a cradle and wrapped itself around her. One moment she was a huddled mass, the next she was gone, the shape of her still visible as a child-sized form just under the bark. Then the tree reabsorbed her, shuddering before resuming its normal shape.

As he stood watch, torn between awe and grief, the hawthorn's leaves fell over him in a gentle green rain.

❧ SIX ❦

RACE's wet hands smelled musty from rolling up the tent. Turning away from Moira, she finished stuffing the tent into its impossibly compact bag. The struggle predisposed her to irritation. She really didn't want to deal with Moira's flight of fancy right now.

"You're kidding, right?" She turned to stare at Moira.

"Afraid not," replied Moira, looking her in the eye.

Grace waited, hoping the other woman would start grinning and admit she had been pulling her leg. But Moira just looked back at her, her expression halfway between resignation and embarrassment.

The backpack leaned against an oak tree, its dull green canvas melting into the background of bark and bush. Grace walked over and began stuffing the tent bag into the pack. A squirrel scolded her from a branch above her head.

"You're telling me that we got here by... by what? Magic?" Grace took a deep breath, trying to quell her rising anger. The anger was tinged with panic. What kind of game was Moira playing? Grace glanced over her shoulder at the other woman.

Moira winced, but nodded. "A rhyme, in a book."

Grace flushed and turned away. She removed the stove from the pack, trying to find more room for the tent.

Moira hadn't bothered to thank her for taking down the tent. She had come running from the creek like Robin Hood riding to Maid

Marion's rescue, only to stop suddenly when she saw Grace. Then she had ignored Grace's questions, insisting that they had to leave right away.

But Grace had had enough. She refused to budge until Moira told her what was going on, which was when Moira came up with the whopper about missing brothers, a Faerie king, and an old family oath.

She knew that Moira had always considered herself the more quick-witted of the two, but it smarted that she expected Grace to believe a ridiculous story like that. Grace's ears grew hot with anger. Since she had no idea where she was or how to get home, she had no choice but to follow Moira. Frustration made her clamp her teeth tightly over a foul word. She wouldn't give Moira the satisfaction.

"Look, Grace," said Moira, taking the tent away from her and re-arranging the contents of the backpack. "I know how it sounds. I've heard these stories all my life and I'm having trouble believing this. Maybe there is another explanation." She tightened the drawstring on the now neatly packed backpack, pulled the flap over the top, and straightened. "But I honestly don't know what it could be."

Grace examined Moira's face, looking for any hint of amusement behind the sincere expression. For the first time, she noticed a small scar by Moira's temple. When did she get that?

All the O'Rourkes were striking rather than good-looking. At twenty-seven, Moira had never looked better. She kept her dark hair shorter now that she was in the Army, allowing the natural curl to run riot. The lines crinkling the corners of her deep blue eyes softened the determined set of her mouth. She looked tanned and fit, and held herself with an assurance Grace envied.

Grace swallowed a sigh and turned away to get her coat. She bundled the parka into as tight a ball as she could, using her belt to keep it so. Her feet were already too warm. It was going to be a miserable walk.

She turned just as Moira came up behind her.

"Grace—"

Grace put up a hand. "Drop it, Moira," she said. "It doesn't matter. One way or the other, I'm stuck with you." Until I can find my way home, she amended silently. "Where are we going?"

Moira sighed and pointed toward the creek. "Down there. I found Mack's sign when I came back from washing the pan."

Reminded of Moira's precipitous return, Grace was about to question her again when a movement caught her eye. She turned, looking for the source, but saw only leaves and flowers and trees.

"What is it?" whispered Moira.

A breeze played over Grace's straight, fair hair, and she pushed the strands away from her face, her eyes trained on the trees. "Something..." she said. "I thought I saw something."

After a moment, she relaxed. Whatever it was, it had been out there all morning, staying out of sight. She wasn't too worried. There had been ample opportunity to hurt them, if it was so inclined. She figured it was shy, and probably curious. Maybe a deer? She turned to Moira and was shocked to see the hunting knife in her hands.

Was she going to pull a knife every time they heard a noise? Just how stable was Moira?

"Come on," said Moira grimly. She clamped the knife between her teeth and shouldered her backpack. She didn't secure the waist belt, probably in case she needed to shed the pack quickly. With the knife in hand once again, she gestured down slope. "Let's get going."

A wave of absurdity swept over Grace, leaving her giddy with hilarity. Moira O'Rourke, warrior woman, jumping at shadows. "What are you so nervous about, Moira?" she said. "I thought you were expected. Isn't the King of Faerie a friend of the family?"

To her immense—and she admitted it, petty—satisfaction, Moira blushed.

They followed Mack's blazes through a forest that went from park-like to primeval within a few miles, the underbrush gradually transforming from airy ferns and dots of wildflowers to dense willow thicket and springy moss.

When Moira finally called a halt for lunch, three long hours later, Grace was all out of hilarity. She stumbled to the nearest log and sat down, waving the mosquitoes away from her face. She tried to calculate if the energy she would expend in taking off her boots would be worth the relief she would feel.

"Here." Moira handed her the canteen and Grace took a long swallow. The water was stale and warm, but it felt like silk going down her throat. They would have to find water soon. Grace looked up and was surprised to see clear blue in between the top branches of the trees. The light didn't reach the forest floor, which explained the perpetual dusk in which they traveled. The forest smelled of soil and damp and cool decay. Grace suppressed a shudder. Hopefully they would find Moira's brothers before nightfall. She didn't think she could stand another night in the woods.

Moira accepted the canteen from Grace and handed her a strip of leather. Grace looked at it.

"It's jerky," said Moira. "Chew it well and swallow it down with water."

Grace reluctantly tried a bite and found she had to tear the piece off. It had the consistency of shoe leather, and just about as much flavor. She looked around hopefully. Maybe there were berry bushes...

"We'll have a better meal tonight," promised Moira. "But I don't want to waste daylight."

Grace didn't answer. Although exhaustion had diminished her anger, she was growing more baffled by the mile. Why was Moira doing this?

Despite carrying the thirty-pound backpack for three hours, Moira still looked fresh. She had removed her sweater as the day progressed to reveal a navy blue T-shirt.

Grace eyed Moira's slim, muscular arms. Next to her, Grace felt like a lumbering ox. She was out of shape. Not surprising, since she didn't spend her days running around on field exercises. However, she was willing to bet that Moira couldn't tell the difference between Georgette crepe and crêpes Suzette. She probably didn't care, either.

If Grace were to remove her wool blazer—which was her only protection against the mosquitoes—her white silk shirt would be plastered against her body with sweat.

And her feet were too hot.

"Time to go," said Moira cheerfully, hoisting the pack effortlessly onto her back.

"Right." Grace stood up more slowly, but refused to show any reluctance. She slung her bundled coat over her shoulder.

As soon as Moira turned her back, Grace sagged against a tree. At one point, she had actually considered taking a turn at carrying Moira's pack. Thank goodness sanity had reasserted itself in time.

As the miles crept by, Grace had to admit that Mack—or whoever—was good at signing. They could always follow his trail, each blaze within sight of the last one. She tried to remember him, but he was older than Moira and had been at military college by the time she reached high school.

She remembered Aidan more clearly. He competed ceaselessly but good-naturedly with both his brothers. He was a few years younger than Mack, a few years older than Will.

Will. The thought of him still made her heart falter. What a crush she'd had on him. Thank God he'd never known.

Moira released a pine branch and it swung back at Grace, its needles brushing by her cheek like a caress. She allowed Moira to get farther ahead. The next branch might not be so gentle. The trees were opening up again, allowing more light to reach the forest floor. An anxiety she hadn't known she was carrying lifted from her shoulders.

She almost bumped into Moira before noticing the woman had stopped.

"What is it?" asked Grace.

Moira didn't answer, but pointed. Grace's gaze followed Moira's pointing finger to a big maple tree. At first all she could see was Mack's blaze, a straight, narrow area at eye level where he had removed the bark. It wasn't enough to harm the tree, just enough to be noticed.

Then her gaze caught on something swaying among the leaves in the slight breeze. She stared for a second before her brain could make sense of it.

Someone had hung a pair of shoes off the lowest branch of the maple tree.

Moira turned to look at her. "Someone must like you."

Grace almost snorted. Now she *knew* they were on some kind of exercise. She had inadvertently been caught up in it, and they—whoever "they" were—were trying to atone, or at least give her a fighting chance, by giving her something decent to wear.

But just how did they know her size?

She walked over to the tree, dropped her bundle at its base, and reached up. The moment she touched one of the shoes, both fell to the ground. Two small, curved twigs had been hooked into the shoes and twisted together above the branch, leaving one shoe hanging on either side of the branch.

She stared down at them for a moment. They looked the right size.

With a grunt of satisfaction, Grace sat down at the base of the maple and took off her boots. She imagined she could see heat shimmering off her nylon-clad feet.

If the organizers of the exercise had left the shoes for her, that meant they were watching. Why didn't they just call a time out and get her out? Were they testing some top secret equipment out here? Judging by Moira's supplies, it wasn't her team that got the new equipment.

She reached for the nearest shoe and examined it. There were no laces. It was a slip-on style, made out of a glossy green, smooth fabric unlike anything she had ever seen. The designer had cleverly cut and stitched the fabric to make it look like tree leaves. Enchanting, but she would have been satisfied with a pair of Nikes.

She slid it on and jumped when it shifted, massaging her foot. "Ah..." she said, at a loss for what to do. Then it stopped, having adjusted itself to the shape of her foot. After a moment, she tentatively flexed her toes. The shoe fit better than anything she had ever worn. Experimentally, she tried to remove it. It slipped off easily. As soon as she replaced it on her foot, it readjusted itself again.

Grace gulped and reached for the other shoe. She brought it up to her face and sniffed cautiously. There was an unmistakably organic odor. Real leaves. The inside was lined with a thick cushion of moss and the sole consisted of woven strips of birch bark. She couldn't tell how it was all stitched together, but was willing to bet it wasn't with polyester thread.

No Army supply master had ever ordered these.

"Moira," she said softly, "come take a look at this."

Moira moved closer to Grace for a better view. As she did, Grace glanced past her and caught the gaze of the oddest creature she had ever seen.

It was a man, dressed in a brown, short-sleeved tunic that fell to just above his bare, knobby knees. He stood half-hidden by an oak tree, staring at her with round eyes too big for his face. His nose was huge, a great bulbous mass that shadowed his wide, thin-lipped mouth. He had a scraggly brown beard and hair to match, neither of which looked as if it had been washed or combed in the last decade.

Something in her sudden stillness alerted Moira. She turned and saw the man.

"Hey!" she yelled.

At once, he slipped behind the tree. Moira shrugged out of her backpack and was running after him before it thumped to the ground.

Grace struggled to her feet. "Moira!" She clutched the soft shoe in her hand and hurried after Moira, hobbling on one shod foot and one bare one.

Moira crashed through the underbrush of alder bushes and fallen trees. Grace followed the swaying branches marking her passage. What did Moira think she was doing, chasing after a strange man in the woods? What if he was some kind of deranged killer? What if she got lost?

"Moira!" she called again, but the sounds were diminishing. Grace stopped. Now what?

"You like?" came a deep, rusty voice.

Grace stood still for a long moment. Finally, she turned toward the voice.

The brown man stood less than ten feet from her, one arm wrapped around a fir tree as if for support. Grace got her first good look at him and forgot to breathe. From this close, it was obvious that something was wrong with his face. His features were disproportionately huge, crowding each other on his small face. His ears were great flaps of flesh that no amount of hair could hide.

He was shorter than her, but his arms, well-muscled and graceful, were too long for his body.

"You like?" he said again, nodding at the shoe in her hand. His words sounded odd, accented, but she couldn't tell from where. She stared at his eyes, unable to find her voice. His expression was stern, almost angry. Finally, something about the way he was fixing her with those great brown eyes penetrated her shock. He was anxious, she realized. About Moira? Or her?

She held the shoe out tentatively. "Did you make these?" Her voice was barely a whisper.

He nodded, not taking his gaze from hers.

"Why?" she asked.

He straightened, for the first time releasing the tree. "You help bird," he said with great dignity. "I help you. No debt." He looked at her fiercely. "No debt," he repeated, reinforcing his words.

"Okay," gulped Grace. "Thank you for the shoes."

The brown man nodded gravely. "You like?"

Grace looked down at the shoe in her hand, at its marvelous, intricate construction. "Oh yes," she said. "Very much."

The brown man relaxed visibly. "No debt," he said again, and turned to leave.

"Wait," called Grace. "Please?" When he paused, she continued. "Where am I? How can I get back home?"

"Fin Bheara," he said, nodding at her as though that was answer enough.

When Moira returned from her fruitless chase, Grace was still standing where the brown man had left her, turning over and over in her mind the name he had left behind.

Fin Bheara. The Faerie king.

❧ SEVEN ❧

SOUTIEN lost Moira's scent at the end of the second day.

The loss troubled him, although he didn't need her scent to track her. She followed her brother's signs. There was no reason to believe she would deviate from the trail Mack had left. Still, her scent had comforted him and its absence left him oddly bereft.

There was another scent accompanying Moira's, an elusively familiar one. It had been present in the study at Kirwan. Did someone accompany Moira? Or follow her?

In the middle of a copse of oak and thorn trees, he stopped, accepting the inevitable. Night had fallen, filling the sky with a wash of stars. Although he could walk safely, he could too easily miss the faint blazes marking the trail. He would wait until morning.

Now that he had finally stopped, exhaustion caught up to him. He knelt, stretching out his back, rounding it to relieve the tightness.

Moira's trail was at least twelve hours old. A lot could happen in twelve hours.

The night wind ruffled his hair, bringing with it the scent of wild roses and fir trees, but no Moira. A few acorns dropped to the ground with soft thuds.

For the first time, doubt filtered through his resolve. Fin Bheara had sent him to find Will and bring him to Kirwan, not to chase after

Moira. Will was Fin Bheara's best hope now that Amadan had Mack and Aidan. *Probably* had them.

Amadan had slipped through the door held closed by Fin Bheara, and without the king's knowledge. Only Soutien had been granted access to both worlds, and that only through Knockma, the center of Fin Bheara's power. Amadan had certainly not come to Knockma. So how had he crossed over? How had he lured Mack and Aidan?

Amadan was old, older even than Fin Bheara. Perhaps he had powers unsuspected by the king.

The weight of Soutien's concern for the two eldest O'Rourkes kept him on his knees. Mack and Aidan were strong, but they did not know the Fey world and the traps it held. And right now, there was nothing he could do for them.

Soutien's duty was clear—he should return to Kirwan and try to locate Will before Amadan did. The magazine Will worked for would know how to reach him.

Even as he thought through the logical steps, Soutien knew he wouldn't take them. Moira was here, in the Fey world, in more danger than she knew. Although she wasn't a "son" of Kirwan, she could bear one. Once Amadan had dealt with the sons, he would turn his attention to her.

Soutien would make sure she was safe before going back for Will.

Hopefully, the blazes would lead him to Mack, Aidan, and Moira...and he could bring them safely to Knockma before looking for Will.

He spread his cloak over a carpet of clover at the foot of a thorn tree. The tree was inhabited but he knew from experience that the wild folk did not mind his presence.

He needed sleep. He had spent the day and most of the night following Moira's scent. This after spending two days in the human world searching for Mack and Aidan. His thinking was growing muddled and his reflexes slow.

At times like these he cursed his half-heritage. While his human blood allowed him to sense other humans, it lacked the stamina of a full-blood Fey. His last waking thought was a comforting one. Moira needed sleep, too, more than he did. He would catch up to her tomorrow.

Hours later, he awoke to a sudden disturbance. Heart racing, he rolled out of his cloak and onto his feet in one continuous motion. A dull roar swept through the forest, spreading from tree to tree with the inevitability of oncoming thunder. Then Soutien realized it was the wind scouring the trees. It blew through the copse, flattening his tunic against him and trailing icy fingers over his skin. Then it was gone.

Soutien glanced at the sky. The moon was up, half full, sharing the night with brilliant stars. It was hours until morning.

A thin wail cut through the distress of the trees, so close it startled him. It came from the hawthorn tree under which he stood and momentarily silenced the rustling of leaves and sighing of pine needles.

He turned toward the hawthorn. "Little cousin, what grieves you?"

The faint weeping grew louder. The bark of the thorn tree rippled in the moonlight as the nymph surfaced, her head, shoulders, and torso projecting from the trunk. As he watched, the bark smoothed into flesh. Long hair flowed over her small breasts and tears coursed down her high cheeks, sparkling in the moonlight. Like all her sisters, she was beautiful. Even in grief.

"A life taken," she sobbed, her shoulders shaking. She freed her hands from the tree to hide her face. "Amadan-na-Briona has stolen a life."

Cold seized Soutien like a foe and he almost reeled with shock. Amadan had killed. Willfully?

Feeling returned to his legs and he stepped up to the nymph. "Hush, little cousin," he whispered, stroking fair hair bleached by the moon. "Tell me what happened."

It took a few minutes of holding her and whispering comfort, but she finally calmed down. By the time she was ready to talk, she was fully out of the tree and sitting on the ground before him, tailor-fashion, unselfconscious about her nudity. With her small breasts and young face, she looked like a human child just entering puberty. But her dark eyes gave lie to that assumption.

"A human came to my sister," she began. "He was looking for Fin Bheara but was heading away from Knockma. She told him where to find the king, and warned him to beware of Amadan, whose domain he was approaching." Here her face crumpled up again, and Soutien held her hands, waiting. Finally she regained her composure.

"She allowed the man to carve a symbol on her tree, as a warning for those who might follow him. Then he left. Another human male followed him, but Breeana did not show herself to him."

Soutien's human curiosity overwhelmed his patience. "And then?"

A great shudder coursed through her. "And then Red Cap came. He accused her of betraying Amadan."

A cold chill shivered through Soutien. Red Cap had been Amadan-na-Briona's lieutenant in the Unseelie Court in the old days, before the Fey came here.

"How did he know she had spoken to the man?"

Bitterness entered her voice, like a bass note thrumming. "The one with the white hand whispered it to him, on the wind."

The one with the white hand. Another member of Amadan's Unseelie Court. More witch than Fey, she lived in birch trees and her long fingers could render a man mad if she touched him on the head, or kill him if she touched his chest.

The night seemed colder somehow, as if he teetered on the brink of an abyss from which welled an icy fear. He remained silent, trying to understand this new development, but the nymph hadn't finished.

"Then Red Cap tore Breeana from her tree." For a moment, it seemed as if the forest leaned in to hear her words. "He took a knife and cut her on the belly, with the same symbol as the man had used on her tree."

Soutien shuddered. Red Cap had attacked a nymph, after six centuries of peace. And the nymph believed Red Cap had acted on Amadan's orders.

Suddenly, the full impact of the nymph's tale hit him. A knife. Red Cap had used a knife.

"How could he touch it?" he asked, his voice low. "How could he touch the knife?"

The nymph turned her too-old gaze on him and he saw that she understood the importance of it, too.

"I do not know," she said, her voice calm. "But it contained iron, there is no mistaking it."

The great wind had passed, leaving behind only loss, and fear. Soutien rose to his feet, needing to move. Iron and murder. The two had gone together since man discovered how to mine the earth. But iron had always been inimical to the Fey. Even he, with his half-human blood, had taken centuries to overcome the weakness that came with proximity to the metal.

It would seem that Red Cap had also trained himself.

Soutien sighed and looked down at the nymph, still seated on the ground. A breeze toyed with the ends of her long, fair hair. Beneath his feet, crushed pine needles released their sharp scent.

"And so she died."

But the nymph shook her head. "Not at once. Red Cap chose to let her suffer." Her eyes closed in pain. "She remained in the tree until another man found her. He tried to help her live, but could only help her die."

"Ah, little cousin," said Soutien softly. What could he tell her that would help? He suspected that words of encouragement would be lies. Red Cap had killed, with iron, in Amadan's name. The Unseelie Court was stirring again. There was no cause for optimism. Then he looked into her eyes and saw that he didn't need to say anything. In all likelihood, she was older than he, and remembered the days before King Fin Bheara brought the Fey to this place. She had no illusions.

All of the Fey world knew the king had to die. Why then was Amadan trying to prevent it by luring the two eldest O'Rourkes to him? Would he kill Mack and Aidan to prevent them from doing their duty?

Soutien shook his head. Amadan was the oldest creature in the Fey world. Even King Fin Bheara couldn't pretend to understand his motivations.

"Thank you," he finally said.

With a nod, she rose gracefully to her feet. Her face was still wet with tears, but she faced him with weary dignity. "Tell the king that we await the word," she said calmly, and without a backward glance, stepped into the tree and out of his sight.

❧ EIGHT ❦

WILL spent a sleepless night not far from the tree that had been the girl's home. As soon as it was light enough, he located the next blaze and set out, but not before taking one last look at the thorn tree. Bereft of leaves, it looked old and shrunken.

He took a picture of it, wanting a tangible reminder of the girl's existence.

Her death knocked the complacency out of him. The adventure no longer felt like a lark. There were no guns here, but people were still dying.

Whoever had hurt her was out there, somewhere. Mack knew there was danger—he had marked the tree with the warning symbol. But the girl hadn't been hurt when Mack left, or he would never have abandoned her. So, what had he been trying to warn of?

Three blazes later, Mack changed direction. Will stopped under a maple tree, studying the blaze in the bark. It was clearly Mack's, but it was leading him northwest now, rather than east.

Frustrated, Will quickened his pace to a ground-eating lope. It was time to find his brothers and get some answers.

As he ran, he forced the questions out of his mind, searching instead for the almost Zen-like state he had learned to adopt when running with rebels—or soldiers, or guerillas—over the years.

Too many years. For a man who had rejected the military herit-age of his family, he seemed to spend a lot of time around death and war. The thought nagged at him. His mother, even more than Aidan, had been bitter about his choice of career as a war photographer. To her way of thinking, in the military he would have had a weapon with which to defend himself. Instead, he faced death and danger with only a camera. He couldn't tell her that he loved the thrill of the action, the adrenaline rush that came with the risk of death and pain. He couldn't explain that he didn't dare carry a gun.

It wasn't something he was proud of.

The day aged, and Will found himself traveling on rockier terrain. The trees—mostly fir, pine and oak—grew gnarled. They hugged the ground as if to protect themselves from the cold wind that had sprung up. When he stopped to eat, Will dug out his sweater and put it on before resuming his run.

Clouds moved in, following the wind. The land grew harsher, the moss doing little to cushion his feet against the rocky mantle of the earth. Except for the larger trees, the landscape reminded him of Ontario and Quebec, where the Precambrian shield dominated the landscape, especially in the north.

Small pockets of water multiplied. He jumped over or skirted most of them. Sometimes lakes stood in his way, invariably inhabited by a pair of loons or a family of ducks. Whenever he encountered one of the bigger lakes, he scouted either side to find which way Mack had gone. He stayed well away from the shores of the bigger lakes, the memory of the water woman still fresh in his mind.

Black flies and mosquitoes had no trouble keeping up with him. He flushed so many deer that he was no longer startled when one bolted before him. He refused to think about bears.

By mid-afternoon, Will realized that Mack was going east again. He stopped, completely confused. What was going on?

The blazes were fresher, sticky with sap, indicating that he was catching up to his brothers. With renewed determination, he increased his pace, ignoring his protesting calves. He would catch up to them by nightfall.

But sunset found him on the edge of a lake so wide he could make out the far shore only as a dim outline. He sat on his haunches, resting, and examined the water. The rocky shore dropped away into sudden depths, uninvitingly cold and dark.

He peered at the lake through the gathering darkness. There was something out there... He squinted, trying to make sense of what he saw.

Then his photographer's eye took over, forcing his mind to override assumption, and he finally made it out. "I'll be damned." Surprise drove him to his feet.

In the middle, far enough to make him doubt his ability to swim the distance, was an island. On it stood the ruins of an old castle. Now that he knew it was a building, he could easily make out walls. Its existence, after days of wilderness, caught him by surprise. He hadn't expected this sign of organized, cooperative work.

The ruins were huge. He estimated that in its glory, the castle would have stood two stories tall, and at least two hundred feet to a side. Three Kirwans would have fit comfortably within its walls. How many people had lived there, and how long ago?

Even in the failing light of a dying day, it was plain to see that the ruins had been abandoned for a long time, perhaps centuries. Of the four towers that had stood at the corners, only two remained standing. One was roofless, but so was the remainder of the keep. He couldn't see past the front of the castle, but he suspected most of the walls were no longer standing. Great stone blocks had tumbled at the foot of the remaining wall, looking absurdly like a child's toys.

The massive wooden doors had long ago fallen from their hinges, leaving an opening like a black cave.

Will had scouted either side of the lake, but found no more blazes. The trail ended here.

***

The encounter with the brown man left Moira badly shaken. She thought she had accepted that her father's stories were true, that she and Grace were now in the Fey world. But when she looked up from Grace's leaf shoes to see that improbable face peering out at them from the woods, every atavistic instinct in her reared up.

She didn't even know why she had chased it. She shuddered, remembering its long arms.

Her first encounter with one of the Fey folk, and she had wanted to capture it. Or worse.

Her pulse still pounded, and her hands still shook. What would she have done if she'd caught it?

"Hey, Moira—are you okay?"

Grace's voice brought Moira back. She looked at Grace in irritation. There she stood in that ridiculous, sap-stained wool suit, one shoe on, one shoe off, and she had the nerve to sound concerned about *her?*

Grace waited, but Moira remained silent.

"He wasn't dangerous, you know. I talked to him."

Moira suppressed another shudder. Not dangerous. Big eyes, big teeth, big nose... Then she registered what Grace had said.

"You *talked* to it? When?"

Grace shrugged. "While you were off chasing him, he doubled back. The shoes are a gift. He just wanted to thank me for helping the bird."

"What bird?" Moira was completely lost. Either she was going crazy, or Grace was.

"This morning," said Grace patiently, waving the boot in her hand. "It fell out of a tree."

"Never mind," said Moira abruptly. "We have to get out of here." They had to get some distance between themselves and that thing. She reached for her knife, then checked the impulse, rubbing her thigh instead.

"Moira." Grace placed a hand gently on her arm. "It's all right. He wanted to pay off a debt, that's all."

Moira shrugged off Grace's hand, mortified that the other woman felt she needed reassurance.

"Come on." Without waiting to see if Grace would follow, she set off again.

The late afternoon slowly faded into evening, but the sky was clear and the trees were smaller, allowing more light to filter through. Moira pushed on, ignoring Grace's silent reproach.

After a while, she realized she couldn't hear Grace behind her and whirled. But Grace was there, a few steps behind, and she stopped in surprise. Moira said nothing, only stared down at Grace's Fey shoes. Either they had special properties, or Grace was less clumsy without her boots.

They walked in silence for nearly an hour. Moira couldn't shake the feeling that they were being watched. It was as if the trees held their breath until she and Grace passed, and then whispered behind their backs.

For the first time since joining the military, she missed her brothers. Most of all, she missed Will. They had been close growing up and had stayed close as adults. She wished now that she had left him a message. He might never know what had happened to her.

The ground grew mossier, and the trees more gnarled. She could smell moisture in the air, as if they were approaching a bog. She waved absently at the black flies surrounding her, trying for a clear breath. After eight years of field exercises, it would take more than a few bugs to distract her.

"Moira?" Grace's voice sounded tentative.

"What?"

"Can we stop now?"

"It's still light," said Moira stubbornly. "We can go on for another—"

A soft whinny startled her into silence. She looked around, hand hovering over the pocket containing the knife. In a small clearing to her right stood a shaggy black horse. It was grazing on tufts of coarse grass, tail and ears flicking at the black flies, skin twitching in reaction to the bites.

By the look of the animal, he hadn't missed too many meals. But his back was straight, in spite of his wide middle, and he was big enough to carry two. Moira almost crowed her delight.

"Transportation!" she cried, immediately heading for it.

"Transportation?" echoed Grace. She followed Moira but stayed well away from the animal.

"Yes, transportation," said Moira, approaching the horse carefully. She murmured softly, and he allowed her to lay a hand on his neck. She proceeded to rub his nose and shoo the black flies away from his nostrils.

"You poor thing," she murmured. "Are those nasty bugs hurting you? Let's get away from here and they won't bother you anymore."

As she spoke, she led him to a stump. She clambered onto the stump and placed her hands on the horse's warm back. Grace cleared her throat.

"Moira, don't... we don't know anything about it —"

"Are you kidding?" scoffed Moira. "This is the only break we've had in two days. Come on, Grace—he's strong enough for the two of us, but too big to be fast. Aren't you tired of walking?"

Even in the fading light, Moira could see the skepticism on Grace's face.

"What if he belongs to someone? And don't you think it's awfully convenient to find a horse just waiting here for us?"

"No more convenient than finding shoes for you!" retorted Moira, tired of the argument. She wanted to find her brothers and this horse would help her do that faster. Besides, she'd been riding for twenty years and was a good judge of horse flesh.

"But what if his owner comes looking for him?"

"We'll send him back as soon as we find the boys."

Grabbing hold of the horse's mane, she swung herself up lightly. His back was a bit wide for comfort, but it would do. He shifted a bit, then resumed his interrupted meal.

"Come on, Grace," said Moira, full of glee. "Don't tell me you're afraid!"

"No," said Grace, "but what if the horse's a phooka?"

A phooka?

Moira looked down at the bent head of the horse and dredged through her memories for the term. *Phooka.* At around nine or ten, she and Grace, along with all their female classmates, had gone through a period when everything Fey had fascinated them. She had read every book she could put her hands on.

Phooka. What the hell was a phooka?

And then the description filtered back. A creature that disguised itself as a horse or pony. It offered a lift to unwary travelers, but once on its back, the poor rider often ended up dumped in the middle of nowhere.

Suddenly uncertain, Moira wondered if Grace could be right. As though sensing her hesitation, the horse lifted his head and looked back at her, blowing softly through his nostrils.

"Are you a phooka, boy?" she asked, leaning over and gently rubbing along his nose. Almost as if he understood, the horse shook his head and turned back to the grass.

Moira made up her mind.

"I've been sitting on him for two minutes, Grace. He hasn't done anything. In fact, I'm beginning to wonder if we can even get him to move. This is no phooka."

But Grace was shaking her head. "It doesn't feel right, Moira..."

Abruptly, Moira lost patience. Grace's knack for worrying about nothing had irritated Moira throughout school. She'd been putting up with Grace's inability to face the truth all day. Now that Grace had finally come around, Moira wasn't about to let her turn good fortune into another cause for worry.

"Look," she said, not bothering to disguise the hostility in her voice. "If I can get this horse to move, I'm going to go find my brothers. You can come with me, or you can stay behind. Which will it be?"

Grace stared up at her for a long time, long enough for Moira to regret her outburst. She thought of apologizing, but the words caught in her throat. Not to Grace. She would not apologize to Grace.

Finally Grace shook her head.

"You go ahead," she said, crossing her arms. "I'll follow on foot."

Damn the woman! She knew very well Moira couldn't abandon her. Just as she opened her mouth to argue, the horse suddenly reared up. With a gasp, Moira threw herself forward to wrap her arms around the animal's neck. His front hooves sliced through the air and she felt herself sliding off.

"Moira!" Grace screamed, rushing toward her.

Then the hooves hit the ground, snapping Moira's teeth together and lifting her bottom a foot in the air. Before she could even cry out, the horse took off at a mad gallop through the trees, with Moira clinging to his back and hiding her face against his neck to protect herself from the whipping branches.

❧ NINE ◈

Soutien sat out the remainder of the night on the damp
ground at the base of the nymph's tree, listening to the
rustle of fear spread through the forest, waiting for the
light. There was no point trying to sleep.

Starlight paled as the moon rose. In the distance, a bullfrog
croaked an eerie accompaniment to the uneasy night. Soutien could
almost smell the fear riding the breeze. Not surprising. When Amadan's
lieutenant murdered the nymph, he effectively declared war on Fin
Bheara and any whose loyalty he could not claim.

Add to that the presence of humans, a presence the Fey world
hadn't seen in over six hundred years...

Soutien waited for dawn with only his bleak thoughts for com-
pany. Why was Amadan raising his Unseelie army? What had ended
the uneasy truce between himself and Fin Bheara?

Fresh pain squeezed his heart as the likely reason came to him.
Oonagh. Amadan-na-Briona loved the queen. Did he blame Fin Bheara
for her loss? Would he attack Knockma in revenge?

If so, Amadan was too late. Fin Bheara had already decided to die.

Soutien shied away from the thought, unable to contemplate losing both Oonagh and his liege. He needed to rest. As soon as dawn
came, he would find Moira and bring her to Knockma. Once she was
safe, he would return to Kirwan and try to find Will.

Then, in a heartbeat, Soutien's thoughts stilled and he focused his attention outward. He was being watched. He turned toward the trees to his right and almost missed the movement when it came. A Fey flitted from one moon shadow to another, but not before Soutien spotted the wings. His breath caught in his chest. The winged ones were the shyest of all.

"Little cousin," he said softly into the night. "Can I help you?"

She came out then, a shimmery, wild thing, eyes and wings glimmering with starlight, unable to remain still. She circled once, twice, then apparently making up her mind, hovered ten feet from him.

"Is it true?" came her voice, high but strong on the night air. "Does Amadan seek war?"

Soutien kept his gaze steady, though he could barely see her. Her wings were a blur of movement.

"It seems so." He wanted to reassure her, but resisted the urge. Despite her appearance of youth and fragility, this small one had survived for centuries in the wild, lonely place to which Fin Bheara had brought them. Assurances would not be believed. Nor were they his to give.

The winged one nodded once, as though he confirmed her suspicions. Her wings slowed as she came closer, alighting a few feet in front of him. Now that she was still, he could see clearly that her glow came from within, not from moonlight. She stood no taller than a foot, with long silvery hair that looked white under the moon. Her limbs were thin and shapely, her features fine as silk.

"My kin and I will await the word." She looked at him for a moment, her eyes unfathomable. "Will you accept my oath?"

Something in the deep, still center of Soutien's being stirred. He climbed to his feet. One should not accept a Fey's oath sitting down.

"I will accept on behalf of my lord, King Fin Bheara."

The winged one smiled bleakly, knelt on one knee, and still looking up at him, spoke.

"I, Elin, daughter of Aucom and Sava, swear allegiance to you, Lord Soutien." She rose and bowed.

A grief almost overwhelming in its suddenness threatened to swamp Soutien. He stared down at Elin, hands trembling by his sides, fighting for composure. She had sworn to him. Not him as the king's representative, but *him*, Soutien.

As if the king were dead.

"When the time comes, Lord, my kin and I will be at your side." And with one graceful surge, she was airborne. A moment later, she disappeared into the night, leaving behind a faint scent, sweet as chocolate.

Before Soutien could regain his balance, another wild cousin came to him. And after that one, another. Over the next few hours, dozens came to him, in ones and twos.

Some of them sought reassurance, which he couldn't give. Some pledged allegiance to Fin Bheara. Most swore loyalty to Soutien himself.

"Why?" he finally asked a tall Fey whose long ears and far-seeing eyes marked him as elderly. "Why do you swear to me? My lord Fin Bheara is your rightful king."

In the darkness, the Fey's stillness was that of a forest shadow. Finally, he stirred, moving closer to Soutien.

"Fin Bheara's heart is no longer with us."

Soutien's own heart almost stopped from the pain. It was true. With Oonagh's departure, Fin Bheara had lost his heart. It was pointless to swear allegiance to a dead man.

But why swear allegiance to *him*, then?

With the moon low and dawn almost there, Soutien set out again, following the trail left by Mack and chased by unanswered questions. By luring Mack and Aidan to the Fey world, Amadan had effectively declared war on Fin Bheara. Why? And why now, after all these centuries of peace? Could it really be Oonagh?

Finally, he gave up on the questions. Right now, he needed to concentrate on Moira. With any luck, he would catch up to her in a few hours. He would be able to go faster once the sun rose.

Walking kept him warm, despite the cool wind. Beneath his feet, yielding earth turned to moss-covered rock and his path led him past small, secreted lakes that glistened with moonlight. In the bogs, night flowers released their tantalizing scents. The soil itself had given up its sun-warmed odors for the cooler ones of mist and damp. The moon finally set, leaving only a pale wash of light in the sky.

The closer he came to the site of the nymph's murder, the fewer wild folk approached him. Those living in Amadan's shadow did not wish to call attention to themselves.

Then, as the sun finally broke night's hold, one came to him who had actually spoken to the humans.

The brown man stepped out from behind a tree into Soutien's path. Even in the poor light, Soutien recognized him as one of the shy Fey who tended the small beasts of the forest. He had never met this one.

Soutien stopped as soon as he saw him. The little man looked ready to bolt, clinging to the oak tree with one oversized hand.

"Little cousin," said Soutien, by way of greeting.

At his words, the brown man seemed to gather his courage. A look of determination settled on his face, as if he were steeling himself for something unpleasant, yet necessary. He took a deep breath and, never letting go of the tree, spoke.

"You seek humans," he said.

It wasn't a question, but Soutien nodded nevertheless. "Yes."

"Two I saw. One was taken by a phooka. One follows behind."

A chill caught hold of Soutien. Phooka. Not intrinsically evil, but following its own logic, which might lead to a death. And one followed... to help or to hinder? He looked at the brown man, willing him to continue. The little man seemed ready to flee into the trees. Only his hand on the oak anchored him to the spot.

"The phooka took one to Fir-na-dhag."

"Ahh..." The castle at Fir-na-dhag had been built by the Fey when they first came to this place, and abandoned in grief for their homeland soon after. Red Cap now lived there.

The cold worked its way deeper into Soutien's heart.

"Which one did the phooka take?" he asked, trying to mask his desperate urgency.

Was it Moira?

But the brown man only looked at him, and Soutien understood that the Fey was beyond describing a human. To him, they would all be big and noisy.

He chose a different tack. "Did you speak to them?"

The brown man nodded. His features were becoming more distinct as night crept away. Brown eyes, enormous nose, small mouth—all squished together in the center of his face.

"How?" asked Soutien, spreading his hands helplessly to show he meant no disrespect.

"I remember their words. From before," said the brown man.

From before. Did he mean from six centuries ago? How many of the old ones remembered? How many of the old ones were *left*?

But already the Fey was edging away, having said what he had come to say.

"Cousin, do not go yet," urged Soutien, resisting an impulse to step forward. "Was the one you spoke with a man or a woman?"

"Female," said the brown man. "Childless but fertile."

At this, Soutien caught his breath. The Fey's words were tinged with the sadness of a dying race.

The Fey turned away.

"Wait!" called Soutien, forgetting to be gentle. "Why did you speak to her?"

But the brown man slipped into the shadows between two trees, leaving behind only silence.

With deep foreboding, Soutien turned toward Fir-na-dhag and broke into a run.

᧚ TEN ᰄ

A T DAWN, Will left his rocky bed to examine his surroundings. A low mist rose like ghost streamers from the water, covering the lake. In the gray light, the island looked ghostly, too, and its ruined castle floated on the mist like a dream. Water lapped at the shore, sounding like someone swimming. Long fingers of fog extended from the lake, reaching almost to his small camp.

He shivered in the damp air and reached for his camera. He took a few pictures of the castle and the lake, then let the camera hang by its strap around his neck while he examined the shoreline. No bridge had magically appeared during the night.

He had just about decided to push on and look for better access to the island when he heard the drumming of hooves on rock. He looked up just as a horse rounded a bend in the shoreline a quarter mile away. It galloped toward him, muscles rippling under its black coat. Will automatically brought the camera up and took a couple of shots. Only then did he notice something clinging to the animal's back. Someone, he corrected. Someone wearing a backpack and whose arms were wrapped tightly around the horse's neck.

The horse moved impossibly fast, growing bigger and more threatening by the second. Then, between one breath and the next, it was bearing down on him. Will jumped out of the way, his hand wrapped protectively around the Nikon. The animal stopped abruptly in a clatter of hooves, close enough for Will to smell its hot sweat. The suddenness of the stop sent the startled rider sailing through the air. Only when she tucked and attempted to roll on landing did Will recognize her.

"Moira!" He ran to his sister, his mouth suddenly dry. The horse reared over her and Will threw himself over his sister's body. The hooves slashed perilously close to his head before landing on the rock. Then the animal wheeled and galloped off, the drumming of its hooves fading as it disappeared into the trees. As he bent over his sister, Will thought he heard the faint sound of laughter accompanying the hoofbeats.

The backpack that had kept Moira from rolling now pinned one arm under her body. The rest of her was curled into a tight ball. Her clothes were torn and scratches covered her arms and hands. Dried mud covered her pants from the thigh down. Twigs and leaves littered her hair. Her face was turned away, her eyes closed tightly.

He brushed the hair away from her face and she groaned. Will blew out a breath he hadn't known he was holding. Alive, then.

Moira moaned as Will ran his hands over her body, looking for breaks or bleeding. She remained tucked, with her eyes closed, seemingly oblivious to him. When he had palpated every bone within reach, he sat back on his heels.

He itched to straighten her limbs and examine her more carefully, but if she had damaged her spine, moving her might cripple her. He had to get that pack off of her.

"Can you move?"

She opened one eye and looked at him. "The question is," she said grimly, "do I want to?"

Will grinned, almost giddy with relief. "Come on, then," he said. "Let's check you out."

Aside from dizziness and trouble focusing, the only damage to Moira—not counting the bruises she was sure to develop—was a small bump and gash on her forehead and a scrape along one cheekbone. She had also wrenched her shoulder when she fell, and it would be stiff for a few days.

Will used the small first aid kit in Moira's pack to clean the gash and applied a butterfly bandage to it. He tried not to think of the last time he had used one. His bandages had done precious little for the tree nymph.

"You may get a shiner," he finally announced, turning her face this way and that. "But your eyes look all right. You probably have a mild concussion. Don't fall down again."

Moira turned a forbidding frown on him, but he'd seen her practice it in front of the mirror too often to be intimidated.

"Now," he continued mildly as he closed her first aid kit, "what are you doing here?"

This time the look she gave him was more troubling. "I could ask you the same thing, Will. What's going on?"

The mist had disappeared under the sun's touch by the time they had finished recounting their stories. Will chewed on his third granola bar, washing it down with water, thinking over what Moira had told him. Now the entire O'Rourke clan was here, not to mention Grace. This was not an improvement.

Moira sat on his rolled-up sleeping bag, arms around her raised knees. He'd seen her wince as she sat down. He didn't envy her the next few days.

"You should have called me," he said at last. He wasn't upset, even though they had promised to wait for each other if ever Fin Bheara sent for one of them. It had been a childhood promise, a game. Even Dad hadn't known for sure that the Fey existed, let alone how dangerous they could be.

"Excuse me," said Moira tartly. "You were busy getting shot at and couldn't be reached. At least I tried. What's your excuse?"

Will grinned at her, unrepentant. It was good to see her again. Her new haircut suited her. He hadn't seen her or his brothers since Christmas at Mack's, when his brother had announced that he and Edna were going to have a child. The announcement had turned the first Christmas without their parents from somber to joyful.

"I never got a chance, remember?" he said, rising from his rocky seat. He stuffed the food back into his pack. "So, why *did* you ride the horse?" he asked. "Didn't it seem suspicious to you?"

Moira gritted her teeth. "It was a stupid move, okay? I paid for it by riding all over hell's half-acre all night." She raked her fingers through her hair, wincing as she brushed her bruised cheek. "I tried to get off the damned thing a dozen times, but I couldn't. Until I landed at your feet, that is."

Will looked at her thoughtfully. "It did feel like the horse was delivering a package."

"Thank you so much."

"I'm serious," said Will, ignoring her sour mood. "That horse delivered you to me. I wonder why?"

"Whatever reason the phooka had," retorted Moira, "I'm here now. How can we get across to the island? Are you sure Mack and Aidan went there?"

Will shrugged. "As sure as I can be. The signs end here. I think they found a way across." He stood up and held a hand out for his sister. "Come on. Let's go find Grace."

"Do we have time?" asked Moira. Then, obviously realizing how she sounded, she shrugged. "She's probably still waiting for me to come back. We'll lose the better part of the day if we backtrack all the way back there, only to turn around and return. Let's check out Mack and Aidan first, then go find her."

Will looked at her curiously. She and Grace had never been good friends, but still...

"Do you really want to leave Grace all by herself, in these woods?" He nodded at the wall of dark trees behind her, which the sun hadn't yet managed to penetrate. "She probably followed your trail. I bet we'll meet her along the shore. She never struck me as the waiting-to-be-rescued type."

Moira looked unconvinced. "Mack and Aidan..."

"...can take care of themselves. They have all that training, remember? Do you want to wait here until I get back with her?" suggested Will, hoping she wouldn't agree. Couldn't she see that there was no choice? He couldn't leave the woman alone out there. This was an O'Rourke problem she'd stumbled into. Nor could he leave Moira behind.

"We'll both go," said Moira finally. "But you don't know her the way I do. She'll still be at that damned clearing, waiting, and we'll have wasted all day."

Will said nothing. Moira angry was never reasonable. Let her work it out for herself. Instead, he pulled her gently into his arms and held her until her tense body relaxed into a hug.

"I'm glad to see you, too," she murmured.

They packed up Will's sleeping bag and camera, and within minutes were tramping back the way Moira had come.

A breeze sprang up, still cool from the night but warming to the sun. Will breathed deeply. The air smelled like nothing he had ever smelled before—thick with the scent of pine sap and sharp still with morning damp. It was clean, he finally decided. No pollution, no haze.

He slowed his pace in deference to Moira and stopped once, briefly, to examine her carefully. He suspected she was still a bit dizzy from the fall, but she didn't complain.

Will realized he had stepped up his pace again and glanced back. Moira was right behind him. By the scowl on her face, he judged she had a headache and he grinned at her encouragingly, wishing he could have left her somewhere safe.

The sun on the lake banished shadows and helped lift his spirits. He looked back the way they had come and the castle looked small, a child's toy, no more forbidding than a sand castle at the beach.

They moved fast. After a while, his feet in their hiking books began to ache from the hard rock. His gaze kept straying to the wall of trees less than ten feet to their left. He knew it was his imagination, but he felt watched, as if the trees were sentient. Not threatening, exactly, but aware. The breeze grew stronger as they walked, keeping the bugs at bay.

Just ahead, the shoreline curved into the trees, hiding the path from view. This was where the horse had first appeared. Will automatically walked more softly. It was a good spot for an ambush. He glanced back at Moira and although she still frowned fiercely, her eyes were trained on the woods ahead.

Then, as if they had planned it, they both stopped and turned toward the forest.

With a soft laugh, a woman stepped out of the trees. Her hair gleamed like honey in the sun and she wore what had once been an expensive navy woolen suit. The jacket was covered in sap, to which were stuck bits of leaves. Her pants looked as if they had been slept in. In one hand, she trailed a belt buckled around a pair of boots and what looked like a down coat. She stared at them in obvious relief for a second, then grinned wickedly at Moira.

"I see you didn't get eaten," she said.

"Very observant, Grace," muttered Moira, glancing away.

Grace turned to Will and smiled. Will caught his breath at the transformation. What had happened to the shy, skinny girl he remembered?

"Good to see you, Will O'Rourke," she said, her color high. She looked as if she wanted to say more, but instead she turned to Moira. "I thought we were only looking for Mack and Aidan."

"We were," said Moira stiffly. "Will is a bonus." She shifted the pack on her back and nodded. "Come on. We can talk as we walk."

They turned around and headed back for the island. Under Grace's prodding, Moira explained about her wild ride and unceremonious dumping at Will's feet. Then Will picked up his side of the story, starting again with Soutien and Oonagh's appearance in the presidential palace in Grozny. When he told about the wood nymph and how she died, Grace's face lost its light.

"Poor woman," she murmured. Then she looked into his eyes. "Poor Will." Her sympathy was absurdly comforting.

By the time they returned to the spot where Will had camped, it was time to eat again. Moira pulled out her camp stove and set it up on a flat rock. There was a dent in it the size of an egg, but it still worked. Will used the contents of his canteen to reconstitute stew while Grace rummaged through the pack and found dried fruit. She ate it as if she were famished.

Apparently Moira thought so, too. She stared at Grace, then her face cleared. "Good God, you haven't eaten since that jerky yesterday!"

Grace swallowed a mouthful of dried apple and shrugged. "There were berries along the way."

Moira was forgetting to stir the stew, so Will nudged her aside and took over the meal preparation.

"How did you know which way I'd gone?" asked Moira.

Grace looked at her curiously. "The phooka left a wide trail. It was a direct line to the lake, and then it turned east. I would have caught up to you much sooner if night hadn't stopped me."

It was Moira's turn to look puzzled. "I was on that phooka all night," she said. "We rode through bogs and forests and swamps..." She looked over her shoulder at Will. "We rode for miles, never in a straight line."

They all stared at each other in silence for a few moments. Then Will shrugged. "I don't think we should expect our rules to apply here."

Under her scrapes, Moira's face looked pale. Will knew exactly how she felt. The foundations of his world had been shifting since Soutien first appeared to him.

They ate in silence. The stew was terrible, but Will ate every bite and browbeat Grace and Moira into eating theirs, too. He had learned from years of traveling with soldiers to eat when he could. As they ate, he tried to judge the distance to the island.

"That looks like almost half a mile," said Grace, startling him. He looked at her, but she was examining the expanse of water between them and the island. "I'm pretty sure I can swim that, but not with my clothes and dragging my coat. I doubt either of you could swim it with your packs."

Or without, thought Will. Swimming had never been his best sport. Moira glanced at him and he knew she was thinking the same thing. The point was moot, anyway. They couldn't abandon their packs. They might not be able to come back and get them.

"Did you try calling across?" asked Grace, turning to look at him.

Will stared at her blankly. "No," he admitted. He looked across the water at the ruins. Why hadn't he yelled? What if Mack and Aidan were camping just the other side of that wall?

"I don't think you should," said Moira slowly. When he looked at her, she shrugged. "They might not thank us for calling attention to them."

Before the ensuing silence could become uncomfortable, Grace stood up.

"I'll swim across," she said. She looked into the water and her face grew expressionless. "I'll check it out, see if I can find sign of them. If they crossed over, there'll be a boat and I can come back and get you. If they're not there, I'll swim back."

Will went to stand by her. Of course there'd be a boat at the island. How else would Mack and Aidan have gotten across? He looked into the water and his memory conjured up the river woman. "No," he said, more sharply than he had intended. "Nobody's swimming."

Grace looked up at him, one eyebrow raised, and he told them about the green woman, about her claws and sharp teeth. When he finished, Grace shuddered, staring at the water with loathing.

"You never told me that part," said Moira, staring at him.

Will shrugged.

He stared at the island, willing it to provide an answer. The sun beat down on his head in sharp contrast to the cool wind. It was just past noon, he figured. They had a good seven hours of daylight left, enough to get to the island, explore it, and move on. If they had a boat.

The wind ruffled the waves, slapping them against the rocky shore. The far side of the lake was a shimmer of green against the blue sky. An eagle soared on an updraft, lazily enjoying the day. And the damned island stayed out of reach.

Unbidden, Oonagh's words came back to him. "See with your heart, not with your eyes," she had said.

What had she meant? He'd never been good with metaphors.

On impulse, he pulled the camera out of the pack and looked through it at the island. His heart might not have eyes, but his camera often revealed a truth his eyes alone couldn't see.

He scanned the water through the aperture. He had come too far to be turned back for lack of a boat. Oonagh had rubbed ointment on his eyelids. Why? So he could see truly?

Sometimes, he thought, the reason you don't see something is because you don't expect to...

A sound like wood scraping on stone began to impinge on his awareness and a chill ran down his back. Slowly, he turned the camera to look down.

Tethered to the shore by a rope around a boulder was a wooden rowboat, scraping gently against the rocky shore.

– ELEVEN –

GRACE sat rigidly in the center of the rowboat's seat, her hands tucked between her knees to keep them from reaching for the gunwale. She didn't want any part of her sticking out over the water.

Will handled the rowboat as if he rowed every day. The craft skimmed smoothly through the water, the oars barely making any sound.

She didn't see how he could be as relaxed as he seemed. They were traveling in a boat that hadn't been there half an hour ago, over water that might or might not contain dangerous creatures. She kept expecting a green, clawed hand to reach out of the water and pluck her out of the boat.

Moira sat in front, keeping an eye on the water. Her back was to Moira, but Grace was willing to bet that Moira would be as stoic as Will was.

She pulled her gaze away from the water, afraid staring would summon trouble.

There was something solid about Will, as if once he planted his feet, nothing would budge him. It was absurd to feel safer with him here. Will was just a man, as vulnerable to this strange place's mysteries as she was.

But she couldn't help being glad of his presence.

He looked much the same as she remembered. Where Moira's dark hair was curly, his was straight and thick. It needed a cut and looked unruly, as if he had combed it by raking his fingers through it. He kept it straight back, away from his forehead.

Grace had never seen him with a beard before, and she decided it looked odd, especially as the rich auburn contrasted with his hair.

He kept his head turned away as he peered over his shoulder to steer the boat. He had filled out over the years, fulfilling the promise of a tall, skinny teenager. A dirty T-shirt tucked into even dirtier jeans did little to conceal his flat abdomen. With every pull on the oars, his shoulders and arms corded with muscle, then relaxed.

The hands gripping the oars were bigger, harder looking, than she remembered.

Will turned back and caught her staring. She shifted her gaze to the island, but the heat in her cheeks betrayed her.

No one spoke as the island grew bigger and the ruins began to loom over the beach. Grace found herself wishing they had been quieter on the shore. Anyone hiding on the island could have seen them. Anyone could be waiting for them behind the ruined facade of the castle.

Or anything.

The bottom of the rowboat scraped along the sand and Moira slipped into the water to pull the craft ashore. She had removed her boots and socks and rolled up her pants to her knees in preparation for the landing.

Grace stared at Moira's muscled calves as the other woman hauled on the rowboat. When had Moira started running?

Then Will jumped onto the wet sand and it was her turn. She stood up, but before she could jump into the water, he lifted her by the waist and swung her effortlessly onto dry sand.

Mortified, Grace stood like a statue while he and Moira hauled the craft onto higher ground. Did she have "helpless" stamped in big letters on her forehead? What was it with these two?

With the boat safely moored to a tree, Moira retrieved her socks and boots.

At close range, the ruins were forbidding, even in bright sunshine.

From the beach, all they could see were the two remaining towers, moss and ivy covered, jutting out of the forest. Small, dark openings in the stone towers suggested windows. They looked like eyes.

Rapunzel, Rapunzel, let down your hair, thought Grace.

They were about one hundred yards from the base of the nearest tower. Grace studied the wall of trees facing them, and her heart sank. They would need a machete to get through.

"We should see if we can find a blaze," said Will in a low voice. They walked up and down the beach, searching for a sign that Mack had been there, but found nothing. The wall of trees remained impenetrable.

Not Rapunzel, decided Grace. Sleeping Beauty, waiting for Prince Charming to hack his way to her.

Finally, Will shrugged and turned back to Moira and Grace. "Why don't you two wait here? There's no sense getting all three of us scratched up."

Grace and Moira glanced at each other, then turned to stare at Will silently. Finally he shrugged again. "It was worth a try." As a precaution, both he and Moira donned their sweaters and Grace buttoned up her blazer.

The trees and brambles fought Will every step of the way, ripping at his clothes, catching at his pack, tripping him up. After half an hour and less than fifty yards, Moira took the lead, and found herself getting the same treatment.

There was a malevolence to these woods that was hard to pinpoint. It was as if the trees were aware of their presence and resisted their advance as best they could.

Still, they ploughed on.

Grace, walking behind, hardly got any scratches. She avoided the worst of the roots automatically, leaving her eyes free to watch for low branches and prickly vines. After a while, she tapped Will on the shoulder. When he stopped to look at her, she slipped in front of him and tapped Moira on the shoulder.

"What?" said Moira testily. She glanced over her shoulder, but kept going.

A long scratch trailed from her temple to her chin. On the other cheek, the scrape she had acquired when the phooka threw her was beginning to darken into a bruise. Suddenly, she tripped on a root and pitched full length into a prickly bush.

Trapped as she was by the weight of the pack and the trees pressing in on either side, it took Will and Grace a few minutes to disentangle her. By the time she was standing again, flecks of blood spotted her sweater and there were more scratches on her face and hands. She looked like she wanted to swear.

Those scratches will probably get infected, thought Grace. "Let me go first," she whispered, unwilling to raise her voice in this place.

"By all means," said Moira. "If you think you can do better..."

As soon as Grace took the lead, the way became easier. She gave herself over to intuition and found she was taking a tortuous path that nevertheless allowed them to move faster than before. The trees didn't exactly move aside, but branches no longer plucked at them, and the brambly bushes no longer caught at their clothes or skin. After a while, Grace's suspicion was confirmed. The shoes were helping her find the best path.

And then they were out of the trees, face-to-face with the ancient stone wall of the castle. Grace had expected a moat, but the forest grew right up to the ruins, with no break. The trees grew so close that she couldn't see where the wall became a tower, nor could she see the main portal they had spotted from across the lake.

"It's over there," said Will, pointing to his right.

So they set off again, and this time Will led. To Grace's surprise, clouds had covered the sun while they fought their way through the woods. It could have been the overcast sky, but it seemed much later in the day than it should have been.

Tree roots had worked their way under the wall, heaving it up in places and buckling it in others. As they worked their way along, they had to negotiate huge blocks of stone that had toppled from the parapet. Grace glanced up often, aware that the wall was not as solid as it looked. The trees by the ruin weren't as big as those by the beach, but they were probably hundreds of years old nevertheless. The ruins had been abandoned a very long time.

She unbuttoned her blazer, suddenly aware that she was sodden with sweat. The air had grown close and insects had discovered their presence. The trees to one side of them seemed to press closer, as if to crush them against the stone wall.

Grace found herself breathing faster and tried to control her rising panic. It was only an old, ruined building. They would check it out, make sure Mack and Aidan weren't there, and leave. This wasn't a big island. No matter which way they struck out, they would come to a beach, which they could follow back to their rowboat. They would be back across the lake before nightfall.

But the castle pulled at her. A deep sadness seemed to emanate from it, overlaid by a frisson of horror. Did the others feel it, too?

Will kept walking, skirting obstacles when they were too big, stepping over them when they weren't. He seemed tireless. Grace was so tired she wanted to curl up somewhere and sleep. But not here.

"There," said Will, and she looked beyond him to see the portal just ahead. Sometime in the distant past, the huge wooden doors had fallen away from the castle. The shape of them could still be distinguished in the gorse bushes before the portal, which were smaller and less dense than the surrounding vegetation.

The three of them stood for a moment, examining the dark entrance. Grace could see a stone stairway just inside, where a lookout would have climbed to get a good view out of an upper window.

"Let's go," said Will in a low voice, and before she was quite ready, they were moving again, heading for the yawning interior. Will lead the way, and Moira brought up the rear. Grace realized without being told that they were trying to protect her. She couldn't tell if that made her feel better or worse.

The arch of the entranceway, and hence the wall, was deeper than she had expected. The stone stairway pierced the arch and disappeared into the gloom of the upper level. Beneath the thick moss underfoot was stone. Aside from the moss, no vegetation grew there. Not enough sunlight, she surmised.

If the castle had stood this long, chances were it wouldn't come tumbling down on her at this precise moment. She took a deep breath and followed Will inside.

It took a moment for her eyes to adjust to the dimness. She

went from being too hot to shivering in the sudden damp. Something smelled bad. She looked around. Some small creature had crawled under the archway to die. Something had fed on it, some time ago, and hadn't finished the job.

Grace looked away, her stomach unhappy.

They passed through the archway into a labyrinthine nightmare. The upper floor of the castle had collapsed onto the main floor, leaving walls tilting crazily against each other and massive blocks of squared stone and marble filling the spaces in between. Daylight penetrated the maze in shafts, illuminating in pinpricks, like sunlight through a sieve. Even so, Grace could tell that someone had been working at clearing the wreckage. She studied two huge blocks that had been carefully set aside, one on top of the other, and shivered. It would take an army of men, or a crane, to move those blocks. She doubted either had been at work here.

"They can't be in here," whispered Moira in her ear, startling Grace. She turned to look at the other woman. Moira's face was in shadow, but a shaft of light hit the back of her hair, giving her a halo.

Grace had her doubts, too. The ruins were a surreal landscape of dirty white marble, stone blocks, and darkness. Why would anybody venture into it?

"Over here," said Will, and both women turned to find he had climbed the steps on the inside of the archway.

They followed him up the narrow steps, and Grace for one was grateful to leave behind the evidence of destruction. What could have destroyed such a massive structure?

"Careful," said Moira, pulling on her jacket to hold her back.

Grace squinted and saw what Moira was pointing at. One whole side of the staircase had crumbled away when the inner wall fell against it. By the outside wall, the stairs seemed solid enough. Will had already disappeared up them. Dim light filtered down from the upper windows, but as Grace climbed gingerly up the staircase, she saw that most of the light was blocked by a huge slab of inner wall that had fallen against the outer wall.

There was only enough room beneath the canted wall to crawl up the stairs. With Will already gone ahead and Moira waiting patiently behind, Grace took a deep breath, crouched and went through the opening.

It was only a few feet, but it felt like a mile. At every inch, she was aware of the weight of the wall pressing down against the outer wall. Rubble bit through the cloth covering her knees and into her palms, although she could tell that most of it had already been swept aside. By whose passage? Will's? Or his brothers'?

Then it was over. She emerged from the tunnel to find only a few more steps left to climb. Gray light filtered through the ivy-covered window openings of a long stone hallway. Here the inner wall still stood, except for the part that had fallen in on the staircase. Grace looked down at the crumbled section of the wall and the darkened ruin beyond it. From this vantage point, the stone ruins looked like huge blocks of foam set in an enormous foam pit, nothing more than a big kid's playpen.

Moira emerged from the staircase behind her, but the window had caught Grace's eye and she moved over to it. She hoped to see across the lake, but the trees were too tall. The sky above them threatened rain.

Behind her, Moira sneezed.

"Over here," said Will.

He stood at the end of the hallway, before a dark opening that had once framed a door. It led to one of the towers.

All three stood in front of the opening, staring up. A flight of stairs disappeared through the floor of an upper level. Somewhere above, a window let in enough light to see that the tower was in good shape.

"Well," said Will softly, staring at the stairs, "we didn't come here just to turn back." And he stepped into the tower.

"Wait!" said Grace, suddenly unsure. "Do you have a gun? Any kind of weapon?"

Will looked at her strangely. "No. If I had a weapon, I'd end up using it."

As he started up the stairs, Grace glanced at Moira, who rolled her eyes.

"Give me a break," whispered Moira, and she pulled out her knife, holding it ready.

But there was nothing at the top of the tower except a large room open to the sky. The roof had fallen in, destroying whatever might have been the purpose of the room. Dirt and debris covered the floor. Flowers and grasses had taken root in the dirt and formed a colorful counterpoint to the sad remnants of the tower.

Grace stood in the doorway and turned her face to the sky. Dark clouds massed against each other, rumbling. This high, the wind chased the bugs away and kept the dust from clogging her nostrils. She took a deep breath.

Will clambered over the debris to the far side of the tower and looked down.

"Just more of the same," he reported when he made his way back. His face was covered in scratches, and his beard looked like someone had back-teased it. There were snags in his sweater.

"I guess that leaves the other tower," said Moira with a distinct lack of enthusiasm.

A drop of rain fell on Grace's cheek and she sighed.

They negotiated the stairs and the long hallway in silence. The far tower was lost in the gloom. As they approached, they realized that vines completely covered the nearest window to the tower. It was only when they came to within a dozen feet of the tower that they saw this one had a door.

A new one.

***

Moira heard the moaning as soon as Will opened the door. She hesitated outside the tower, but Will began to climb the stairs quickly and quietly, Grace right behind him.

Moira took a deep breath and, clutching the knife tightly, followed them.

The smell hit her the moment she entered the stairwell, a cloying stench so thick she could taste it.

The stone stairs looked as if they had been cut yesterday. Whoever had built them hadn't had time to wear them down. They curved around the wall of the tower, cutting through a small hole in the floor above. Gray light flooded down the hole, a beacon compared to the darkness of the lower stairs.

The moaning never stopped.

Will paused, then cautiously climbed the step that would bring his head above floor level. A heartbeat later, he climbed the rest and disappeared. Grace hesitated a moment, then followed him.

A fear so cold it hurt gripped Moira's insides and twisted. She didn't want to go up there and face what they would find. But she had the only weapon. Trembling, she forced herself to place one foot before the other and climb.

She didn't look around until she reached the top of the stairs. Then one quick glance revealed a single, large, round room with only one window. Someone had hacked away the vines to let the light in. The vines, dry and dead, lay on the floor where they had fallen. Moira had time to see a small table standing away from the curved wall and a heap of foul-smelling rags underneath it before her attention caught on Will and Grace.

They stood side-by-side with their backs to her, perfectly still. Moira finally realized they were staring at something. She stepped closer, peering over Grace's shoulder.

"Mack!" she cried. Pushing past the other two, she ran to her oldest brother. He was sitting on a tall wooden chair, his arms bound to the wide arms of the chair, his torso roped to the back. His head sagged to his chest, leaving only his profile to recognize him by. He was unconscious.

"Mack," she repeated and went to fall on one knee by his side. Then she saw what kept Will and Grace frozen in place.

Mack's hands were missing. His arms ended in ragged stumps that looked as if they had been cauterized by a blowtorch. She stumbled back and, in growing horror, looked down. His legs ended just above where his ankles had been. Someone had shoved his bloodied pant legs up over his calves. Bone protruded from the ragged, burned flesh of his stumps.

Below the stumps was the source of the stench, a deep stone basin full of blood, the surface clotted and filmed like milk gone bad.

Moira clamped a hand over her mouth and turned away, willing herself not to retch. When she finally turned back, Will was kneeling by their brother's side, gently pulling his head up.

"Mack," he said, "can you hear me?"

Mack's face was so white it looked phosphorescent. In spite of herself, Moira glanced down at the basin again. So much blood...

She couldn't... Mack... Her mind skittered around the sight of her oldest brother, unable to grasp what she was seeing. Grace moved past her, toward the back of the room. Only then did the continuous moaning register. With quick, jerky steps, Moira followed Grace.

The light from the window barely reached this far in, but there was enough to see a stone fireplace set against the wall. Next to it, someone huddled, arms wrapped around legs, face buried against knees. Moira's training kicked in and she reached for Grace's arm. She pulled her behind, placing herself and her knife between Grace and the creature on the floor.

By the muscled arms and wide shoulders, Moira decided it was a man. He rocked on his hams, moaning almost inaudibly, lost in his own private hell. With dawning awareness, Moira touched his shoulder.

Aidan lifted his head, and looked blankly at her. Then he buried his face against his knees again, moaning.

Moira and Grace stared down at him. The sight of her brother physically unharmed but obviously in distress helped pull Moira out of her shock. Her brothers needed her.

She looked around. Aidan would hate knowing she had seen him this way. Behind him, the remnants of small bones gleamed in the ashes and dead coals of the fireplace. A faint odor of cooked meat clung to the walls.

"He's still alive," said Will. Moira turned away from Aidan with relief and went to help Will. While they cut through Mack's bonds, Grace shifted the foul-smelling basin away. Moira saw pieces of cloth floating in the thick liquid, but had no time to wonder about them.

Mack's eyes flickered open. They were glazed with shock and looked very dark against the pallor of his skin. He turned from face to face and recognition dawned in them.

"I knew you'd come," he whispered.

But too late, thought Moira as hot tears flooded her eyes. Too late.

"Oh Mack." She swallowed a sob. "Let's get you out of here." They had to get him back home, to a hospital.

Mack shook his head minutely, as though trying to conserve his energy.

"Is Aidan...?" he trailed off, looking at Moira.

"He's okay," she said quickly.

Mack closed his eyes. "Good," he whispered. "Don't hold it against him."

Before anyone could ask him what he meant, Mack's eyelids struggled open again.

"You have to leave," he said, urgency lending strength to his voice. One arm stump lifted, then fell back and Mack bit back a groan of agony. After a moment, he continued, his voice faint as an echo. "Take Aidan. Get out before he comes back."

"Who?" asked Will. Moira recognized the burr in his voice, the sharp edge that revealed his anger. "Who did this to you?"

Mack shook his head, then stopped. Moira could tell the movement had made him dizzy.

"No time," said Mack. "Big, too strong for us, insane. Ate my feet." For the first time, he seemed to realize the enormity of his situation. His face twisted in a rictus of horror. "He ate my feet!"

Next to Moira, Grace put a hand over her mouth. "Dear God!" she said. She swayed as if she would faint, and Moira put an arm around her.

"Not yet," she told Grace roughly. "First we get them out of here, then you can get sick."

Grace removed her hand from her mouth and nodded. Her eyes were bright with tears and her face was white, but she moved over to Aidan, and helped him up. Aidan followed her docilely, moaning the whole time.

Will picked up his older brother and carried him like a child to the staircase.

"Leave me," whispered Mack. "I'm dead anyway. I'll slow you down."

Will shook his head. "You're coming with us."

"No," said Mack with a hint of his old fire. "Save those you can, Will!"

But Will only shook his head grimly and started down.

Halfway down the tower, Mack fainted.

Despair crept toward Moira on rational feet as she followed her brother to the bottom of the staircase. How would they carry Mack through those woods? And even if they made it, what then? Give him back his feet? His hands?

When they reached the hallway, she looked down on her brother's ashen face and knew. He was going to die here, in this place of mystery. He would never see his baby.

"Come on," said Grace, shaking Moira's arm. "We have to get out of here."

"She's right," came a voice from the end of the hallway. Adrenaline shot through Moira. She whirled, crouched, and swept the knife out in front of her before she recognized the figure standing less than ten feet away.

Soutien. Somewhere inside her, a little knot loosened.

Next to her, Will had started to lower Mack to the floor before he recognized Soutien. Now he straightened.

"Where the hell have you been?" he said, his voice harsh.

Soutien looked at him strangely. "We can discuss that when we're far away from here. Let's go." He moved to take Mack, but one look at Will's face warned him off. With a curt nod, he led the way back to the staircase.

Moira watched the cloak swirl around Soutien's knees and tried to get past her relief to question the miracle of his presence.

How had he known where they were?

Will walked past her and Mack's hair brushed her arm. She helped Will lower him to the top stair of the archway staircase and supported the unconscious Mack while Will crawled past the obstruction on the stairway. Soutien had already disappeared.

It took both women at his head and shoulders, and Will and Soutien at his feet, to get Mack through the blockage on the stairs. By the time they got him down, all of them were shaking and pale. They had been as careful as they could, but one leg stump had caught on an obstruction and ripped charred flesh away, causing fresh bleeding. Mack and Soutien were covered in Mack's blood.

Through the grisly procedure, Aidan sat on the top step, arms on his lap, eyes closed, moaning. Moira didn't blame him. She wished she could do the same.

We'll get you out, she silently promised her troubled brother. Don't worry, Aidan, we'll get you out.

Finally, after what seemed like an eternity, they were at the bottom of the stairs, with the jumbled mass of destruction on one side and the forest on the other. Clouds now filled the sky, and rain fell in a steady downpour guaranteed to soak them the moment they left the protection of the arch. It would be dark soon. Moira thought of the way back and suppressed a shudder.

It would be hell. But it was still a better option than remaining here.

Will clasped the unconscious Mack to him as though he were weightless, but at almost two hundred pounds Mack was the biggest of the O'Rourke brothers. Will wouldn't be able to carry him all the way back.

"We'll need a stretcher," said Grace.

Moira glanced at her, then away. The look on Grace's face reflected Moira's thoughts exactly—a stretcher wouldn't make it through those woods.

"We don't have time," said Soutien. He looked at Moira as though the words pained him. "We have to get off this island before nightfall."

The word seemed to trigger something in Aidan. His moaning rose in volume and his eyes darted around in panic. Moira and Grace moved to either side of him, ready to restrain him if they had to.

For the first time, Moira realized that Aidan was saying "No, no, no," in a continuous stream of fear. What had happened to him? He was physically intact, with only a few bruises on his face. His wrists bore burn marks, as if he had struggled against bindings. Had he helplessly witnessed Mack's torture, knowing he was next?

Then why had they found him unbound?

"It's all right," she said to her brother, running a gentle hand up and down his back. "It's all right, Aidan."

Her voice seemed to calm him. He resumed his low-voiced moaning, wrapping his arms around himself and rocking from side to side.

Soutien and Will had watched the incident in silence. Now Soutien turned to Will.

"The creature who did this to Mack will return at nightfall. If we're not gone before then, we'll have to fight him. Someone could die."

Will's lips thinned and color stained his cheeks above his russet beard. Moira quickly stepped forward before he could say something he would regret later. Will might believe Soutien had betrayed him—and their brothers—but she didn't.

"What do you suggest?" she asked Soutien.

Soutien looked at the wall of forest that began on the other side of the archway. Then he looked at Will. "You won't let me carry him?" Will shook his head and Soutien sighed. "Then at least let me carry your pack." When Will just stared at him, Soutien raised an eyebrow. "Do you want to get out of here, or not?"

The strain of Mack's weight was already beginning to tell on Will. His face looked etched by a knife and his hands where they clasped Mack against him were white.

"Moira, help me here," he growled. Between the two of them, they supported Mack while Grace removed the backpack from his shoulders.

Finally, Soutien removed his cloak and tied it to the pack. Then he shrugged the pack over his shoulders, adjusted the straps to his liking and looked up. "Let's go," he said, and started to move out from under the archway.

"I'll go first," said Grace. She moved to stand beside Soutien.

"No!" said Will, and Grace turned to him in surprise. "It's too dangerous."

Too dangerous? wondered Moira. As opposed to what?

Grace gave Will a curious look but before she could say anything, Soutien spoke up.

"She's right," he said, looking down at Grace's shoes. "She should lead."

And before Will could object further, Grace turned and stepped out into the rain.

❧ TWELVE ❧

RAIN plastered Will's hair to his skull, trickling down his face and into his beard. He carried Mack over one shoulder, leaving himself a free hand with which to fend off branches. It was no different than every other time he had carried someone out of the line of fire.

Except that this time, the wounded man was his big brother.

The trail they followed could barely accommodate one person at a time. The trees protected them from the worst of the downpour, but drops collected on the cupped leaves, then fell all at once when the silent travelers jostled branches.

Will placed one careful step in front of the other. The rain brought out throngs of mosquitoes and black flies to attack the exposed flesh of his face and hands. He didn't want to think about what they were doing to Mack.

He tried not to feel Mack's arms brushing against the back of his legs with every step.

Soutien walked ahead, where Will could keep an eye on him. The man was careful of the branches, making sure Will had them in hand before releasing them. He turned around often to make sure the others were all right.

Will didn't know what to think of Soutien. The man looked the same as ever—tall, lean, and graceful, blond hair darkened by rain, green eyes darkened by concern. He acted like the man Will had always known. But he hadn't acted like that in Grozny.

Your brothers are in danger.

It didn't matter that Soutien had known where to find Will. It didn't matter that he had disappeared before Will's eyes in the presidential palace.

He had known that Mack and Aidan were in trouble, and hadn't helped.

Will was honest enough to understand that his anger was misdirected, at least in part. He knew who was really to blame for Mack's mutilation.

If he had been faster... if he hadn't waited for the nymph to die... if he hadn't turned away from the island to find Grace...

He stopped thinking then, and concentrated on walking.

***

Grace's every step released an odor like mildew and rotting leaves, as if she waded through a compost heap. She walked as fast as she dared. They were nearly out of the forest, but night—or at least darkness—was creeping in faster than they were creeping out.

She was wet, tired, and scared. She wanted to see the open shore and feel the sandy beach beneath her feet. She even looked forward to the boat trip.

Behind her came the sound of people crashing through the brush. Why couldn't they be more quiet? Even Aidan's moaning was swallowed by the noise of snapping branches and rustling leaves.

She hoped Moira was all right with Aidan, and Will with Mack.

Oh God, Mack...

She couldn't bear to think of his poor legs and arms. That poor man. Even if he lived...

She was past being nauseated. Tears pricked her eyelids and she swallowed hard. There was no time for tears. They had to get away from here, now.

At least they had Soutien. They would need every able body to get Mack and Aidan safely away.

Soutien had said the creature would come back at nightfall. Was it already on its way? Where was it coming from? Would the creature be on the beach, waiting for them?

Just get me off this island, she prayed. Just get *us* off.

Then she heard a sound not caused by their passage, and stopped.

To her right, something was rustling in the trees, the sound growing louder by the second.

Grace's lips parted as she struggled to breathe past the fear. She turned to look behind her and found Soutien already moving, pushing her ahead, urging the others on.

"Hurry," he whispered.

She broke into a stumbling run, trusting the shoes to steer her away from the most treacherous roots. Behind her, the others began running, too, Moira tugging Aidan on. Grace heard Will's labored breathing and Mack's unconscious grunts every time Will's shoulder jammed into his gut.

The rustling grew closer and Grace ran faster. Something in this godforsaken forest was stalking them. Fear lent strength to her legs. She leapt over fallen logs, twisted around huge trees, and ducked under branches. All the while, she prayed that the others were right behind her.

And then she broke out of the woods and stumbled through a few brambles onto the sandy beach. There was more light once she was out of the trees, but the rain was fiercer. Trying to control her panic, she looked around the beach. Nothing but the boat, exactly where they'd left it. She took a deep, shuddering breath and turned back to help.

Moira came first, pulling Aidan by the hand. He was frantic with fear, looking over his shoulder and grimacing. White showed all the way around his irises. He was breathing too hard to keep up the moaning.

"Come on," urged Grace, and helped pull him to the beach, where he immediately curled up in a ball on the wet, hard-packed sand, hiding his face. Grace left Moira frantically removing her backpack.

It was hard running through the wet sand and Will was already stumbling out of the trees by the time she returned to the forest edge. He still held Mack securely clasped over one shoulder, but his face was flushed with strain and he was panting with exertion. Soutien emerged right behind him, his gaze taking in everyone's position before returning to the trees.

The rustling turned into the sound of snapping twigs and low grunting. A trembling like fever began in the pit of Grace's stomach.

"Hurry!" she whispered, to everyone and no one. The boat was high on the sand. Then she took a good look at it and turned to Will in despair.

"It's too small."

"No, it's not," said Soutien, turning her around and pushing her toward the rowboat. Grace stumbled in amazement. It was no longer the small craft she had seen a moment before, but a sturdier one at least three feet longer and a foot wider.

"How...?" she began, staring at it in confusion.

"Help me!" called Moira, giving up on secrecy. She had tossed her backpack into the bow and was trying to shove the rowboat off the sand by herself.

Grace ran to help, leaning her shoulder into hard wood and pushing. Behind her, in the trees, the grunting rose above the sound of rustling leaves and snapping branches. Where was it? It sounded close enough to burst out of the trees at any moment.

The craft slid into the water and Grace ran back to help Aidan, leaving Moira to hold the rope.

Aidan sprang to his feet at the touch of Grace's hand and followed her to the rowboat. He clambered in and sat on the aft bench. At once he began moaning.

"Hurry!" said Moira, glancing over her shoulder at the forest.

Soutien waded into the water and dropped Will's backpack at Aidan's feet. Grace couldn't take her gaze off the trees. Her mouth was dry. What was taking it so long?

"Get in," Soutien told her.

Grace slipped into the craft and sat next to Aidan while Soutien and Will lifted Mack over the gunwale. One arm stump caught on Will's backpack, causing a slow trickle of blood. Mack groaned but didn't come to.

The crashing in the trees stopped suddenly. They turned as one toward the forest as a wild pig emerged from the trees. It stood staring at them, blinking and snuffling.

Grace sagged with relief, already starting to feel foolish. But before she could say a word, Soutien whirled, picked up Moira, and dropped her like a sack of flour into the row boat.

"Get in!" he shouted at Will, who immediately hauled himself into the boat. He almost stepped on Moira on his way to the oar bench.

As Will hurriedly got the oars in the water, Grace looked around in confusion.

Then she saw it. Something was approaching them from the other end of the beach, less than sixty feet away. The pig's noisy arrival had covered the creature's advance.

Grace pressed a trembling hand against her mouth to keep a burbling cry from escaping. Too big. Oh God, it was so big!

It was man-like, as wide in the hip as it was in the shoulder. Its arms hung to below its knees, ending in huge, taloned hands that twitched. One hand carried a long-handled axe that looked like it was made of sharp-edged stone. Both its eyes protruded, barely held back by the thin skin surrounding them. Beneath its beak of a nose was a wide, thin-lipped mouth. The lower jaw extended beyond the upper, to accommodate large, pointed tusks. Its skin, including its face, was covered in short bristles, like a boar. The head was at least twice the size of a human's. It stood two heads taller than the tallest man she had ever met.

Discovered, the creature broke into a loping run that covered ground at a frightening pace.

Moira untangled herself and raised her head above the gunwale, catching her first glimpse of the creature. She gasped in alarm, attracting Aidan's attention.

"No-o-o-o-o!" he wailed, and tried to scuttle back, stopping only when he almost fell overboard. Grace couldn't help him. She was paralyzed by fear.

Then Soutien gave a mighty shove and they floated free. Immediately Will turned the boat and applied himself to the oars. As he pulled away from shore, Soutien hauled himself dripping from the water, flinging one leg over the gunwale. Moira scrambled to help him. He made his way to Will, and sat next to him, grabbing one of the oars.

On the beach, the creature stopped and sniffed the air, turning its head this way and that.

A red skull cap covered its stringy gray hair and a grimy brown tunic haphazardly hid its genitals.

He. It was a he.

The creature followed their progress with his gaze, then took a step in the water. He immediately retreated. Then, as if finally realizing he was thwarted, he raised the axe above his head and roared.

Just as Grace thought they were going to get away, the beast's arm swung forward and he released the axe.

As though in slow motion, the axe traced a graceful, deadly trajectory toward the rowboat. It was going to hit them, in spite of the distance. Grace tensed, ready to fling herself into the water.

Then Soutien stood up. He lifted his arm as though about to wave and caught the axe. The momentum swung his arm back and he traced a half circle forward in the air with the axe, releasing it at the top of the arc.

"No!" cried Moira as the axe left Soutien's hand. "Don't give it back to him!"

The axe hurtled back to the island, heading straight for Red Cap.

"Row!" said Soutien, catching up the oar again. At the same time, the axe cleaved the air where Red Cap had stood and thunked into the trunk of a tree, splitting it in two.

"The axe is tied to him," said Soutien grimly, pulling in rhythm with Will. "It always returns to him."

By the time Red Cap had retrieved his weapon, they were well out of range.

❧ THIRTEEN ❦

I T WAS almost dark by the time they reached the far side of the lake. The boat scraped against the rocky shore and Soutien pulled in his oar to avoid trapping it. He held fast to a boulder, steadying the rowboat while Grace climbed out and tied the rope to a tree.

The rain had slackened to fitful showers but it didn't matter. They were all soaked. Soutien glanced at Will, noting how the man's shoulders and arms trembled with fatigue. Or was it grief?

Soutien looked away, steeling himself against the rush of pain. If he gave in, grief and guilt would swamp him, rendering him incapable of doing what had to be done.

In spite of his resolution, his gaze found Mack's still form. What would Fin Bheara think if he saw Mack?

He would think he had chosen poorly when he trusted Soutien to bring back Kirwan's sons. Those great, fierce eyes would fill with contempt, and with good reason. How could Soutien hope to save the Fey when he couldn't even protect his charges? His friend?

He took a deep breath of damp air. Self-pity was a waste of time. He had to get them all to Knockma, and quickly. Amadan was on the move. The longer they tarried, the greater the chance of Red Cap, or another of his ilk, catching up to them.

"I'll help you with him," he told Will, indicating Mack. To his relief, Will didn't object and they lifted Mack out of the boat while Grace braced it against the rocks.

"Grace," said Soutien as Moira coaxed Aidan onto shore, "stay in the boat until I get back."

She gave him a narrow-eyed stare but nodded. He looked at her a moment longer. Hers was the scent that had nagged him. He had all but forgotten this old friendship of Moira's. She had changed, young Grace. No longer the shy, coltish teenager, time had firmed her jaw and steeled her gaze. Or perhaps the change dated from her arrival here.

He and Will carried Mack up the rocky shore and laid him, unconscious, on the hard ground. Will arranged his brother's arms carefully over his chest.

Soutien turned toward the island to give Will more privacy. After moment, Will came to stand beside him.

"He's still there," said Soutien, gesturing at the island. "Pacing up and down."

Will squinted at the ragged outline of black trees against gray sky.

"Good eyes," he said. "I can't even see the beach."

"He's waiting for the rowboat to come back." Soutien didn't look at Will, but felt him stiffen. Without a word, Will turned and walked back to the rowboat.

With a sigh, Soutien followed him. Why was Will so angry with him?

Moira stood up as they approached, her back to the lake. Soutien couldn't see her expression. Was she angry, too? No. She had been relieved to see him at the castle. Whatever Will's reasons, she didn't share them.

Aidan sat on a nearby boulder, a few feet above water level, blessedly silent. He didn't even look around as they clambered down to the shore.

Grace looked expectantly at Will and Soutien from her seat in the rowboat. Her hands were tucked between her knees and she was shivering.

"Now what?" she asked.

"We have to destroy the boat," said Will harshly.

"Why?" said Moira. "What if—"

"Its magic ties it to the island and to this shore," said Soutien, from behind Will. "If we leave the rowboat, it will reappear at the island where Red Cap waits."

Moira waved at the boat. "Then let's burn the damned thing and get out of here!" She glanced over her shoulder at the dark bulk of the island.

"Fire won't do it, Moira," Soutien explained. "The boat is spelled against the normal dangers. Otherwise the first storm would have pulled it from its moorings."

"Spelled?" said Moira.

"How do you know so much about it?" demanded Will at the same time.

"Iron," said Grace, interrupting them both. "Iron." She looked at Moira. "Use your knife."

Iron. Soutien's glance slid over to Grace as she sat patiently in the bow of the rowboat. The unreality of the situation suddenly hit him like a slap in the face.

The only humans in the Fey world were about to use iron to keep a monster away.

How had the past become the present?

Moira plucked the hunting knife from her cargo pocket. The blade seemed to sigh as she pulled it free from its sheath. She climbed in with Grace and attacked the wooden hull of the craft as if it were Red Cap himself. Will came closer to examine her progress but Soutien could see she'd barely scratched the surface. Already she was breathing hard from the exertion.

"Let Soutien do it," said Grace suddenly.

They all turned to look at him, even Aidan.

Soutien stared at the ground for a moment, wondering how she knew. Then he slipped into the cold water and waded over to the boat. Without a word, he took the knife from Moira and in half a dozen deft, powerful strokes, chopped a four-inch hole in the bottom of the rowboat.

It sank so fast Grace and Moira had to jump out. From the island came a faint roar of anger. Red Cap's eyes were as good as his.

Soutien handed the knife to Moira, turned, and climbed back onto shore.

Shivering in the breeze from the lake, the others followed him to where Mack lay. They stared down at the maimed man for a long moment before Grace finally broke the silence.

"We have to get out of here," she said, her voice firm. She was nothing more than a shadowy outline against the sky. She turned to Soutien. "We have to get him to a hospital. How do we get out of here?"

Soutien's stomach knotted in dismay. They thought he could bring them back. They thought Mack might survive. He swallowed hard before speaking, feeling as if he were ringing a death knell. "The only way I know is through King Fin Bheara. And he's days from here."

"Mack doesn't have days," said Moira, her voice almost a whisper.

I know, thought Soutien. He bent to retrieve Will's backpack. "You'd better let me carry Mack for a while," he said gently, handing Will the pack. "We can go faster."

❧ FOURTEEN ❧

WILL and the others followed Soutien for two grim hours, stumbling under a moonless sky. Soutien set a slow, steady pace, never faltering, never hesitating. Still, they could barely see where they were going and made poor progress.

Although the rain had stopped some time earlier, everything was still wet. Walking kept Will warm, but he worried about Mack. Even wrapped in a blanket, he was getting too cold.

All of them save for Soutien went sprawling more than once, adding bruises and lumps to the strain of trying to see. As the hours wore on, Will's grudging admiration of Soutien's stamina turned to bleak wonder. The man could see in the dark and had extraordinary strength. What else would he surprise them with? Even Grace stumbled with fatigue, despite her shoes.

When Moira took a particularly bad fall on her already sore shoulder, Soutien called a halt.

"We can't stop now," protested Moira, her voice catching with the pain. "Mack..."

"Mack won't get to help any sooner if one of you breaks a leg," said Soutien. "There's a stream a little ways from here. We'll camp there."

Will wanted to add his protests to Moira's, but logic kept him quiet. Soutien was right. It would only compound their problems if someone got seriously hurt.

"I'll make a fire," said Moira when they finally reached the stream.

"Don't take branches from a living tree," warned Soutien. "Only what you find on the ground."

A heavy silence descended on the group, but nobody questioned him. Will didn't like it, but he would follow the man's lead for the time being. As mysterious as he had become, Soutien was their only guide in this strange land.

Moira and Grace worked at building a small, smoky fire while Will dug through his backpack and Moira's for sleeping bags. He and Soutien made a bed of moss close to the fire and covered it with a light tarp and a sleeping bag. Then they gently placed Mack on it and covered him with the other sleeping bag. If Soutien saw the bloodstains on Will's bag, he didn't mention it.

Aidan sat with his back against a tree, watching them. The smoky fire sent shadows dancing on the planes of his face, turning him into a stranger. He hadn't made a sound in hours and Will wondered if he was finally coming back to himself. Then, as they tucked the bag around Mack, Aidan stirred.

"It's no use, you know," he said. "He's going to die."

Will turned and stared at his brother. More than the words themselves, it was Aidan's tone of voice—so casual, as if he were commenting on the weather—that chilled Will's blood. This was the first thing he chose to say after his long silence?

Moira finally broke the spell. "Not if we can help it, Aidan."

Will crossed the few feet separating them and hunkered down by older brother's side.

"Aidan," he said gently, "what happened back there? How did you...?" He stopped, suddenly at a loss for words. He couldn't ask his brother why he hadn't been hurt, while Mack had.

But it was too late. Aidan had retreated to his private little world, and sat staring blindly at the fire.

Will clasped his brother on the shoulder, wishing he could do something to help him. He had seen this kind of shock before. Only time would help. And safety. With a sigh, he stood up. There was someone else he wanted answers from.

"Maybe it's time you told us what's going on," he told Soutien.

Moira turned, a second lightweight tarp in her hands. Grace entered the circle of firelight with an armful of twigs and deposited them a few feet from the fire. She looked expectantly at Soutien.

Will and Soutien stared at each other across the unconscious figure of Mack.

"Maybe you can start with who you really are," prompted Will.

Soutien shook his head, and although it was too dark to be sure, Will thought he saw the familiar sardonic smile flit across his face.

"I'm Soutien de Navarre," he said. "Friend to the O'Rourkes. The same man I always was."

"But that's not all you are," said Grace quickly.

There was a brief silence. Then, "No, that's not all I am."

Moira abandoned her tarp and approached Soutien. He turned to address her.

"I am the adopted son of Fin Bheara and Oonagh. They took me in when my human mother died in childbirth."

"Your *human* mother?" said Grace.

Soutien sighed. "Yes. My father was of the Fey. He crossed over when my mother died."

"Crossed over?" said Moira.

"Died," said Grace.

"Not died," corrected Soutien. "He went where all Fey go when they are too tired or heartsick to live. It is not death. It is… somewhere else."

His voice seemed to catch and he turned his face to the shadows. Moira abruptly sat down on the ground. Before Will could reach her, Soutien held out a hand to her.

"It's too wet, Moira." He effortlessly pulled her to her feet, then spread her abandoned tarp over the uneven ground and helped her to sit.

"Half-Faerie," murmured Grace.

"We prefer Fey."

"That makes you…" began Moira.

"Still your friend," finished Soutien.

In the ensuing silence, Will tried to rearrange his worldview. Who the hell was this stranger among them? Despite all the years he had known the man, Will had never suspected his true strength, or known that he could see in the dark. Half-Faerie... Half-Fey, he corrected. Will struggled, but everything Soutien had done since they left the castle supported his statement. Not to mention that little disappearance act in Grozny.

Half-Fey.

The wet wood finally caught, sending a shower of sparks into the air. In the flickering light, Will examined Soutien, looking for any clue that should have tipped him off to Soutien's heritage. Soutien stared back calmly, the same Soutien who had always been there.

Always been there...

Before he could even put the chaotic thought into words, Grace spoke up.

"Soutien..." She hesitated, then her words rushed out as if she were afraid of running out of courage. "Just how old *are* you?"

Her ability to cut straight to the heart of the matter took Will's breath away. No beating around the bush for Gracie.

Soutien took an audibly deep breath. "I am two hundred and seventy-nine years old."

Will's mind went momentarily blank, then flooded with disbelief. Almost three hundred years old...! Then he remembered everything that had happened since he arrived here and realized that maybe it wasn't so far-fetched, after all.

He could grapple with that one later. Right now there was one question that needed answering.

"Why didn't you help them?" he asked, and was surprised by his lack of anger. Sometime during their flight, his rage had leached away, leaving only bewilderment. He nodded down at his brothers. In the ruddy light, Mack looked as though he were sleeping. "Why get them into this only to abandon them?"

Soutien's eyebrows rose. "I didn't." There was no disguising the surprise in his voice. "Why would you think so?"

Exasperation sharpened Will's tone. "You came to me in Grozny and told me they were in danger!"

In the ensuing silence, Will felt Soutien's attention like a prickling on his skin.

"What are you talking about?" asked Soutien. "You saw *me* in Grozny?"

"Were you there?" asked Moira, her voice hoarse with exhaustion.

"No," said Soutien slowly. "No, I wasn't."

"Well, somebody sure as hell was!" said Will, frustration finally stripping him of patience.

He felt more than saw Soutien shake his head. "Likely it was Amadan-na-Briona."

"Who?" said Grace, drawing closer to the fire.

"Tell me exactly what happened," ordered Soutien. Something in his tone finally convinced Will that the man was telling the truth. Relief washed over him—Soutien hadn't betrayed them. This one anchor, at least, remained.

Will quickly sketched out the details of the Grozny apparition, his encounter with Oonagh, his brother's blazes, and his discovery of the dying wood nymph.

"Ah," said Soutien. "I had hoped it might be you. You were very kind to her. The wild folk took notice."

Will found nothing to say. What did he care about these wild folk? His delay had cost Mack his hands and feet. If not his life.

As though guessing his thoughts, Moira stepped into the silence, recounting her and Grace's adventure since arriving. When she finished with meeting Will on the shore of the lake, Grace took up the questions.

"Why are we here?" She spread her hands to indicate the woods around them. "What do you want from us?"

Will waited patiently while Soutien gathered his thoughts. Finally the other man looked up, but it was Moira his gaze settled on.

"I didn't call you here. Nor did the King. I came after you when I discovered what had happened. I believe Amadan tricked Mack and Aidan into coming here."

"For what reason?" demanded Will. "Who is this Amadan, and what does he want? And how is it any different from Oonagh getting me to come?"

Soutien shook his head. "I'm not sure why Oonagh came to you, Will. I suspect she learned that your brothers were in danger. If she helped you cross over, then Amadan wouldn't have you under his control. As for Amadan, I don't know very much about him, except for the stories. In the old days, he was known as the Fool of the Forth, for the place that spawned him. He is the last of his kind, and the most powerful. I'm told that his touch can cause madness." He sighed. "I thought he was gone, like most of the old ones."

"Old ones?" said Grace.

"From before. Before we came here," replied Soutien, his voice suddenly sad.

"If Amadan tricked them," said Grace slowly, "how did Mack and Aidan end up on the island, and not with Amadan?"

Soutien shook his head. "I don't know, Grace. Red Cap—the creature on the island—was Amadan's lieutenant in the old days. We can assume that he held Mack and Aidan on Amadan's orders. But I thought I was the only one to travel between the two... worlds. I didn't know Amadan could."

Two worlds. Will heard Moira's sharp intake of breath and knew how she felt. Traveling between two worlds. It seemed impossible, despite everything he had seen and been through. Then he shrugged it off. It was enough that they were here.

For the first time since Soutien started talking, Will remembered Aidan. He turned to his brother, but Aidan still sat beneath the tree, expressionless, staring into the flames.

Soutien rubbed his face. "We need to post a guard tonight," he said. "This is unfriendly territory. I'll take first watch."

"But..." started Moira. She glanced at Will, then at Soutien. "You haven't told us anything."

Soutien sighed. "I've told you what I know. Anything else would be guessing." He looked at her for a long moment, then relented. "It does look like Amadan-na-Briona is raising the Unseelie Court again. Otherwise, he wouldn't have killed the tree nymph. He may want to take over Knockma—he hates King Fin Bheara."

"Why?" asked Grace.

Soutien shrugged. "Because Knockma is filled with order, with beauty and light and music. Because Fin Bheara is strong and brought the Fey folk here, when iron and the new god became too dangerous to us. Because Oonagh loved Fin Bheara and not him."

He paused, then continued more slowly. "Whatever the reason, you can be certain that Amadan-na-Briona is a powerful foe. He sent Red Cap to capture your brothers. We'll be in danger until we get to Knockma."

"But why was it so important to lure us here?" asked Will. "What does Amadan want from us?"

"And why didn't he come to me," asked Moira quietly.

The ensuing silence stretched uncomfortably as they waited for Soutien to speak. When he did, however, it wasn't to answer their questions.

"It's only a few hours until dawn," he said. "I suggest you get some sleep." And he stepped out of the circle of light into the shadows.

***

The rain clouds dispersed as the night wore on, and the temperature plunged. Grace shivered, despite Will's sweater on top of her suit jacket. Where was her down coat, now that she needed it? Lost somewhere on the island, no doubt, along with her belt and her boots. Certainly nowhere that would do her any good. At least her feet were warm in the brown man's shoes.

Sleep, Soutien said. What a joke.

She shifted on the hard ground, trying to find a comfortable position. The tarp might keep her dry, but it wasn't a mattress.

Next to her, Moira slept on her side, her fists tucked under her chin, her legs curled up. Grace listened to her even breathing with envy.

She hadn't said a word when Moira lay down next to her, although her lips had trembled with the need to ask why she didn't use the tent. The urge died when she realized that nobody had suggested putting Mack in the tent.

It looked too much like a sarcophagus.

The night pressed down on her like a damp blanket. She wanted to go home, to her warm bed and her safe life. But Soutien had said only Fin Bheara could send them home and Fin Bheara was days away.

Every time Soutien mentioned the king's name, his face closed up. What wasn't he telling them?

Her mind reeled with questions, but after a moment, one separated itself out, crystal clear and demanding an answer.

What did the Fey want from the O'Rourke family?

Losing the fight to control her shivering, Grace clamped her teeth together to keep them from chattering. It was no use. She wasn't going to sleep tonight. She opened her eyes and noted   sourly that the sky was barely lighter than it had been—what? Five minutes ago? It was the dawning of another wonderful day. What joy.

Maybe she should let Will get some sleep by taking a turn at watch. There he was again, moving quietly around the camp, from Mack to Aidan, to her and Moira. His vigilance was comforting and no doubt the reason Moira slept so well.

Her eyelids fluttered shut over eyes gritty with exhaustion. Will hadn't said a word, but when the others turned in, he had stayed up with Soutien. Grace couldn't decide if it was for added security, or out of a lingering suspicion of the other man.

Fear-tinged wonder swept over her. Soutien's story was absurd. Impossible. But impossible things seemed normal here. Her shoes. The phooka. And that thing on the island...

Too many impossible things. She wanted to go home.

They must have found her car by now. The storm would have covered her tracks, but the police would surely have checked out Kirwan and found the broken glass. What would they make of it? Would they think she was dead under the snow somewhere? Would they assume foul play?

Were Mom and Dad mourning?

What about Moira? Would anyone mourn her? Mack was married, but as far as she knew, none of the other O'Rourkes had special people in their lives.

And then Grace was crying, great fat tears of self-pity and fear and exhaustion. She made no effort to control them, allowing them to slide silently down her temples to trickle coldly through her hair. After a few minutes, she sighed raggedly, wiped her face with her hands, and sat up.

"I'll bet that felt good," came Will's low voice from the darkness.

She looked up. He was leaning against a tree, arms folded, staring at her. There was just enough light from the banked campfire to see the sympathy on his face.

This should be embarrassing, thought Grace. But it wasn't. She felt relaxed and loose, as if something that had been wound up too tightly had finally sprung free.

"It did," she admitted, swallowing the remnant of a sob. "You should try it."

Will grinned, his teeth a flash of white. "Wouldn't do, you know," he affected a terrible British accent. "Stiff upper lip and all that."

Grace smiled and wiped the last of the tears away. "Why don't you sleep for a while," she suggested. "I certainly can't." For the first time, she looked around. One, two, three recumbent forms. "Where's Soutien?"

"Outer perimeter," said Will.

The military language jarred Grace, reminding her of all the time Will had spent in war zones.

"Lie down," she said, accepting his hand. "I'll walk around and keep an eye on things."

Will pulled her to her feet. "Thanks, but it's almost dawn—"

A cramp clutched at her feet and traveled like lightning up her calves. With a cry, she fell over, landing painfully on her hip.

"What?" cried Moira, rolling over with the knife instantly in her hand.

Grace could only gasp as cramp after cramp crippled her.

"What is it?" Will dropped on one knee by her side, hands half-raised as if to fend off an attacker.

Her feet were tortured iron and a ghostly blacksmith was trying to hammer them into shape. Her hands clawed at the tarp. She tried to straighten her legs to ease the pain but her muscles no longer obeyed her.

Then Will's hand landed on her leg. "Jesus! She's cramping up!"

Immediately he and Moira pushed up her pant legs and, one at each leg, began to massage the long muscles in her calves.

Grace screamed and tried to twist away from them. Not the legs, she wanted to say, but her voice no longer obeyed her.

"The shoes," came Soutien's voice from the dark. "Remove them."

At once her feet were freed. Will's warm hands engulfed one foot as he pressed and kneaded and stroked, moving slowly up her leg to the knotted calf muscle. Moira's hands were small and deft, with strong thumbs that unerringly found the center of the cramp and massaged it out.

Another spasm struck, and Grace clamped her mouth shut on a scream, but couldn't keep her back from arching and her head from twisting back. The whole world was upside down, a kaleidoscope of torment and darkness, with a blurry red smear where the campfire was.

As the pain rippled through her lower limbs, a shadow moved near the campfire. Through the haze of agony, she saw Aidan bending over Mack.

Then another cramp, and another.

By the time the cramps stopped coming, the sky had paled to indigo from black and the stars had faded away. Grace was wrung out and trembling, too weak to stand up.

Moira squatted on her heels, resting her forearms on her knees. "Are you that out of shape?" Her voice was more worried than accusing, however, and Grace decided to let her live.

"It's not that," said Soutien from his position at Grace's shoulder. He smoothed the sweat-soaked, tangled hair away from her forehead. "It's the shoes."

A measure of strength came stealing back, tentative and careful. "How do you mean?" whispered Grace.

"Humans always pay a price for magic."

"Wait a minute," said Moira, rising to her feet. "Those shoes were a gift."

Soutien nodded. "But humans are not meant for magic. Only the best intentions keep them from being lethal. If the brown man hadn't meant well, Grace might be dancing her way across the continent right now."

Grace stared blankly at him. She vaguely remembered a children's story about a young woman whose thoughtlessness had earned her a pair of dancing shoes that never came off and kept her dancing until she dropped dead.

Will swore and grabbed the guilty shoes. "I'll burn the damned things!"

Soutien's hand on his arm stopped him. "Never spurn a Fey gift."

Goosebumps sprang up on Grace's arms. Or else what? She'd find herself danced to death?

"It's all right, Will," she said, accepting Moira's help to sit up. "I'll keep them, but I think I'll go barefoot for the next little while." Until she found a real pair of shoes.

"As soon as we've eaten, we should go," said Soutien.

"I'll be ready," lied Grace.

"I'll get breakfast," said Moira and she headed for the campfire. "I think we could all use some hot tea."

Privately, Grace thought a stiff scotch would do more good. "Help me up," she said, holding her hands out to both men. She wanted to see if her legs would support her weight.

They carefully pulled her to her feet and she stood unsteadily on trembling legs. She accepted the shoes back from Will and stuffed them in her waistband. Then she concentrated on forcing her foot forward a few inches. She didn't see how she'd be able to walk.

"Will—" Moira's voice held so much grief that they turned as one to look at her.

She knelt by Mack's side, cradling his head on her lap. As Grace watched, Moira pressed her cheek to his.

Will and Soutien ran to her, leaving Grace tottering on uncertain legs. She stared at them, peering past the campfire. In the gray light of dawn, she saw Soutien straighten slowly away from Mack.

With a sinking heart, she turned to find Aidan staring at her from his seat under the tree, where he had spent the night.

"Can't we do something?" whispered Moira. Grace forced herself to take one step. She knew first aid. Maybe...

"It's too late," said Soutien, his voice rough with grief.

Into the ensuing silence came a rustle in the trees next to Grace. She jerked away in fright. The move was too sudden and her legs buckled. She landed in a heap just as something leapt over her, tumbling in an aborted spring. Oh God, what now?

"Watch out!" she cried, and then the air filled with shrieks and yells as the woods came alive with attackers.

Something clattered against the trunk of a tree a few feet away. Grace looked up to find a small creature grinning at her with a mouth full of sharp teeth. She stared for a split second at its pointed ears and greasy black hair before her frantically scrambling brain identified it.

Goblin!

She screamed and tried to scuttle away. The creature vaulted through the air and landed on her back, wrapping its reeking legs around her neck. With an instinct born of fear, Grace knew it was about to sink those terrible teeth into the back of her neck. She reached up, grabbed a fistful of greasy hair, and yanked with all her might.

With a shriek of anger, the goblin flew through the air, tumbled, and landed running. Without pause, it aimed itself at Will's back.

"Behind you, Will!" she yelled, struggling to her feet. He turned in time to fend off the creature with the burning end of a branch. Behind him, a pack of the creatures swarmed Soutien, biting and clawing at him. He seemed impervious to them, plucking them off his body and throwing them with casual strength against the nearby trees.

Then Moira was by his side, her arm scything rhythmically through the creatures as they fell away beneath her sharp knife. It was still too dark to see if anything stained the blade.

If she drops it... thought Grace.

Something heavy landed on her back and she fell again, automatically rolling to unseat the creature. It clung to her with fierce determination, grunting as it searched for skin to claw. This one seemed bigger than the others and its weight kept her down. Its bites couldn't penetrate through Will's sweater and her jacket, but they hurt and she yelled in rage, redoubling her efforts to shake it off.

Then Will pulled the goblin off her back. He pitched it as hard as he could against a tree, only to see it roll to its feet, barely dazed.

Will pulled her to her feet. "Back to back!"

She turned her back on him and immediately felt the comfort of his wide shoulders and back against hers. Then she looked around in the increasing daylight and lost her optimism. They were surrounded. The ground between the trees heaved with scurrying and leaping bodies. She had a quick impression of clawed hands and nasty little faces with mouths filled with teeth. Big, ugly rats, she thought. Complete with tails.

And their only weapons were a firebrand and a knife.

"Aidan!" called Moira, her voice piercing the low grunting that filled the glade like a hum.

Grace spared a glance at the spot she'd last seen Aidan. Where was he?

Then the goblins crowded her and Will tightly together and she concentrated on staying upright and fending off the sharp claws and teeth.

"Take this!" called Will.

She glanced over her shoulder and saw that he was handing her the now spent firebrand. Even without a fire, it made a good club. She grabbed it and hit the nearest goblin on the head. It backed off a step, black eyes momentarily dazed, then it rejoined its brethren in the attack.

"Hang on, Will!" cried Moira. She and Soutien slowly made their way toward Will and Grace, following the path created by Moira's knife. Then a goblin threw itself at Moira's feet, sending her sprawling. The knife flew from her hands to land a few feet away. With a yell of triumph, the goblins swarmed over her.

Immediately, Soutien threw himself on top of Moira, trying to protect her with his body.

Panic threatened to overwhelm Grace's tightly controlled emotions. If Soutien and iron couldn't stand against these creatures, what chance did she and Will have?

Stop pulling your punches, she told herself fiercely. You have to *try* to hurt them!

With the inexorable approach of daylight, she saw her opponents clearly. No more than three feet tall, filthy and ugly, an unholy glee in their faces.

They fought on, Grace fuelled by adrenaline, Will apparently by fury. His roars of rage sent chills up her spine and triggered in her a berserker strength. She swung the club with all her might, connecting with an arm here, a head there. Each time she heard a bone snap under her blows, she grunted with satisfaction.

Then a movement in the trees caught her eye and she looked up to see tall shadows filtering through the trees, creeping nearer.

"Will!" she cried.

The shadows slipped through the trees and into the clearing, re-solving themselves into tall men and women with drawn swords. They were uniformly slender, with silver hair and tunics and leggings of dappled brown and green. Despite the grim set to their features, they were breathtakingly beautiful.

Their silent approach caught the goblins by surprise. One by one, goblin cries of alarm were cut short by a sharp blade. Finally, one goblin managed to scream a warning. The new arrivals gave up on stealth and set about them with blades shiny with blood.

Seeing his chance, Will dove for the fallen knife and rose fighting.

Within minutes, the remaining goblins fled, leaving behind their dead and dying.

As the sun finally rose past the horizon, Grace looked around at the remains of their camp. A goblin had fallen on the embers of the fire and smoke billowed around him like a shroud. The smell of singed hair and burning meat filled the clearing.

Mack lay on his bier of boughs, undisturbed. Aidan was nowhere in sight.

Soutien stood next to Moira. Both were scratched and bloody, and unsteady on their feet. Will stood astride a dead goblin, staring at his bloody knife as if it had suddenly appeared in his hand.

Beyond their small circle was a greater one, composed of tall, si-lent men and a few women. Grace took a closer look and saw pointed ears peeking through the fair hair.

They were beautiful.

And they looked angry.

ॐ FIFTEEN ॐ

SOUTIEN stood in the middle of the sunlit clearing, looking at the carnage in all its grotesquerie. A dozen goblins sprawled over stumps and in bushes, their black blood drenching the earth in shadow. In death, the goblins looked like broken and abandoned toys. The stench was that of a slaughterhouse.

Amid the goblin bodies, the dé Danann stood like bright dappled statues, untouched by the gore. The illusion broke when they turned as one to the dé Danann nearest Grace.

He recognized her at once. Ilyane, daughter of Lord Cathel, the leader of the Tuatha dé Danann. There was no mistaking those blue eyes, so unusual among the Fey. That particular shade only appeared in the Tuatha dé Danann tribe. He wasn't sure she would remember him. He hadn't seen Lord Cathel in almost a century and a half.

Was she leading this war party? Had the dé Danann stumbled upon the goblin attack, or had they been looking for the humans?

Next to him, Moira reeled in the aftermath of the fight and he automatically took her elbow, steadying her. As though unaware of his touch, she stepped forward, out of his reach, and looked wildly around the clearing. She wasn't exhausted, after all.

She was frantic.

"Where's Aidan?" she asked, turning to Will. "He disappeared during the fighting!"

Will looked around, too. "Aidan!" he called loudly. "Aidan, where are you?" He moved toward the tree where Aidan had spent the night.

Immediately, three tall elves surrounded him. He stopped, frowning at them, and his shoulder muscles bunched up as if he were about to take a swing at one of them. Instead, he looked over his shoulder at Soutien.

"What's the problem?"

Yes, thought Soutien. What *is* the problem?

Slipping into diplomat mode, he bowed to Ilyane. "My Lady," he began, speaking in the original tongue. "My companions and I are deeply grateful for your intervention. Yet one of our party remains missing. We must search for him."

Ilyane shook her head decisively. "That one is lost to you. You are to come with me."

Soutien stared at her. What did she mean—that Aidan had lost his way, or that he was dead?

"What did she say?" demanded Moira, turning to him. "Did you tell her about Aidan?"

"Yes, but she wants us to come with her."

Blood suffused Moira's cheeks, replacing the unhealthy pallor put there by shock. She turned to Ilyane and, fists on hips, tilted her head to look up at the dé Danann.

"Look," she said, "we need to find—"

Her words were cut short by the soft sighing of Ilyane's sword leaving its scabbard. Soutien moved a split-second before Will roared a warning and swept away the startled dé Danann surrounding him.

Soutien had time to see Moira's eyes widen in surprise and hear Grace's shocked gasp; then he was between Moira and the blade, staring into Ilyane's mad eyes.

"Lady Ilyane," he said softly, holding her with his gaze. "We will be pleased to accompany you, since Lord Cathel awaits." He *hoped* Lord Cathel awaited. "All we ask is that you send trackers to search for our lost companion."

The madness in Ilyane's eyes receded at the mention of her father's name. She stared back at Soutien, then looked at Moira, her expression hard with dislike. She spoke curtly and two dé Danann, a man and a woman, melted into the surrounding woods.

Soutien knew better than to thank her. She did not want thanks. She wanted blood.

ᕭ SIXTEEN ᕭ

GRIEF was like a fast-moving river, pulling Will under every time he came up for air.

Mack dead. Aidan gone. All because he hadn't moved fast enough to find them.

Dusk crept through the forest, blurring the edges of trees, merging shadows. Will rotated his shoulders, missing the familiar weight of the pack. An elf now carried it, somewhere up the line. Or, a *dé Danann,* as Soutien called them. He wanted to see Moira, but she was too far up the line.

They had stopped only once all day, to eat, drink, and rest. Moira had looked pale then, and Will had wondered if the strain was too much for her. When he had looked at her eyes, however, he had seen only grief.

Just ahead of him, Grace managed to keep up, despite her bruised, cut feet. He watched the gold in her hair fade with the day and promised himself he would find a way to make it up to her.

Behind him, two of the strangers carried Mack. Will wanted to push them away and carry Mack himself. But they walked with such solemn dignity, with such respect for their burden that Will turned away from his brother's shrouded body, hands clenched by his sides.

As he walked, the ground beneath his feet gradually softened, and the terrain grew hillier. They were leaving behind the land of rock and lakes, heading back in the direction from which he had come, all those days ago, when Oonagh first set him on this path.

"Fin Bheara needs you, as do your brothers," she had said.

But he hadn't acted quickly enough. Hell, he hadn't acted at all. He had thought this was an adventure and that his brothers were invincible. Now Mack was dead, Aidan wandered the forest out of his mind, and he and the others were prisoners of sword-toting, pointy-eared strangers.

The smell of goblin blood clung to him like a pall. He wished he could bathe.

With an effort, he pulled himself out of the spiral of self-pity. He had to be ready.

They had to get out of this strange, terrible place.

The trees they passed were huge. Mostly oak, pine, and ash, they towered over the travelers, some bigger around than the clasp of three men. Their tops disappeared into the darkening sky. It would be easy enough to disappear into this forest, especially with Soutien's help.

It was almost dark. Even the strangers were showing signs of fatigue, a drooping shoulder here, a less-than-nimble step there. They would want to stop soon. As soon as they settled down for the night, he would find a way to slip away. Moira would be on the lookout, as would Soutien. All they had to do was rescue Grace. With a little luck—and a diversion—they would escape. It was time to find this Fin Bheara and get Moira and Grace out of here. Once they were safe, he would come back for Aidan.

Then something brought him out of his grim thoughts—not a sound so much as a feeling, a ruffling of air over his skin, an awareness of difference. He stopped.

The forest was quiet, with only the chirping of a grasshopper to heighten the silence.

Something was watching them.

The guard to his right stepped closer, motioning him on with one hand. Will ignored him, searching the growing darkness for what had alerted him. Then the guard touched him on the arm and drew his attention upward.

Will followed the man's pointing finger and whistled softly.

The treetops were lost to darkness but, like night blooms, dozens of silvery, dé Danann faces gazed down at them from the shadowy heights. After a moment, Will made out what appeared to be platforms on which they stood, staring silently at the group on the forest floor.

They had arrived.

***

In the last forty-eight hours, Grace had been chased by a cannibalistic ogre, attacked by goblins, and rescued—or was it kidnapped?—by elves, or dé Danann.

And somewhere in there, she'd watched a good man die.

So how on earth had she ended up perched on a swaying platform twenty feet by twenty, a hundred feet off the ground?

She sat cross-legged in the center of the platform, as far from the railless edges as she could get. It wasn't really wood, she decided. More like tightly woven vines. How did they remain rigid? More magic?

She kept her eyes firmly closed, even though it was now night, with only a half-moon providing half-hearted illumination. She wouldn't even be able to see the ground if she were to look down. Not that she planned to.

A light tread caused the platform to shudder and she dropped both hands to the rough surface in an effort to keep it stable.

"Please sit down," she said through clenched teeth.

The movement stopped.

"Grace..." Soutien sighed. "Don't tell me you're afraid of heights?"

Grace cracked open one eye. In the light of the rising moon, Soutien's fair hair gleamed dully. The sympathy on his face belied the exasperation in his voice.

She closed her eye again. "Where are Moira and Will?"

"I don't know," answered Soutien, a shrug in his voice.

They had this particular level of airborne hell all to themselves. Were Will and Moira on another platform, somewhere else in this gigantic tree? In a different tree? Again she listened, straining to catch the sound of their voices, but couldn't hear anything past the rustling of leaves.

What a perfect prison, she thought with grudging admiration. They were perched far out on a fat limb and the only way off—short of jumping—was past a tall, grim-faced dé Danann who kept his hand on the pommel of his sword. He stood at the fork of branch and tree, which seemed a much sturdier perch than their flimsy platform.

A thought occurred to her and she opened her eyes again to peer at the dé Danann's sword. The blade was short and hidden in a scabbard. She tried to remember the swords she had seen that morning as the dé Danann fought the goblins. They had shimmered in the dawn light, pale and white.

"I thought the Fey couldn't stand iron," she said, looking up at Soutien. "How can they have swords?"

Soutien dropped down next to her, drawing one long leg up and wrapping an arm around it. He, too, studied the dé Danann.

"It's not iron," he said. "It's *sesmael*. Like silver, only stronger. It is mined in the north."

Grace stared at him for a long moment, suddenly awash in a sense of unreality. What was she doing here, for God's sake? What was she doing in a *tree* discussing mining with a three-hundred-year-old half-Fey?

She clenched her fists, digging her nails into her palms.

Focus. That's what she needed. Focus on anything but the weird turn her life had taken and the little voices gibbering hysterically at the back of her mind.

"What the hell are we doing here?" she said abruptly, pinning Soutien with her gaze.

His eyebrows rose and she realized that she had been rude. Too bad. Niceties belonged to the world of her fabric shop.

If Soutien resented her tone, he didn't show it. "I'm not sure why we're being kept here," he said slowly. "I have asked to speak with Lord Cathel. He's the leader of this... tribe, I guess you would call them. He's always been friendly to King Fin Bheara." He nodded at their guard. "I don't know what this means."

A very literal answer. And probably true, as far as it went. No doubt he had told them nothing but the truth since they first ran into him on the island. It was what he wasn't telling them that worried her.

The breeze riffled through the leaves and the platform beneath Grace's clutching fingers shifted as the branch swayed. She swallowed hard.

"Then tell me something you do know. Why do we need Fin Bheara to get back home? Why can't we go back the way we came?" Her breath caught on the words. If a spell had brought them here, why couldn't one take them back?

Soutien sighed and drew up the other knee. He turned his face up to the night.

"Fin Bheara *is* the way you came," he said. "He created the spell that brought you here. A very powerful spell, and very old." He sighed again, almost imperceptibly. "Almost six hundred years old."

When he didn't continue, Grace looked at him. "And?"

Sadness kissed Soutien's face, drawing down the line of his mouth, aging him briefly. "He can no longer make such powerful spells. His strength is now concentrated at Knockma, the keep where the Seelie Court sits. We must go to him there if you hope to get back."

She felt his reticence like a tug on her curiosity. What wasn't he saying?

"So what's different now?" she asked, plucking at his reluctance. "Why can't he make powerful spells anymore? Is he too old? Has he lost his abilities?"

Soutien flashed her a look full of irritation. "Fin Bheara is as strong as he ever was."

"Then what?" said Grace. "Why can't the all-powerful King of the Fey send us back home?"

"He has too many demands on him," said Soutien sharply. "The Fey depends on him to keep them here—"

His abrupt silence, more than his words, alerted her that he had said too much. Keep them here. What did he mean, *here*?

She had been too busy to give it much thought, but *here* looked a lot like home, only cleaner. Less built up. Heck, *not* built up. It was hard to believe that there was any place this pristine left in North America. Sure, there were lots of parks, but even in the remotest cor-ner of the Yukon there was always some sign of civilization. A contrail in the sky. The distant whine of a highway. A maintained path with markers. Something.

She shifted carefully, trying to ease the tingling in her legs, with-out disturbing the platform. The guard straightened attentively.

In the three days since arriving with Moira, she had seen nothing remotely resembling the civilization she had left behind. The crumbling castle on the island was the only structure she had seen. But this place, with its gigantic trees and dense underbrush, was her idea of what old-growth forests would have looked like in eastern Canada before people came.

Her mouth suddenly went dry and she looked at Soutien. He was studying the stars, ignoring her. The breeze whispered past her ear, lifting the short hairs off her neck.

"How long has Fin Bheara kept the Fey here?" she asked softly.

Soutien didn't look at her but she felt his body tense. For a moment, she thought he wouldn't answer. When he finally did, his voice was a whisper.

"Almost six hundred years."

Six hundred years.

"Soutien... where is *here*?"

She held her breath, but he remained mute. His profile might as well have been chiseled in marble.

"Soutien..." She placed a gentle hand on his arm. The muscles beneath the thin cloth were rigid, and his flesh was so hot she doubted he could feel the cool breeze. "It's not *where*, is it? It's when."

After a long moment, the muscles beneath her hand relaxed and he turned to look at her, his expression hovering between relief and surprise.

"Yes," he nodded. "It's when."

A trembling started in the pit of Grace's stomach.

When. Not where, when.

"Okay. Tell me," she said calmly, crossing her arms. Under her hands, her heart thudded uncomfortably hard against her rib cage.

Soutien shrugged. "There were no wild places left in the old world. Man's iron had forced the Fey out of all of them. So they followed the ships to the new world."

"How long ago?"

"Those who could no longer survive in cities came with the first settlers. The wilder ones followed as humans pushed them out of the last wild places."

His gaze grew brighter and he turned away again, hiding his face.

"It made no difference," he continued, his voice carefully neutral. "Within a century, iron had swept over this continent, too."

Grace tried to imagine what it had been like to be chased from their homeland to a strange, wild place. Lonely, she decided. It must have been lonely.

Soutien took a deep breath. "And so, Fin Bheara brought us here, to a time before humans peopled this land."

The trembling spread to Grace's limbs and she hugged her ribs in an effort to control it.

The breeze carried a sweet, peppery scent. She breathed deeply, hoping it would calm her. Their guard glanced at them curiously, but as he made no move to interrupt, Grace ignored him.

"How...?" She cleared her throat, finding it suddenly constricted. "How is it possible...?"

Soutien shifted to face her, sitting tailor fashion. "I don't understand it all, but think of it this way: If time is like a long thread, then it loops around itself and tomorrow can touch yesterday. Or, maybe different times—past, present, future—are as close to each other as drops of oil in a glass of water."

Once begun, he seemed to warm to his subject. His long-fingered hands caught moonlight as he sketched the imaginary thread of time. Grace listened in silence, unable to tear her gaze from his mobile face.

"Fin Bheara, though not as old as Amadan, is one of the old Fey, and one of the most powerful. He found a way of penetrating the barrier that keeps time streams apart. He forced open the way between past and present. Those who wanted to, came here." He swept a hand toward the trees, the ground, the sky.

Grace opened her mouth to ask how many had remained behind, but Soutien kept going like a man finally released from his vow of silence.

"But he couldn't close the doorway he had opened." Soutien shook his head, his words coming faster. "Time itself knows we don't belong here. The past seeks to expel us back to our proper timeline. That's why Fin Bheara remains in the doorway, at Knockma. The past constantly pushes at him while the present constantly pulls at him. Yet, he remains, year after year, century after century. As long as he does, keeping the doorway blocked, so to speak, the Fey remain on one side, in the past, safe. Without his presence, the Fey world would return to the present, to the world you left behind."

He stopped talking abruptly and they both sat in silence, looking at each other. She stared at the handsome, ageless face of the man she had known for close to twenty years and wished she could stand up. She desperately needed to stretch her legs. She always did her best thinking standing up.

As if hearing her thoughts, Soutien stood up and began to pace. His steps were so light that she barely felt the trembling in the platform but he walked right up to the edge before turning away and pacing to the other side. She turned away from the nerve-wracking sight and focused on the Fey guard. He was looking down at the shadows surrounding the tree. She couldn't see his expression.

"I still don't get it," she finally said. "What does all this have to do with the O'Rourkes?"

"The Fey are dying here," said Soutien. "We are safe, but no Fey have been born in centuries. Despair is slowly killing us. Fin Bheara needs the O'Rourkes to help get us back to our proper time. Your present."

Grace stared at Soutien, nonplussed. What could the O'Rourkes do? Certainly, they were a capable family, but they had no special powers.

"But what about the iron problem?" she asked. "That was one of the reasons for coming here. And if you think there were no wild places left six hundred years ago..."

Soutien stopped with his back to her. "I know," he said softly. "Many will die."

"But..."

He turned to look at her. "If we remain here, *all* will die."

She remained silent for a few minutes. They could stay here, and die. Or they could go back to their proper timeline. And die. What kind of a solution was that?

"Wait a minute," she said. "Didn't you say that Amadan called Mack and Aidan here?" She thought it through. "If Amadan and Fin

Bheara are enemies, why would Amadan help Fin Bheara?"

The guard spoke suddenly and they both turned in his direction, but he was talking to someone below the platform's level.

Soutien listened for a moment that stretched into a minute as the murmur of voices continued. From his intent expression, Grace understood that Soutien's hearing was much better than hers.

"What are they saying?" she asked softly.

He looked down at her. "They've come to bring me to Cathel." He leaned down and placed a hand on her shoulder. "Amadan's *not* helping," he said. "He only needs one O'Rourke, and he's chosen Aidan. Mack and Will are expendable. Aidan is probably with Amadan right now—that's why the goblins attacked. To take Aidan, and kill Will."

Soutien's words landed on Grace like hot embers. "But why? Why kill the O'Rourkes?"

A movement caught her eye and she jumped, making the platform jump, too. Soutien straightened. Another dé Danann clambered up the tree to stand next to their guard. Pale moonlight streamed through the branches above the dé Danann, casting faint shadows over her features. She looked at them and spoke, her voice carrying clearly.

"She wants me to go with her," said Soutien.

Alarm shot through Grace. "Just you?"

Soutien spoke to the woman, his voice lilting and musical. When she answered, he turned back to Grace.

"Lord Cathel wants to see me alone." Something of Grace's distress must have shown on her face. He squatted down next to her and took her hands in his. "I won't make promises I might not be able to keep, Grace. But you must know by now that I am a friend of the O'Rourkes, and yours. If it is at all in my power, I will get you home safely."

Grace closed her eyes briefly and decided not to point out that he was hardly in a position to offer safety. Still, his intentions were good. She squeezed his hands. "Don't worry about me," she said. "I'll be fine."

He smiled and, releasing her hands, rose to his feet.

"Wait," said Grace. "You didn't finish. Why does Amadan want the

O'Rourkes dead?"

The woman spoke again, more sharply, and Soutien nodded and said a few words. She looked at the guard, who shrugged.

"I don't know for certain, but I believe Amadan wants to make sure none of them reach Fin Bheara before he is ready. I believe he wants to be king of the Fey."

None of this was making sense. In her agitation, Grace stood up. The guard looked at her in surprise. Before she could stop herself, she looked down at the inky well beyond the platform's edge and abruptly sat down again. She kept her eyes closed until the dizziness passed.

"He wants to kill the king, then?" she asked, more to keep her mind off the reeling darkness beyond her eyelids than because she really wanted an answer.

"No. Or at least, not yet."

Grace did open her eyes, then, to look at him in irritation. Before she could ask, however, Soutien spoke again.

"He needs the king alive while he gathers and trains his Unseelie army. Only then will he want to return to our own time."

The answer did little to clear away Grace's confusion. "Well, why doesn't Fin Bheara get out of the doorway, or whatever it is, and let the Fey world go back to its own time? Since that's what he wants to do anyway?"

Soutien smiled, but it was an odd smile, one that sent shivers crawling up her scalp. "He can't. Fin Bheara *is* the barrier. The only way he can open it up again is by dying." He took a deep breath. "And the only way he can die is if the eldest O'Rourke son kills him."

The muscles in Grace's face went slack and astonishment robbed her of words.

"*Bannet!*" This time, the imperative tone of the woman's voice brooked no argument. She took a step onto the platform.

"Yes, yes, just a moment," said Soutien impatiently, ignoring the look she gave him. He turned back to Grace.

"I don't believe you," Grace finally managed to say. But she did. Oh, God, she believed him.

"It doesn't matter what you believe, Grace," said Soutien. His eyes were suddenly fierce as he knelt on one knee and grasped her by the upper arms. "Your belief system doesn't matter here. Know this: The king must die, and soon. If Amadan has enough time to raise the Unseelie court, he will force Aidan to kill the king. Then Amadan will be the one to lead the Fey back to the present. Back home, Grace. To your home and that of your family. If we don't reach Knockma first, and soon, there's no telling what madness will be added to humanity's."

"But..." Grace still struggled against the enormity of Soutien's words. "Who...?"

"Will, of course," said Soutien with pity. "Will must kill the king."

"But Aidan is the eldest now," she objected.

He nodded. His eyes filled with infinite sadness. "The king will order him killed, if we can't rescue him from Amadan."

Grace's mind went blank with shock.

Soutien finally stood up and walked to the edge of the platform where the woman waited for him.

"Wait!" cried Grace suddenly as the thought struck her. "Does he know? Does Will know?"

"No." Soutien sighed. "If he refuses..."

Without finishing the sentence, he jumped onto a lower branch and disappeared from sight.

ॐ SEVENTEEN ॐ

MOIRA'S two escorts jumped the last few feet from the gnarled branch onto a platform. It barely moved. It was larger than the one on which she had been held, and could easily accommodate a dozen people.

Although the platform looked sturdy, Moira lowered herself to it instead of jumping. These dé Danann might be taller than she was, but they looked like they were made of mist and imagination.

She kept a hand on the rough bark of the branch as the woven platform sprang back under her weight. Branches from adjacent trees overhung the platform, frustrating the efforts of a ring of torches placed at uneven intervals.

One of her escorts waited, his face impassive, while Moira looked around and surreptitiously tested the solidity of the platform. She hadn't been able to check out the underside of her holding platform and she dearly wanted to know how they were built.

At the far side, a woman stood waiting, hands folded in front of her. Something about her, maybe the calm in her eyes or the sense of patience she exuded, told Moira she was old. Physically, she looked no different than the other dé Danann she had seen so far. Tall and willowy slim, with green eyes and silvery hair.

The woman's gaze seemed to soften for a moment. Then she stepped aside, drawing Moira's attention to the figure at her feet.

Mack rested on a narrow, raised bier made of woven branches covered in moss. The sleeping bag had been cut away from him, and his clothing removed. Naked, his mutilations stood out in stark contrast to his ashen flesh. His limbs were streaked with dried blood.

Pain squeezed Moira's heart and she struggled to breathe. "Oh, Mack," she whispered. She wanted to go to him, but her legs refused to move.

A rustle of leaves announced a new arrival and she turned to see Will dropping from the branch to land on the platform. It heaved gently, then settled. The vibrations of his footsteps traveled through the soles of her boots. His two guards remained perched in the tree.

"You all right?" said Will in a low voice when he came abreast of her. Then he saw Mack and his expression grew bleak.

Before Moira could say anything, the dé Danann woman stepped forward and took her by the hand. She led Moira to Mack and pointed at several different-sized willow baskets placed at his head and feet. The bigger ones were filled with fragrant white blossoms. Two baskets, lined with leaves, contained sweet-smelling water, while still others held cloths and combs.

Moira closed her eyes in anguish. Then she looked at Will. "They want us to wash him."

Will tensed, as if he would argue. But he didn't say a word, only stared at Mack's body. Finally he removed his sweater, revealing a once-white T-shirt. He folded the sweater and placed it on the platform, then walked over to the bier and knelt by his brother's side. After a moment, Moira followed, kneeling on the other side.

The woman picked up a cloth, dipped it in the water, and began to wash Mack's body. Will and Moira looked at each other over their brother's body, then followed suit.

Moira had never seen Mack naked, and she was uncomfortable at providing such an intimate service for him. When her parents died, the funeral home had handled everything, and Moira had felt like an outsider more than anything. It had taken a few times of returning to Kirwan and finding them gone before she could finally accept their death.

That wouldn't happen with Mack.

She methodically washed the dirt and blood from Mack's body, her salty tears mingling with the sweet water, and found herself thinking of her childhood, of the time they were all home, before Mack went off to officer school.

Eight years older than her, he had always looked out for them, even as he led them on camping trips in the surrounding woods.

Mack was a born leader, while Aidan was the daredevil. As much as he wanted to lead, Aidan was no match for his older brother. Even as a teen, Mack already showed the resourcefulness and calm attention to detail that would make him a good officer.

On their camping trips, Mack gave Aidan ample opportunity to take the lead, to shine. But something always went wrong. Aidan would forget the compass and they would be lost, or he'd hang the food pack in the tree on a rope that would then break, attracting bears, or he'd wear new hiking boots that raised blisters on his feet, forcing them to trail blaze shortcuts through the woods.

Mack's camping trips were models of organization, but Aidan's were adventures. His trips were the ones that were told and retold at family dinners.

She stole a glance at Will. The grimness had left his expression, to be replaced by a look of peace.

Finally, they were done. They covered Mack's body with the blossoms, a blanket of fragrance.

When they finished, the dé Danann woman rose gracefully and nodded to one of Moira's guards. He signaled and suddenly four dé Danann descended from the trees. They carried ropes and moved with purpose to Mack's bier.

"What are they doing?" asked Moira.

Will moved as if to stop them, but the woman placed a slender hand on his forearm and he looked at her gravely.

"*Bannet*," she said gently and motioned them to follow her. Moira and Will hesitated, looking back at their brother's body.

The dé Danann had tied ropes at either end of the bier, and one in the middle, all joined in an intricate knot over Mack's body. In a branch above the platform, two more began hauling on the rope. The bier lurched up a few feet, spilling a dozen blossoms. The dé Danann on the platform quickly stabilized it.

Moira turned away. "I don't want to watch this," she said. "Let's go."

***

If not for the guard's hair gleaming in the pale moonlight, Grace wouldn't have known he was there. His soft green, long-sleeved tunic and dark brown pants blended into the shadowy tree trunk like another shadow.

Wind ruffled her hair and danced in the leaves with a sound like silk sweeping against silk. Branches rose and fell and dizziness swept over her as leaves swayed against the starry sky.

She closed her eyes.

The urge to lie down was almost overwhelming and she fought it with all her determination. Lying down would be giving in.

Her fingernails dug into the woody platform, and she tried to concentrate on the texture of the vines beneath her fingers. One hand stole to her waistband, checking for the brown man's shoes. Still tucked safely away.

The ridges of the platform dug painfully into her buttocks and bare feet, and the pain in her feet suddenly reminding her of Mack. He'd been a good man, with a good life ahead of him. Certainly he didn't deserve the terrible death he got.

And yet... and yet, his death gave them a better chance at survival.

And Aidan... She had seen him bending over his brother as wave after wave of cramps beset her. Had he been checking on Mack? Or had he decided that his brother couldn't hold them back if he were dead?

An immense weariness stole over her. All she wanted was a good night's sleep, and to wake up in her own bed, away from all this.

The platform suddenly shook beneath her and her eyes flew open in alarm.

The dé Danann guard had stepped onto the platform. When he saw he had her attention, he gestured.

"*Bannet*," he said, and stood waiting.

The gesture was unmistakable, and it was the same word the

woman had used when summoning Soutien. Ironic that such a music-al voice could issue from such a sour-looking face. Like the others, he had green eyes, pale skin, and silvery hair. His beauty made his grouchiness all the more noticeable. He probably wanted to be sleeping, too.

I'd better get up before he comes to get me, she thought glumly.

She briefly considered crawling to the relative security of the tree trunk, but immediately rejected the idea. She didn't care if it meant falling to the ground—she would walk.

It had been easier walking onto the platform than it was to walk off. In the pre-moon darkness, she hadn't even known what it was until she tripped over the edge and landed on it. That was when she learned how precariously anchored it was to the branch.

She fixed her gaze beyond the stern dé Danann to the dark, solid trunk of the tree and rose shakily. Without giving herself a chance to think, she took one step, then another. When she finally reached the man, she looked him in the eye.

"Well?"

A hint of amusement crept into the depths of his eyes, but he turned silently and led the way to the trunk. Grace envied his careless agility and followed more carefully. She looked straight ahead, praying she wouldn't trip on a protrusion.

The tree limb was safe, she finally admitted. It was wide enough for two people to pass, with room to spare, and it widened as it joined the trunk. Still, it wasn't as if it came with handrails.

When she reached the trunk, she leaned against it gratefully, her body trembling with relief. The tree was a huge, old-growth maple. A good, solid tree. She patted it and glanced over her shoulder at the platform she had just left. In the dim light of the moon, it looked bigger than it had felt. The branch beneath it seemed to split into three, providing a stable base. The platform was cupped securely, not perched. She tried to remember if she'd ever seen a maple tree branch do that and finally shook her head. It didn't matter. All that mattered was that she was getting out of the tree.

The dé Danann started climbing up.

Grace stared at his backside with horror as he climbed nimbly from toehold to branch. He glanced down at her, his face lost in the shadows.

"*Bannet!*"

No, thought Grace grimly. No, no, and no. She looked down the trunk to search for the best way down.

An impassive dé Danann woman stared back at her from her spot on a branch just below Grace. She silently pointed upward.

Grace snarled and followed him.

***

The trip up took forever. Her hands hurt from gripping handholds too tightly. To her surprise, the rough bark didn't hurt her feet. In fact, her bare feet clung more readily to footholds and branches than if they had been shod. Then she remembered the brown man's gift and reconsidered. The Fey shoes would do even better than bare feet, but at greater cost.

The higher she climbed, the more moonlight filtered through the canopy of leaves. Her hands grew sticky with pungent sap and she caught a faint sweet smell that she thought might be wild roses. She saw more platforms on different levels. Although her concentration remained on the climb, she couldn't help scanning each platform she passed. Empty.

The dé Danann woman kept well below her. To prevent Grace's escape? Or to better avoid her falling body?

Grace shuddered. It was best not to think about falling.

Their arrival at the tree had been frightening enough. Several woven, basket-like contraptions had been lowered from the tree—from fifty feet up. Each of the prisoners had to clamber in, one at a time. The contraption was then pulled up swiftly, and the person disgorged on a branch to climb the rest of the way.

Will had made a caustic comment about freight elevators, but Grace had been too busy fighting nausea to appreciate the humor.

She looked up at the moving shadows above her. Where were they going? They had been climbing for an eternity, at least, and still there was more tree looming above her.

As if her thoughts were his cue, the man above her stopped and waited for her. She reached the branch on which he stood and leaned her forehead against the trunk, breathing hard. Her legs still trembled, but from exertion now rather than fear.

A gentle hand on her shoulder turned her around. She blinked slowly at what looked like fireflies hovering just before her. Then perspective reasserted itself and she saw that the lights were actually lanterns dispersed throughout a vast expanse of canopy.

"Wow," she breathed, as understanding finally dawned. This was the top of the forest and before her was a community of trees, many of them connected by platforms. Bridges linked branches that were too far apart.

Moonlight limned the branches and leaves in silver, while torches provided golden pools of contrast. The greatest number of torches seemed clustered to her left. She peered through the leaves, trying to make out what was attracting so much interest.

Just ahead of her, dim in the immediate gloom, was a footbridge. Strung between two tree trunks, it seemed to consist of cobwebs and hope.

The other guard joined them and nodded at the man. With a hand on Grace's back, the dé Danann gently nudged her forward.

Grace resisted.

"You're kidding," she said, dragging her gaze away from the insubstantial bridge to stare at him.

The ghost of a smile flitted across his face. Obviously the sentiment came through, even if the words were strange to him. With a shrug at the other woman, he stepped onto the bridge and within seconds was urging Grace on from the other side.

Grace examined the bridge more closely, hoping that a railing had magically appeared. It hadn't. The bridge was nothing more than a bunch of branches side by side, strung together with skinny rope. It was barely two feet wide. It swayed in the wind. It had no handrails.

I can't do it.

Without a doubt, this was beyond her ability. Wiping suddenly damp palms on her pants, she plastered her back to the trunk of the maple and shook her head.

"No," she said. To her shame, her voice trembled. "No," she tried again, but her voice was too faint to hear. Bile rose in her throat, burning as she swallowed.

The dé Danann woman took her arm and tried to pull her toward the bridge. Grace tensed her legs and braced her feet.

"No!" she said, and the word came through loud and clear, with a definitely hysterical edge to it.

Suddenly, strong hands pulled her away from the tree and before she knew what was happening, she was slung over a hard shoulder, knocking the breath out of her. She frantically pushed at the back, trying to free herself. She caught a glimpse of the woman's surprised expression and realized the man had her.

And then they were on the bridge and the darkness beneath her swung sickeningly and she knew she was falling, falling...

The world stopped spinning and rocking and she was on her feet again with his steadying hands on her shoulders. She tried to control it, but in the next moment she was on her knees, vomiting bile.

Immediately he knelt beside her, holding back her hair while she retched helplessly. When the paroxysms finally abated, he pulled a small skin container off his belt and unstoppered it. He handed it to her and made motions toward her mouth.

Tiredly, Grace poured some water into her hand and washed her face. She managed to squirt some directly into her mouth without touching the skin and rinsed her mouth out. Finally, she handed the waterskin back to him and struggled to her feet, refusing his help.

The dé Danann woman crossed the bridge and came to stand by the man. They both looked down at her as if she were an odd specimen that had washed up on the beach.

"No more bridges," said Grace weakly. "You people are terrible at them."

She felt better after throwing up, and the rest of the trip passed without incident. There were no more bridges. Most of the transitions from tree to tree took place on platforms. When they had to jump from one branch to another, the man always stood on the far branch with his hand held out. Since the branches were always sturdy and wide, it was a simple matter to step from one to the other. As long as she didn't look down.

They made their slow way toward the center of light. As they approached, a low musical hum impinged on Grace's awareness. She focused on it to distract herself from the journey. After a while she realized she was hearing voices, many voices raised in discussion. The dé Danann, she thought, as wonder washed over her. They were talking in their language, and it sounded like music.

Then she started seeing dé Danann perched in trees around them. Grace counted and got to twenty-three before they stepped off the final branch onto the huge platform that seemed to be the center of activity.

The canopy of stars was like the roof of a vast hall and she lost herself in wonder for a moment. When she finally lowered her gaze, it was to see dozens of tall dé Danann standing in a circle.

She and her escorts drew closer and the outer ring parted, revealing an inner cluster of figures.

Moira and Will stood with their backs to her. Soutien stood a little apart from them, before a man sitting erect on an intricately carved, raised wooden throne. The stranger's white hair flowed over the silvershot black velvet of his tunic and contrasted with the polished ebony of the throne. His pants, tucked into elegant, knee-high leather boots, were of the same rich fabric.

Even without the throne, Grace would have known this was the leader. Authority emanated from him like a scent and was etched in the hollows of his cheeks, the steadiness of his gaze. To her surprise, his eyes were blue, unlike the others.

He was listening intently to Soutien, his eyes attentive. She was still too far away to catch Soutien's words.

Then a shimmer around the leader's head caught her attention and she stared hard. It was blurry, almost like a double exposure in a photograph—was there an image beneath?

The dé Danann on the throne looked up as Grace's escorts finally pushed through the last of the onlookers. A figure at his side stirred and for the first time, Grace noticed the woman who had led the fighting against the goblins. And noticed that she, too, had blue eyes. Unlike his, her eyes crackled with an inner light, like a sparkler, or a firecracker.

The woman pointed at Grace and Will and Moira turned around, seeing her for the first time. Grace's escorts led her to stand with them, then stepped back into the group of onlookers.

Will took her hand in his and squeezed. "You all right?"

Grace nodded and squeezed back. "What's going on?"

Moira looked away from Soutien and the dé Danann on the throne. Her mouth was a thin line and there were deep creases between her eyebrows. "I think Soutien is pleading our case."

Grace glanced from one grim face to the other. "What do you mean, 'our case'?"

But Moira turned away and it was Will who answered. "The man on the throne rules over these dé Danann. As near as I can figure out, that's his daughter who helped us this morning." A mirthless smile crossed his face. "Although I don't see why. She's arguing that they should kill us. Soutien is trying to convince them not to."

Great, thought Grace. Just bloody great.

ᐛ EIGHTEEN ᐖ

A GENTLE wind tugged at Soutien's clothes, bringing with it the scent of hot resin from the torches. He held himself straight and relaxed his shoulders. Beneath his feet, the woven platform shifted under the massed weight of many.

He knew the moment Grace stepped through the ring of watchers. He allowed himself a moment of relief but kept his gaze on Lord Cathel.

Why did the high lord cover himself with a glamour? Soutien saw past the spell to the humble willow chair that served as throne, to the plain, if well-made, spider-silk tunic, to the elongated ears indicating advanced age.

If Soutien, half-human, could see through the glamour, surely the dé Danann could. Or was it solely for the benefit of the humans?

"My Lord," he said, keeping his voice even. "My charges are no danger to you or your people. On behalf of King Fin Bheara, I seek safe passage to Knockma." There, it was out, the formal request. According to the unspoken covenant between the peoples of the Fey, Cathel must honor the request, or risk war.

"No danger!" Ilyane, Lord Cathel's daughter, stepped forward. Her blue eyes flashed eerily in the torchlight. Soutien almost expected to see the light reflect from her pupils like an animal's. But, of course, she wasn't an animal. She was simply mad.

"These outsiders are enemies!" Her hands twitched at her sides like caged birds. "We cannot allow them free passage—Amadan seeks them. If you will not destroy them, then give them over to him. It will prove our friendship."

Alarmed, Soutien glanced at the high lord, but Cathel remained impassive.

Amadan? Dé Danann seeking alliance with Amadan?

"My Lord," said Soutien, "if Amadan is a concern, King Fin Bheara's army can be here in less than two days."

If the spark of amusement in his blue eyes was any indication, the high lord understood the implied threat winding through the promise. Before he could speak, however, his daughter sprang forward, her body barely containing her tightly coiled anger.

"Father, I brought you these strangers that we might witness your strength, not to watch this half-breed trick you into doing nothing!"

A challenge. Soutien sensed the collective tensing in the sudden silence. Was this the first time daughter challenged father? Or simply the first time she had done so in public?

Cathel turned to look fully at his daughter. Slowly, one eyebrow rose.

"Indeed?" he said gently, his voice carrying in the silence. "I had thought it was because I ordered you to bring them to me."

"They will destroy everything!" cried Ilyane. She waved an arm wildly at the trees, the stars, the Fey. Her short, spiky white hair stood out from her head like a harsh halo. "Would you stand by as they do it?"

So she knew. Soutien took a deep breath of the cool night air and regained control of his pulse. True, it was dark and the torchlight was uncertain, but of the Fey, the dé Danann had the sharpest eyes. He wouldn't want an untimely flush to betray him.

Did the rest of the dé Danann know? By the questioning murmur rising all around him, he suspected they didn't. But Cathel knew something. Soutien could see it in the fathomless sorrow in the high lord's eyes.

"My Lord—" began Soutien and was interrupted by the arrival of a dé Danann, who bowed to the high lord.

"Yes?" said Lord Cathel.

"My Lord," said the newcomer. "It is ready."

This time the hush that descended on the assembly was respectful. The high lord looked at Soutien. "It is time to honor your friend."

Soutien nodded, struggling past the surfacing grief to a more clinical reaction. A man who arranged for an honorable burial for one was not prepared to order the death of the others.

Of course, Lord Cathel was not a man.

Soutien turned, acknowledging Grace with a brief smile before addressing Will and Moira.

"The pyre is ready. It's time."

Will nodded abruptly, turned, and walked away. Two of the dé Danann scrambled to catch up to him. Most of the others left, too, like ghosts disappearing into mist.

When Soutien made to follow, Lord Cathel put out his hand in a restraining gesture. "Stay for a moment, envoy."

Moira looked over her shoulder at Soutien just before she stepped out of the circle of light, but there was nothing he could offer her as reassurance, so he simply watched until they disappeared into the gloom. He thought he heard Grace's voice raised in objection.

"Father."

Soutien turned back to the throne, surprised to find that Ilyane was still there. A dozen dé Danann remained, standing close to the throne. Factions in the high lord's court?

Ilyane spoke to her father in a voice too low for Soutien to understand. He could tell by her sharp, controlled gestures that she was angry.

He knew she was insane, but still struggled to understand her motivation. Why had she saved them from the goblins? Did Amadan want them alive? Or did some remaining shred of honor dictate that she bring them to her father for him to overrule her objections?

And they had carried Mack all the way back here, perhaps out of sympathy for the family or out of respect for a strong man who died horribly.

Or perhaps out of fascination for death? When was the last time any of these had seen death? A century? Two?

Suddenly Cathel raised a hand, silencing his daughter.

"Enough. I will speak alone with Fin Bheara's envoy."

Ilyane opened her mouth, then closed it at a warning look from her father. For a moment, Soutien thought she would defy him, but then she whirled and strode into the gloom beyond the torchlight. Half a dozen dé Danann followed in her wake, but the rest were already filtering back into the trees, much to Soutien's relief. It meant that Lord Cathel still held sway.

The high lord sighed and relaxed against his throne. The shimmering glamour suddenly disappeared, leaving only the willow chair—lovely in itself—and a simply garbed, tired old Fey.

Soutien wondered if he should feel honored or worried.

In spite of himself, he sympathized with the high lord. When Soutien first met him, Lord Cathel had been in his prime. With his Lady by his side, he had ruled over the Tuatha dé Danann with a firm, kind hand. That was before the slow poison of sterility seeped through the Fey world. Ilyane was Soutien's age. Did she go mad when she realized she would never have children? Or when she realized that all the dé Danann, like the rest of the Fey, would eventually die out?

"What Fin Bheara proposes is terrible," said Lord Cathel, startling Soutien.

Soutien's instincts told him it was time for honesty. In any case, the thought of lying to this one was repugnant.

"My Lord," he said, "Amadan took the choice out of the King's hands."

At the high lord's raised eyebrows, Soutien continued. "Amadan called Kirwan's sons here, not Fin Bheara. I believe his purpose was to destroy them—except for one son—before Fin Bheara could claim them."

Lord Cathel watched him for a long time with those strange blue eyes. He was not as old as Amadan or Fin Bheara, but he was old enough to remember the ancient rivalry between them. He would understand the implications of Amadan's actions. Finally, Cathel sighed.

"I knew the time had come, but I thought Fin Bheara had decided. Does he then still cling to life?"

The implied criticism sent heat to Soutien's cheeks, and he felt like a youth again. And yet, the rebuke was justified, at least in part. He had known for a long time that the Fey's salvation lay in reuniting with humanity.

Which meant Fin Bheara had to die.

"King Fin Bheara brought the Fey here," said Soutien. "He had to be sure returning was the right decision." He paused to marshal his thoughts. "My Lord, Ilyane is right. The reunion will cause chaos."

At the mention of his daughter's name, a flicker of emotion crossed the high lord's face, too fast for Soutien to identify it.

"I would be careful to whom I admitted that," said Lord Cathel. "There are factions in my court willing to do anything to keep us where we are."

Meaning his daughter, thought Soutien. "Even if remaining here means the death of all things Fey?"

Lord Cathel studied Soutien's face for a long time before answering.

"There is comfort in the known," he said finally. "Some will struggle to retain that comfort until it is torn from them."

Soutien was uncomfortably aware that Lord Cathel spoke on more than one level. Fin Bheara had grown old, too, and fond of his comforts. It was much easier to turn a blind eye to the slow decline of the Fey than to contemplate dying to renew it. Oonagh had seen it, had grieved for the loss of the High King she had loved. Had crossed over in order to remove his greatest comfort, to shock him into action.

And it had worked, but too late. Amadan had already lured Mack and Aidan, killing one and destroying the other's mind. But Oonagh—from wherever she now existed—had stepped in to help Will.

And Moira and Grace? Wild cards. Amadan hadn't planned on them. Neither had Fin Bheara.

Weariness descended on Soutien like a hand pressing down on him. It took an effort of will to keep his shoulders square, his back straight.

"The time for comfort is past," he said. The words came out brusquely. He tried to modify his tone. "If we are to save anything at all—of the Fey or of humanity—we cannot let Amadan win. Will you help us, Lord Cathel?"

The high lord's gaze went past Soutien to the shadows beyond the torchlight. The expression on his face grew grim as his body gradually straightened.

"I will help you, envoy," he said.

But the words sounded more like a warning than a promise.

❧ NINETEEN ❦

WILL allowed one of the dé Danann to precede him off the platform. The remaining dé Danann kept pace above them and on surrounding trees. Moira and Grace followed more slowly.

They're both tired, thought Will.

He worked it out and realized it had been two days since they had slept. They would need rest before escaping.

The moon rode low in the sky, peering at him through the branches. Three of the dé Danann carried torches, including the one ahead, and their movements left a glowing trail in the night like a blur of motion on a photograph.

He itched to take a picture of the scene, of the ghostly Fey flitting from branch to branch, their silvery pallor contrasting with the flaming torches against the night.

But his camera, along with his pack and Moira's, had been confiscated on the march here.

It occurred to him that he might blithely be leading Moira and Grace to their deaths. Cathel's daughter and a bunch of her followers wanted them dead. Just because Cathel had put his daughter back in her place was no reason to trust the high lord.

And yet, he did.

The high lord was honorable and Will trusted honor in a way he would never trust politics. The dé Danann leader would not dishonor himself or his family.

Unless he had to.

Will shook his head. There was no point trying to second-guess the man. He would wait until Soutien reported back to them. Soutien would do everything he could on their behalf. If it wasn't enough, Will would do what he had to when the time came.

For now, it was enough that Mack would be taken care of. He wouldn't be buried on O'Rourke land and he wouldn't lie next to their mother and father, but at least he would be respected in this strange place.

Then Will thought of Edna, who wouldn't even have a grave to visit, and her baby, who would never know a father. Grief rose, swelling his heart, constricting his throat. His vision blurred and he blinked rapidly. It wouldn't do them any good if he fell off the damned tree.

His hand brushed against the rough bark of the tree trunk, and he paused to wait for Moira and Grace, and to compose himself. The dé Danann ahead of him turned back to look at Will. Between the moon and the glow of his torch, there was enough light to reveal the questioning expression on the man's face.

"Hang on," said Will. He looked over his shoulder. At the other end of the platform, Soutien stood before the seated Cathel, one hand rising and falling as he made a point. He was too far away for Will to make out his expression, but something about the throne made him stare. Hadn't it been bigger?

Moira clambered up to the branch and stood next to Will.

"What do you suppose they're talking about?" she asked.

Will shrugged. "Hopefully, how to get us out of here." By the look on her face, he realized his tone had been anything but hopeful. Where was Aidan while they stood around talking? Ilyane had sent someone to look for him, but they wouldn't find him if he didn't want to be found. Will and Moira could. They knew all of Aidan's tricks, just as he knew theirs.

"Did you see the way they walk when they're on the ground?" asked Moira. "As if they're afraid of getting their feet dirty. They must live in the trees most of the time."

Before he could comment, the sound of a commotion caught their attention.

"Damn it all!" came Grace's voice. "I'm not crossing!"

The thread of panic in her voice propelled Will past Moira, to the bridge he and his sister had just crossed. Grace stood on the far side, her back against a tree, her arms by her side. Will couldn't be sure, but he thought her fingers were digging into the bark of the tree. By the look on her face, it would take some serious convincing to get her across that bridge.

The two guards who had originally accompanied her to the platform stood on either side of her. They looked helplessly at Will and he felt a twinge of sympathy for them.

The other guards silently arrayed themselves on branches above and to either side of him. Will ignored them. He couldn't take his eyes off the mixture of stark fear and stubborn determination on Grace's face.

When had she grown so beautiful?

"Grace?" he said gently.

She glanced at him, then quickly back at the two dé Danann next to her, as if afraid they would rush her.

"What?"

"Are you afraid of heights?"

She spared him a furious, contemptuous look, and he winced.

"Good guess, Einstein," whispered Moira, joining him.

"I'm not crossing that damned thing again!" said Grace angrily.

Will studied the bridge. It was made of branches tightly woven with rope and it was at least two feet wide, with a span of four feet. Safe enough, if you didn't mind the absence of handrails and were sure on your feet. He had been in enough jungles and crossed enough makeshift bridges to recognize relative safety when he saw it. And Moira's military training had accustomed her to heights and to flimsy bridges.

Then his gaze caught on the dark abyss below them. Shadows met and parted beneath the bridge and only reason told Will they were branches and leaves moving in the wind. To someone half-crazed with fear, what did those shadows conceal?

"You won't have to," he said finally. He crossed over the bridge, moving with the sway. Grace's eyes closed tightly so as not to watch him. As he stepped onto the branch, Moira stepped onto the bridge, crossing easily.

He had seen this fear before, had seen it paralyze strong, brave men. It said a lot about Grace that she was still standing.

He reached her side and placed a hand on her cheek. She opened her eyes and immediately some of the panic left them.

"I'm not—"

"Shush," he said, pressing his thumb briefly against her lips. "It's all right."

He turned to the dé Danann who had led them and who remained on the other side of the bridge.

"We're going down," he said, pointing to the darkness below.

The ensuing discussion between the Fey didn't sound musical at all. Finally, one of Grace's guards turned his back on the others and jumped to a lower branch, landing cleanly on both feet. He looked up at Grace, said *"Bannet!"*, and without waiting for her, began clambering down the tree.

Will immediately warmed to him.

"Come on," he said before the others could object. He pulled a trembling Grace away from the tree trunk, released her into Moira's clasp and jumped down to the next branch. Then he turned and held his arms out.

"Better hurry," Moira said to Grace. "Before they make up their minds."

Moira held Grace's arm until Will's hands closed around her waist and he lifted her down to the branch. Then Moira jumped down to join them. In this fashion, they made their slow way down the tree. The remaining dé Danann quickly spread out, some staying above them, some hurrying past to await them on the ground.

The branches were wide and strong, and grew larger as they made their way toward the ground. But every time Will's hands closed around Grace's waist, her hands clutched convulsively at his shoulders and he could feel her trembling.

She didn't say a word all the way down.

When Will's feet finally touched the ground, he found half a dozen dé Danann waiting for him. In the light of their two torches, he caught a glimpse of large trees and stern faces. Well, they weren't about to stop him now. He held his arms up for Grace. The last branch was a little too far for him to reach her.

"Jump," he said. "I'll catch you."

Without hesitation, she jumped off the branch. He caught her and absorbed her momentum against his chest, wrapping his arms around her and stepping back a little to counter the impact.

She remained in his arms for a long moment, shuddering. Finally she pulled away and he reluctantly released her.

"Thank you," she said, her voice clear in the silence.

Moira landed in a crouch next to them. "Oh, he didn't mind at all, did you, Will?" she said, her voice ripe with amusement.

Oh, shut up, thought Will.

They followed the Fey through the dark forest for what seemed like a long time. Will insisted on carrying a torch, to light Grace's path as she picked her barefooted way around stones and twigs. It was a warm evening, but the ground was damp. Maybe he should offer her his socks.

Then he considered the state of his socks and decided she was better off with the damp.

He examined her as they walked. She'd had no sleep the night before. Then she'd suffered waves of cramps, fought off goblins, and marched all day. No wonder she walked like a zombie.

Finally, he saw what looked like a gathering of fireflies up ahead.

"What is that?" asked Moira.

"Torches," replied Grace.

As they approached, the trees thinned out until they finally reached a large clearing. Every tree surrounding the clearing contained half a dozen dé Danann perched on branches. Torches flared, illuminating the pile of brush and branches stacked ten feet high in the center of the clearing.

Will stopped. His reluctant gaze traveled up the pyre to the top. There, nestled atop the pile, was the bier with Mack's body. The blanket of pale flowers covered his entire body, save for his head. Will traced his brother's profile with his eyes, refusing to think.

A breeze caressed his face, bringing with it the fragrance of the flowers, the smell of living wood and moist soil, the stronger odor of his own unwashed body.

Moira stopped next to him and he heard the faint catch of her breath. Her arm pressed against his comfortingly.

Grace came up behind them. "Ahh..." she said when she saw Mack.

Will picked out individual faces among the dé Danann perched in the trees. The high lord's daughter, Ilyane, sat on a low tree limb, one leg drawn up. Even from that distance, anger radiated from her.

"What's she got against us?" wondered Moira aloud, following his gaze.

Before Will could answer, Soutien dropped from a nearby tree, landing on his feet. The two dé Danann who had accompanied him remained in the tree.

"They're ready," said Soutien without preamble. "Are you?"

Moira looked up at Will. "Should we say something?"

Like what? wondered Will. Sorry I didn't show up early enough to save you? Sorry you were cheated out of your life?

When Will didn't answer, Moira turned to Soutien. "Go ahead," she said.

Soutien turned toward the clearing and nodded at someone in the trees. Only then did Will see Cathel. The high lord stood in an oak tree, on a branch that should have been too flimsy to hold him, one hand braced on the branch above him. Torchlight caught the silver thread of his velvet cloak, like starlight twinkling from a black sky.

One long, elegant hand gestured and from the far side of the clearing a woman's voice rose in song. Will held his breath as the pure voice filled the clearing and rose to the heavens. The voice called up an ache in him that he refused to acknowledge. In it echoed all the losses in his life, all the good men he had seen die. He stared stoically at the bier, steeling himself.

Next to him, Moira caught her breath. He glanced down to find her weeping. He wrapped an arm around her and held her close.

More voices joined the first one, some rising in celebration, some deep with sorrow. Out of the corner of his eye, he saw Soutien move to stand next to Grace. They remained a respectful distance from brother and sister.

Then, as if at a signal, all the Fey surrounding the clearing rose to their feet. In one sweeping motion, a dozen torches dropped onto the pyre. The dry wood and kindling caught in a whoosh that reminded Will of gasoline-soaked brush catching on the first match.

But this wasn't burning brush in a South American jungle. This was Mack.

The flames rose high above the bier, illuminating the clearing with a ruddy, flickering light. Even from this distance he could feel the searing heat. He tried not to think of what the flames were doing to Mack's body.

The fire burned hot for a long time. Will and Moira watched in silence while the Fey sang. Mack's body was barely visible through the flames.

Will tried to think if Mack would have appreciated a cremation. He couldn't remember ever discussing death with him. It had seemed so improbable.

Mack wasn't supposed to die. Not like this. He was going to have a long, successful career in the army, have lots of kids and grandkids, and eventually die peacefully. He wasn't supposed to die in this impossible place, at the hands of an impossible creature.

Moira tensed beneath his arm and he realized he'd been squeezing too hard. He released her and tried to bring himself under control. Mack was dead. There was nothing he could do about it. But Moira was alive and, hopefully, so was Aidan.

As the flames consumed Mack's body, Will swore to his brother that he would get Moira and Aidan—and Grace—out of here if he had to die doing it.

When the flames began to abate, the high lord suddenly appeared at their side. He looked at Moira and spoke. When he finished, he glanced at Soutien.

"He's inviting us to join him for a meal, unless we would rather be alone."

Will examined the high lord's face for a moment before turning to Soutien.

"What's going on? Are we prisoners, or aren't we?"

Soutien shrugged. "I don't know. He said he would help us, but I'm not sure what that means." He gave Will a crooked smile. "If it's any consolation, I believe we are safer as his guests than his daughter's."

Moira looked up at the High Lord, her eyes bright with tears. "I'm not very hungry," she said.

Neither was Will, but this was an opportunity to find out more about Cathel and maybe figure out a way to get out of here.

"Tell him yes," he said.

Grace and Moira looked at Will in surprise but Soutien only nodded. He bowed formally to the high lord and relayed their acceptance.

With a nod and a backward glance at Moira, Lord Cathel left. Two torchbearers accompanied him. Will looked around but couldn't see Ilyane or any of the dé Danann he associated with her. What was she up to?

"An invitation to dinner?" he said finally, when they were alone save for their patient guards.

Moira picked it up. "First they make us prisoners, then they discuss whether or not to kill us, and now suddenly we're dinner guests? What's going on, Soutien?"

Soutien shrugged. "Dé Danann politics," he said. "Ilyane and her father are struggling for the leadership, but they're being genteel about it."

"That girl is crazy," said Grace, as if she were commenting on the price of eggs. She slapped at a mosquito on her arm.

Will studied her face. She would need to sit down soon.

"So where does that leave us?" continued Grace.

Again the shrug. "With a good meal to look forward to," said Soutien.

Will frowned. "We don't know if they'll help us or kill us. We have to get out of here as soon as possible." He turned to Soutien. "How do we get to Fin Bheara?"

Soutien stared at him, his eyes unreadable in the uncertain light. "His castle is by the sea, due east from here." He smiled slightly. "As a son of Kirwan, you are tied to him. You'll probably sense it when you're near."

A sudden shiver raced up Will's scalp. "What exactly is this con-nection?"

The smile left Soutien's face. "That is the King's story to tell," he said and turned to follow Lord Cathel.

Will and Moira looked at each other, then they looked at Grace. She looked as if she wanted to be sick. Will moved to support her, but she held up a hand.

She stared at Will for a long moment. "I hate this place," she said at last, then she turned and followed Soutien.

As Will and his sister followed the others, it occurred to him that Cathel's invitation came before they had to witness the destruction of his brother's body by fire. He squelched a sudden, fierce gratitude. The High Lord might be honorable, but he had his own reasons for the things he did. Best not to forget that.

***

They followed Cathel to a small glade surrounded by fir trees that met in a dark canopy far above their heads. Wind sighed through the fir needles, sounding melancholy to Grace's ears. Queer shadows danced on the trees, cast by torches hung in rope holders all around the glade.

"*Sithan*," said the High Lord as they entered the glade. He stood by a table heaped with food, and as he beckoned them forward, torch-light caught in the silver folds of his cloak. Again, Grace caught a blurring just beneath the surface. She tried to concentrate, but her tired eyes refused to focus. Instead, her attention settled on the table.

A huge platter of cakes held center stage. Surrounding it were bowls of fruit, pitchers filled with a pale, creamy liquid, and loaves of fragrant bread. Two candelabra cast a soft, appetizing glow on the as-sembled food.

Grace doubted that Cathel normally dined at ground level. Was this all for her? Did that mean they weren't prisoners?

Cathel was alone, but she knew that if she looked up, she would find a dozen Fey faces peering down at her from the trees. And a dozen Fey hands would be hovering near swords.

"Lord Cathel invites you to eat," said Soutien, gesturing at the table.

Grace glanced at Moira and Will. Neither one made a move toward the table.

"I'm not hungry," said Grace finally. The ground beneath her bare feet felt damp and soft and infinitely comforting. He had set his table at ground level and here she was, spurning his offer of food. Still, this was no time to let politeness stand in the way of common sense. They didn't know where Cathel's loyalties lay. "Besides, you know what they say about accepting Fey food..."

"I think we're past worrying about enchantment, Grace," said Moira, a hint of condescension in her voice.

Grace shrugged, too tired to rise to the bait.

"We may be here for a while," said Soutien seriously. "You'll eventually have to eat something you didn't bring yourselves."

Will nodded. "Better eat," he said. His tone was casual, but the gaze he turned on Grace was full of meaning.

Better eat, thought Grace, because they might need all their strength to escape in the next few hours. Better eat because they didn't know when next they would have a chance. Better eat, even if Mack was turning to ashes.

She picked up a small, heavy platter that looked like it was made of solid gold and put some cheese and bread on it. When she looked around for a place to sit, Soutien pointed at the trees.

For the first time, Grace noticed two ropes hanging from a branch, ending in a woven seat.

A swing, one of half a dozen clumped on the same side of the glade. Some hung crookedly, as if they had been erected in haste.

In the silence that followed, Cathel poured the creamy pale liquid from the pitcher into goblets. After handing a goblet to each of them, he spoke in a low murmur to Soutien, then turned to the others. He said a few words, then raised his goblet expectantly.

"This is *misan na*," said Soutien, raising his own goblet. "A wine made of *misa* berries picked at midsummer. It is served only on rare occasions. Lord Cathel offers it to honor Mack."

The others raised their goblets, but Grace hesitated. Why were they blithely trusting Cathel? Was she being paranoid?

Moira glared at her. "We're drinking to my brother."

What good is honoring a dead man, thought Grace, if it gets us into trouble? She glanced around and found Will looking back at her expectantly. Should she tell him what she had learned from Soutien? Surely he had the right to know the whole story? It wasn't really her decision to make.

Was it?

Finally, she raised her goblet. Nobody else seemed to think there was a risk.

"To Mack," said Soutien, and drank deeply. Grace hesitated a moment longer, then followed suit. The drink tasted of summer and love, rich with sunshine and warmth. She wished Mack could have tasted it.

Will set his goblet down by his feet and turned to Soutien. "It's time. Ask him what he wants in return for helping us." He nodded at Cathel. "Ask him."

Soutien's expression smoothed to neutral. He set his plate and goblet at his feet, straightened, and bowed formally to the high lord. When he began to speak, his words rose and fell in a rhythm reminiscent of poetry.

Staring at Soutien, Grace shivered. His face seemed carved of wood, lacking even the shadow of a beard. In spite of everything they had gone through, he still looked elegant and clean. His hand swept out to encompass the group, but he kept his face turned toward Lord Cathel.

The high lord replied, his voice rising on a question. After a moment, Soutien replied.

A sense of unreality swept over Grace as she watched Soutien petition a Fey lord for help. The face she had known as a girl suddenly seemed strange, harder, older. What did she know of him, except that he had always been at Kirwan?

Only a few days ago, she had been happily planning her next buying trip. Only a few days ago, Mack had been alive, and Aidan sane.

"Well?" said Will, startling her. Soutien had turned toward him, his expression grave.

"He will supply food and water for your trip to Knockma. At the same time, he will send more of his folk to look for Aidan—"

"No," said Will. "I want you to take Moira and Grace to Fin Bheara. I'll go with the dé Danann to find Aidan and join you later."

A sudden irritation flared up in Grace, but before she could say anything, Moira spoke up.

"Excuse me, High and Mighty Warrior," she said tartly. "I am but a lowly female, but I have been known to speak for myself."

Grace almost laughed.

"Moira —" began Will, impatience tingeing his voice.

"Don't *Moira* me," said Moira.

"It doesn't matter what either of you wants." Soutien's voice cut through the argument with finality. "You have no choice. Lord Cathel wants Will to get to Knockma as soon as possible. When they find Aidan, they'll bring him to Knockma."

Grace's heartbeat faltered momentarily at Soutien's choice of words. Again, Moira gave voice to her thought.

"Wait a minute. You make it sound as if Will's going to be on his own."

Soutien shook his head, but his expression was grim. "Not alone. Grace is to go with him."

"Me?" said Grace. Her stomach plummeted and she spilled some of the wine.

"Grace?" Moira turned to stare at her. "She can barely put one foot in front of the other. And what am I supposed to do while the two of them are traipsing around the countryside? Knit?" She took a long shuddery breath, and Grace could hear the panic bubbling through the anger. "And you? Are you going, too?"

Again, Soutien shook his head. "No. I am to stay with you, here."

"For what earthly purpose?" cried Moira.

"As insurance," said Grace, suddenly understanding. She was glad she hadn't eaten. What the hell did they want from her now?

"Insurance?" said Will, turning to Cathel. The high lord stood his ground under Will's cold anger. "Insurance against what?"

"Lord Cathel supports the king, and since the king needs you, the high lord will do everything in his power to help you."

"But if that's not enough..." said Moira, obviously beginning to understand.

"He may be able to buy time for his people by throwing you and Soutien to Amadan," finished Grace, the last trace of exhaustion disappearing as her mind went on full alert. She looked at Lord Cathel with contempt.

"Why me?" asked Will, staring at Soutien. "Why send me to Knockma, and not Moira? We're both O'Rourkes."

He asked the question calmly, almost idly, but Grace saw the thinning lips, the tightness around his eyes. They had lost Aidan, and cremated Mack. He didn't want to be separated from his remaining sibling.

But with his question came another realization. Will thought staying with the dé Danann was dangerous, more dangerous than a trip through unknown terrain, facing unknown enemies. That's why he wanted Moira to go, if they had to be separated at all.

Would he still feel that way once Grace told him what he was expected to do at Knockma?

She turned to look at Soutien, but he avoided her gaze. He sighed so softly that she might have missed it if she hadn't been watching him. "The spell calls on the son of Kirwan, not the daughter," he said.

"And he's beginning to run out of sons of Kirwan," said Will grimly. "What exactly does Fin Bheara need me for?"

Tell him, prayed Grace. Tell him so I don't have to make this decision.

This time Soutien's sigh was audibly ragged. "He will tell you when the time comes."

Grace looked away from Soutien, suddenly loathing him.

"What happens if I fail at whatever it is I'm supposed to do?" asked Will.

Soutien looked at him, sadness in his eyes. "You must succeed, Will," he said. His words came as if from a distance. "Cathel's scouts have spotted Amadan's army. They move only at night, but they move fast. Amadan is less than three days from Knockma. You must reach Knockma and Fin Bheara before they do. Cathel cannot stand very long against Amadan. He may not even try."

You bastard, thought Grace.

"And that's where we come in," said Moira bitterly.

This had gone on long enough. Will and Moira deserved to know what they were getting into. If Soutien couldn't do it, then she would.

Grace opened her mouth to speak, but a strange lassitude stole over her, robbing her of the ability to form coherent speech. Her nose began to prickle, then her fingertips and toes.

To her surprise, her chin nodded against her chest. It was a struggle to raise her head but she did. The first face her glance encountered was Moira's.

She tried to say, "I told you so," but her lips refused to move. Then the goblet slid from her fingers, spilling its contents on the ground.

Bloody hell. She tried to stand, but only managed to lurch forward a step before toppling to the ground.

❧ TWENTY ❧

SOUTIEN at in his swing and watched Moira pace the length of the sunlit, uneven platform, turn sharply, and pace back. It was a large platform, at least thirty feet across. He wouldn't be able to reach her in time if she took a wrong step and fell off. He glanced down at the green forest floor at least thirty feet below, then back at Moira as she turned for another lap.

"How can you just sit there?" she demanded, continuing what was so far a one-sided conversation. "I'm sick of waiting here."

She had been saying that since they awoke in daylight to find Will and Grace gone. Two hours, he judged. She was working herself into a fine frenzy, one of the few unsavory habits she had retained from childhood. Unfortunately, there were no indulgent parents here, and Soutien could do very little to protect her.

At least ten guards perched above and below the platform, silent presences that loomed over his every thought. Their faces were hard and unsmiling—Ilyane's followers. Did that mean Cathel was no longer leader of the dé Danann? Was he also a prisoner, somewhere in this treetop community?

Or did it mean that he was the consummate politician and had allowed his daughter to guard her insurance policy?

Moira's agitation was hard to resist. Part of him wanted to get up and pace with her. The other wanted to snap at her to stop acting like a child. He deliberately relaxed his shoulders, trying to remain alert despite his growing irritation.

Finally, he faced the truth. Moira wasn't the source of his irritation. He was. His duty was clear. He should step out of the Fey world and into his room at Kirwan. From there, he could step into the king's study at Knockma. He could then alert the king to the growing danger, tell him of Mack's death and of the disappearance of Aidan and Will. By morning, there would be a host of armed Fey looking for Will and Aidan, and even more heading toward Lord Cathel.

But that would mean leaving Moira alone.

He scowled, shifting in his swing. A knot dug irritatingly into his left hip.

None of the guards had responded to his inquiries. He desperately wanted to talk to Cathel, to see if reason—or self-preservation—could convince the high lord to let them go.

He should have expected this move. Between Fin Bheara, Amadan, and Ilyane, Lord Cathel walked a razor edge of need. Instead of being cautious—especially in the face of Grace's obvious misgivings—Soutien had blithely trusted the high lord.

He and Moira would have to escape. He wasn't sure how yet, but it would have to be at night. The dé Danann were creatures of daylight. Although their night vision was better than a human's, they didn't like to travel at night. If he and Moira escaped under cover of darkness, they might have a chance.

A dragonfly flew by, in hot pursuit of a mosquito. Soutien absently admired the dragonfly's iridescent wings. They caught the light only to disappear into shade and reappear a second later as the insect moved through dappled shadows.

All they needed was a distraction.

Moira reached one end of the platform, turned sharply, and strode toward the other end.

"You're only making them more nervous," said Soutien calmly. "They'll never relax if you keep acting like a prisoner planning to escape."

Moira glared at him, but finally stopped, to his immense relief. She ignored the swing next to him and flopped down on the platform itself, drawing her knees up and wrapping her arms around them, as though trying to contain the need to move.

***

Morning crawled toward afternoon and clouds moved in, bringing with them a cold wind that shook branches and sent rude fingers up Moira's T-shirt.

"This is nuts!" she finally said, jumping up and resuming her pacing. At least it kept her warm. And sane.

Soutien looked up at her and she turned away from the understanding on his face, irritated beyond measure. How could he sit there so calmly? Didn't he *care*?

He had let them drink that damned wine. He, of all people, should have been suspicious. Or maybe he had known all along that it was drugged. Maybe he was in on it with Cathel.

She was being unfair, and she knew it. But Aidan was lost in the woods, or worse, and Will was out there, somewhere, bushwhacking his way to Fin Bheara. There was no telling what kind of trouble her brothers were facing while she *rotted* on this damned platform. While Soutien just sat there.

"You should try to relax," said Soutien.

She whirled on him. "Relax? When one of my brothers is dead and the other two are in danger?" Frustration roiled up in her, gathering meanness. "Why aren't *you* more upset, Soutien?"

"You forgot Grace," said Soutien mildly.

His words caught her off guard. "What?"

"Grace. She's in danger, too."

Heat crept up her cheeks. "Of course she's in danger," she replied. "I haven't forgotten."

"Even if you would like to," said Soutien.

Moira glanced at him. He was artfully deflecting her anger. She was almost grateful. It was easier to talk about Grace than to face Soutien's potential disloyalty.

Finally she shrugged. "She irritates me."

Soutien raised an eyebrow. "Grace?"

"Yes, Grace," she mimicked.

"What did she do?"

Just as suddenly, the irritation melted away. "Nothing. Everything. It's just the way she is, always careful, always reasonable. I don't think that woman's ever done an impulsive thing in her life."

"Yes. Well. We can see where impulse brought you."

Surprised, Moira looked at Soutien. "What do you mean? I had to come. Mack and Aidan were in trouble."

Soutien looked at her and sighed. "Just once, Moira, would it have killed you to wait? You didn't wait for Will. You didn't try to talk to me." He shook his head. "Grace may be too cautious for your taste, but you are too impulsive."

Moira opened her mouth to refute the accusation, then closed it without saying anything. He was right. She hadn't thought things through. She had landed herself here unprepared, dragging Grace along for the ride.

Maybe it wasn't irritation she felt, so much as guilt for entangling Grace in a dangerous situation.

Goosebumps sprang up and she rubbed her arms absently.

Hell. She hated feeling guilty.

Warmth suddenly enveloped her shoulders and she whirled in alarm, only to relax when she saw Soutien standing in front of her. He had placed his cloak over her shoulders.

"Thanks," she said, not meeting his gaze. She tried to suppress a massive shiver. "I have a perfectly warm sweater in my backpack, wherever that is."

She didn't want to think about Grace any more. She would think about it when she was back home and could put this whole sorry mess behind her.

Soutien smiled. "My tunic is warm enough," he said. "You are welcome to the cloak."

Then, to her amazement, he gathered her in his arms, rubbing her back as if to warm her further.

"Soutien?" she said, her voice coming out more like a squeak than she would have liked. All thoughts of Grace fled. She was uncomfortably aware of the dense, hard planes of his body, the smell of wood smoke and fresh air that clung to him.

"Shh," he whispered in her ear. The warm breath sent a shiver of a different kind coursing down her neck and she stiffened. What was he doing?

"We're going to have to move soon," he murmured, still rubbing her back.

For a moment, she was lost in the sensation his warm breath and stroking hands produced, then his words registered.

He was planning their escape.

At once, she relaxed into his embrace and nodded imperceptibly. Above her, dé Danann faces peered down at them. Was their hearing better than hers? Could they overhear Soutien's whispered words? It didn't matter. None of them spoke English.

Unlike Soutien, who was the king's man, and friend to the O'Rourke family for almost three hundred years.

She almost pulled back as the realization hit her. Forcing herself to feign calm, she turned her face toward Soutien's ear, almost nuzzling his smooth cheek.

"You can travel back and forth, can't you? Between here and Kirwan?"

Soutien remained silent for a long moment, his body very still. His hands stopped stroking her, coming to rest on the small of her back. Finally, he answered her.

"I can get to Kirwan from any spot in the Fey world. From Kirwan I can only go to Knockma."

Hot anger spurted through her. "You wasted all this time!" She pulled out of his arms and moved away, still facing him.

"You could have left this morning and been on your way back with help by now." She tried to keep her voice low, but the day's pent-up frustration worked against her.

A rustling in the trees announced the dé Danann's growing interest, but Moira ignored it. Let the damned Fey listen.

"Moira—"

"Jesus, Soutien," said Moira fiercely, her anger finally finding a close target. "Will and Grace are out there! Why the hell are you still here? Go find help!"

"No."

Moira stepped back as if she had been struck. No?

"I am not leaving you."

"Not...?" Moira stood before him, suddenly at a loss for words. What did that mean, not leaving her? Because she was incapable of looking after herself? Because the danger was even greater than she thought?

Her body remembered the pressure of his body against hers, the long, slow caress of his hands on her back, the sensual whispering in her ear, and she closed her eyes tightly.

"If anything happens to them," she said softly, her voice almost lost in the wind, "I will never forgive you."

***

Grace woke slowly, gradually becoming aware that she was in bed, and that someone was shaking her.

She raised her hand to stop the shaking, then opened her eyes. Will was staring down at her, eyes so dark they looked navy, hair tousled and soot-black against the cornflower blue of an early morning sky. He smelled of damp earth and grass.

She sat up sharply, her hand still clutching his thick wrist, her mind completely blank. She could make no sense of his presence in her bed. Then it all came flooding back—the fight with goblins, the march, the cremation.

She released his wrist and groaned.

"The drink," she said, her voice coming out as a croak. She pushed the hair away from her face. She wasn't in bed. She was lying on prickly grass.

Will nodded, but said nothing as he sat back. Now that she was fully awake, she became aware of other smells—the clean scent of morning breeze over damp grass, the odor of her unwashed body mingling with his, and underlying it all and emanating from Will, a spicy, musky odor that was infinitely attractive.

With a jerk, Grace turned away from him.

They were on a knoll in the middle of rolling hills lush with wild grass and surrounded by stands of trees. The hills looked like grassy knees poking out of a forest bath.

The nearest woods stood half a mile away. She couldn't be sure at that distance, but they looked like chestnut and oak trees, with the occasional ash tree thrown in. Not a fir tree in sight.

Without a word, they both stood up to get a better view. An occasional glimmer through the trees caught Grace's attention. At least there'd be water.

"Any idea where we are?" she asked Will, facing him once more.

He shrugged. "Hopefully, less than three days from Knockma." There was a thread of steel in his voice, belying the casual shrug.

Three days. She glanced down at her naked, filthy feet peeking out from the ragged hem of her pants. Would she last? Would she be able to move fast enough? What if they encountered more goblins?

"Let's go," said Will. He held his pack in one hand and stuffed a blanket into it with the other. Belatedly, she realized she was standing on the blanket's twin.

"They left me my pack," said Will, hefting it. "There's enough food in it to last three or four days. The same in yours."

She followed the direction of his nod and saw a lump a few feet down the knoll. She took a step toward it, then realized it was a bag. Made of tightly woven willow twigs, it was gathered at the top with a leather drawstring. A carrying strap had been incorporated into the design to enable the wearer to carry it cross-wise on the back, like a quiver.

Grace squatted next to the willow bag and opened it. There were packets of what she assumed was food, some carefully wrapped in leaves, some in cloth. Something bladder-like sloshed as she moved the bag. A water container of some kind.

She moved things around in the bag, hoping to discover a pair of running shoes. Instead, a small round ball rolled to the bottom of the bag. She fished it out and held it out in the sunlight. It sat on her palm, a small lumpy, malleable ball of...

"What is that?" asked Will. "I've got one, too."

Grace sniffed the ball. There was something familiar about the fragrance.

"Soap!" She barely restrained herself from dancing a little jig. "It's soap!"

Will stared at her long enough for her to regain her composure. "The next river we come to," she told him, "I'm taking a bath." If they had time.

If nothing lived in it.

A small smile tugged at Will's mouth, still visible despite the whiskers.

"It takes so little to please you," he murmured.

Grace popped the soap back into the bag, not deigning to answer him. She stood up and swung the bag up and over her shoulder. Then she slid it off again, gathered her blanket, and stuffed it into the bag. As she closed the bag, she glanced up at Will, who was staring out at the forest.

Soutien hadn't told him what Fin Bheara wanted of him. That meant she had to.

Grace closed her eyes tightly. Soutien was afraid Will would refuse. What sane man would agree to murdering a man he had never met?

Will might have to kill Fin Bheara or humanity and the Fey would die. But Will was a pacifist. If the man couldn't kill in war, could anyone truly expect him to kill in cold blood?

Besides, it might never come to that if Aidan was rescued and brought to Knockma.

Still. She had to tell Will. Even if she doubted Soutien's story—and she didn't—she didn't have the moral right to keep the information from Will.

But he was already planning to go to Knockma. It wasn't as if she had to convince him. If she told him, he might decide not to go to Knockma at all. Whether he found out now, or once he got to Knockma…

And if Aidan had been found and rescued by then, Will would never need to know.

With a sinking feeling, she realized that she couldn't take the chance.

"Soutien said you'd feel it," she said finally, feeling like a hypocrite. "He said there was a connection between you and Fin Bheara. Do you feel anything?"

Will's smile vanished. "Not a damned thing."

"I don't suppose we have any idea where Soutien and Moira are?"

"No." His anger returned full strength, leashed but still dangerous.

Grace decided she didn't want to be around if Will found Cathel. She sighed, looking east at the vista of hill and forest. He would be angry with her when he found out she'd withheld information.

"Soutien said Fin Bheara's castle was by the sea, due east from...." She faltered to a stop.

"Exactly," said Will grimly.

Grace stared at him for a moment, then turned back to the sun. A hint of warmth rode on the dew-fresh air.

The castle was due east when they were in Lord Cathel's forest home. But they had no idea where they were now, or how far they had been moved while unconscious. They might travel due east forever and never find Knockma.

Well, maybe not. Presumably they would hit the sea first. But then what? Right or left?

"Why didn't he send some of his people with us, if this is so bloody important?"

Will shrugged. "I don't think Cathel knows which of his people he can trust. If there's a power struggle between him and his daughter..."

If Cathel didn't know which of his dé Danann secretly supported his crazy daughter, then Grace was just as glad not to have any of them here.

She shook her head. "I can't believe we were just dumped here, with no directions and no protection. What if a hungry wolf happened to walk by while we were sleeping?"

For answer, Will pointed at the ground. At first, Grace couldn't figure out what he was pointing at. All she could see was wild grass nodding under the breeze and little clumps of bluebells. Then she looked closer. There were an awful lot of bluebells. Again she turned slowly, this time looking at the ground. The entire top of the knoll was circled by bluebells.

"I can't remember," she finally murmured. "Are they for protection?"

Will shrugged. "I can't remember, either," he said. "It doesn't matter. Nothing ate us."

Grace nodded. He was clearly impatient to get going, but she was reluctant to set off barefoot on another long trek.

As if the thought triggered the sensation, her feet suddenly felt cold. It would be a while before the sun burned off the dew. She would be traveling with cold, wet feet over rough ground and through tall grasses. There was no telling how many sharp stones lurked in those tall grasses.

Her hand crept to her waistband, to the soft shoes safely tucked there. On the island, the shoes had led her back to the beach. There was no need for a guide—Cathel knew the shoes would lead them to Knockma. They would at least protect her feet and allow her to move faster.

Even if it meant paying for that protection and speed with excruciating pain.

She pulled the shoes out of her waistband and sat down on the damp ground.

"No," said Will, wrapping a hand around her forearm. "Let's try something else."

"They'll lead the way," explained Grace.

Will shook his head. "We'll go east and take our chances without those damned shoes."

Tempted, Grace considered his suggestion. If it were at all possible to avoid the cramps... Finally, she sighed.

"As soon as we stop for the night, I'll take them off." She looked at Will. "I probably wore them too long the first time."

Will shook his head. "At least try it my way." He shrugged out of his backpack and, crouching down, rummaged through it. He finally withdrew three pairs of gray woolen socks.

"We'll pad your feet," he said and handed her a pair.

Grace looked down at the socks and then at him. His face grew red. "I'm sorry," he said stiffly, "I don't have any clean socks left."

Over the next fifteen minutes, they tried different variations: one pair of socks stuffed with grass; two pairs of socks, one over top of the other, with grass in between; three pairs of socks stuffed with grass and Will's T-shirt. They tried tying on the socks with long grass.

Finally, they tried letting Grace wear Will's boots and stuffing the toes with the socks. She took one step and tripped.

"This isn't working," said Grace, brushing the dirt from her hands.

Still on the ground, she removed the boots and reached for the brown man's shoes.

"No," said Will, once again putting a hand on her forearm.

Grace looked up at him. "We're wasting time, Will. The shoes will help us find the way. They helped me find you after the phooka took Moira, and they helped on the island."

Will's jaw tightened visibly under the beard. "I don't care if they helped you find your way out of Oz," he said quietly. "You are not wearing them."

Grace stared at him for a long moment, then stood up and tucked the shoes carefully into the waistband of her pants.

"I will assume you're being a presumptuous jerk out of concern for me." She smiled at him sweetly.

Without a word, Will picked up her pack and his, turned and led the way down the knoll, stepping deliberately over a clump of bluebells.

With a sigh of exasperation, she followed him. Isn't that just like an O'Rourke, she thought.

He was as bad as Moira, assuming she was an idiot and incapable of looking after herself. She had warned Moira about the phooka. She warned them about accepting Cathel's drink. But would either of them admit that she was right? Of course not. Especially Moira. She wouldn't admit Grace was right if it killed her.

The sudden tightness in her chest surprised Grace. She couldn't believe she was worried about Moira. It was silly. Moira was more than capable of looking after herself, especially with   Soutien to help her. Grace had a sudden memory of Soutien and Moira fighting the goblins side by side. Moira was smart and strong, and Soutien was just as capable. They would be all right.

But what if she and Will didn't make it to Fin Bheara in time? What if her bare feet slowed them down too much?

She caught up to Will and made him give her her willow bag. She dug through it for something to eat. She found some bread and a chunk of cheese, which she ate while walking, even though she had no appetite. *Hey Moira*, she thought, *look, I'm learning.*

She slowly became aware that Will was picking the easiest route, avoiding thorns and thistles. Despite never once turning to look at her, he seemed to know exactly where she was and never allowed the distance between them to grow.

He's trying to protect me, she thought. *But we can't afford to detour around everything that could hurt me.*

"We have to move faster than this," she called to Will.

Without a word, he lengthened his stride.

Surly bugger.

She developed a rhythm of scanning the ground for pitfalls, then looking up to watch the grasslands to the south, where the grass grew thigh high. A few times she caught a ripple of movement that wasn't caused by wind and guessed that some animal, perhaps a rabbit, or something bigger, was making its way under cover of the grass. Once, she saw a bald eagle circling high on a thermal, a sight that inexplicably cheered her.

Twice she turned around, convinced that something was behind them.

Exertion quickly warmed her feet. The sun rose higher, cajoling her into removing her wool jacket and wrapping it around her waist. A few clouds crept in from the west, heralds for the rising humidity.

Her sweat seemed irresistible to a variety of bugs that all came to investigate. Some stayed to dine. She distracted herself by trying to count the number of black flies circling Will's head like miniature buzzards.

But no matter how she tried not to think about her sore feet, she grew increasingly aware of each nick and bruise. Within half an hour, she was hobbling and trying to favor her left foot, which had landed on a prickly burr.

She was slowing them down.

Once a black bear emerged from the forest to the north, stood up on its hind legs to sniff the air, and quickly disappeared into the forest again. Aside from an occasional deer and curious blue jay, the wildlife kept well away from them.

Almost an hour after setting out, they entered the first stand of trees. The temperature immediately dropped. Grace walked through pockets of warmth interspersed by wide bands of cool humidity. She shrugged her coat back on.

Their passage startled a sleeping owl, which glided silently past them on ghostly wings. Grace didn't know if they should be making noise to alert wildlife to their presence or go as quietly as they could in case there was more than wildlife around.

They threaded their way around clumps of sturdy birches, past maple trees and a few ash trees, their glossy red fruit lush and abundant. She walked on a spongy carpet of leaves, dry on the surface, but damp just below. Tall, delicate ferns grew in shafts of sunlight, competing with buttercups and wild sage.

Grace took a deep breath of the intoxicating essence of flower, wood, and leaf. Then her heel landed on something sharp and hard.

"Ow!" In an effort to remove the weight from her injured foot, she hopped on the other one, slipped on wet leaves, and lost her balance.

She twisted in midair to protect her bag. Her head grazed the ground as she landed on one knee with her clenched fist jammed between thigh and diaphragm. The air whooshed out of her.

Through the roaring in her ears she heard Will running back to her, but she was too busy trying to breathe to pay him much mind.

"Grace!" A warm, rough hand pushed the hair away from her face. He gently turned her over.

"Can you breathe?" he asked. She shook her head, trying desperately to force air inside. She'd had the breath knocked out of her once before, during gym class in grade school, so she knew what was happening, but her eyes must have looked wild to Will. To her horror, he bent over her, pressed his mouth against hers and forced air into her starving lungs.

She tried to push him away, partly in panic that he was making things worse and partly in mortification. But then she gasped and he sat up, and she could breathe again. She lay on the damp ground, eyes closed, taking cautious sips of air, reassuring herself. Her cheeks felt warm and she desperately didn't want to open her eyes.

When she finally did, Will was studying her feet.

"It's not going to work, is it?" he said.

Grace sat up and looked at her poor, abused feet. The soles were black with dirt. Where the dirt had dried to gray, cuts and scratches crisscrossed in a bloody pattern. What she couldn't see were the bruises that made walking so painful. Those would appear later.

She had never seen her toenails filthier.

"No," she finally sighed. "We're not going to make it if I go barefoot."

"I'm sorry, Grace," said Will, taking her hand in his. "I'm sorry for all of it. If I could, I'd..." He stopped, shook his head, obviously at a loss for words.

Grace felt absurdly comforted by his concern. She squeezed his hand. "I'll take them off as soon as we stop for the night. There may not even be any cramps. Let's find a stream or something, okay? I'd like to wash my feet before I put the shoes on."

Will nodded gloomily and stood up, pulling her up with him. He gave her a brief hug and released her. "We should stop for a bite anyway."

But it was at least half an hour before they finally found water. The trees had thinned out and knee-high grasses were beginning to replace the mulched forest floor when Grace stepped in a puddle of water. She looked down at her feet in surprise. Water seeped around her soles, limning her feet in glistening liquid.

"Will."

A few feet ahead of her, Will stopped and turned to look at her. She pointed at his feet. Immediately he retreated, joining her where the water wasn't so deep.

"I hate wet boots," he said, lifting up one foot to check the extent of the damage.

Grace examined the grass, but could find no telltale break to indicate a stream. However, there were enough trees nearby to provide a vantage point. Will obviously had the same idea. He set his backpack down on dry ground, then headed for a willow with branches low enough to climb and strong enough to support his weight.

Grace rolled up her pant legs before following him. Wool shrank when it got wet.

In one powerful heave, Will lifted himself to the branch and carefully stood up.

Grace caught her breath as he stretched to full height, one hand resting on the branch above, his attention on the view. Through the curtain of shimmering willow leaves, he looked like something conjured from her longings. Was it only last night she had felt the strength in his hands as he gently lowered her from branch to branch? She had held on to those powerful shoulders as if he were a life buoy in a sea of terror. He had held her pressed tightly to him, to the strong, hard feel of him, and she had felt safe. And wanted.

It occurred to Grace that a woman might do silly things to recapture a feeling like that.

Then he turned to look at her, grinning, and she decided that first he would have to lose the beard.

"It looks like a spring," said Will, dropping effortlessly to the ground. He immediately began unlacing his boots. "I'll check it out. If there's no problem, you can wash up. Quickly," he added as a warning.

Grace nodded. Definitely quickly. She wondered if they should even be taking the time, but her whole body cried out for the feel of clean water over her grubby skin. And her hair—oh, how she wanted to wash her hair.

Then she thought of Moira, a prisoner of the dé Danann, counting on her and Will.

"Damn," she muttered under her breath.

"What's that?" asked Will.

Grace closed her eyes. "I've changed my mind," she said carefully. "Let's go."

When Will didn't reply, she opened her eyes. He was watching her, his blue eyes even darker than usual. "You're sure?" he said.

She nodded, and thought she saw a flicker of relief cross his face.

He took up his backpack again and waited while she slipped the brown man's shoes over her dirty feet. Despite the puddle, they were still gray with grime. The shoes tightened comfortably over her aching feet. She wiggled her toes in relief, then stood up.

"Let's go," she said to Will. He stared at her for a moment longer, his eyes unfathomable. Then he turned and walked way.

They traveled the rest of that morning and through the long afternoon without stopping for more than a bite and to relieve themselves.

The shoes not only protected Grace's feet, they nudged her toward the easiest routes. After a while, they realized they were constantly veering off the due east course they had set themselves. Discussing it briefly, they decided to trust the shoes and adopted a more northeasterly route.

By the time the sun began to set, Grace figured they had traveled at least ten miles. She should have been exhausted instead of feeling ready for another ten. She dreaded removing the shoes, knowing the price she would pay.

"We need to look for a place to spend the night," said Will, startling her. They hadn't spoken more than twenty words since leaving the spring, and now his voice sounded out of place.

"We can see better from up there." She pointed at the knoll visible through the thinning trees. They had reached the third "knee" on their journey. As they began the climb, Grace again felt the prickling on the back of her neck. She stopped and turned around, studying the trees they had just left.

"You, too?" asked Will quietly.

She looked at him in surprise. He had turned and was studying the trees. Half a dozen times through the afternoon she'd been positive that if she just turned around quickly enough, she would catch someone following them. She hadn't told Will, in part because she never saw anything, and in part because she felt the way she had when the brown man first appeared to her.

Expectant.

"How long have you known?" she asked Will.

He glanced at her. "At our last break. I had the feeling someone was watching us."

Grace nodded and they resumed climbing. Unlike Moira, Will seemed prepared to wait and see.

The view from the top of the hill was disappointing. It revealed more of the same—forest and grassy clearings and hills that gradually flattened into undulations.

When a sigh escaped her lips, Grace realized that she'd been hoping for a glimpse of the sea, or at least a hint that they were nearing their goal.

"Looks like a river," said Will, pointing.

She followed his pointing finger and saw a thread of silver gleaming through the trees.

"It's as good a place as any to make camp," continued Will. "Besides, we need water."

Grace nodded and they set off down the hill and into the trees again. As they walked further into the forest, she saw that she had been fooled by the amount of light on the hill into thinking they had lots of time. It was much darker in the trees.

A squirrel scampered up a tree next to her, startling her. She didn't want to spend the night in the trees. She'd rather be out in the open, where she could see danger coming. But that would leave them too exposed.

Ten minutes later, they stood on the leafy bank of a river. The water flowed quickly, a deep pewter with brassy troughs. The banks were rich, loamy soil, about two feet high. She wondered if the river ever flooded.

Judging by the restlessness she felt, Grace knew they would have to cross the river. She told Will.

"It'll have to wait until morning," he said. "Let's see if we can find a better place to ford."

Grace followed him along the riverbank. The river was at least twenty feet wide, much wider in spots. Maybe she could cross it with her Fey shoes on, but she had no idea what water would do to them. And although she was a good swimmer, she didn't think either she or Will could cross without getting their packs wet—the food would be ruined. Better to find a shallower place to cross.

The sun cast long tree shadows on the water by the time Will called a halt.

"This looks like a good spot," he said. "We might as well camp here, and try crossing in the morning."

The river had cut through the soft bank to form a miniature bay where the current was more leisurely. Boulders poked out of the swirling water. Perhaps they would extend all the way across. It was hard to tell, as the far bank was lost to shadows.

Slender aspens dominated the area, their trunks almost phosphorescent in the fading light. Leaves trembled in the growing breeze, making a shifting pattern against the darkening sky. There were wild flowers growing in profusion on the banks, some among tree roots exposed by the swirling action of the water.

"Not exactly the Hilton," said Grace, "but it has charm."

Will grinned at her feeble attempt at humor. Then he grew serious. "We're going to have to take turns at watch."

Grace nodded. Another night of broken sleep, but it was better than no sleep at all, which was exactly what she'd get if no one was on watch.

"You should get some sleep first," continued Will. "You'll need it. First, you should take those shoes off."

Grace stifled a sigh. She'd worn the shoes much longer the last time. Maybe there wouldn't be any cramps.

"First, we set up camp," she said firmly. "Then I'll take them off." If she ended up debilitated by the cramps, she wouldn't be of any use to him.

It didn't take very long to set up camp. Will found a relatively flat spot and laid the tarp from his backpack on the ground. He dumped his rolled-up sleeping bag and the blanket on it. Grace pulled out her own blanket and spread it on top of Will's. By the time he set up the camp stove and began heating water in a tiny, square pan, it was almost completely dark.

"We'll have tea in a minute," he said. "Let's get those shoes off now."

Yes. It was time.

With an assurance she didn't feel, she walked to the tarp, sat down, and rolled up her pant legs. Will knelt before her, sitting back on his heels. There was no reason to believe she would even get cramps. She'd worn the shoes for a much shorter period today.

She took a deep breath and removed the first shoe.

The cramps were just as fierce as she remembered, but didn't last as long. She didn't know if it was because they were doing one foot at a time, because there was a half-life to the pain the shoes could extract, or because Will's big hands untiringly sought out and worked out each cramp before it had a chance to fully form. When the last one subsided, Grace sat up and grimly removed the other shoe. Her hands shook.

When it was all over, Will brought her tea and they both sat on the tarp, exhausted, and watched the river.

So much water. So dark and yet so invitingly clean. And she was so dirty. Her hair was matted and snarled. Her clothing filthy with dirt and sap. At this moment, the only thing she wanted was to be clean.

Surely it would be safe enough to bathe here? According to all the books she and Moira had read, back when this place was just a legend, most Fey did not like running water.

"I'm going to wash up," she said suddenly.

Will looked up, his face lit from below by the tiny flame of the camp stove. Neither of them had suggested lighting a campfire.

Amadan's army traveled at night.

She could tell by the stillness in him that he didn't like the idea and she tried hard to marshal arguments to convince him, but all she could think of was that she wanted to be clean.

When he finally spoke, it was to say, "Wait a sec. I'll turn the stove off, then I'll keep watch."

The thought of him keeping watch while she bathed sent shivers up her body, even though she knew he was doing it out of necessity, not lust.

While he finished with the stove, she took off her pants and jacket and tossed them onto the tarp. The tail of her silk shirt barely covered her underwear. She dug through her bag for the ball of soap. "Ready?"

By now Will was only a dark shadow. He had turned off the camp stove, and the absence of its hissing emphasized the rising chorus of crickets.

"Take the gourds," came his voice out of the dark.

Grace dug through her bag again and pulled the nearly empty gourd out. How would he keep watch if they couldn't see anything? But even as she turned back to the river, her eyes began to adjust. She could make out the flat silver of the water, the dark humps of the boulders.

"Here."

His voice in the darkness, so close to her ear, sent a shiver up her arms. He handed her his gourd.

With an abrupt nod, she took the gourd and headed for the river-bank. She waded in to the shallow part until she was knee-deep, then began to fill the gourds. She tried to see if the boulders in the river reached to the other side but it was too dark.

"Don't take too long," warned Will. She was surprised to find that he was so close—far enough that she could pretend at privacy, yet close enough to help, if need be.

She used the gourds to wash her hair, pouring the water from one to thoroughly wet her hair, lathering with the soap, and using the other gourd to rinse. She refilled the gourds and placed them on top of the nearest boulder. It was still warm from the day's sun.

After squeezing as much water as she could from her sopping hair, she straightened.

"Please don't look," she said to the tall figure in the dark. He turned his head away. Quickly, she took the rest of her clothes off. Then she knelt again and washed her bra and underwear, after which she used her underpants to scrub herself, dipping time and again into the cold, swirling waters to rinse, lather, and rinse again.

Finally satisfied, she donned her shirt, grateful for its length. She wished she could wash it, but then she would have nothing dry to wear. As it was, she hadn't been able to dry herself before putting it on, and it was growing damp.

"All done," she said, more cheerful than she'd been in a long time. Amazing how being clean could change a woman's perspective. "You want to take a turn?" She plucked the gourds from the boulder and waded back to shore.

Will hesitated. "Yes."

When she finally set foot on soil, his big frame seemed to relax. He tossed something to the ground and she realized that he had been holding rocks.

She hastily donned her wool jacket and her pants, grateful for the sudden warmth on her bare legs. The bra and underwear she hung from branches to dry overnight.

The sound of the water lapping against the shore merged with the song of the crickets and the hooting of a nearby owl. It was hard to believe they were on anything but a campout.

Okay, stop stalling, she told herself. Will had watched out for her; now she had to watch for him.

But when she looked at the water, he wasn't there.

She came closer, her heart pounding. Then Will rose from the water, shaking his head free of excess water and exhaling loudly. Her lips parted when she realized that she could see him remarkably well. The moon was rising, and although it wasn't full, it still cast enough light to let her see broad, gleaming shoulders, arm muscles rippling as he lathered his body, a flat belly.

She turned away, embarrassed at ogling him. Her glance fell on the tarp, with its waiting blankets.

Good grief. Next she'd be pouncing on the man.

A few minutes later, Will joined her and she silently poured the rest of the tea into their cups. He pulled some kind of travel cake—sweet with berries and honey, with seeds and nuts thrown in—out of his package and shared it with her. It was heavy and consistent.

They ate in silence and when the tea was gone, Will sighed.

"You'd better get some rest," he said.

Grace nodded and slipped under the blankets while he went to the river to rinse out their cups.

***

She woke suddenly, startled. The half-moon rode high in the sky. A few clouds had moved in while she slept and she could smell rain coming. The only sound came from the river rushing inexorably past her feet. The crickets and owls had fallen silent. Although not a breath of air stirred, there was a shivery feel to the air, as if invisible beings surrounded her, their papery wings vibrating in a subsonic hum.

She sat up, suddenly frightened. "Will?" she whispered.

"Shh," came his whisper from the tree above her head. A quick movement, a gentle thump, and he landed next to the tarp.

She scrambled to her feet, the blankets falling away from her. Before she could speak, he placed a finger against her lips. In his hand was a heavy stone. She glanced down and saw one in his other hand.

When he was sure she understood his warning, Will pointed at the sky.

Grace glanced up and had to bite back an exclamation. Against a moonlit backdrop, darkness writhed in the clear sky to the north, as if an enormous, amorphous creature approached. Then she saw that it wasn't one creature, but dozens.

Hundreds. '

Her hand flew to her mouth to keep the fear from taking voice. They had to be Amadan's forces. They were heading southwest, in the direction from which she and Will had come.

Were they already too late?

The creatures flew in silence, so low some barely cleared the tops of the trees. The only sound was the beating of their wings. Some had long, leathery wings like bats. Others had seemingly useless wisps on their backs, but still managed to fly. There were tiny creatures the size of monkeys and tall ones the size of full-grown men. All had spindly legs and arms that seemed to flail around aimlessly, as if the flyers didn't know what to do with them.

The host flew so close to the camp that Will and Grace flattened themselves against the tree and looked down at the ground so the pale gleam of their faces wouldn't betray them. Grace worried that one of the creatures would spot her underwear drying in the tree. Will stayed close to her, but always kept his right arm free, in case he needed to throw a stone.

After what seemed like an eternity, the host passed. When the sky remained clear for long minutes, Grace and Will relaxed their vigil.

Grace rotated first one shoulder, then the other, hoping to ease her neck muscles. For the first time since waking up, she noticed that her legs were trembling. She couldn't tell if it was from fear or from the residual effects of the cramps.

She turned away from the river. How much time did they have? Was the host traveling toward the dé Danann or to meet up with Amadan? Were those creatures all of Amadan's army?

It was still so very dark. How long until morning? The adrenaline slowly subsided, leaving her exhausted. But she no longer wanted to sleep.

She turned toward Will, a suggestion that he should get some rest hovering on her lips. Then a shadow stepped out of the trees beyond the tarp. Grace gasped in fear.

A stone flew past her, and she jerked back, startled, her eyes trying to focus in the darkness.

First came the sound of something hard striking flesh, followed immediately by a soft grunt of pain, and then the thud of a body falling to the ground.

"Got you," said Will with satisfaction as he strode past her.

Damn, thought Grace. Damn, damn, damn!

❧ TWENTY-ONE ❧

IN THE guttering torchlight, Soutien watched Moira sleep. She had fallen asleep in spite of herself, leaning against a tree, her back to him.

It was too late to recall the words spoken, to hide the betrayal of his body holding hers. She knew now how he felt, and she had rejected him as completely as a woman trapped on a platform could.

He sat next to her as she slept, offering her the meager windbreak of his body.

You should have known, he told himself scornfully. You are the Soutien of her childhood, the one who cleaned her scraped knees and listened to her girlish secrets. She could never see you in a different light.

But he had hoped.

He put the ache aside, turning his attention to the night and the dé Danann. Already one of them slept at his post. With the three who had left earlier and not been replaced, only six guards remained. That he was aware of.

Were any of the remaining ones loyal to Cathel? Would they help or hinder an escape attempt?

He waited, biding his time. Hours later, when the moon cast shadows on the night, he lifted his face to the sky. Clouds scuttled over the stars, sending goosebumps of awareness down his arms. He could almost hear something, a subsonic shivering in the air.

A voice in the distance cried a warning and suddenly all the dé Danann were awake and talking.

The shivering grew, buzzing through him like electricity. Now, he thought.

"Moira?" he said, so low it was almost soundless.

But she was awake. "Yes."

He studied the surrounding trees. All the dé Danann were looking up at the sky. Leaning close, he whispered, "Follow. Quietly."

He slipped off the platform onto a tree branch. Risking a glance to make sure she followed, he continued down to the next branch, and the next.

Moira followed closely and silently. Far above, voices rose in excitement and he paused, afraid they were discovered. But the voices grew no closer and he realized they were reacting to the new arrivals.

How much farther to the ground? Once down, they could move faster, find hiding places. In the trees, they remained vulnerable.

A sudden hiss from Moira made him stop and look up. She crouched on a branch, one hand clutching it, the other on the trunk. A dark figure loomed over her.

Soutien surged up the tree, his heart hammering against his ribs. Moira rose to her feet just as he reached her and together they turned to face the threat.

Now that he was closer, Soutien saw that the dark figure was a dé Danann, not one of the Unseelie Fey, as he had feared. Why hadn't he called for help?

"Be quiet," murmured the dé Danann. He glanced up, then back down, a suggestion of movement. "From Lord Cathel."

He held something out and Soutien took it. It was a heavy bag, fragrant with the smell of willow and food.

"You must hurry," said the Fey. Before Soutien could thank him, he melted back into the darkness.

Next to him, Moira sagged imperceptibly. "What was that all about?" she whispered.

"Cathel," said Soutien. "We have to hurry."

Moira turned to follow him. "What's going on?"

"The Unseelie Court is arriving," said Soutien. "Be quiet and move fast."

ಒಾ TWENTY-TWO ಣ

THE river was a silent thunder rumbling beneath Grace's knees. In the calm just before dawn, night flowers perfumed the air and somewhere nearby, an owl hooted. The clouds that had earlier threatened were gone, leaving behind a black sky strewn with stars.

Grace knelt over the brown man, gently palpating his head. His eyes were open and he was breathing, but he gave no sign of awareness. He smelled of rich, dark earth. It was too dark to see if his pupils were the same size.

Her fingers threaded through hair stiff as straw until she encountered a lump the size of a robin's egg just behind his ear. He winced as her fingers brushed it, and she finally sat back on her heels.

"Is he all right?" asked Will.

Grace looked up at him, straining to make out his features.

"No, he's *not* all right. You hit him with a rock." The rational part of her understood Will's instinctive act, but she was still upset that he had struck down the little man. She didn't know what to do if he had a concussion. Her first aid was limited to applying pressure on wounds.

The memory of Mack came rushing back, robbing her of breath. His injuries had been so severe... would he have survived if they'd gotten him home?

"I'll make tea," said Will, turning away from her.

Were you supposed to give liquids to someone with a concussion? She couldn't remember.

With a soft grunt, the brown man sat up suddenly, startling her.

"No..." Before she could finish, he pulled himself to his feet and stumbled over to Will.

Grace stood up quickly, half-afraid he would attack Will, but the little man stopped a few feet away and began talking.

Grace could make no sense out of his words. He spoke too fast and the words were too guttural. But every once in a while, she caught a word: "eat," and "fire," and "food."

After a few moments, Will looked over the top of the man's head at Grace.

"Do you understand what he's saying?"

Grace shook her head, and realized at the same time that it was getting lighter. She could make out Will's puzzled expression.

"Not really. Something about eating and a fire."

"Is he hungry?"

At this, the brown man grew more agitated, waving his thin arms as if to make a point. Worried, Grace placed a hand on his shoulder. He immediately stopped talking and looked at her.

"No," she said slowly. "I don't think he wants to eat." She peered into the brown man's huge eyes, searching for meaning. "What is it?" she said softly. "Is it the birds?"

"What birds?" asked Will.

"He gave me the shoes in payment for a debt he felt he owed me. The only thing I did was replace a bird in its nest. Maybe he wants our help with a hurt bird."

"We don't have time," said Will, resuming his tea-making. "We have to get going."

He was right, of course, but at that moment Grace didn't like him very much.

As night receded, the outline of the trees became clearer and birds began to chirp a welcome to the day. The damp of the morning worked its way through her layers of clothing and Grace shivered.

The brown man seemed to be listening to the birds, head cocked to one side. Finally, he straightened and looked at Grace.

"Come," he said, taking her hand in his. His accent made the word sound more like "coom."

His skin felt paper dry and warm. She squeezed his hand. "I can't," she said. "We need to find Fin Bheara."

A look of anguish settled over the little man's face. He released her hand to pull at the scraggly hair escaping from under his brown cap.

"No food," he said. "Much debt." He looked as if he wanted to cry.

The man's obvious distress frightened Grace. She didn't know what to do.

"We can share our food," said Will, appearing by her side. "If he's hungry..."

"No food!" cried the brown man, pointing at the woods. He turned back and pointed at the shoes Grace had left on the tarp. "Debt! Much debt!"

Shaken, Grace walked to the tarp and picked up the Fey shoes. She needed them, despite the toll they exacted. But if he wanted them back... She handed the shoes to the brown man but he pushed them away in frustration.

"What does he want?" said Will, his tone mirroring the little man's expression.

The brown man took a deep breath and a look of intense concentration settled over his strange features. He turned to Will. "Kill," he said. "Man kill."

A shiver ran up Grace's scalp. A man killing? Or a man killed?

"Who?" she said softly. "Who is it?"

The brown man pointed at Will. Will's eyebrows rose.

"Me?" he said, his voice tinged with dread.

Again, the brown man shook his head and turned to Grace with a beseeching look.

"Not Will," she said softly. "But someone else, a man, is killing." And then, "For food?"

The brown man's posture relaxed and she knew she was on the right track. Grace turned to Will.

"I think someone is killing the animals he protects, for food. I think he wants us to stop them."

In the growing light, she could see the weariness etched on Will's face. He hadn't slept at all.

"How can we?" He swept a hand toward the river and she knew what he meant. They were running out of time.

As though guessing what was left unsaid, the brown man whirled on Will, his face contorted by anguish.

"Man!" he cried. He pointed a long, skinny finger at Will's chest. "Kill!"

And suddenly, Grace understood. There were no other men here. Mack was dead, and Moira and Soutien were prisoners of the Fey. That left only one person.

"Aidan," she whispered.

Will turned to her, his face draining of color.

"Aidan? He's talking about Aidan?"

The look on Will's face alarmed Grace. She took a step toward him, but he turned away, moving jerkily to the tarp. He immediately began rolling up the blankets and stuffing things into his backpack.

"Will," said Grace helplessly. "What are you doing?"

"Aidan's out there." He went to the camp stove. "We're going to find him."

Grace watched him empty out the unused tea and stash the small pot into his pack. When he finally straightened, she took a deep breath.

"What about Moira?" she said. "And Soutien?"

He turned to her, despair etched in his face. "Do you think I don't know? Moira and Soutien stand a better chance of surviving than Aidan. He's all alone out there, Grace! And he's out of his mind."

Grace dropped her gaze, hating what she was about to do. "The brown man followed us all day before he worked up the nerve to approach us. There's no telling when he last saw Aidan. And no telling what might have happened to your brother since then." Her voice dropped as she told Will what he didn't want to hear. "If you go looking for Aidan, you risk finding him dead. And then you'll have lost him *and* Moira."

A heavy silence settled over the camp. The brown man stood looking from Grace to Will. The sun crept over the horizon, flooding the world with light, and still Will remained silent. When Grace finally looked at him, he was staring at the river.

"Will?" she said timidly.

Without looking at her, he tightened the drawstring on his backpack, closed and tightened the flaps, and swung the pack onto his shoulders. "We'd better get going," he said, with no inflection in his voice.

Then he set out for the river.

As soon as the brown man understood that Will wasn't coming with him, he looked at Grace.

"I..." She stared into his impossibly big eyes, at a loss. What could she do?

You could go with him, she told herself. Will doesn't need you. You could go with the brown man, find Aidan, and bring him back.

Fear washed over her like ice water. She didn't want to go. She didn't want to leave the security of Will's presence. But finding Aidan would be more useful than tagging along behind Will.

Before she could change her mind, she called him. "Will!"

At the riverbank, he turned, his face carefully impassive.

"I'll go with him," she said in rush. "That way you can still make it to Knockma."

In three swift strides, Will was at her side. Grabbing her by the upper arms, he shook her roughly.

"Don't be stupid!" he said. "You're coming with me."

His grip would leave bruises, but Grace was too startled to protest.

"If I can find him..." she began.

Will's hands tightened on her arm and she bit off a cry of pain.

"Do you honestly think I'd let you go?" he demanded, his face contorted with anger.

His rage sent a thrill of fear coursing through Grace. She knew the anger wasn't directed at her. She understood that Will was angry at the situation, at Cathel, at Amadan... not really at her. Or maybe he was, for telling him what he knew was the truth but couldn't accept.

For the first time, she saw him not only as Will, whom she had known most of her life, but as a big, powerful man whose character had been formed by forces and events she didn't understand. He was no longer the easygoing, friendly boy she'd known as a teenager. He was a man tempered by war and atrocity, whose family was now in danger.

Would he go over the edge, too?

"You're hurting me," she said softly, not taking her gaze from his.

At once, he released her, but he remained close, looming over her. He stared down at her, his expression fierce, the anger banked but not gone.

"You're staying with me. Is that clear?"

She nodded jerkily, not daring to do otherwise. Without another word, Will picked up her bag and tossed it to her. She slipped it over her head and across her shoulders. Only then did she remember the brown man.

She turned to look for him, but he was gone.

***

The thud of her feet hitting the ground was like a drumbeat resonating through the forest. It served as loud counterpoint to the rasp of her breathing. Moira tried to control both, but was too busy straining to see roots and branches—while running as fast as she could—to concentrate on much else.

She had been running for two hours. Two hours of following Soutien while dodging branches, leaping deadfalls, and listening for pursuit. Two hours of wondering if Will was alive or dead.

The dense canopy filtered the moonlight, shrouding the forest in ghost fog, forcing Moira to glance up often to keep Soutien in view. Every time she did, the sight of his silent figure only a few steps ahead sent hot anger rushing through her. He had risked Will and Grace, for her.

The anger never lasted. It always dissipated in the need for control and concentration.

The man moved like a wraith, silently flowing over, around, or under obstacles.

She, on the other hand, moved like a rogue elephant crashing through the bush. She'd lost count of the times she had fallen. Fatigue dragged at her legs. How long before she took a serious fall, one that would cripple her? If the dé Danann followed—*surely they followed?*—they would have no trouble finding her and Soutien.

Soutien's dark form stopped and waited for her. She came to a halt, grateful, her legs trembling. Silently, he handed her the water bladder. She sank to the ground, ignoring twigs and dirt, and took a sparing sip. She wanted more, but this one small bladder might have to last them a long time.

Three days east, that's where they'd find Fin Bheara. If they kept moving at this pace, they would be there sooner. Hopefully, Will and Grace would already be there. Maybe Fin Bheara could find Aidan.

And maybe she'd wake up in the morning to find this was all a bad dream.

As she handed Soutien back the bladder, she caught a whiff of her own body odor, familiar from so many Army exercises. The night chill leached away the heat of exertion, and she shivered.

"That was too easy," she said when she finally caught her breath. Soutien wasn't even breathing hard.

How could she have known him all these years and not known how he felt about her?

"I know." Soutien held out the travel bread for her, but Moira shook her head. Her stomach couldn't handle food right now. Dampness seeped through the cloth of her pants but she was too tired to care. She breathed deeply of the forest, a cool smell on which lingered the memory of sun-warmed flowers. Beneath it was deeper note of danger and decay.

Soutien broke off a chunk and chewed silently for a few moments. "Either they let us go, or something is keeping them occupied," he finally said.

Moira wondered what would keep Ilyane so occupied that she wouldn't chase them. She didn't give up easily, that one.

Soutien had said the Unseelie Court was arriving, but she didn't really know what that meant. They were bad news for humans, that much she remembered from childhood reading. And they flew at night, kidnapping innocents. It was never clear what they did with them.

But maybe not all the members of the Unseelie Court could fly. Maybe some walked, and were winding their way through the forest toward a rendezvous with Ilyane.

Or maybe they had already reached the rendezvous and had been sent to find her and Soutien.

She scrambled to her feet at the thought, looking around nervously. Red Cap was Amadan's lieutenant in the Unseelie Court.

"What if the dé Danann sent someone after us? Instead of coming themselves, I mean."

"Someone like Red Cap, you mean?"

Moira looked sharply at Soutien, but the night hid his features. Was he telepathic, too? No, of course not. He couldn't possibly have hidden *that* all those years.

"Yes, like Red Cap."

"Let's worry about that problem when we come to it. *If* we come to it." There was a shrug in his voice.

Easy for him to say. He could always blink—or whatever it was he did—and be back at Kirwan, safe.

Immediately she was ashamed of herself. Soutien had had ample opportunity to escape during the day.

But apparently, it wasn't honor that kept him by her side. She shied away from the memory of his body pressing against hers, the intimacy of his breath on her ear. Long tendrils of anger penetrated the memory, clouding her thinking.

All around them, the forest brooded in darkness so dense it felt like a presence. She could almost hear it breathing. Maybe Red Cap was creeping up on them even now...

The smell of rotting vegetation seemed suddenly much stronger, almost overwhelming her empty stomach. She looked around, trying to see beyond the few feet her night vision allowed. Was that a sound? A shiver raced up her arms.

Oh, stop it, she told herself firmly. There was no point in spooking herself. Of course they were still in danger, but at least they were free, and *doing* something.

"Do you think Cathel will be able to help us?" she asked Soutien.

He remained silent for a long moment. When he finally spoke, his voice held no emotion.

"Moira, Cathel may not be an enemy, but he is certainly not a friend. If we hadn't escaped, we would be in the hands of the Unseelie Court right now."

Moira swallowed. "He helped us... had a dé Danann waiting..."

"What did that cost him?" asked Soutien gently. "One dé Danann with a bag and some supplies. If Ilyane found him, the dé Danann could plausibly say that he was on his way to help look for Aidan." He took a deep breath and his face, visible under the half-moon's glow, looked somber. "Cathel has had hundreds of years of practice at politics. We are pawns to him."

"You're wrong!" blurted Moira. She was ready to concede that the High Lord was in a tight spot, but the moment he'd seen a chance to help them, he had.

"And why would you think that, Moira?" asked Soutien softly. "Because he was charming and his eyes looked into your soul? Because someone so fair could not possibly be so calculating?" He shook his head. "You were deceived by the glamour he donned."

"What glamour?" asked Moira, stung. Soutien was being a jerk. Cathel was on their side. She knew it, and so did Soutien. Why was he bent on smearing the High Lord?

"You remember glamour, don't you?" Soutien stepped closer to her, his eyes suddenly darker, deeper than she remembered. "The ability to make others see something other than reality?"

Moira stared at him. In the moonlight, he seemed taller, his shoulders broader, his smile more dangerous. She tried to step back as he approached, but her feet felt rooted. Her breathing quickened as he leaned down, suddenly so close she could smell the heady scent of him.

"The ability to make yourself so attractive, you become irresistible?" he whispered, and her gaze clung to his mouth as he drew even closer, his breath fanning warmly on her face.

She closed her eyes, and her face tilted up to his.

And then he laughed, a harsh, ugly sound. Startled, she opened her eyes, and it was only Soutien—no taller, no broader than usual. Just Soutien.

The smile on his face was self-mocking. "And that, my sweet innocent, is glamour."

Heat bloomed on her face but before she could say anything, Soutien bent down and gathered up the willow bag.

"Time to get going," he said, swinging it onto his shoulder.

Moira's training kicked in and she followed him into a run. Her heart still raced with the expectation of his kiss and she wanted to hit him, but now wasn't the time. Then another thought occurred to her. He could have used his ability to make himself irresistible at any time.

Later, she promised herself. *Later I'll think about this.*

Her legs wobbled, but they would soon warm up and she would find her rhythm. If she didn't trip over anything.

At least she wasn't running obstacle courses with a fifty-pound pack on her back. Eight years of twice-yearly Army exercises left her grateful for the small mercy of carrying only her own weight.

They ran and rested, ran and rested, through the better part of the night. Miraculously, Moira kept to her feet, raising one increasingly heavy leg after another, following Soutien. By the time dawn diluted the inky night, her eyes burned from the strain of trying to see in the dark.

Then she slammed into a tree, ramming her shoulder hard and rapping her head on the trunk. She instinctively wrapped her arms around the thick trunk, struggling to keep to her feet, shaking her head to get rid of the ringing.

"Are you all right?" Soutien's hand landed on her back, heavy with concern.

Light crept slowly through the forest, turning trees and stumps the same blurry shade of gray. Or maybe that was concussion.

Moira leaned her cheek against the rough bark of the tree. Blood trickled down her other cheek from a gash in her temple. Her shoulder felt numb, but would soon hurt. It was the same shoulder she had injured when the phooka tossed her. Her head already hurt.

Soutien's hand on her back burned like a brand.

"No," she finally said, pushing away from the tree. An oak tree. "But I'll live."

Soutien's face relaxed its worried lines and he squeezed her good shoulder before cupping her chin in one hand and turning her head to examine her wound. She wanted to pull away, but his demeanor brooked no argument. Just this way she had turned to him as a child, when she needed comforting or help.

But she was no longer a child. And she didn't want him touching her.

They both heard it at the same time, a creaking like the sound of branches rubbing together in a storm.

Soutien's hand dropped from her face. Silently, as one, they turned toward the sound. Moira's tired eyes strained in the uncertain light, trying to find the source of the noise.

The sun wasn't up yet, but dawn had chased away the night shadows. A thousand shades of gray now filled the forest and it was impossible to distinguish individual trees.

Then the forest swayed and she blinked hard. "What—?"

"Run!" cried Soutien, grabbing her hand and jerking her away from the tree. Something clutched at her hair and she screamed, then staggered when Soutien yanked her forward. She regained her balance and, tightening her hold on his hand, forced her exhausted body to match his breakneck pace.

"What is it?" she yelled, fending off branches with her free hand. One caught in her hair again and tore her scalp as she jerked free.

"Goblins!" called Soutien over his shoulder, never slackening his pace.

She risked a glance. Less than a hundred feet away, moving shadows resolved themselves into dozens of small, dark shapes. They flitted between trees, swarmed up trunks, flung themselves from branches.

As soon as they saw they had her attention, the goblins raised their voices in a cry that was halfway between hunger and rage. The sound almost robbed her of strength.

Soutien suddenly swerved toward the north and Moira gave him her full attention.

An elm tree blocked their way. Just beyond it, Moira caught a scuttling movement.

Still running, Soutien angled off toward the west. A movement in the trees resolved itself into half a dozen goblins running parallel to them. Startled, Moira and Soutien veered off.

Night receded like the tide, leaving behind only trees. Soutien's hand was crushing hers. Her breathing harsh in her ears, her legs threatening to fail her, Moira looked around.

They were surrounded.

***

Will finished lacing his boots and stood up without looking at Grace. The boulders ended halfway across the river, and he'd had to remove his boots, stuff them in his pack and wade the rest of the way through the icy water, his pack held high above his head. Now his clothes were soaked from the waist down, but at least his feet were dry.

Grace, still barefoot, had removed her pants and jacket before entering the water, and tied her shirt under her breasts. He ignored her while she put her pants back on and slipped on the Fey shoes.

He knew he was being unfair. It wasn't her fault that Aidan was lost. And she was right—going back with the brown man would have placed all of them at risk.

But she'd asked him to leave Aidan behind when she knew that leaving him almost surely meant his death.

"Ready," she said.

Without a word, he shouldered the backpack and set a punishing pace toward the northeast.

As the morning wore on, the terrain gradually shifted to low, rolling hills, and the ground softened underfoot. Aspens dominated, with the odd oak and spruce breaking up the white wall. Birds flitted from tree to tree, calling and singing noisily. Even the sun conspired to turn this into a walk in a park, shining warmly on the side of his face, streaming long shadows through the woods.

But this was no park, and he wouldn't drop his guard again. The last time he had allowed himself to be seduced by this place, his delay had cost Mack his life.

Now, Aidan and Moira were in danger, not to mention Grace and Soutien. Oonagh should never have drawn him here. He was a photographer, not a warrior. He was completely useless in this place.

Except for the task he was supposed to accomplish for Fin Bheara. But Will didn't see how it would help them get home because Soutien refused to tell him what the task was. For all he knew, it might involve mucking out the stables.

Or maybe the king wanted his picture taken.

Grace followed silently behind him, keeping up with his harsh pace thanks to the shoes the brown man had given her. She would pay later for the privilege. The thought filled him with conflicting emotions—resentment that she was here, suffering for his family; respect for her stoic endurance; and a deep abiding wish that he could take the suffering away from her. And underneath it all, the knowledge that, because of her, he might lose another brother.

Every once in a while, she would call out a course correction and he would silently veer in the direction the shoes indicated.

A few hours later, the glint of sun on water caught his attention and he turned toward it. Grace followed uncomplainingly. They came to a sunlit glade through which a brook burbled. A depression allowed the brook to form a pool ten feet across before spilling out on the other side in a wider stream. The water had undercut the banks on either side.

"Water," said Grace, startling him. She hadn't spoken to him since crossing the river and now her voice sounded loud against the murmuring of the water.

"I need to refill," she continued. He looked around. The willow bag lay at her feet, open. She waved an almost empty water bladder at him and headed for the pool. His hand shot out and he clamped his fingers around her arm, stopping her.

"No. There's no telling what—"

Grace pulled her arm out of his grasp. "That pool is too shallow for anything but fish," she said.

"Grace..."

She whirled on him, eyes crackling with anger. "Leave it, Will!" She swept the hand carrying the bladder toward the water. "It's just a damned hole in the ground! Not everything is out to get you!" Turning her back on him, she stalked to the pool.

For a second, he was too taken aback to do more than stare at her retreating back.

Grace knelt by the side of the pool to fill the bladder. He reached her in three long strides and hauled her to her feet. The bladder slipped from her fingers and landed in a sodden heap on the ground. He turned her to face him, barely controlling an urge to shake her.

"Where do you get off talking to me like that?" he demanded. The face she turned up to him was white with fury and the rage in her eyes almost made him step back.

"Stop manhandling me!" She stomped on his instep, surprising him, and in two deft movements, broke his grip on her upper arms. He stared in astonishment at her, vaguely aware that he was gaping.

Then she stepped up to him, hooked her leg behind his, and shoved. Arms flailing, overbalanced by his backpack, Will landed with a splash in the pool.

He gasped and got a mouthful of water. He spluttered and water went up his nose. He struggled with the backpack and almost panicked. Finally, he found the release on the belt and the backpack fell off, freeing his arms. He beat at the water, surging toward the surface. Long grasses trailed against his bare arms, spurring him on. Then he broke through the surface and stood up, panting.

Grace wasn't there. He heard a snicker and whirled. She stood on the other bank, hands on her hips, a satisfied smile on her lips.

For the first time, Will realized that the water was only waist deep.

"That wasn't funny, Grace!"

She raised an eyebrow at him. "Really? I thought it was hilarious."

With as much dignity as he could muster under the circumstances, Will felt around the bottom of the pool with his foot, finally locating the backpack. Only then did he remember the camera.

That bloody woman would be the death of him.

Taking a deep breath, he plunged into the pool, grasped one of the pack's padded belts, and hauled. Maybe if he took the camera apart and dried it thoroughly... He broke through the surface in a loud spray of water, shaking his head to sluice off the water.

"Will!"

He glanced up, alarmed, but she was looking past him. He immediately released the pack and turned. Before he could complete the turn, something splashed in the water behind him. He caught a glimpse of huge round eyes peering through grass before something caught him by the legs and pulled him under.

He struggled against whatever held him, but it was too strong. Then he heard a second splash as another creature dove into the water next to him. He redoubled his efforts and the water grew murky from his thrashing as mud stirred up from the bottom. Still he peered into the water, trying to see what held him and what had dived in to join them.

His lungs burned with lack of oxygen. To hell with the second creature—he had to free his legs or he'd drown. He jackknifed, reaching down his legs. His hand encountered a hard, round object with long tendrils of grass on it. He stared into the murky depths, trying to decipher what it was. Then it turned in his hand, tilting up to him and through the disturbed water, he saw two huge, saucer-round eyes staring up at him.

Breath left his body in a blast of bubbles. He straightened up just as something grabbed his shoulder. He swung around, lashing out with his fists. One connected and his shoulder was released. But his legs were still trapped and he reached down again, fighting his revulsion. Something brushed by him in a wash of bubbles and he instinctively shied away.

Then, miraculously, he was free. He propelled himself toward air and life, kicking hard, and broke free to fill his burning lungs with great gulps of air. He stood uncertainly, legs trembling, watching the still surface of the water changing color, from mud brown to ocher. Blood.

Suddenly, he whipped around. "Grace!"

As if in answer, her head broke the surface of the water. She blinked, dirty water streaming down her face, hair plastered to her skull. Then she slowly rose out of the water and waded to the shallow end of the pool.

She held the backpack in one hand and his knife in the other.

❧ TWENTY-THREE ❧

SOUTIEN tightened his grip on Moira's sweaty hand as they ran, afraid she would slip out of his grasp. Her breathing was ragged and loud, and the drag of her weight on his arm grew increasingly heavy as fatigue overtook her.

He glanced over his shoulder. In the early morning light, the goblins looked like large, hungry rats swarming through the forest.

Large rats that were slowly gaining on them. The goblins' short legs were no match for his and Moira's longer ones, but they were lighter and faster. And they hadn't been running half the night.

Soutien scanned the forest ahead, wary of ambush. Although the goblins were a threat, they weren't the most dangerous denizens of these woods. Over the centuries he had explored much of his Fey home, but he had always avoided this area. This was Amadan-na-Briona's domain. Even Fin Bheara kept a respectful distance.

The trees—oak, pine, and the odd maple—grew far apart, long past their sapling days of competing for sunshine. In spite of the growing openness of the forest, the thick branches filled the sky with concealing leaves and whispering needles, adding to Soutien's unease.

Sunlight shafted through rents in the clouds, filtering through to the spaces between the trees, encouraging him to greater speed. More room for him and Moira meant more room for their pursuers.

He tuned out Moira's panting and the thundering of his pulse, straining to hear all around him. Leaping over a deadfall, he landed safely on the other side and pulled Moira along. A branch broke as she landed.

He spared her a quick look. Her face was red with exertion and already purpling with a bruise from her encounter with the tree. They'd been running from the goblins for almost an hour. How long could she keep up this pace?

As if to answer his question, Moira tripped and stumbled, recovering only because of his firm hold on her.

"Can't... go on... much longer!"

Soutien nodded but kept running. She was past the point of endurance while the goblins showed no signs of slackening. Stopping now would be suicide.

His human side, always slow to emerge, now rose up to swamp his Fey nature with fury. He swallowed the rage with difficulty. Moira needed him cool-headed, not blinded by emotion.

But he was sick of running.

He wanted to turn and fight, wanted bones to break beneath his hands, wanted to see black goblin blood seeping into the ground. But he couldn't indulge, not while Moira was in danger.

He needed to get her out of here.

Elin. The memory of the winged Fey flitted through his mind like a will-o'-the-wisp. Elin had said she and her kin awaited the word. Would she come if he called for her? Did he have the right to endanger the wild cousins to save himself and Moira?

His feet thumped against the ground, keeping pace with his thoughts. He had to get to Knockma and warn the king that Amadan was on the move. And he couldn't do that while Moira was in danger.

Ahead, a line of darkness appeared through the trees. It took a moment to understand that he was looking at the lip of a ravine.

He realized he'd stopped when Moira ran into him. He automatically wrapped an arm around her to keep her from falling.

"What?" she gasped. Then she saw the ravine. "Oh."

Soutien glanced around, but the goblins had stopped now that they had their prey trapped. He saw more than a few leaning on trees to catch their breath. What they lacked in human endurance, however, they more than made up for in numbers.

Tugging on Moira's hand, he led her to the lip of the ravine and they looked down. Tangled brush and stunted trees led the way to a bottom lost in shadows, at least a hundred feet down. A wave of cool air rose from the depths, fetid and damp. Even rested, he would have hesitated to lead Moira down those steep walls. The other side of the narrow ravine beckoned, eighty feet too far. Perhaps there was a bridge?

A movement to his right caught his eye. The goblins were creeping in. Their stench preceded them, clinging to the surrounding trees like a miasma. Those who had regained enough breath called out insults through bristling teeth, like human thugs circling and taunting their victims. Soutien allowed himself a small smile. The goblins, for all their bravado, were slow to approach. They had learned caution around humans.

Moira looked around, her lips tightening. Her breath still came in long, dragging gasps, and her body swayed. The nearest goblin grinned at her. Its oversized, pointed ears barely peeked through the tangled mass of its hair. Except for the filthy mat of fur covering its body, it was naked.

Moira shuddered. "Where's Knockma? Which direction?" she asked Soutien.

He nodded to the east. "That way."

That way were a dozen goblins, now less than fifty feet away.

"Then let's go through them."

Startled, Soutien looked at her. "Through them?"

"Yes." She nodded, still staring at the creatures, and for the first time, Soutien noticed the light in her eye. "We can't let them trap us there." She nodded at the ravine. "And I've had about as much as I'm going to take from a bunch of overgrown rats."

She looked at him and grinned, a grin so full of recklessness that he tightened his arm around her. Despite his alarm, a fierce elation rushed through him, threatening to overtake him. He struggled with reason.

"Moira, they're small but they can kill you."

Moira slipped out of his clasp to reach for a fallen branch. It was bone white, thick, and relatively straight. A series of broken twigs studded the knobby end like a mace. She hefted it, looked at the goblins, then back at him. She grinned again.

"What have we got to lose?" And with a bloodcurdling scream, she turned and raced toward the goblins.

The nearest goblin scrambled out of her way, but the second one wasn't so lucky. Moira's club landed with a sickening thud on the side of its head, sending the goblin flying. Soutien caught a glimpse of blood on the club before the remaining goblins swarmed over her.

He launched himself into the fray, plucking goblins by their greasy hair and tossing them against the nearest trees. The air filled with screams of pain and rage, and above them all, Moira's wild ululation as she spun like a dervish, clearing a space for herself.

"Elin!" shouted Soutien to the forest. "Elin, daughter of Aucom and Sava! In the name of Fin Bheara, I call upon you now!"

Then a goblin sword pierced his thigh and he roared with rage, turning to block a return jab. He grabbed the goblin's forearm and plucked the sword out of its hand. The goblin barely had time to register fear before Soutien sliced open its throat.

Before he could move, three goblins landed on his back and he reeled, almost falling into the ravine. "Watch out!" he yelled, his voice puncturing the goblin cries as he glimpsed Moira's danger. She turned in time to knock a goblin sword aside.

For every goblin he disabled, three took its place. The smell of crushed pine needles spiked through the goblin stench, now heightened by the acrid smell of fear.

Soutien managed to peel two goblins off him and toss them over his shoulder into the ravine. Their yells ended abruptly as they landed. He swung the third by one leg, smashing its head against a tree. The goblin scrambled to its feet, shaking its head, and Soutien despaired of reaching Moira.

Rage had apparently replaced Moira's exhaustion. She swung the club with brutal abandon, crying in exultation whenever it connected. Her bruised face stretched tight, as if her skin were made of mottled marble. Soutien looked into her eyes and saw nothing there of the Moira he knew. It was the same look Will had worn when fighting the goblins a few days earlier.

Berserker.

For the first time, Soutien understood at a visceral level why the Fey needed humanity. He watched in awe as the goblins fell away beneath Moira's onslaught, some falling to her club, some unwilling to risk getting caught by it. The Fey world had nothing like the raw power upon which she drew.

He worked his way toward her, knocking goblins out of his way, knowing that her single-mindedness blinded her to danger. Only a few feet more and he would at least be able to protect her back. A goblin launched itself at him with a shriek and Soutien long-armed it into the ravine. If nothing else, the ravine's steep walls would delay the goblin's return to the fight. Catching fire from Moira's insane rage, he tossed goblin after goblin into the ravine, roaring his challenge.

Then a sudden shimmer appeared in the air before his eyes and he reared back. He tried to bat it away but it eluded his blows.

"My lord!" came a small, vaguely familiar voice, penetrating his fog of rage.

Only then did see the winged Fey hovering in sunlight.

Elin.

A goblin slashed at the small Fey, but she swooped toward the ravine, leading the creature forward. As the goblin tried to stab her again, Soutien booted it over the edge. The goblin's cry became lost in the sound of breaking tree limbs and thrashing undergrowth.

"Lord Soutien," said the small Fey urgently. "You must leave here, now!"

"I am trying!" Soutien pointed out, tossing another goblin over the edge.

They were still vastly outnumbered. Had the winged Fey brought reinforcements or was she just here to point out the obvious?

Moira's adrenaline-fueled berserker rage was slowly burning itself out. Her blows were slower and took more effort, although the goblins still maintained a cautious distance. Of the goblins surrounding her, most had suffered broken bones or other disabling wounds.

There were no catcalls now, Soutien noted with grim satisfaction.

"Did you bring help?" he asked the Fey cousin.

She dipped in the air. "Yes, but you must not remain here!"

Then a cry of a different sort reached him and Soutien looked down. The underbrush rippled like a wave, starting from the east and traveling west along the floor of the ravine. Again, the cry came, sending a shiver up his scalp. It sounded like a woman's cry. Then another cry, guttural with pain, abruptly cut off.

A small tug on his sleeve. He looked up.

"Now, my lord!" said Elin, her small face drawn with worry. "They came at our call, but they are not ours to control."

A third time the cry came, this time very close.

The goblins stopped pressing against Moira and all eyes turned toward the ravine. Suddenly, a sleek tan shape surged out of the underbrush and flowed up the ravine wall as if it were a staircase. It screamed again as it launched itself over the lip of the ravine to land on a goblin. The goblin had time for only one cry before the cougar snapped its neck.

A collective shudder ran through the massed goblins, but they stayed in place, staring at the big cat. Then the cougar lunged with a snarl into the crowd of goblins and they scattered in all directions, some even falling into the ravine. The goblins' shrieks raised the hackles on the back of Soutien's neck.

A low grunting dragged his attention away from the cougar's pursuit. To his left, two grizzlies negotiated the ravine wall, their powerful haunches propelling them at a terrifying speed. Their muzzles were dark with blood.

And beyond the grizzlies, more rustling in the underbrush as gray shapes slunk toward the battle. Soutien caught his breath as a wolf looked right at him, its yellow eyes knowing.

Gaze still on the wolf, Soutien stepped back, reaching behind him for Moira. His hand found her forearm, slick with blood, and closed over it.

He glanced to either side of the ravine. Everywhere he looked, goblins ran, trying to escape the cougar and the bears.

"Follow me," he told Moira, as the first of the running goblins fell under grizzly claws. He pulled her toward the ravine.

Elin flitted above as Soutien and Moira half-stumbled, half-ran down the steep ravine wall. Above them, growls and screams inter-mingled, and Soutien tried to shut out the sounds of bones crunching beneath massive jaws. The wolves swept up the slope next to them. Soutien and Moira paused as the big animals passed them, but aside from a long sideways look from the pack leader, the wolves ignored them.

When the wolves had passed, Soutien and Moira resumed their descent to the bottom of the ravine, watching for goblins. But the only ones they saw had been killed by fang or claw. As they approached the bottom, Elin flew into the thick forest and it was only then that Soutien noticed the shimmering among the branches. He squinted to see more clearly. The tightening of Moira's hand in his told him she had seen them, too—hundreds of small, winged Fey, balanced on tree limbs, bowing to them.

❧ TWENTY-FOUR ❧

GRACE and Will walked quickly and quietly for several hours after leaving the pool. Grace led, her Fey shoes guiding them past thorns and hidden roots onto barely visible animal trails. The forest was hushed, with little of the birdsong and squirrel chatter that had become background noise for her. As she walked, her gaze ranged between tree branch and forest floor, searching for the cause of her unease.

But the miles passed and the trees grew fewer and farther between. Besides startling a deer, they saw nothing. Even the insects seemed less voracious.

After a while, the land began to slope upward, so gently that at first they didn't notice. It was only when they glanced back that they saw how high they were getting.

They finally stopped to rest at a fallen oak whose trunk was nearly lost in the profusion of yarrow and lupine growing on either side. It wasn't as big as the trees growing nearby and its bark had fallen off long ago. The wood was gray and smooth with time. Grace sat down, shifting away from a knot, and wondered if she should take the shoes off now to minimize cramping later. Instead, she rummaged around her willow bag for a cloth-wrapped piece of cheese. Her stomach rumbled in anticipation.

Will settled down next to her and she glanced at him, then looked away quickly. The flowers had closed in around him, and for one terrible moment, his legs had looked like they ended at the knee.

The air felt heavy with impending rain, but an occasional tangy breeze cut through the humidity. Her tattered shirt clung to her like a damp second skin. She didn't even want to think how her hair must look. Would she ever be able to comb it again, or would she have to shave her head and start over?

With a soft sigh, she pulled out her water bladder for a sparing sip. It was almost empty. They had found no other water since leaving the pool.

She shook her head and took a deep breath, trying to dislodge the memory of the creature floating in the pool as the water slowly turned pink.

"Well, at least now we know," said Will.

Grace looked at him. He sat on the dead tree, elbows resting on his knees, hands dangling among the flowers, staring at the ground between his feet. His face above the beard was red from exertion and the strip of neck she could see between overgrown hair and collar was covered in black-fly bites.

"At least we know what?"

"That your shoes can survive a dunking." He nodded at the brown man's shoes and Grace stared down at them. He was right. Not only had they survived her plunge into the pool, they had kept her feet dry.

Grace handed Will the water bladder and rubbed her hot face with her hands.

Now that she had stopped, the horror of seeing the creature's humped back breaching the surface of the water rushed back to haunt her.

The pool was too shallow to sustain such a big creature. But then, the creature's presence in the pool might not have been accidental. Maybe it had stalked them. According to Soutien, Amadan needed only one O'Rourke male for his plans. And he wouldn't want Fin Bheara to have the other.

Which meant that Amadan would keep sending creatures like that water *thing* after them.

Grace shook her head again. It had wanted to drown Will. She had tried to pull it away but it was too strong. That was when she'd gone for Will's pack, and found the pocket in which he kept his knife.

Her gorge rose as she remembered the feel of the knife sliding into flesh. Like slicing into a pumpkin—at first a little resistance, then nothing.

"Hey."

Will's gentle voice brought her eyes open. He was staring at her, his eyes compassionate. Apparently, he was no longer mad at her.

"We should get going," she said, unwilling to respond to the tacit invitation. She couldn't talk about it, not when he might have to kill, too. Again the impulse to share Soutien's secret almost overwhelmed her, and again she struggled to find the right path.

She stared at him, watching the curiosity in his eyes change to concern as the silence lengthened.

He might have a touchy temper, but Will was still the most honorable man she knew.

It occurred to her that he made life-and-death decisions every day in his work. Who was she to make this decision for him?

Relief washed over her like cool water on hot skin. She would tell him. Of course she would tell him. Will would decide for himself what he should do.

He would do the right thing.

"Will," she began, then stopped as a scent on the rising breeze caught her attention. She sniffed, trying to capture the elusive smell. Where had she smelled that almost-unpleasant earthiness before?

"What is it?" asked Will, rising from the log. She noted distantly that the knife was in his hand, blade open. The breeze ruffled her hair, bringing a shiver to the back of her neck.

Above their heads, treetops receded into the sky. The lowest branches were at least thirty feet up. There would be no climbing these trees.

"Nothing," she said finally. "I thought I smelled..." She shook her head and rose, too. "We should keep moving."

Will nodded and shouldered his backpack, but kept the knife in his hand. The sun was just beginning its slow descent toward the west. It would be a while before lengthening shadows brought relief from the heat and humidity. Gathering clouds in the north hinted at possible showers.

Again she caught the fleeting scent. She turned, trying to locate it.

And there, no more than ten feet away, was Aidan.

She stood like a statue, staring at the disheveled man, too amazed to think. She couldn't have spoken if her life depended on it.

Seeing her confusion, Will turned and caught sight of his brother.

"Aidan!" he cried, his face breaking into a smile of delight and relief. "Thank God!" He took a step toward Aidan, his hands reaching out.

Aidan stepped back, staring at the knife in Will's hand.

Will stopped. "It's all right, Aidan," he said softly, as if gentling a horse. He flipped the blade shut and pocketed the knife, turning his palm out to show it was empty. "Come with us—are you hungry?"

Aidan stood half-hidden by an oak tree. His clothes were torn and dirty and he had a dark, scruffy beard. His glance darted around fearfully. He looked as if he would bolt at a sudden move.

The smell came from him. As Will tried to persuade his skittish brother, Grace stared at Aidan, trying to work out what was wrong. After everything the man had been through, it was understandable that he would be afraid. But something about his behavior bothered her.

"Aidan, have some food," said Will. He pulled out a travel cake and took another step toward his brother. Grace tensed, but Aidan stepped back.

"Will, wait," she placed a hand on his arm.

"What?" Will spared her a glance.

"I don't know," Grace said, frustrated. "Something's not right."

He pulled his arm out of her grasp. "Well, while you figure out what it is, I'm going to get my brother."

And then she had it. The scent was the same one she had experienced her first night in this place, when she and Moira arrived. It all came rushing back—Moira's terseness, her own confusion, the sense of danger, heightened by that strange, almost-offensive smell, like damp earth and composting leaves.

Will continued his slow approach, talking gently, offering the food.

Grace looked again at Aidan, and now she could see the insubstantiality of his body, as if all the effort went into making his features believable, as if that was where the attention would focus.

"Will, stop!" said Grace. He glanced back at her in annoyance. "Please," she continued, dropping her voice. "That's not Aidan. It's Amadan."

Will closed his eyes. When he opened them again, the look in them was hard.

"Not this time, Grace," he said grimly. "I won't turn my back on him again."

Instead, he turned his back on Grace and stepped closer to Aidan. "Come on, Aidan, it's time to find Moira and go home."

For every step Will took forward, Aidan took one back. There was something calculated about his movements, something cunning behind the fear in his eyes. If this truly was Amadan, thought Grace, what was he waiting for? Why didn't he attack?

Because he can't, she suddenly realized. He wasn't really there, or at least, most of him wasn't. And because he wasn't physically present, he couldn't hurt them.

But he could delay them.

With a sinking heart, she realized that she couldn't hear anything but the sound of Will moving through the underbrush. Not even the drone of insects.

And then she did hear something. Something big, breathing too close to her. She slowly turned to look behind her.

She barely had time to shout "Will!" in warning then Red Cap reached out a clawed hand, picked her up, and flung her at the nearest tree.

Pain exploded through her body as her head slammed against the maple. She slid to the foot of the tree, striking her head again on an exposed root. She struggled to remain conscious, every instinct screaming at her to stay awake.

She forced her eyes open, squinting past the pain. Red Cap was ten feet away. He shambled toward her, axe clutched in one hand, pig snout snuffling, eyes bloodshot. He grinned, revealing small tusks. He smelled of old, clotted blood and rotted meat.

Ignoring the roaring in her ears and keeping an eye on Red Cap, Grace pushed herself to her knees, gasping as pain lanced through her side. With fear spurring her, she used the tree to haul herself to her feet. She groaned and clutched her ribs.

Five feet away.

Keeping a hand on the tree, Grace edged around the bole, keeping it between herself and the beast.

Was Will hurt, too? Was Amadan circling around behind her? Instinctively, she glanced over her shoulder.

At that moment, the axe thudded into the tree next to her face. She recoiled in terror, screaming as the sudden movement sent fire stitching through her ribs.

"Hang on, Grace!" shouted Will and she looked up in time to see him hurtling through the air to land on Red Cap's back. The creature roared and spun around to dislodge Will, but Will had wrapped his legs around Red Cap's waist and one arm around the beast's massive neck.

It'll never work, thought Grace in despair. He's just too strong for Will. As she watched, one huge hand reached behind and groped for Will.

Only then did she notice the knife in Will's free hand. He stabbed at the hand groping for him, then sank the blade to the hilt in Red Cap's chest.

Bright red blood stained the beast-man's tunic and streaked his arm where Will had cut him. Red Cap bellowed in anger and wrapped a huge hand around Will's forearm. Will grunted with pain, but re-doubled his stranglehold on Red Cap's throat.

He's going to get killed, thought Grace. With a surge of adrenaline, she grasped the handle of the axe and pulled with all her strength, ignoring the agony in her side. As she worked the axe free, she glanced around, but there was no sign of Aidan. Of Amadan.

With a sigh, the axe finally slipped out of the tree. Grasping it tightly, she turned toward the struggle. Red Cap had one hand on Will's head, and the other was clawing at Will's choke hold. Blood ran freely from deep scratches on both of Will's arms. He had dropped the knife and his right arm hung uselessly by his side. By the angle of his forearm, Grace could tell it was broken.

A fresh spurt of adrenaline surged through her, and with it, fury. With a scream of rage, she launched herself at the beast. Just as she reached him, she swung the axe at Red Cap's legs, overriding the ominous pain in her ribs. At the last second, the axe twisted in her hands and the flat part of the blade smacked into Red Cap's hairy shin.

Too late, she remembered Soutien's warning. The axe was magically tied to Red Cap. It would always return to him. Obviously, it was also spelled not to hurt him.

With a grunt, Red Cap looked down at her. Ignoring Will as if he were a gnat, he reached out and grabbed Grace by the front of her shirt. To her horror, he lifted her off the ground and held her up to his face.

He was going to rip into her with his tusks. She glimpsed Will's haggard face just behind Red Cap's head and wanted to tell him to run while he could. But terror kept her mute. Then she felt the silk fabric of her shirt start to give way, cutting into the flesh of her underarms, twisting around her neck. With a final surge of energy, she braced one knee against the creature's bloody chest and with the other leg, kicked with all her might.

Her foot connected with his genitals, and with a roar of fury, he shoved Grace away from him just as the shirt finally tore free. The arc of his thrust could have impaled her on a fallen oak's branches. Instead, she flew ten feet into the air, the longest two seconds of her life, and landed on the trunk itself.

Something gave way in her chest and she felt the sharp end of a bone poking into internal organs. Terrified, she remained very still. The pain of breathing was excruciating. She could still move her head, however, and she slowly lifted it to look around.

Will was shouting her name. He wasn't looking at her, however. He stood before Red Cap, knife in his left hand. The blood must make that slippery, she thought. A small part of her recognized she was going into shock and she fought against it.

Will's face contorted with fury as he faced the beast-man. His chest heaved and blood ran down his face and arms, giving a ghoulish cast to his expression. Grace shivered at the raw emotion on his face. Red Cap stood two feet taller and outweighed Will by at least two hundred pounds, but even he took a step back under the onslaught of such rage.

Then Will sprang at Red Cap, his knife slicing through the beast-man's leather tunic into his gut. With a roar of pain, Red Cap stumbled back and shouted a word.

To Grace's horror, the axe, which had remained on the ground where she had dropped it, now began to move, sliding on the forest floor toward Red Cap. She tried to crawl toward it, only to stop when the blackness at the edge of her vision crept closer. She tasted blood but couldn't spare the energy to wipe her mouth.

She struggled against the darkness, pushing it away. A spark of anger helped clear her mind. She knew she was dying and it enraged her to go like this, a poor pathetic thing broken by the likes of Red Cap. She wanted to go out like Will, fighting.

Tears welled up in her eyes.

She didn't want Will to die.

"Oh please," she whispered into the ground, her tears falling into the loam. "Please help him."

As though the words had dropped into a waiting ear, the ground trembled in response. It took a moment to recognize the sensation as the thud of hoofbeats. Somewhere close, a horse was galloping. In the next instant, she heard it...them. She looked up just as Red Cap turned around. Two big black stallions came hurtling out of the forest, eyes rolling as if the fiends of hell were after them. On the back of the nearest one was a familiar figure.

The brown man.

Will stepped back at their appearance, but the horses didn't even pause. The first one barreled into Red Cap, sending him reeling. The brown man vaulted off the stallion's back just as the second one rammed into the beast-man. Red Cap landed with a thud that shook leaves.

Incredibly, Red Cap struggled to his feet, and this time, he had the axe in hand. With an inarticulate shout, he took a lumbering run at the nearest horse. The horse's eyes suddenly flared red and it snorted, rearing and lashing out at Red Cap. Phooka.

Red Cap stumbled back, and swung to face the other phooka.

"Be careful," whispered Grace as Red Cap swung the axe in a deadly arc. Miraculously, the horse danced back just out of range. The first phooka snorted again and Red Cap whirled to face it.

Then the air was full of whirring sounds and bright movement, and Grace blinked furiously until she could make out small, winged shapes, some as tiny as six inches, flying through the air.

Winged fairies, she thought, and in spite of everything, wonder filled her for a brief, shining moment.

Red Cap waved his axe and his free hand around madly. Grace stared at him, then turned to look more carefully at the fairies. The Fey.

Each one carried a small bow and a quiver. While Red Cap fended off one set of flying attackers, another sent tiny darts pricking into his skin.

Red Cap's roars grew increasingly frantic as he tried to bat away his tiny foes. Then a stone landed on his head with a fearful crack.

Grace looked up. The trees were full of Fey, each carrying a sack full of rocks.

As the stones flew through the air, Red Cap finally gave up. Without another sound, he turned and lumbered into the forest, away from his attackers. Snapping branches and rustling underbrush accompanied his departure.

A loud cheer rose from the various rescuers, then the Fey swarmed after Red Cap.

It seemed Fin Bheara was looking out for them.

With a ragged sigh, Grace let her head rest against the cool trunk and closed her eyes. It was all right. Will would be all right.

Before she could sink into oblivion, however, she felt hands tugging at the remnants of her silk shirt. She opened her eyes. The brown man crouched before her, his scrunched-up face close to hers.

"Come," he said. Next to him, one of the phooka sniffed her hair. Its breath felt warm and moist.

"Wish I could," she whispered. The bloody taste in her mouth was growing more pronounced. "I can't seem to get up."

"Then we'll help you," said Will, kneeling on her other side. He looked more dead than alive, and there were deep gashes in his chest where Red Cap had slashed him. Remember to disinfect those, she wanted to tell him, but the look on his face chased all thoughts out of her head.

He looked scared. Scared for her.

With a nod at the brown man, they each placed an arm under her shoulders and lifted her to a sitting position. She must have passed out for a moment, because when she became aware again, she was on her feet and the world was a kaleidoscope of pain. She noticed distantly that the brown man looked grim, a comical expression on him, and that Will's face was ashen.

Then one of the phooka knelt before her and somehow, she was on its back. When she came to again, Will was behind her, his good arm keeping her from falling. Although the phooka walked gently, she felt every step like a hot poker in her side.

She was so cold.

The sounds of the forest receded from her awareness and blackness stole over her. She needed to sleep.

"Look, Grace," said Will in her ear. His voice seemed to come from far away. She looked and, in a moment of clarity, saw that they had crested a rise and that there were very few trees to impede her sight. From here, the slope swept downhill for a quarter mile until it stopped at a cliff that overlooked the sea.

And at the head of the cliff stood a large stone building that looked like a castle.

"We made it, Grace," said Will. "We made it to Knockma."

Grace nodded, and kept nodding until consciousness fled and she could finally rest.

҈ TWENTY-FIVE ҈

THE hum of Fey wings filled the tiny glade with a false sense of purpose. Half the Fey rested in the trees in preparation for the final push to Knockma, but even at rest their wings moved lazily in the late afternoon sunlight. Those not resting flitted between trees or hovered high above, watching for goblins. Or bears.

The stirring of so many wings brought different scents to Soutien's attention—wild rose, pine needles, wet leaves. He even caught the faint whiff of a long-gone deer.

With a sigh, he looked down at Moira sleeping on the forest floor. She had kept going for two hours after their rescue. The moment Elin announced a stop, however, she had collapsed and was asleep before her head hit the moss. Soutien had tucked his cloak around her for warmth, but her skin still felt cold, and her pallor worried him.

He squatted by her side and stroked her cheek, willing some of his strength into her. They weren't safe yet. Knockma was still three hours away at a hard march. They could make it before nightfall. But looking at Moira's drawn features, he doubted she would have the stamina.

"My lord," said Elin, by his ear.

As he turned to face the Fey cousin, he caught a flicker of motion out of the corner of his eye, but did not bother following it. It was another of the smaller ones, come for a closer look at Moira. The small ones moved as fast as hummingbirds. They made him dizzy.

Elin alighted and glanced down at Moira before turning her gaze on him. Her wings moved in lazy sweeps, and her feet barely touched the ground. Even in the long shadows of the setting sun, her silver hair shimmered.

"I have word from the scouts." Her wings shivered and Soutien gave her his full attention.

"What is it?"

"Red Cap attacked two humans almost within sight of Knockma," she reported. "He was driven off, but not before harming the female."

Soutien rubbed his face with his hands. "How seriously?"

Elin now hovered off the ground, as though she couldn't bear the contact. "She is dying, my lord."

Oh, Grace. Grief rose up to choke him and he fought to control himself. Grace.

"And the man?" he finally asked.

"Hurt, but not fatally. They were taken to Knockma."

She waited patiently while he absorbed her news.

"Will King Fin Bheara send help?"

"Yes, my lord, but he cannot spare many defenders. Only a small troop."

Soutien nodded his thanks. Will was at Knockma and help was on the way. Moira would soon be safe. He should be grateful for that much.

Elin looked at him a moment longer, then at Moira. She flitted closer, then, as though sensing his displeasure, she swooped back to the main camp.

Soutien sighed and stood up, the wound in his thigh protesting. He knew Elin couldn't help her curiosity, any more than the other Fey who kept finding reason to come near. Moira attracted them like salvation attracts a dying man. None of the Fey folk had seen a human in centuries.

And they had seen her fighting the goblins, had seen firsthand the berserker fury.

Now Moira lay deathly still and pale on the cold ground, her reserves of strength so depleted that Soutien worried she might not recover.

And Grace was dying. Was perhaps already dead.

Beyond that sorrow, the brazenness of Red Cap's attack worried him. How close was Amadan's army if Red Cap could attack so near Knockma? At least King Fin Bheara now knew that Amadan was on the move.

Then all movement in the glade ceased and Soutien looked up in alarm. The winged Fey, big and small, had settled on various branches and were staring down at him, wings completely still.

A soft sound sent Soutien whirling around. In the shadows between the trees stood the brown man. A sparrow perched on his shoulder, staring gravely at Soutien. Then the shadows moved and Soutien realized that the brown man was surrounded by animals—rabbits, deer, a fox, weasels. The trees above his head were filled with squirrels and birds—blue jays, cardinals, owls, sparrows... he even saw grouse.

Soutien's eyebrows had climbed up his forehead. He controlled his expression with difficulty. *Now what?*

"You must come," said the brown man.

Before Soutien could do more than open his mouth, the little cousin continued.

"The human hunts."

Soutien closed his mouth as relief swept through him. It could only be Aidan. Had he escaped from the goblins? Maybe he'd never been a prisoner.

Then the sobering thought: Aidan was hunting. That explained the grim expression on the brown man's face, not to mention his accompaniment of wildlife. The Seelie did not hunt—could not conceive of killing for nourishment when food was freely available everywhere. Only the Unseelie ate flesh.

And Aidan.

He felt a sudden pang of sympathy for the man. He was only doing what he had been trained to do to survive. And now, here, it might get him killed. Soutien looked at the brown man's face, noting the tightness in his jaw, the set to his mouth.

Moira would expect him to find her brother. Yet Soutien couldn't leave her. She was vulnerable, maybe even sick. She needed him at least as much as her brother did.

"I…" he began, fully intending to tell the brown man he couldn't help right now, that his first responsibility was to Moira.

Then the memory of the last time he had seen Fin Bheara crept back to haunt him. He had promised his liege he would bring him Kirwan's sons. Instead, he had allowed the eldest one to die and managed to lose the other two.

He had promised, fully understanding the weight of the promise, as well as the urgency of finding the O'Rourke boys and bringing them safely to Knockma.

Fully understanding that on them rested the safety of the Fey and Humanity.

Soutien took a long, ragged breath and expelled it slowly.

"How far?" he asked the brown man.

"Not far."

Soutien stared at him. "Wait," he finally said, and turned back Moira. Elin swooped down to meet him.

"I must accompany him." He saw the question in her eyes. "If she awakens—" he nodded at Moira "—tell her…" He stopped for a moment, suddenly realizing that if Moira knew he was looking for Aidan, she'd come after them. "Tell her I will be back soon."

Elin nodded. Soutien hesitated, then reached out a hand to the winged Fey, only to let it drop by his side.

"Elin…" He swallowed.

"It is an honor to serve you, my lord. You have but to ask." Somehow, the Fey managed a graceful midair bow.

He hadn't earned her loyalty. He hadn't even thanked her for saving their lives. Nevertheless, he had no choice.

"Then I would ask that you protect her until I return."

"Of course, my lord." She looked mildly offended that he even thought to ask.

Despite his misgivings, Soutien bowed in return. "If I am not back by dawn, take her to Knockma. You are but half a day away."

"If you take too long, my lord," said Elin firmly, "we will come looking for you."

Soutien shook his head. "No. Your first duty is to her. The king's reinforcements should be here soon. Take her to Knockma. Tell the king that I went after the eldest Kirwan."

Elin looked puzzled, and uncertain, but finally she nodded. Soutien hoped the king received his message before demanding that Will kill him.

He took a last look at Moira, at the Fey in the trees, then turned to the waiting brown man.

"Show me where," he said.

Without a word, the brown man turned and disappeared into the forest.

***

Tree shapes blurred as twilight eased daylight out. Although his eyes were better than a human's, Soutien paid strict attention to where he put his feet on the uneven ground. It would be too ironic to fall and break a leg now.

The brown man flitted from shadow to shadow like a firefly, forcing Soutien to follow closely. The animals had all melted into the forest, leaving only two owls flying silently between the trees, accompanying them. They were already an hour away from the camp where Moira slept, and Soutien chafed at the growing distance.

The scent of night orchids mingled with the smell of his sweat, reminding him that he hadn't bathed in a long time. Or slept.

He should have stayed with Moira. There was no point in chasing after a ghost in the night. Better to have waited until morning and daylight.

But the brown man stayed barely within sight, giving Soutien no chance to change his mind.

After another hour of struggling to see his way while keeping the brown man in sight, Soutien gave up. He stopped by an ancient oak, breathing deeply and trying to quiet his worries.

The brown man's idea of "not far" might be another mile, or ten. Soutien couldn't risk being away from Moira for so long. It was time to get her safely to Knockma. Then would he come back for Aidan.

The tricky part would be convincing the brown man to wait for his return before approaching Aidan.

A rustle announced the return of the brown man. "Come," he said. His voice floated out of the deeper shadows between two trees.

Soutien squinted into the darkness. "Too far," he said, finally pin-pointing the other's location.

"He hunts." The wild cousin's tone held a note of warning.

Soutien strained to see the brown man's expression. His stillness suddenly seemed threatening.

An owl hooted above Soutien's head and he started. The winged Fey had called bear and cougar down on the goblins—could the brown man do the same to stop Aidan?

He tried to imagine Aidan facing down a grizzly bear but all he could see was Mack, strapped to the chair and bleeding to death in Red Cap's ruins. He shook the vision off and was formulating a cautious response to the brown man when he caught a faint scent on the breeze. His head snapped up.

Wood smoke! Atavistic fear surged through him and he straightened away from the oak, suddenly trembling. Even King Fin Bheara was powerless before a forest fire.

Soutien controlled himself with an effort. It couldn't be a forest fire—the smell was too near, too faint. It could only be a campfire. It could only be Aidan. The sudden relief left him weak.

Another fear occurred to him as he turned toward the faint whiff of wood smoke. Was Aidan burning deadwood or had he taken living branches?

Then the brown man stepped out of the shadows and for the first time, Soutien saw the determination etched in the strange, small face.

"Come," said his wild cousin.

Soutien came.

They found Aidan within fifteen minutes, huddled half-naked around a small fire. He sprang to his feet when Soutien stepped into the firelight. Soutien frowned. Aidan was almost unrecognizable as the Air Force officer he had known.

A black beard covered the young man's face. Like his hair, the beard was snarled and thick with twigs and bits of leaves. He wore a pair of heavy canvas pants torn down the length of the right leg. He was bare-chested and his ribs showed clearly through the profusion of scratches and bruises.

Before Soutien could speak, Aidan darted to the fire and snatched up a burning brand. He leaped back, keeping the fire and the waving torch between himself and Soutien.

Soutien's heart sank as he looked into those dark eyes. There was no recognition in them. Nothing but fear.

At least the fire had been built of dry deadwood. He wondered briefly where the brown man was, but couldn't spare the time to look around for him.

"Aidan," he said gently. "It's me, Soutien."

Aidan jumped at the use of his name, but the brand remained high. If anything, he looked even more frightened.

"I've come to bring you to safety," said Soutien quickly, hoping to allay some of that fear. He held out his hand. "You recognize me, don't you?"

Too late he remembered that Amadan-na-Briona had stolen his guise to deceive Will. Likely he had done the same with Aidan and Mack. How could Soutien convince Aidan that he was who he said he was?

Then, to his surprise, Aidan lowered the torch.

"Soutien?"

"Yes." Soutien nodded and tried a smile.

Aidan hesitated a moment longer, then dropped the brand into the fire. His shoulders slumped and Soutien realized with a start that he was going to fall. He leapt over the small campfire and caught the young man around the waist, supporting him until he could sit on the ground.

"I thought you were *him*," said Aidan. "I thought you were going to kill me."

Soutien squatted by Aidan's side and laid a hand on his trembling back.

Him. Amadan. Or Red Cap. "How did you know?" he asked, relieved that Aidan was talking. The last time he had seen him, the young man had been almost catatonic. "How did you know it was really me?"

Aidan drew a long, shuddering breath. "*He* smells like death."

Dread trailed a cool finger down Soutien's spine. He stood up. "Can you walk?"

Aidan looked up at him, and the drawn expression on his face told Soutien that he was near the end of his endurance. Still, he struggled to his feet.

"Is Will safe?"

Soutien nodded. "He is at Knockma, with Grace." He shuddered at the thought of Will trying to murder the king. It wouldn't work. Soutien had to get back to Knockma with Aidan, quickly.

"Grace?" said Aidan.

The other man's puzzlement filled Soutien with uneasiness. Aidan had seen Grace at Red Cap's castle.

Soutien answered carefully. "She got caught up accidentally when Moira crossed over."

As though hearing her name for the first time, Aidan turned sharply toward Soutien. "He tricked Moira, too?" Despair laced his voice and Soutien automatically placed a hand on the other's arm.

"Moira is safe for now, but we must get back to her." He examined the darkness of the surrounding woods, refusing to let despair overtake him. Aidan would slow him down even more than the lack of moonlight. "She's only a few hours away."

"I'm ready."

Soutien avoided looking at Aidan, knowing he was anything but ready. He kicked dirt onto the fire, and suddenly they were in darkness.

"We should pour water over it," came Aidan's strained voice out of the darkness.

"It won't be a problem," promised Soutien. He decided against telling him about the brown man. Aidan was spooked enough already.

The return trip was even more grueling than Soutien had anticipated. Aidan was clumsy with fatigue and had to be led around or helped over most obstacles. Soutien consoled himself with the knowledge that Moira had been exhausted, too, and probably wouldn't wake for many more hours. He ignored the small voice that wondered just how safe she was sleeping in the woods, in spite of her Fey guardians. Hopefully, Fin Bheara's reinforcements had arrived.

Finally, in spite of his growing anxiety, he called a stop.

"Why are we stopping?" asked Aidan, his voice thick with exhaustion.

"You need to rest."

"I can keep going—"

Soutien put up a hand. "Rest. We still have a long way to go."

As though the words gave him the permission he needed, Aidan immediately sank to the ground and sat with his arms wrapped around his drawn-up knees. He laid his forehead on one knee, hiding his face.

Soutien looked around. Next to a huge maple grew a hawthorn, slender by comparison. He sat at the base of the hawthorn, wondering if a nymph inhabited it. He drew comfort from the possibility.

The familiar noises of the nighttime forest wrapped around him, a cocoon of safety. Each chirp of a cricket and croak of a bullfrog told him nothing dangerous crept around his immediate vicinity. An owl hooted in the distance, hunting, and Soutien wondered if it was one of the ones that had accompanied him earlier. The forest floor was alive with the stealthy rustling of mice and vole, searching for seeds, avoiding predators.

Soutien found himself wishing the brown man had accompanied them. Strange as he was, the little cousin would have been a welcome presence.

"Tell me what's been happening."

Aidan's voice sounded muffled, as though he hadn't the strength to lift his head. Soutien examined the dark, bent head and the straining shoulders of the younger man.

Was this a moment of lucidity? Did Aidan truly want to know what had happened?

Why else would he ask?

Soutien allowed the peaceful forest sounds to wash over him while he marshaled his thoughts. Finally, he took a deep breath.

"After the dé Danann rescued us from the goblins, they took us prisoner."

"What dé Danann? What's a dé Danann?" Aidan raised his head and looked at Soutien.

Was he gone before the dé Danann arrived or was this more evidence of Aidan's flimsy grasp of reality? Soutien examined Aidan's expression and decided that the other man was fully there, at least for the moment.

He backtracked, sketching out the events of the past few days. Aidan listened in silence, absorbing every word. Soutien thought he would ask why Amadan had tricked them into coming to the Fey world, why Mack was killed, why Grace, Moira, and Will had to fight for their lives. If he had, Soutien would have had to tell him what he had told Grace about the O'Rourke/Kirwan duty to kill the king. With Mack dead, that duty now rested on Aidan's battered shoulders.

But Aidan didn't ask, and Soutien didn't press. Aidan was too fragile... and Soutien too tired. First he would get the young man to Knockma. Then he would destroy his life.

When he finished, Soutien waited in silence. After a while, he realized Aidan wasn't going to say anything. Sometime during his tale, the young man had buried his face against his knees again. Soutien stared at the bent head, eyes narrowed.

"Why did you run, Aidan?" he asked softly. "We thought the goblins took you. Where did you go?"

For a moment, he thought Aidan wouldn't answer. Then he raised his head and looked directly at Soutien.

"I killed him."

And Soutien knew exactly what he was talking about, but the name still flew from him, expelled on a gust of horror.

"Mack?"

Aidan nodded. His gaze never wavered. "You knew Mack. Would he have wanted to go on living?"

The familiar, impotent grief washed through Soutien as he faced the question. Would Mack have wanted to return to his world, his family, his life, to the daily horror of knowing that Red Cap had *eaten* his hands and feet?

He shuddered. No. Of course not.

But after a moment, an insistent thought surfaced. Who was he to decide what Mack would or wouldn't have wanted? Mack had been one of the strongest men Soutien had known, physically and mentally. He had a good life waiting for him, and a wife with a baby on the way. He couldn't have remained on active duty, but Mack would have found a way to surmount the psychological and physical horror of his wounds.

Soutien returned the other man's gaze, keeping his own expression neutral. Aidan had always competed against his older brother, but he had loved him, too. He had known Mack at least as well as Soutien had. Had he killed his brother because he himself would not have wanted to live with such wounds?

"Why run?" he asked again.

Aidan looked at him. "The goblins came after me. I didn't have any weapons, so I ran. Then I got lost."

The ensuing silence stretched on uncomfortably, and Soutien dropped his gaze. So far, he had done a poor job of protecting his charges. Finally he rose, signaling the resumption of their journey.

The eastern sky was growing pale by the time they stopped for the last time, within a mile of camp.

They should have run into Elin's scouts by now.

Aidan sat where Soutien had placed him, at the base of an ancient maple. Legs splayed out and hands by his sides, he leaned against the rough bark, eyes closed.

Bare-chested, Soutien shivered in the pre-dawn cool. He had given Aidan his tunic hours earlier, when the other man's shivering became uncontrollable. The added warmth seemed to help.

"Isn't it funny how fast the snow melted?" said Aidan. He opened his eyes and looked around. "It must have been quite the Chinook."

Soutien sighed. Aidan had been weaving in and out of lucidity most of the night. He treated their stumbling march as if it were one of his boyhood camping trips with his siblings. Then, in the next breath, he would ask Soutien for more details about the Fey.

"How far do you suppose we are from home?" asked Aidan, turning to look at Soutien. "Nothing looks familiar."

Soutien found a moss-covered log and sat down. His thigh throbbed where the goblin sword had poked him. There would be no infection, thanks to Elin's ministrations, but the wound nagged at him. He leaned his elbows on his knees and expelled a breath, hoping to dispel some of his tiredness with it. A squirrel, disturbed in its sleep, chittered at him from a branch above.

"Not far," he said finally.

"I'll be glad to get home," said Aidan, yawning. "I'm tired."

Yes, thought Soutien. *So am I*. He tried to remember when he last slept—two days ago, a drugged sleep courtesy of Lord Cathel. It was hard to believe that only two days ago he was drinking wine and hoping he had found a refuge for his charges.

He watched Aidan slowly sink into sleep, watched the lines of exhaustion and puzzlement smooth from his face, watched his legs twitch as tired muscles finally relaxed.

He would give him ten minutes, no more.

A doe stepped between two trees and stopped when she saw him. Her ears flicked as she tried to decide what his role was in her particular food chain. When he made no move toward her, she took another step, still watching him carefully.

Although she stepped lightly, her hoof landed on a dry twig that snapped loudly in the pre-dawn stillness.

"Agh!" Aidan exploded to his feet, arms flailing at an imaginary enemy, screaming with mingled rage and fear.

Soutien sprang to his feet. "Aidan!" The young man whirled, hands balled into fists, eyes shifting back and forth, his mouth a grimace of fear.

"Aidan!" repeated Soutien more forcefully. "It was a deer!" He kept repeating it until his words penetrated Aidan's wall of terror. Finally, Aidan's fists lowered slightly.

"A deer?" he said, glancing around in doubt.

"A deer," repeated Soutien firmly. "Long gone now," he added when he saw Aidan still looking around.

The adrenaline rush suddenly deserted Aidan and he fell, more than sat, back on the ground. "A deer. Oh God."

And suddenly he rolled onto his side on the ground, wrapped himself into a ball, and began to cry in great, racking sobs.

Soutien stared in amazement for a full five seconds before going over to the young man. He crouched by his side, ignoring the pain in his thigh, and tentatively placed a hand on his back. Aidan trembled violently under his hand.

"You're tired and hungry," murmured Soutien softly. "You've been in great danger, but it'll soon be all right." It felt strange to be consoling Aidan like a child. He hoped he wasn't lying.

"Let's keep going," he said when Aidan quieted. "We aren't far from Moira now."

But Aidan remained curled up, although his trembling abated. Just as Soutien was about to slip a hand under Aidan's elbow to help him up, he began to talk.

"It took me three days to catch up to him," he said, so low that Soutien had to strain to hear him. "He'd left me the message, the one we'd worked out as kids, but I didn't get it right away. His trail was easy to follow, though. Mack was always a good marker."

Aidan continued speaking in a monotone and after a while, Soutien sat on the damp ground, his heart heavy. He wasn't sure he wanted to hear what Aidan was saying.

"I was pretty spooked by the time I caught up to him. There were things sniffing around my camp at night, and I kept catching sight of creatures that would disappear as soon as I turned around. Once I was with Mack, though, I felt safer. My big brother was there, and everything would be all right."

He paused. "Thing is, I hated it. I hated feeling safe because I was with him. I was just as strong, just as smart."

"Maybe Mack felt safer having you around, too," said Soutien gently.

Aidan laughed without humor. "Then he was a fool." His voice caught on the word and he was silent for a long time. When he finally continued, his voice was under control.

"I took first turn at watch that first night. We were both tired. I'd barely slept for three nights. I fell asleep." His voice dropped and Soutien leaned in. "I woke up when something entered our camp, something..." His breathing quickened and his shoulders tensed. Soutien reached out to touch him but stopped just short of his shoulder. He didn't want to interrupt. Not now.

"It was big—low and wide—and it looked wild, almost like a tree. Then I blinked, and it was you."

Soutien closed his eyes and waited.

"It wasn't really you, but he looked so much like you, and even though he smelled strange, I was so glad to see you. I tried to get up but he signaled me to be quiet. Then, this... thing came out of the trees behind where Mack was sleeping." He cleared his throat and his voice came out a whisper. "It was big and it had a snout... I was so scared I *couldn't* talk. Then I saw the axe in its hand and I yelled a warning to Mack. And then you—Amadan, I guess—hit me over the head. When I came to, Mack and I were prisoners."

Soutien's hands clenched into fists and his insides tightening in apprehension. Oblivious to his audience, Aidan continued.

"Mack was already tied to the chair. He was conscious and we were alone. I was tied up, too, trussed up like a pig and left in a corner next to the fireplace to wait my turn."

Aidan suddenly pushed himself up and sat up. His eyes were unnaturally bright in the dawn's gray light, and with his tousled hair and week's growth of dark beard, he look dangerously unpredictable. Soutien tensed, but Aidan only wrapped his arms around himself as if he were cold, and began to rock.

"Mack tried to get me to back up to him so we could untie each other's hands, but I was groggy. I took too long. Before I could reach him, the door opened and... that... it came back."

He abruptly stopped rocking. The eyes he turned on Soutien were full of despair, but his face was completely expressionless. He spoke clearly and calmly.

"It shoved me back in the corner. Then it raised its axe and chopped off Mack's hand. It took a burning piece of wood from the fireplace and cauterized the wound. Then it cooked Mack's hand and ate it, like it was some kind of delicacy."

Soutien listened in grim silence as Aidan listed Red Cap's horrors. When Aidan finally stopped, Soutien was too exhausted to even feel relieved. He had seen Mack. He knew what had been done to him. But to have Aidan tell him in a brutal purge was almost more than he could bear.

No wonder Aidan had gone out of his mind.

Soutien forced himself to his feet, heavy with the burden of the other man's confession. He should say something, comfort him in some way, but absolution wasn't his to give. Aidan blamed himself for what had happened to Mack. He couldn't forgive himself for surviving.

"We have to go." Soutien held out his hand. "Let's go find Moira."

Aidan stared at Soutien's hand for a long minute before finally taking it.

As they set off through the dew-laden underbrush, Soutien promised himself he would never tell Moira or Will what Aidan had told him. They had enough nightmares to live with.

They moved slower than ever. Soutien finally kept his arm around Aidan to support him. He had been away from Moira for most of the night. Too long. He began to search the trees, watching for the telltale flicker of Fey wings.

Within a quarter mile of the camp, he knew something was wrong. There should have been guards. He should be able to hear the whirring of so many winged Fey in one spot.

Forcing himself past tiredness, he pulled Aidan into a stumbling run.

He smelled the camp before he reached it—a thick, cloying scent that sent fear shooting through him. "Wait here!" he said, abruptly releasing Aidan. Soutien ran the last hundred yards, leaping fallen trees, weaving between maple and fir. Sunlight sparkled on a thousand dew drops, shattering them prism-like as he crashed through the underbrush.

Then the sun caught a shimmer in the trees and his heart soared with relief. He turned toward the Fey, words of reproach on his lips, only to swallow the words in horror. The shimmer was caused by the aimless fluttering of wings in the morning breeze. The Fey attached to the wings was impaled on the tip of a hard maple branch. Her sightless eyes seemed to stare right through him.

Soutien slowly turned and examined his surroundings. On almost every tree, a dead Fey hung impaled. Some were missing their heads or limbs. Small corpses dotted the forest floor like crumpled up flowers.

A wordless grief fought to batter down the barrier of ice that shot up around his soul. With feet that no longer felt like his, he walked past the honor guard of the dead, looking for Moira. He placed each foot with precision, avoiding small corpses.

The forest floor was slick with pink-tinged dew. This battle was hours old. The goblins had found them, caught them by surprise.

How? And how had goblins managed to catch so many winged Fey?

Moira wasn't where he had left her, but Elin was.

She rested on her side, curled up on a bed of leaves brown with dried blood. Her eyes were closed and her silver hair streamed out behind her as if in an invisible wind. Soutien dropped to his knees next to the small Fey, hands reaching for her. He stopped short when he saw that the dried blood had come from her.

Someone had torn off her wings.

A trembling started deep in the pit of him, shaking free the ice that surrounded his soul, allowing grief and rage to take hold of him. Somehow, hers was the worst outrage. All the other Fey had kept their wings, but in an ultimate act of contempt and cruelty, hers had been ripped off.

Then Elin opened her eyes. For the first time, he noticed that they were pale blue. She looked at him in dull incomprehension, then recognition sparked in her eyes, clearing the pain momentarily.

"My lord," she murmured. She tried to rise, but Soutien placed a restraining finger against her ribs. She winced and settled back. Blood trickled in a thin line out of the corner of her mouth. Soutien wiped it clean, but more blood appeared.

"What happened?" he whispered. He stroked the gossamer hair at the crown of her head, trying to comfort the dying Fey.

He became aware of a presence behind him and knew that Aidan had disobeyed. He ignored the other man, concentrating on Elin.

"Amadan-na-Briona," she said. Her voice gained volume as anger lent her strength. Her ice blue eyes sparkled with passion. "He came as you, Lord. We saw through his disguise within moments, of course, but it was long enough to distract the guards." She paused to take a few shallow breaths. "They were all around. They were in the trees..."

"But..." *But you have wings*, he wanted to say. *Why didn't you fly away?* The words died on his tongue as his gaze unwittingly strayed to the torn, bloody membrane on the shoulder blade he could see.

"It was the Unseelie Court, Lord," said Elin, as if hearing his thoughts. The light left her eyes and she began to weep. "The winged ones. Please forgive me, my lord. We tried to protect her, to keep her from them—" She took a long, shuddery breath. It sounded liquid. "We failed."

"Elin," he whispered, suddenly not trusting his voice. "You have nothing to be forgiven. I..." He was about to ask for her forgiveness for putting her and her kin into danger when he suddenly realized that her eyes were staring at him unseeingly and her chest no longer moved.

Dead. All dead. Because he had set aside his duty once too often. He had betrayed the O'Rourkes, his king, and now the winged ones who had sworn allegiance to him. All for the love of Moira.

For her, he postponed his duty to the king. For her, he delayed looking for Mack and Aidan. For her, he risked the lives of the Fey.

He stood up. Behind him, Aidan breathed heavily and Soutien knew the young man was reliving his own personal nightmare. But the guilt, rage, and grief that filled Soutien left no room for compassion.

Without another word, he set out through the corpse-strewn glade, heading for Knockma.

❧ TWENTY-SIX ❧

WIND buffeted Moira's dangling body, ballooning up her T-shirt and roaring in her ears. The world below rushed by, a blur to her wind-stung eyes. She had an impression of trees, and flashes of lakes like dark diamonds in the moonlight. The sight made her dizzy.

Looking up was even worse. She'd caught only a glimpse of talons and a huge, furred body before the creature carried her off by the shoulders. Now she had a good view of the vast, leathery wings and the all-too-human head that swiveled down to leer at her. She fought down terror and nausea, concentrating on the pain in her shoulders.

Pain was good.

Pain kept her from thinking about the winged Fey, impaled on the trees.

The creature adjusted its hold and almost dropped her, tearing a scream out of her.

"You son of a bitch!" she shouted, more angry than frightened. In answer, the creature dipped down and Moira quickly pulled up her knees to keep her legs from smashing into the tops of the trees.

The creature laughed, a high liquid sound suggestive of ravens.

Leaves whipped the soles of her shoes and an upthrust branch scraped her hip. She twisted away from it, causing the creature's talons to pinch her armpits.

Moira cursed her captor with words she had left behind at boot camp. She tried clawing at its body, just out of reach of her hands.

Then something nipped at her heels and she yelped in surprise. It came again, a sharp pain like a needle thrust in her Achilles tendon. She twisted to look down and almost moaned in dismay. The flying monsters from the Fey camp had caught up and now surrounded her, blotting out the trees below. They came in all sizes, from the big one that tirelessly carried her to ones no bigger than a bat. All seemed to have teeth.

A dozen of the smaller ones surrounded her, nipping at her heels and legs and pinching her arms and buttocks with their claws. She swore at them and tried to kick them away. Her flailing feet never connected and she grew increasingly frantic as the small creatures, emboldened by her failure, stepped up their attack. A particularly nasty bite on her calf drove Moira past the edge of caring. With a roar of rage, she bucked and twisted, lashing out at her tormentors.

To her amazement, her right shoulder came free. With a sickening lurch, she plummeted, dragging her off-balance captor with her. It screamed at the smaller creatures and they fell back. Then it frantically beat the air to regain altitude, dragging her by one shoulder.

But she had one hand free now. Ignoring the tears streaming down her face, she forced her cold, stiff body to turn in mid-air. Her left shoulder screamed in protest but she clamped her teeth over the pain. Grabbing one of the claws still holding her, she glanced down. The lake was right below her.

She yanked with all her strength on the claw and a small bone gave way. The monster screamed in pain and released her.

Arms flailing as if that would slow her fall, Moira searched past her pointing feet for the glimmer of water.

It wasn't there.

"Oh shit!"

She had misjudged the size of the lake and was going to smash up against the rocky shore. Struggling against gravity, she forced her body into a tuck before she could hit the hard ground now less than twenty feet below.

Then a sharp claw raked her back and talons clamped onto her belt, digging into her flesh and tearing a scream of mingled fear and pain out of her. Above her, great leathery wings beat the air, slowing her fall.

The monster's cries of anger merged with her own screams as she dangled helplessly, watching the killing ground rushing up at her. She glimpsed an open flame and dark figures standing still, then she was falling again, abruptly released. She fell ten feet, landed on a mossy patch by the lake, and rolled to her feet, ready to fight.

Blood pounded in her ears as she waited for an attack that didn't come. Instead, the night air filled with cries and the sound of beating wings as the winged creatures converged on the camp.

Moira took a deep breath and examined her surroundings while she could. Less than thirty feet away, dark winged figures joined the wingless shadows hovering by the campfire. The Unseelie.

The attack had come so fast... One moment she was sleeping, the next she was on her feet, fighting for her life. Only her life wasn't in danger—at least not immediately. But the little winged ones... She blinked rapidly, chasing away the grief. There was no time for that now. Nor was this the time to wonder about Soutien, who was nowhere to be seen during the attack.

In the center of the assembled creatures stood a man. He seemed to be listening as monster after monster landed next to him, spoke briefly, and was dismissed—a general taking field reports.

Moira studied him carefully in the firelight, frowning. There was something odd about him. He was short and extremely wide, so wide he was out of proportion. A sleeveless tunic bared his massive shoulders and powerful arms. He wore pants that went down to his muscular calves. His feet were bare and filthy and his hands were huge.

He turned to study the sky and Moira blinked. Viewed from the side, he looked two-dimensional, like a sheet of paper, impossible to keep in perspective. He shimmered in the firelight, his form wavering and uncertain.

Then he turned toward her and for the first time since waking up to the confusion of battle, Moira felt true fear. She looked into his eyes and felt the world pitch toward oblivion.

The trembling started in the pit of her stomach and traveled out to her limbs. She was going into shock. She sat down abruptly to keep from fainting.

The wide man approached her, his entourage following with a rustling of claws, wings, and paws.

From the man came a smell of compost, of damp, turned earth, of algae-rich ponds. His was the smell she had encountered on the first night in this strange place.

The monsters ranged themselves around Moira in a threatening circle. She swallowed, aware of hard eyes staring at her.

Stay calm, she told herself. *Stay calm. They haven't killed you yet, so they want something.*

As silence descended on the camp, Moira began to hear other sounds—water lapping at the shoreline, the crackling of the fire, the hooting of a faraway owl. She became aware of the almost overwhelming stench of the creatures surrounding her, a stench like that of an animal den after a long, hard winter.

She was cold. She knew it was a symptom of shock, but couldn't give in to it. Showing weakness would mean her death.

Taking a deep breath, she got to her feet again, fighting to suppress her trembling. If she was going to die, she would do it on her feet, not cowering on the ground.

And she would take some of them with her.

Ignoring the menace of the creatures, she faced the wide man. They stared at each other for a long moment. He spoke first.

"You are a female of Kirwan blood." His tone was certain.

Moira allowed one eyebrow to rise. "Really? And how did you arrive at that conclusion?"

The wide man looked at her, his expression mild. "You smell like Kirwan."

Moira examined him openly. His face was like a cliff come to life, all blunt and craggy, as though the sculptor hadn't had time to finesse the work. She couldn't tell what color his eyes were, but they had a hypnotic quality. She avoided staring into them too long.

His hair was a black tangle of twigs and leaves. She wasn't sure, but she thought she caught the glitter of small eyes staring at her from the cover of snarled hair.

He was wide, so wide that it made her flesh crawl. And suddenly, she knew that this was Amadan-na-Briona. As wild and as wide as a hill, Will had said. Yes, she thought now, that was exactly right. There was something about the creature standing before her that made her think of the beginning of time.

She raised her chin and looked him in the eye, refusing to show fear. "What do you want?"

Amadan cocked that massive head as if to study her from a different angle. The circle beyond them shifted as creatures began to murmur. Almost at once, she broke eye contact. Looking into his eyes was too much like dying.

"Child," he said gently.

She glanced at him again. This time his eyes contained galaxies. She swallowed and turned away.

"You will be that which lures Kirwan's son," murmured Amadan. Bait.

It rankled, this role of hostage. She hadn't liked it with Cathel, and she hated it with this creature. But she was under no illusions. She would live as long as Amadan thought she would be useful to him. Not a moment longer.

She plastered a cool look on her face, though she still avoided looking at him. "Protection, you mean," she said crisply. "My brother and Soutien are going to come looking for me."

"Unlikely. One Kirwan is already at Knockma. And Soutien leads another to Fin Bheara as we speak." He breathed deeply, and Moira heard gales. "Fin Bheara will not allow them to leave, once they are within his walls."

If that was true, how did he hope to use her as bait?

Will—and presumably Grace—was safe. Somehow, Soutien had found Aidan and was bringing him to join Will. The last time she had seen Soutien, they had been settling down for a rest in the Fey camp. Then she'd awakened to battle and Soutien was gone.

Now that her brothers and Grace were safe, Soutien would come looking for her. Even if Fin Bheara kept Will from coming, Soutien would come.

A niggle of doubt pried apart her certainty. Soutien's loyalty wasn't necessarily to her. He had needed to get Will and Aidan to Knockma for this mysterious task of the king's. He didn't need to risk himself again.

But... he had risked everything for her, risked Will's safety, ignored Aidan's danger, to stay with her as Cathel's prisoner.

Only to leave her alone with the little winged ones. Maybe he had come to his senses. Or maybe, something bigger than his feelings for her had drawn him away.

Then she remembered his face as he looked at her, the feel of his arms around her, the warmth of his breath on her ear.

He would come.

She looked at Amadan, but he was studying the sky again. The flying monsters had all landed or were roosting in the nearby trees. The stars grew paler as night slowly gave way to dawn. An owl hooted close by and a frog called to its kin on the far side of the lake. Moira considered making a dash for the water, then thought better of it. Even if Amadan's dominion didn't extend below the water, where would she go?

Assuming she could even get to the water.

And assuming she had enough strength left to swim. Her face throbbed from ramming into the tree and her shoulder hurt. Blood still trickled from the bite on her calf. And she had been dropped ten feet—she didn't feel those bruises yet, but she would.

The wiry hair on Amadan's head waved in the non-existent breeze. A long, pale tail peeked out of the tangle, only to whip back in.

"Why do you want to kill Fin Bheara?" she demanded, stalling for time. "What has he done that you should want him dead?"

And suddenly the creatures around her melted away. Some took to the skies and some slithered away, but most scampered toward the nearest trees.

Moira whirled to see what had alarmed them, but there was nothing. Within seconds, she was alone with Amadan. With trepidation, she looked at him.

He stood very still, staring at her. His eyes were dark whirling clouds that threatened to suck her in. She swayed, dizzy, and struggled to look away. Finally, she placed her hands over her eyes.

"You are so fragile," whispered Amadan. His voice was far away, yet all around her. "You live such short lives, and know nothing of what makes life worth living. You are brutish and lack elegance. And yet, we need you." He was the wind now, his voice a caress in her ear. "We need your primitive vigor, you base energies to replenish our life force. We are dying. Fin Bheara should never have brought us to this time."

Startled, Moira opened her eyes but kept her gaze on the ground. Amadan was no nearer, but she felt his presence like a pulse in her veins. His smell was much stronger now, almost overwhelming.

"What do you mean?" She had to force the words out past the dizziness. "What do you mean, 'to this time'?"

Amadan moved closer and Moira instinctively stepped back. She couldn't let him touch her.

"You have no idea, do you?" he marveled, coming to a stop.

Moira glanced up and breathed a sigh of relief. The swirling clouds were gone, leaving behind only dark eyes. They filled with something suspiciously like pity.

"No," said Moira, deciding instantly to be honest. "I *have* no idea. Tell me."

Amadan turned toward the east again, obviously judging how much time he had. Moira blinked rapidly, trying to keep him in focus. Whenever he turned sideways, it was as if he stepped into a different dimension where breadth didn't exist.

"Come," he said. "Sit by the fire."

Moira looked at the proffered hand, callused, with thick fingers. It was as wide as three of hers. Ignoring it, she walked toward the fire and sat down as close to it as she dared. The heat leached into her and she immediately started shivering.

Trees rustled with dark life as Amadan approached, but the creatures remained hidden. Amadan walked from side to side, almost lurching, but when he sat down, it was with grace.

"You have been duped," he began abruptly. "I cannot kill Fin Bheara. If it were possible, I would have killed him long since." His cliff face hardened and Moira spoke before she could stop herself.

"But why do you hate him?"

Amadan sat still for a long time. When he finally spoke, there was great bitterness in his voice.

"Because Oonagh loves him."

Oonagh. Fin Bheara's wife. Amadan and Fin Bheara both loved the same woman. The traditional recipe for hatred.

"You hate him," she said finally. "But you can't kill him. So what's this all about?" She waved at the trees where feral eyes gleamed in the dark.

"My army," said Amadan, a trace of irony in his tone, "such as it is." He paused. "So many have died in this time, so many are weak. I must make do with such as these."

Right. "To do what, exactly?"

"To return home," he said softly. "To reclaim our time."

And suddenly the night was full of howls and screeches, sounds so full of pain and anger and Moira jumped up, ready to fight or flee. But the Unseelie Court remained hidden in the trees. After a few moments, Amadan raised a hand and the sound died away.

Unsettled, Moira sat down again.

"You see?" said Amadan gently, flames reflecting in his eyes. "They all want to go home."

"What's stopping you?" said Moira. She had to clear her throat before the words could get out.

"Fin Bheara. He keeps us prisoners of this time."

"You keep saying that," objected Moira, frustration overtaking her caution. "What do you mean, 'this time'?"

Amadan's raised eyebrows implied she was slow, but she kept her chin high. So far, he hadn't made much sense.

"We are in the time before," said Amadan. "How could you not know that?"

At once, the world fell away from Moira and she swayed where she sat. *The time before.* Of course. Of course, the past. Nothing else made sense—the vegetation, the animals, the lack of technology, the absence of any signs of civilization—they were in a past before people came to this part of the continent.

She fought against the dizziness, against the impossibility of Amadan's words. There was no doubting the truth of what he said.

"But... how...?"

"Fin Bheara," said Amadan. "He stands at the juncture of past and present, his existence intricately linked to the two. As long as he lives, we remain trapped in this time."

"But..." None of this made sense. "If you want to go back..." She looked across the flames at the strange creature. "The only way you can go back is if the King dies."

Amadan nodded.

"But you said you don't want to kill him."

Amadan shook his head. "I said I *cannot* kill him. Nor do I want him dead yet." He took a deep, shuddering breath. "Not until my army is ready. Only when I can control humanity shall I return. Soon."

He meant every word. Even if he was insane, there was something too raw about him, too powerful to ignore.

"But you can't kill him..."

And then Amadan smiled a terrible smile, full of secret amusement and alien cruelty.

"No. But Kirwan's son can."

And before Moira could make sense of his cryptic words, he rose to his feet.

"Rest while you can. At sunset we march on Knockma."

❧ TWENTY-SEVEN ❦

GRACE slowly became aware that she was standing by a tall, narrow window. Far below, late afternoon sunlight glinted off waves like molten silver. The slanted light merged sea and sky until she couldn't tell where one began and the other ended.

She was rubbing her side.

Frowning, she let her hand fall. The ache in her side nagged at her, prodded her...

Like air filling a vacuum, memory came rushing back. Her side ached because her ribs had been *broken*. She shook her head, trying to make sense of her memories. She remembered the feel of ribs poking into internal organs as she crept toward Red Cap. She remembered the taste of her own blood, the ringing in her ears as her head struck the tree and she struggled to remain conscious.

She remembered Will. And phookas.

And nothing else.

She glanced down, staring in bemusement at the curve of her white breasts pushing against the tight brocade bodice of her gown. The skirt and sleeves were a deep green and made of heavy silk. The low bodice was stiff and cut straight across her breasts, with a dark swirling pattern of blues and greens. A lovely dress.

She wondered how she'd gotten into it.

A moist breeze caressed her cheek, lofting the scent of salt and seaweed up to her. She struggled against panic, scouring her memory.

She had been badly hurt, maybe even dying. She remembered Will's voice telling her to hang on. Then everything was like a series of still pictures: Red Cap's tusks, a phooka's flashing hooves, flying Fey, a castle by the sea.

The last memory helped calm her trembling. Knockma. She must be in Knockma.

But... Again her hand found her ribs. They had been *broken*...

She was in a small round room with one door. The floor was stone and tapestries depicting hunting scenes hung on the walls. A rectangular table made of some pale wood, perhaps oak, two stools, a bed, and a chest at the foot of the bed almost filled the room. The bed alone was huge, with four posts and a tall frame from which were suspended more tapestries. It would have to be *very* cold before she would willingly entomb herself inside all those tapestries.

Beyond the bed, half hidden, was a small fireplace. At the sight, Grace's legs almost gave way. She reached for the stone window sill to steady herself.

There had been a fireplace just like that one in Red Cap's tower room.

"Will?" The name escaped her in a whisper of trepidation.

As if on cue, a soft knock sounded and the door opened to admit a Fey woman.

The woman's eyebrows rose when she looked at Grace and for a moment, a memory parted Grace's swirling confusion. She had seen that same face leaning over her, concerned. Then more memories rushed to the breach: bouts of fever alleviated by a kind hand and a wet cloth, a parched throat eased by a sip of cool water, a nightmare banished at the touch of a gentle hand.

And surrounding all the images was a sense of time passing.

"You are Tivane," said Grace, as the name surfaced.

The woman nodded with a small smile. She wore a yellow tabard over a green tunic and leggings, and short boots on her feet.

Grace raised the hem of her gown to peer at her own feet. She wore the brown man's shoes. The sight reassured her and gave her a measure of self-confidence. She could run if she had to.

Then she wondered how long she had been wearing them.

"My lord is ready," said Tivane.

"Ready for what?" asked Grace, startled. "And what lord?"

Tivane's smile deepened, reaching her green eyes. "King Fin Bheara awaits you in the Great Hall."

Fin Bheara. Of course—this was Knockma, after all.

"Where's Will?" Grace tried to keep the tremor out of her voice, but couldn't keep from studying the other woman's face intently.

"He is well," said Tivane, answering the question Grace was afraid to ask. Then she turned and led the way back out the door.

Grace stared at the empty doorway for a long moment before following her.

They walked along hallways covered in rich tapestries that muffled their steps and past unexpected balconies with stone balustrades.

They met no one, no one sweeping that meticulously clean floor, no one coming out of the closed doors they passed. The air itself seemed still, and yet shimmery at the same time. Grace concentrated on Tivane's back, wondering if she was still sick.

She didn't feel sick, only disoriented.

Her hand twitched and she controlled an urge to feel her ribs again. Somehow, she had lost at least six weeks of her life while her ribs healed. Maybe longer—she had no idea how long it took internal organs to heal.

With the thought came realization. If King Fin Bheara could place the Fey world in a small pocket outside of time, he could certainly place her in a different pocket, giving her time to heal.

The thought made her shiver—had six weeks been stolen from her, or had she been granted an extra six weeks?

Gradually, she realized she could hear the sound of many voices, muted as if by distance, with the occasional strain of music from stringed instruments. Somewhere in Knockma, a great many people were gathered.

Finally, Tivane stopped and waited for Grace. The sound of laughter and music was louder here. It came from the end of the hallway, where Grace could see the top of a stairway.

"Are you ready?" Tivane's voice was like the breeze sighing through grass.

No, thought Grace, but she nodded. They walked side by side down the length of the hallway until they reached the top of the stairs.

Tivane waited patiently while Grace took in the tableau. A hundred richly clad figures milled around an enormous, rectangular room stretching from the foot of the stairs. The room seemed to comprise a separate wing of the keep.

Tivane slowly descended, giving Grace time to absorb the swirl of Fey around tables laden with food and drink. A few winged Fey flitted from one table to another. Musicians circulated through the crowd, filling the room with sweet music. She saw what looked like lutes and a miniature harp. Somewhere in the crowd, someone played a flute.

Grace's foot found the first step. One hand automatically raised the hem of her gown to keep from tripping.

She stared uneasily at the bright clothing, the flashing jewels, the rich wood of the tables and chairs. Blinking, she tried to focus past the blurring of her eyes.

Tivane waited for her at the foot of the stairs and Grace focused on her. Then, halfway down, she realized that the assembly had grown quiet.

She looked up to see a hundred pale Fey faces turned toward her. She swallowed and concentrated on not tripping. Finally, she reached the main floor.

Tivane smiled reassuringly, but said nothing. She turned and stepped into the Great Hall, leaving Grace to follow. Taking a deep breath, Grace raised her chin and, keeping her gaze on Tivane's slender back, followed.

The assembly parted in solemn silence, leaving a wide aisle bordered by tall, silent Fey men and women. Grace darted a glance to either side. On every face was a mixture of wonder and gravity.

Their reaction so unsettled her that her gaze dropped to the floor, which was laid in thousands of tiny round pebbles set in mortar. All blurry.

Murmurs sprang up in her passage. These Fey spoke the same musical tongue as Cathel's tree-dwelling dé Danann. It sounded like water rippling over stones.

Then Tivane stopped, and stepped aside. Grace looked up and

found herself face-to-face with King Fin Bheara.

He sat on a throne of stone, stark with lack of adornment. His fine, pale red hair flowed down his shoulders in thick waves, held back from his forehead with a thin band of gold. The hair contrasted sharply with his clothing which, though black from shoulder to sole, was richly detailed with black embroidery at hem, collar, and sleeve. Even sitting down, he easily dwarfed every Fey in the room.

He looked at her. The stillness in which he encompassed her excluded everything and everyone in the room. Grace forgot to breathe as his eyes searched hers, delving deep into her, examining her weaknesses, appraising her strengths.

Then those heavy-lidded eyes blinked and she was released.

She almost stumbled, but the brown man's shoes came to her rescue. As the noise level of the assembled Fey began to rise again, she resumed breathing.

"You are the one named Grace." Fin Bheara's voice rumbled out of his barrel chest like thunder on a cloudless day. "An apt name."

Grace blushed. She forced herself to meet the king's cool gaze and inclined her head slightly in acknowledgement of the compliment.

"Where is Will?" she asked.

Fin Bheara might as well have been made of the same stone as his throne. Then one golden-red brow rose. "No time for pleasantries, I see."

Humor threaded his voice and warmth kindled in his eyes. For the first time, Grace had the feeling that he was really seeing her, *her*, not the bundle of mistakes and abilities that made her up.

She hesitated, wondering how best to approach this man, this being. Then she shrugged mentally. She had no patience or desire for finesse. She wanted answers.

"Forgive my impatience, my lord," she said. "I need answers." Her hand strayed to her ribs and again the sense of unreality washed over her. "How long have I been here?"

The sudden silence made her turn. The long aisle down which she had walked with Tivane had filled in with revelers. And right now, they were all looking at Fin Bheara.

She turned back to Fin Bheara, wondering if she had said something rude. The king rose and stood staring at the Fey. Grace couldn't read his expression. Then he looked down at her.

"Come, child," he said. As if commanded, she rested her hand on his like a leaf on a lake. He was the biggest man she had ever seen. He towered over her, close to seven feet tall, and although she could sense the immense age of him, he stood straight and moved with the grace of a young man.

Without another word, he led her behind the throne to a plain wooden door banded in copper. As he pushed it open, Grace glanced over her shoulder. Tivane wasn't among the many faces turned toward her. Then a shadow caught her eye and she looked up at the ceiling, only to find that there was none. She gazed uncomprehendingly at the sky, where a lone cloud crossed the sun's path to cast a shadow on the room.

"Oh!" she said. Then she was through the doorway and into a much smaller, plainer room. Fin Bheara closed the door with his free hand and waited patiently as she stared in wonder at the open sky above them.

"How...?" She turned to look at Fin Bheara.

"A simple matter," he said, shrugging. "I did not wish a roof over my head."

"But... why...?"

His expression turned grim.

"I am confined to these walls," he said. "I can no longer roam the world as I see fit. But this much of the world comes to me."

He released her hand and walked to the center of the room, into a shaft of sunlight. Grace stared at him. Confined?

And then she remembered Soutien's whispered tale on the tree platform. Fin Bheara stood at the juncture of past and present. Only his presence kept the time streams touching. And Knockma was where he chose to stand his ground and wrestle with time.

Pity swelled in her as she watched him stride to a small sideboard. He kept all the Fey world safe, at the cost of his own freedom.

Fin Bheara picked up a tray with two goblets and a pitcher and carried it to a low table by two stools. On it was a chess set, all the pieces in their starting positions.

"Do you play?" he asked, looking at her from beneath luxuriant eyebrows. For the first time, she noticed that his eyes were gray. It didn't surprise her, even if almost every Fey she had met in this place had had green eyes. Clearly, Fin Bheara was no ordinary Fey.

"No." Grace shook her head. His face filled with such disappointment that she impulsively added, "But I could learn."

King Fin Bheara, lord of the Fey, grinned like a child and gestured her to one of the stools.

"Sit, Lady Grace, and I shall introduce you to a game fit for kings and varlets."

Grace smiled at his enthusiasm. She sat down, arranging her skirts around her as best she could.

The chess set was simple, the details suggested rather than implicit. The board, too, consisted of simple lines and paint.

"You do not approve of my board?" asked Fin Bheara. He placed the tray on the table next to the chess set and handed her a goblet.

She accepted it with a smile. "No, it's not that. It's just nice to see something clearly." She looked around the room with its simple furnishings, then at the king. "You, too," she said. "In the other room, everything was blurry."

Fin Bheara stared at her for a moment, then sat down opposite. "You see the glamour," he said. "Here, there is none. I choose not to hide behind a veil of trickery."

"But why can I see it?" asked Grace. Cathel had covered himself with a glamour. His feast, too, had been covered with glamour, yet Will and Moira had seen nothing.

Fin Bheara smiled at her. "You must have Fey blood," he said. At Grace's skeptical expression, he continued. "It was not unusual, in the days before we came here, for the two races to... mingle."

Heat rose in Grace's cheeks. Fin Bheara watched her in amusement. His eyes seemed darker suddenly, as though a fire smoldered beneath. He really was a very attractive man and his size made her feel...

Abruptly she caught herself and frowned. What was she doing, succumbing to this one's charm like a schoolgirl?

"I don't mean to be rude, King Fin Bheara," she said firmly, returning the goblet to the tray without taking a sip, "but I must know where Will is."

Another man might have frowned in annoyance at her abruptness, but Fin Bheara gazed at her steadily, as if gauging the true extent of her need. Finally, he nodded.

"He is well and in another part of the keep."

"I want to see him." *More than anything.*

But Fin Bheara shook his head. "Nay, child. Not yet. His time is coming soon enough." The grimness in his voice abruptly reminded Grace of Will's task. She shivered.

"Is it true, then? Do you really expect him to kill you?"

This time, Fin Bheara's eyebrows rose in surprise at her bluntness. Then he smiled. "This I have missed most about humans," he said. "The fearless use of words."

By that, Grace assumed he meant talking before thinking. But he still hadn't answered her question. Before she could open her mouth to repeat herself, he continued.

"Yes, it is true." All trace of levity disappeared from his face. Although he still sat straight on the stool, Grace could almost feel a great weight settle on his shoulders. "If he is the eldest Kirwan son, then he must slay me."

For a moment, the years lay etched in Fin Bheara's face like ghostly scars. Then he took a deep drink from the goblet, shattering the illusion.

Grace stared at him, her hands clasped in her lap. "My lord..." She couldn't believe that someone—Will—would have to murder this man in order to save two peoples. "Is there no other way?"

Giving up on chess, Fin Bheara rose slowly to his feet. He looked tired. He walked over to a window and stared out, straight and tall as a tree trunk.

"Would that there were," he said, his voice so low Grace had to strain to hear him. "But death is the price of my arrogance."

Then he glanced over his shoulder at her and smiled rakishly. "And in my youth, my arrogance knew no bounds."

"But surely..."

He raised a hand to silence her, still with his back to her. Grace didn't even question her immediate obedience. Finally, he turned to face her.

"This is necessary. Not wished, but necessary. The irony, Lady Grace, is that I brought the Fey here to save them. Instead, I only caused our slow demise."

Grace stood up. There had to be another way. She couldn't see death as a solution to anything. All it would do was turn Will into a murderer and deprive the world of Fin Bheara. And if he didn't, he would condemn the Fey to a slow death. Neither option was bearable.

"Won't the Fey be in danger when they return to Earth—to the present?" She tried to put into words her worries. "The world is so different than when you first came here. There is metal—iron—everywhere. Very few wild places are left, and the authorities..." *The authorities will hunt you down, she finished silently. They'll never leave you alone, once they discover you. And they will discover you.*

Fin Bheara's grave expression deepened as he listened to her. When she finished, he nodded slowly.

"True. There is grave danger in returning. But there is certain death in remaining."

The deference she'd felt evaporated. "Do you want to die?" she asked in exasperation. "Can't you at least *try* to find a solution?"

He frowned, and suddenly he was the king again. The look he gave her mingled anger and contempt. Grace caught her breath and took a step back. Then his expression softened.

"No, child. I do not wish to die." He crossed his arms. "I have tried for centuries to find a different solution," he said finally. "By refusing to accept the fate I had crafted for myself, I may have caused the death of both humanity and the Fey."

A chill coursed through Grace and she shivered. Surely not...

As though she spoke aloud, Fin Bheara reached for her hand and led her to a plain wooden chair built to accommodate his size. He gently pushed her into it. It was hard and uncomfortable, but Grace perched on the edge of the seat and watched him as he began to pace.

"I met my first Kirwan many hundreds of years ago. I had taken to bed the beautiful bride of Diarmud, Lord of Kirwan. He accused me of kidnapping her, but the lovely Siobhan had come willingly."

Grace couldn't help herself. "Weren't you married to Oonagh?"

Fin Bheara looked at her strangely. "Indeed. How is that important?"

Grace stared back at him, nonplussed. Finally she shrugged. "If it wasn't important to her, I guess it's not important to me."

Fin Bheara stared a moment longer as if trying to decipher her meaning.

"In any case. Kirwan chased us to my home and threatened to dig up my barrow and ring the pit with iron if I did not relinquish his bride.

"I was impressed with the human's courage, but his behavior was outrageous. If I did not accept his challenge, every human male within miles would see fit to attack me. Therefore, I accepted, but added a wager: If I won, I kept the woman. If Kirwan won, he could name his prize."

Grace's eyebrows rose at this cavalier treatment of women, but she bit her tongue on a scathing remark. It was more important to hear the rest of the story than to vent her outrage.

"I was very sure of myself," continued Fin Bheara. "Too sure, perhaps." He grinned again. "You will recall I mentioned a certain arrogance... Kirwan was big and strong, and his sword contained iron. We battled for three days and three nights."

Here Fin Bheara's step faltered. He clasped his hands behind his back and looked thoughtfully down at the slate floor. "At the end of three days and three nights," he finally continued, "Kirwan won. He claimed his prize: his bride, prosperity for himself and his descendants, and the power to kill me, if they so chose, for himself and his descendants."

Fin Bheara looked up at Grace with a lopsided grin. "Kirwan was not only strong, he was shrewd. He had earned my enmity, and knew it. He wanted some assurance of his descendants' safety. Not to mention his own."

Grace stared at the king, overwhelmed.

Fin Bheara resumed his pacing. "I agreed to the first two conditions but refused the third." The king's eyebrows rose at some private memory. "Kirwan was stubborn—almost as stubborn as I was. Tired as he was, he picked up his sword to do battle again. So did I." He sighed and looked up at the sky. Long shadows had crept into his study while he talked. He flicked his fingers and in the wall sconces, half a dozen small torches lit, bathing the room in the warm glow of firelight.

Grace was beyond wonder. The part of her mind that still noted these things acknowledged that lighting torches without benefit of touching them was cool. The rest of her concentrated on Fin Bheara's words.

"Who knows how long we would have fought had Oonagh not stepped in."

Here the king stopped pacing, stopped moving altogether. He stood looking at the far wall, lost in private memory. A flicker of pain crossed that broad, craggy face.

"Oonagh reminded me that I had given my word." Here the king smiled wryly. "She was always good at reminding me of my obligations."

He resumed pacing, but this time there was tension in his step, and his words came faster.

"She decreed that I would have to live by my word—with two caveats. Kirwan's power over me would reside in only one person at a time—the eldest Kirwan male. And to show his good faith, Kirwan was to agree, on his own behalf and that of his descendants, to come to my aid when I called."

He stopped by the window once again and leaned against the sill, half-turned away from her.

"Oonagh swore her own oath—to be guarantor of our pact. She swore that as long as I lived, and as long as a Kirwan came at my call, the Kirwan clan would be wealthy."

The setting sun turned his red hair into a halo of blazing fire. A cool breeze swept through the room and Grace shivered. She tucked her feet under her, nestling herself far back into the seat as she waited for Fin Bheara to continue. After a moment, he shook himself.

"Kirwan prospered. Although we never liked each other, he was true to his word and passed on to his children the terms of our pact."

Grace's thoughts returned to her first morning in this time, when

Moira told her the story of her family's connection to Fin Bheara.

"Something got lost over the generations," she said slowly. Fin Bheara turned to look at her. "The O'Rourkes—the descendants of the first Kirwan—forgot the reasons behind the pact, even parts of the pact itself." She looked at the king, who stared back.

"I felt no need to remind them of the power they held over me," he said.

"And Soutien...?"

"Oonagh's idea. He is our adopted son, of a human woman and a Fey man. Oonagh sent him to be our eyes and ears in the Kirwan home. He came to care deeply for the Kirwan family. He keeps them— kept them—safe, as much with good counsel as with Fey magic."

The image of Mack's funeral pyre suddenly imposed itself and Grace caught her breath, fighting tears. First Mack, then Aidan wandering the woods, out of his mind... certainly dead by now. Will was safe, but where was Moira? Centuries of caring and looking after the Kirwans, and later the O'Rourkes, only to see them die...

Oh, Soutien.

"So you see," continued the king softly, standing before her, "I must die."

Grace blinked away the tears, a small part of her wondering how he had moved from the window without her noticing. A fleeting thought crossed her mind and she latched onto it desperately.

"But Oonagh isn't truly dead," she pointed out. "She came to Will in Grozny. Can't you...?" She swallowed the rest of her words at Fin Bheara's expression. He placed a hand on either arm of the chair and leaned in toward her.

"He *saw* Oonagh?"

Grace nodded jerkily. "In Grozny. She brought him here...."

The king closed his eyes. Pain suffused his expression and the muscles in his arms and shoulders tensed as if to keep him from falling.

"She appears to my slayer, but not to me."

Grace's heart almost broke at the anguish in his voice. "But... when you cross over... won't you be with her?"

Fin Bheara straightened as if he were made of stone and every movement pained him. He finally looked down at her.

"I cannot cross over. When Kirwan named as his prize the power of life and death over me, I lost the ability to cross over. When Will, son of Kirwan, slays me, I will die."

Only then did the impact of Fin Bheara's loss hit Grace. She stared in dismay at the man before her. He had been immortal. He had foolishly given his immortality away, and for what? A woman? No, worse than that. For pride. Arrogance.

And warring with her contempt was pity. How terrible. To know you could have spent all of eternity with the one you love only to have that snatched away because of your own folly.

An abrupt knock at the door scattered her thoughts.

Fin Bheara barked out a word and turned to face the newcomer as the door opened. It was Tivane.

The Fey woman bowed to Fin Bheara, then looked up, her expression one of deep excitement and fear.

"My lord," she said English, in deference to Grace, "Amadan-na-Briona approaches. He is less than an hour's march away."

Grace looked up at the sky, past the missing roof. The sky was suffused in red, umber, and indigo. It was sunset.

**

For the tenth time in as many days, Will emptied his backpack on the table and examined its contents.

An empty water bottle. A rain poncho. A small bag of trail mix. A space blanket. A broken camera. A pair of light running shoes. A container of matches. A comb. A heavy sweater. Shorts. A seriously depleted first aid kit.

No rope. No hatchet. Not even his Swiss Army knife.

With a snarl of frustration, he stuffed everything back in his pack and threw it against the wall.

Ten days!

As soon as he had regained his strength, the Fey woman stopped coming with his food. Instead, a tray would appear on the floor outside his door twice a day. He kept the door open, trying to catch whoever brought it, but no matter how fast he was, there was never anybody in the hallway. The tray seemed to appear between one blink and the next.

And no matter how often he explored the hallways, or which direction he took on leaving his room, he always found himself back where he had started.

Even the windows were too narrow for him to crawl out. He stalked over to one and glared at the sliver of sea turning red beyond the coastline.

If he had to spend another night in this damned place, he would tear it down, stone by bloody stone.

Controlling a strong urge to shout in frustration, Will slapped the unforgiving stone, as if he could force it to give up its secrets.

At that moment, the floor beneath him shifted. He lost his balance and had to clutch the window embrasure to keep from falling. He blinked hard as the air before his eyes wavered. Just as suddenly, it stopped.

"What the hell...?" His voice sounded too loud. Was that an earthquake?

He spun on his heel and ran to the door. It crashed into the wall with the force of his pull. Only then did he hear the murmur of noise.

What had been so far a silent, ghostly prison now hummed with sound. Fey voices formed the background with, every now and then, a voice crying out what seemed to be an order. The clang of metal and the drumming of hurrying feet filled Will with a sense of urgency.

The hallway was empty. He turned left and followed the voices until he reached a balcony overlooking a great room. A hall. It, too, was empty.

And yet, all around him, he felt the rush of air as people hurried by on urgent errands. Voices rose from the deserted hall like ghosts from the past.

He stepped back against the cold stone wall, unnerved, and the hairs at the back of his neck rose.

"Will!"

He spun toward the voice, relief and hope replacing the dread.

"Grace!" He looked around the deserted hallway. "Where are you?"

"Will!" she cried again and he backed into one of the pillars supporting the balcony. Her voice was so close he should have been able to see her. Then the stone wall at the end of the hallway dissolved like mist and Grace stepped through. Behind her, what had been a solid wall was now a staircase leading down.

"How—?" began Will. He took a good look at her and closed his mouth.

She wore a long dress with a stiff bodice that revealed a whole lot of breast. Her hair was clean and shiny. It was held away from her face by what looked like tiny woven chains of gold and silver, leaving the rest of it to fall loose. With her hair back like that, her cheekbones seemed higher, more aristocratic. Or maybe that was the effect of the dress.

She stopped a few feet in front of him. For a moment longer, Will stood staring at her.

"Where the hell have you been?" The words spilled out of him in accusation, when what he really wanted to do was shout in relief that she was safe.

Her eyebrows rose along with her color. "Trying to find you."

"For ten *days*?"

With a frown, she shook her head. "What are you talking about? I just woke up a couple of hours ago."

Will laughed raggedly. "Well, I've been awake a hell of a lot longer. And I've been trapped here."

"They kept you prisoner?" said Grace, obviously aghast.

He nodded, suddenly wanting to touch her to make sure she was real. She looked healthy and strong. Surely it would have taken more than ten days to heal her.

"Until you showed up," he continued, "all I could see were walls. I couldn't get out of here."

Grace looked at him oddly. "Why didn't you use the camera?"

For a moment, he stared at her, at a loss. Then he remembered. At the lake, looking for a way to Red Cap's castle, he had peered through the camera lens to find the enchanted rowboat.

"Somebody threw me in a pond," he pointed out. "The camera's ruined." No need to mention that it hadn't even occurred to him.

Grace looked embarrassed, then she shrugged, causing an interesting ripple effect. Will dragged his gaze back to her face. For the first time, he admitted to himself that he had feared she was dead. He

wished he had hugged her when she first appeared, instead of practically accusing her of hiding from him.

There would be time enough for apologies later. Right now, he
needed to find Fin Bheara, then find Moira, Aidan, and Soutien.

"How do we get out of here?" he asked. "And what's all the commotion?"

Grace stepped up to the balcony and looked down. Now that he
had pointed it out, the noise seemed to abate. He followed Grace's
lead and looked down. A dozen Fey, male and female, ran purposefully across the Great Hall, heading for a door in the far corner. One
called an order. Three separated from the group and headed toward
the barred double doors at the end of the hall, where half a dozen Fey
stood at attention.

All of them wore swords. Some also carried bows and quivers full
of arrows.

The familiar, dreaded thrill coursed through Will.

Battle.

He stared down at the Fey, fascinated. His blood surged with the
promise of action. From far away, he heard Grace say, "The Unseelie
army is coming. They'll be here soon."

"Why couldn't I see them before?" asked Will. He tamped down
the excitement, controlled the twitching in his fingers. "Why couldn't I
see the stairs? Why were you able to get through, and not me?"

Grace sighed. She straightened, keeping her gaze fixed on the
activity below.

"It has something to do with King Fin Bheara," she said. "If I
understand this correctly, he can manipulate time. He brought the
Fey here, to a past before the Europeans came, before there were any
people here."

Will stared at her. He opened his mouth to speak, but she continued.

"It's what he did with us," she said. She glanced at him, at his
arm. "He kept us separate from this "now" while we healed. Your arm
was broken." Her hand stole to her brocade-covered ribs. "I was hurt,
too. I think they saved my life."

Will had a sudden flash of holding Grace on the phooka, trying to keep her from falling. Deep down, he had known she was dying. She had been bleeding internally and he'd been terrified that she, like the tree nymph, would slip away from him.

It would have taken much more than ten days to heal her injuries.

Grace turned her head slightly and studied his expression. A small smile played about her lips.

"Yes. It's a bit much for me, too. But can you think of a better explanation?"

"That doesn't explain the wall." He waved at the staircase behind her. "Why weren't the stairs there before?"

"I think that's glamour," said Grace slowly. "You know, making you see what isn't really there, or making things appear other than how they really are."

"Why didn't it affect you?"

Grace looked embarrassed. "Apparently I have a trace of Fey blood."

After a moment, Will shrugged. "Well." He stopped again and stared at her. Then he shook his head. "Let's go find this Fin Bheara."

The expression on Grace's face became grave.

"There's something you need to know first."

"Can't it wait?" he asked, suddenly impatient to find Fin Bheara now that he was finally free.

"No," she said. There was a determined tilt to her chin, and she looked directly into his eyes. For a moment, she reminded him of Oonagh. "It's Fin Bheara. You have to kill him."

For a split second, Will thought she had lost her mind. Then he looked at her again.

"You'd better explain," he said grimly.

"It's a long story," she warned.

"Then you can explain on the way."

With a nod, she turned and led the way through what had been, until a few minutes ago, a solid wall.

And Grace told him.

Ten minutes later, they reached the top of a steep, narrow tower staircase that ended at a closed door. From the faint light leaking all around it, the door led outside, onto the parapet. Before Grace could push it open, Will placed a hand on her wrist.

"How long have you known?" he asked. His voice was harsh. He didn't care. "When did you find out?"

"The night of Mack's funeral pyre," said Grace. She tugged slightly against his hold, but he didn't release her.

"Just when were you going to tell me?" Two weeks? She had known for two weeks? Even longer for her, apparently.

"I tried to tell you that night," she said. "But we were drugged. After that," she shrugged. "Things happened. There didn't seem to be a right time."

Rage poured through Will like poison. *A right time.* He stared at her, his hand clamped on her wrist, and struggled with the urge to shake her. She had betrayed him, or at the very least used him, just as Soutien and Oonagh had used him. She was no better than them, no better than this Fin Bheara, the cause of all this.

"Will, you're hurting me," said Grace through clenched teeth.

He looked down at her, seeing the dangerous light in her eyes, and released her. What was it about her that drove him past his normal constraints?

Without another word, he pushed past and pulled open the battlement door. He found himself in a small alcove at one corner of the battlements. Two Fey men who had been standing just outside whirled on him with swords raised.

With a whir of wings, three winged Fey swooped in from the battlement and hovered just before his face, bows drawn and cocked.

He glared at them, refusing to raise his hands to show he was unarmed. The Fey glared right back at him, their faces set in grim lines.

Grace slipped past him and stood between him and the Fey. "Fin Bheara?" she asked, directing her question to the Fey on the left.

The winged Fey lowered their bows and the others relaxed. The Fey on the right turned his back, resuming his scan of the sky. The other one pointed down the battlement. This side of the keep was nearly eighty feet long. Every five feet, a tall, slender Fey stood at the battlement, crossbow in hand, aiming outward. Then the wall turned at a sharp angle. Fin Bheara must be on the other side.

Grace nodded her thanks and moved down the parapet. Will followed, throwing another glance over his shoulder. The winged Fey had resumed their aerial patrol of the grounds.

As Will and Grace moved away from the alcove, the wind caught them, flattening their clothes against them. Grace raised the hem of her skirt and leaned into the wind, heading for the corner. Will noticed that she hugged the inside wall of the keep and was startled. He had forgotten her fear of heights. The Fey along the parapet glanced sideways at them as they passed.

The wind dropped abruptly as they turned the corner and Grace straightened, releasing the fabric she had kept bunched up in her fist. She stopped and Will looked up to see what had caught her attention. The sky over the shore was black with birds. Then he looked again as perspective reasserted itself. Not birds. Flying monsters.

He took an instinctive step toward Grace, remembering their last night together and the fear in her body as they pressed against the tree, trying to remain unseen by the Unseelie flying overhead.

But these monsters stayed well away from the keep. Glancing down the battlement walls, Will could see why. Archers stood ready, crossbows resting against the parapet. Halfway down was a small knot of figures, with one towering above the rest.

"Fin Bheara," whispered Grace, almost to herself. She set out toward the tall figure and Will followed closely. Here then was the king of the Fey. The one to whom his family owed allegiance.

The one he was supposed to kill.

Fin Bheara looked up as they approached and the Fey at his side melted back. He stood head and shoulders above the tallest Fey, and a good eight inches over Will.

They reached Fin Bheara and stopped. Grace carefully didn't look over the parapet, keeping her gaze focused on the floor. After a brief glance at her, Will concentrated on the king, who returned his examination with interest.

The king wore black as if it were a uniform. He had one hand on the parapet and the sleeve pulled away from his forearm to reveal old scars.

Battle scars, thought Will. He examined the king's features, noting the fading color in the hair, the firm set to the jaw, the direct gaze.

A small scar started at the left temple and disappeared under his hair. Will glanced at the king's hands. They were huge and hard, with as many calluses as scars. Calluses earned with a sword, thought Will.

"King Fin Bheara," said Grace suddenly, pulling Will out of his examination. "This is William O'Rourke of Kirwan. Will, this is Fin Bheara."

The king's eyes softened as he looked at Grace, but when he turned back to Will, they were hard as stone.

"Are you ready to do your duty, son of Kirwan?" The words were harsh, the look he gave Will unflinching.

Will's own anger rose to meet the king's. He hadn't asked for this damned obligation. Fin Bheara himself had laid that particular burden at the feet of the Kirwan clan. And now he had the nerve to act as if Will were shirking his duty.

Before Will could retort, a Fey came running up to the king, panting.

The king turned and listened as the Fey gave his report. Still furious, Will looked away, hoping the respite would give him a chance to calm down.

"Do you think you could keep your temper under control?" whispered Grace.

He glanced at her, suddenly baffled by conflicting emotions.

"He wants me to *kill* him!" said Will, keeping his voice low. "Don't you think I'm entitled to a little temper?"

A movement on the ground caught his eye and distracted him. At first, he couldn't make out what he was seeing. When it finally registered, he took a sharp breath. Alarmed, Grace moved closer to him and looked down. Her hands clutched at the battlement as if to keep her from flinging herself over.

"Dear God," she murmured.

What he had taken for shadows of trees swaying in the wind were figures milling around at the forest's edge. The trees were full of dark creatures perched on limbs. As he watched, two launched themselves into the air, climbing high into the lurid sky only to swoop down in a mad dive. A cackle of laughter floated on the wind.

Will glanced at the nearest Fey and saw his eyes fixed on the flying creatures. The Fey's hand twitched on the release of his crossbow, but he didn't let fly. The flying monster was out of range.

And then Will saw a solitary figure standing mid-way between the forest and the keep.

"An envoy," said Grace, staring at the same figure. She glanced over her shoulder to where the King still listened to the late arrival. "I have a bad feeling about this."

So did Will. His gaze roved back and forth among the mass of creatures until he found a knot of relatively still figures. One in particular he stared at for a long moment. The distance was too far to be certain and the figure was sitting down... but that dark hair... Then the figure stood up and certainty landed like a block of ice in Will's guts.

"That's Moira," he said.

Grace looked at him, then turned to follow his pointing finger. She squinted against the failing light, then her face paled.

"Oh God, Will," she whispered. "They've got Moira."

"Yes," came Fin Bheara's voice behind them. "They have the girl."

They turned to face the king. His expression was grave but determined.

"We have to get her back," said Will.

Fin Bheara's expression didn't change, but something in his eyes telegraphed his answer before he spoke.

"We cannot. They want you in exchange for her."

"Then I'll go!" said Will. He didn't relish being a prisoner of Amadan and his Unseelie army, but it was infinitely better than knowing Moira was their prisoner.

The king shook his head slowly. "He must not have the second son, else he wouldn't be so desperate to obtain you. Yet, how can he be certain that *I* don't have the second one?" he asked musingly.

Anger rose in Will like a welcome heat after being cold too long. "His name is Aidan."

Fin Bheara looked surprised. "Whose?"

"The 'second son'," snapped Will. "And the eldest was Mack. I've lost one brother to your insanity, maybe two. I'll be damned if I'll lose Moira, too!"

"You have a duty!"

Will laughed, taking a bitter pleasure in the king's outrage. "A centuries-old pledge? That means nothing to me. My duty is to my family, not you."

Fin Bheara's cheeks grew blotchy and his eyes sparked gray fire. "Can't you see, Kirwan, that killing me is the only way to free her?"

"The name's O'Rourke!" said Will. "And it's not my custom to murder people!"

"You come from a long line of warriors," snapped Fin Bheara. "Will you betray them now?"

"Enough!" cried Grace, stepping between the two of them. Her wind-whipped hair flew in her face and she pushed it away with an angry gesture. She opened her mouth to speak, then her eyes widened in astonishment.

Will turned to follow her gaze. There, walking down the battlement, was Soutien. He was naked from the waist up and his face was grim and forbidding. Behind him stumbled Aidan.

Aidan stopped suddenly, reeling in exhaustion. His clothes were ripped and stained. The flesh on his face was scratched and red with wind and old blood where the whiskers didn't hide it. But it was his eyes that caught and held Will's attention.

They were the eyes of a man who had seen too many atrocities. They carried memory like a hunchback carried his hump. Will looked into his brother's eyes and had to control an impulse to step back. Instead, he stepped forward.

"Aidan." He took another step, then another, and then he pulled his brother into his arms and held him with all his might.

The wind poked and prodded at him, digging cold fingers into his flesh. He held Aidan close and said nothing. Aidan's arms crept up and across Will's back and he returned Will's clasp weakly.

"It's all right," said Aidan, his voice a murmur. "Everything will be all right now." He kept repeating it like a mantra while Will kept quiet, fighting the tears. Then he became aware that Soutien was talking to Grace.

"You live," said Soutien, relief threading through his voice. "I am pleased." He looked as if he wanted to hug her. Instead, he turned to Fin Bheara.

"My lord," he said. "The Unseelie are in force, though not as strong as Amadan would have wanted. Cathel's fealty is uncertain. His dé Danann may yet join Amadan." He stopped to take a shaky breath. "My lord, they have the girl, Moira."

At her name, Aidan stiffened and pulled away from Will. His gaze fixed on Soutien. Will turned to look at Fin Bheara.

"You have no reason to keep me now," he said quietly. He was peripherally aware of Grace's soft "no!", but he ignored her. She was safe. Moira wasn't. "I'll go to Amadan. We can exchange prisoners halfway between the keep and his camp."

Fin Bheara turned toward the parapet and pointed outward. "Look there, son of Kirwan." His deep voice was pitched almost too low for Will to hear over the wind. "Do you see them?"

Will stepped up to the parapet next to the king and looked. Against the darkening sky a few darker figures wheeled lazily. After a moment, he saw that two of them dangled a third figure between them. Even from that distance he could hear faint shouts of rage.

He forced down his own rage and anguish.

"They toy with her in an attempt to draw you out," said Fin Bheara softly beside him. "Amadan may not care whether she lives or dies, but those Unseelie creatures *will* kill her as soon as they have you."

The king turned to the Fey who had brought him Amadan's demand and spoke quickly. The Fey nodded once and took off at a run.

"What did you tell him?" demanded Will.

Fin Bheara watched the running Fey until he disappeared around the corner, then slowly turned to face Will.

"He is to tell Amadan's envoy that I will speak with Amadan himself. I will meet him halfway between the forest and Knockma." He looked over Will's head at Soutien, who nodded imperceptibly. "This should give us enough time."

"Time for what?" asked Grace. Her gaze followed the slow wheeling of the winged Unseelie creatures and the struggling figure between them. Her face paled and she stepped back against the inner wall. "We can't just leave her—"

"Aidan!" said Soutien.

Will looked around in alarm, thinking that Aidan had collapsed, but his brother wasn't on the stone floor.

He wasn't anywhere on the parapet.

Soutien took off at a run, heading for the stairs, and Will took off after him.

He didn't get far. At a sharp word from Fin Bheara, a dozen tall Fey stepped between Will and the staircase.

Soutien glanced over his shoulder at Will, then disappeared through the doorway to the staircase.

❧ TWENTY-EIGHT ❦

THE two monsters dropped Moira. It was only ten feet. She had leapt from taller walls during Army exercises and rolled safely to her feet. This time, with exhaustion and injuries slowing her reflexes dangerously, she barely had time to tuck and roll.

The landing on the needle-covered forest floor jarred her. Before she could uncoil, rough hands caught her up and dragged her backward through the forest.

"Let go!" She struggled against her captors—goblins by the smell of them—but she was off balance and barely managed to keep to her feet. Then her back was slammed against a tree trunk and her hands tied behind it.

Head still ringing, she looked around and tried to catch her breath. Shadows surged with furtive movements as Unseelie creatures flitted between trees and from branch to branch. The darkness seemed lighter to her right. That would be the sea, which meant that the keep would be to her left. Low voices murmured nearby, interspersed by hissing and high-pitched laughter. She thought she recognized the low thunder of Amadan's voice.

Moira closed her eyes tightly, fighting off dizziness. The smell of burning wood reached her. Somewhere behind her was a campfire.

Her legs trembled with residual adrenaline. She needed to sit down, but the tree widened at the base and the rope binding her to it wasn't long enough to allow her that luxury.

She leaned back, surreptitiously testing her bonds. The tree was a young one, but still big. At least sixteen inches of rope played out between her hands. Maybe she could wear the rope thin enough to break it.

Her chin hit her chest and she jerked awake, straightening against the pull of sleep. How long had she slept?

A rush of sound caught her attention and she twisted around to see dozens of dark figures limned by fitful firelight moving into the trees. One of the figures—wide and eerily insubstantial—was Amadan. They were leaving.

Did that mean Amadan was getting ready to attack?

Only five creatures now remained at the camp site—three goblins, one of the small, monkey-like creatures, and something short and squat, indecipherable in the gloom, that dragged its hands on the ground when it moved.

With a start of dismay, she looked back at the group retreating through the trees. Without Amadan to keep the remaining Unseelie in check, what would they do? Already a few dark figures were slinking toward her.

Moira gulped as the squat creature crept into the fire's light. Its face consisted mostly of nose and mouth. It reached long, skinny arms toward her and she snapped her teeth at it. Startled, it jerked back, and Moira laughed. Even to her, the laugh sounded hysterical.

Then sharp fingers poked her in the ribs and she whipped her head around but the goblin skittered away.

The entertainment proceeded for a few minutes more, with creatures slipping in and tweaking here, pinching there. When she was lucky, Moira caught one with a powerful kick, but all too often, they were too fast for her.

Abruptly, her tormentors stopped and melted back into the trees. Moira sagged with relief. Her chin dropped to her chest and she struggled against tears. It was exhaustion as much as pain, but she was damned if she was going to cry in front of these things.

Then a soft sound, like feet brushing aside leaves, made her raise her head.

Less than five feet away stood Red Cap, staring at her. His eyes and snout glistened in the moonlight. Firelight cast fitful shadows over his face. His stench hit Moira like a wave and she gasped.

Fear robbed her legs of strength and only the tree held her up. For a moment, all she could see was Mack in the tower room, and Aidan catatonic by the fireplace.

At the memory, rage replaced fear. This creature might kill or hurt her, but she wasn't going to give in to fear or let it drive her to madness.

She looked up into Red Cap's eyes. "What do you want?" she demanded.

He didn't answer, only stood there as if his feet were rooted, fingering his axe and staring at her. Had Amadan left him behind to guard her?

"Come on, you ugly bastard," she taunted. "What are you waiting for? Set me free and we'll fight."

The trees surrounding them erupted in chittering and hissing. Her tormentors were now her audience. Moira ignored them. The same recklessness she had felt when she and Soutien escaped the goblins now seized her. She was sick of being a prisoner, sick of running, sick of this place.

She could accept that she was going to die. But she refused to do it trussed up like somebody's dinner.

"What's the matter, Red Cap?" she spoke his name like a curse. "Afraid of me?" She laughed wildly. "C'mon, you son-of-a-bitch! Set me free and let's see what you can do!"

She stopped when Red Cap stirred himself. He took one step, then another, until he stood by her side. For the first time, she noticed the dried blood on his arms and shoulders. The fabric covering his chest was slit and also covered in blood. Somebody had tried their damndest to turn him into a pin cushion.

Red Cap's head tilted down and she stared back defiantly, refusing to let his size, stench, or brutality cow her.

Then he wrapped a huge hand around her forearm, whipped the axe around and chopped the rope binding her to the tree.

Moira tasted warm blood from the inside of her lip. Her freed right arm swung forward, stiff and sore from being kept in an unnatural position. But her left arm was still in Red Cap's grasp. Breathing through her mouth to avoid most of the stench, she tried to pull her arm free.

Instead of releasing her, Red Cap yanked her arm higher and pressed her hand against the bole of the tree.

"What...?" Moira gasped in pain as he pressed down on her arm. What the hell was he doing?

She peered up past his chin to her arm. The pale skin of her arm almost glowed in the nighttime forest. Then she glimpsed his axe as he hefted it and suddenly understood.

"No!" she screamed. Without thinking, she braced herself against the tree, shoved her knees between herself and Red Cap, and pushed with all her strength.

With a grunt, Red Cap stumbled back. Suddenly released, Moira landed hard on her back. A root dug into her hip as she scrambled to her feet.

Red Cap lumbered toward her, grunting, his tusks gleaming in the firelight, his axe swinging in a deadly arc. Still winded, Moira staggered to the tree and kept it between them.

Fire. The campfire was only a few feet away. A quick glance at the surrounding trees revealed eyes glinting eerily—the goblins, less eager to play now that Red Cap was involved.

She scooped up a firebrand and whirled toward Red Cap, now almost within reach. She eyed his axe warily. If she moved quickly enough, she could duck under his arm.

Before she could move, something hurtled out of the trees with a banshee scream and landed on Red Cap's back. The force of the blow knocked the axe out of Red Cap's hand.

Moira leapt away, keeping the firebrand in front of her. Red Cap roared with rage and twisted, trying to dislodge his attacker. Fresh blood glistened on his chest and in the light of her torch, Moira caught a flash of metal as a knife slashed down again and again.

The banshee's screams resolved themselves into curses, and with a shock, Moira recognized the voice.

"Aidan!" Where had he come from? How had he avoided the Unseelie army?

He raised a face distorted by determination and hatred. His eyes searched wildly, finally settling on her.

"Run!" he yelled over Red Cap's roars of rage. His forearm was locked around the creature's thick neck and Moira could tell he was exerting all his strength to choke the beast. With his free hand, he hacked at Red Cap whenever he could, avoiding the creature's flailing hand.

Moira ran at Red Cap and with a vicious poke, stuck the firebrand into his belly.

Screaming in pain, Red Cap stopped trying to snatch Aidan's arm away from his neck and swung at Moira. She danced under his arm and stuck the firebrand into his armpit. She whirled away from his frantically clutching hand, jabbing again and again.

Red Cap's tunic caught fire but the blood running down his front soaked the fabric and kept the fire from spreading. *He's getting weaker*, thought Moira exultantly. A few more minutes and they would have him.

"Behind you!" yelled Aidan.

She whirled to see the goblins rushing her. She poked the firebrand into the face of the nearest one. It screamed and clutched its eyes. But the fire at the tip of the branch was nearly out. Wielding it like a baseball bat, Moira clubbed the next goblin and sent it reeling. She glanced over her shoulder to see how Aidan was doing.

To her horror, he had lost his grip on Red Cap's neck and was now gripping the beast's lanky hair. As she watched, Red Cap's huge hands fastened on Aidan's head. In one effortless move, he pulled Aidan off his back and sent him flying ten feet.

"No!" screamed Moira as Red Cap lumbered toward her prone brother. Another, deeper scream echoed hers and she looked up to see Soutien sprinting toward Red Cap, sword in hand.

Then something barreled into her knees, toppling her to the ground. The next few minutes were a flash of knees and fists as she struggled to free herself from the Unseelie creatures. She saw a goblin hand grasping a sword, unwarily close to her. Without thinking, she bit down as hard as she could on the wrist. A gout of bitter blood gushed out on a scream of pain and the goblin released the sword. She grabbed at it and stabbed the goblin.

One down and two to go. She turned on the creature with the long skinny arms just as it clamped a hand on her arm.

"Wrong arm!" she screamed and with all her strength sliced down on the restraining hand. The sword cut the creature's arm in two, sending it staggering with black blood spraying in a wide arc. For a second or two, its hand remained clenched on Moira's arm. Then she pried it off and turned on the other creatures.

There were none. The goblin whose eyes she had taken out with the firebrand was still writhing in pain and the one she had brained lay as if dead on the ground. Already the creature whose arm she had severed was slumping to the ground, growing weaker as its lifeblood pumped out. Of the fifth creature, there was no sign.

Moira turned toward Red Cap and found him circling Soutien. Somehow, Red Cap had found his axe—or it had found him—and he hefted it now as if it was eager to taste Soutien's blood.

"Enough," whispered Moira. Reeling with exhaustion, she gathered herself up for one last spring. When Red Cap's circling had him facing away from her, she broke into a run, sword arm flailing above her head. She released the last of her energy, the last of her rage and fear, into a wild battle yell.

"Enough!" she screamed. "Enough! Enough!" A red haze covered her eyes until she saw the world smothered in blood. She didn't care that she was about to die. She only knew that she was taking that brother-killing, cannibalistic bastard with her.

Her screams finally penetrated Red Cap's concentration and he turned his head to look over his shoulder at her. His small eyes widened and for a moment, she thought she saw fear in them.

Then a grunt escaped him and an expression of faint surprise crossed his face. He looked down at his chest, hidden from Moira's view. Then she was on top of him and stabbing at his neck, even when he toppled over onto his back and she saw the sword sticking out of his chest.

Finally a hand on her sword arm stopped her. She looked up at Soutien, at first not knowing who he was. Then the red haze receded and she shuddered.

"He's dead," said Soutien gently.

Moira gagged, unable to rid her mouth of the taste of goblin blood. Soutien held her arm but made no move to hold her. "Aidan," she gasped when she could finally talk. "Where is he?"

Within moments, they found him. Even as she approached him on unsteady feet, she saw that his head lay at an unnatural angle. Still, she dropped to her knees by his side and gently rolled him over. With trembling hands, she straightened his head, ignoring the loose-ness of the neck muscles. She straightened his arms and legs, noting with distant pride that he still clutched the sword.

Only then did she look at his face. His expression was one of fierce determination, as if even in death, he was ready to fight. She stared at him for a long time.

Finally, Soutien placed a heavy hand on her shoulder.

"Moira."

She looked up at him. He seemed to waver where he stood.

"Moira," he repeated, his voice tight with urgency. "Is that your blood on your face?"

She touched her cheek, growing tight with drying blood. "Goblin," she said thickly. "I bit the bastard."

In the darkness, she couldn't see his expression, but she did hear his sharp intake of breath.

"Moira, we must leave."

Moira nodded. She struggled to her feet, ignoring Soutien's help-ing hand. Her legs trembled and she tasted the goblin's blood like bile. "Help me carry him," she said.

For a moment, she thought Soutien would refuse. Then he leaned over and with a smooth movement gathered Aidan in his arms like a child.

Without another word, they set off through the trees toward Knockma.

❧ TWENTY-NINE ❧

SOUTIEN led the way, Aidan an increasingly heavy burden. Behind him, Moira trudged through the damp leaves, her dragging feet releasing an odor of decay and mold with every step.

The moon had yet to rise, but Soutien's Fey eyes revealed the silvery night and its hidden pitfalls. He found the secret paths between the tall trees that led to Knockma. He pressed on, forcing Moira to move quickly in spite of her exhaustion. He needed her to move while she still could.

They had been lucky, but it wouldn't last. Amadan had obviously sensed that Fin Bheara was willfully delaying him and had sent Red Cap to check on Moira. When his lieutenant didn't report back, Amadan would send more Unseelie creatures. Soutien planned to have Moira safely inside Knockma before then.

An owl hooted, reminding him of the brown man. Would Aidan still be alive if the little cousin hadn't brought Soutien to him?

It doesn't matter, thought Soutien. *The boy is dead. Nothing will change that.*

And finally, the monotony of movement released a thought that had hovered just below his awareness from the moment he found Aidan.

Why hadn't Amadan pursued Aidan? As the eldest living Kirwan,

Aidan was crucial to Amadan's plan. He must have known that it was only a matter of time before Aidan stumbled across one of the more lethal denizens of the Fey world.

Why hadn't Amadan gone looking for him? Why aim for Will?

The weight of Aidan's body in his arms added to the weight of guilt on Soutien's soul. He carried Aidan just as he had when Aidan was a child too tired to walk.

For so many centuries, his role had been clear. He was the eyes and ears of Fin Bheara, and protector of the Kirwans. Oonagh herself had assigned him the duty. Now the nighttime forest breathed strangely, as if all around him the trees were turning into something else. But the forest hadn't changed. He had.

He had carried generations of O'Rourkes, and before that, Kirwans, safely from cradle to grave.

Now, because of him, two Kirwans were dead and two were in mortal danger. The Kirwan line could die out.

As if to underscore the thought, the owl hooted again, so close it startled him. He stopped abruptly and Moira bumped into him. He glanced at her, noting the feverish gleam in her eyes. Without a word, he lowered Aidan's body to the ground. Then he turned to face the wall of trees.

The brown man slipped between two trees, stepping lightly until he faced Soutien. His gaze dropped to the body at Soutien's feet. The Fey creature stared at it for a long moment, his face unreadable. Then he looked up at Soutien.

"Amadan attacks Knockma."

Soutien's heart squeezed in anguish. His home, attacked. After a moment, he regained his balance. Knockma was well armed and Fin Bheara was an experienced warrior. He would destroy Amadan's forces before they could overrun the keep.

Then realization hit him like a blow. Past and present flowed through Fin Bheara, tethering the king to the keep. While he stood in the doorway of Time, he could not lead his Fey into battle. At best, he could travel a few steps from Knockma's walls. Unable to take the fighting to Amadan, Fin Bheara would have to wait for him at Knockma or lead the fighting through his lieutenants.

"Will," came Moira's sepulchral voice from the dark. A shiver coursed up Soutien's scalp and he turned to look at her.

She stood unnaturally still, staring at the brown man, her eyes glittering with fever. Her cheekbones poked sharply under skin grown too thin and there was a spot of color high on each cheek.

"Does he know where Will is?" she repeated herself. This time her voice sounded raspy, like dried reeds rubbing in the wind.

Sick from the venomous goblin blood, pushed beyond her limits, unable to understand the language he and the brown man spoke, she still worried about her brother. Her remaining brother.

Unable to look at her any longer, Soutien looked down at Aidan's ashen face, a well of despair opening up within him.

"Will is in Knockma. He and Grace are all right." A gust of wind trailed cool fingers up his back. Taking a deep breath, he turned to the little cousin. "Has Amadan surrounded the keep?"

The brown man shook his head.

"Fin Bheara's archers keep them away."

There was still a chance, then.

"Take her to Knockma," he said, nodding over his shoulder at Moira. "Stay off the path and circle the keep. If you approach from the sea side, the Unseelie will not see you."

The brown man looked at him steadily, silently, and only then did Soutien realize that he had given the little cousin an order, as if he were a soldier in Soutien's army.

Instead of bristling in resentment, or melting back into the trees as Soutien half-expected, the brown man grew very still. He glanced from Aidan to Moira, then back at Soutien.

"This I will do," he finally accepted. "But know that Cathel's dé Danann are also on the move. They follow closely behind Amadan."

Soutien closed his eyes, tired beyond measure.

"Does Cathel obey Amadan?"

"This I do not know."

Soutien opened his eyes. The wind was rising, riding in on a storm out at sea. It brought with it the smell of fish. A slight movement in a branch above the brown man's head caught Soutien's attention. A barn owl looked back at him. For the first time, he noticed that the branches were full of all manner of birds and squirrels, all watching in unnatural stillness.

"Then you had best go," he said finally. "I will await Cathel."

The brown man stepped past him and looked at Moira. Short as she was, he still had to look up at her. She stared down at him, her breathing ragged, as if she had been running.

"Moira," said Soutien, taking her hands in his. Hers felt hot and dry. "The little cousin will take you to Knockma. To Will. You must remain strong for a little longer. Can you do that?"

She stared at him. "You come, too."

Soutien shook his head. "I need to wait for Cathel."

"You'll need my help," she whispered.

Soutien placed his hands on her burning cheeks.

"Moira. Listen. I must do this alone. Go to Knockma. Find Will and Grace."

A shiver shook her and he dropped his hands from her face. He glanced down at the brown man. In their own language, he said, "Look after her."

Without a word, the brown man took Moira by the hand and led her, stumbling, toward Knockma. A heartbeat later, the birds rose from the trees in a rush of wind and followed them.

❧ THIRTY ❦

Moira's blood felt like lava coursing through her veins. Every running step sent it thudding to her head like a battering ram. Even the air she sucked in with every breath was hot like embers. Only the cool wind of an oncoming storm provided any relief from the fire consuming her.

The world dissolved into blurring trees and tripping roots, flitting owls and thumping feet. Only the brown man's hand enveloping hers kept her from falling. She clung to it with a child's trust. Somewhere behind her was a great sadness involving Soutien, Aidan, and Mack. Somewhere ahead were Will, and Grace. She knew she ran toward them, but she didn't know why.

Her only certainty was the sound of her feet on the uneven ground, the feel of the brown man's hand holding hers, and the sense that she had to keep moving, no matter what.

She was aware, dimly, that the brown man kept looking back at her. Once, he stopped and pulled out a small flask and put it to her lips, but Moira pushed it away. She didn't know why she shouldn't drink, but it had something to do with dancing shoes. He stared at her for a long moment, then put the flask away and pulled her into a run again.

Moira's legs trembled and her shoulders felt as if they had been pulled out their sockets. Her ribs ached. She couldn't remember why she was in such pain.

Finally, the brown man slowed and she fell into a walk. The trees resolved themselves into individual shapes, softened by night. She and the brown man stood at the edge of a forest, at the top of a long rolling hill. In the distance, the last of the light glinted off waves that stood white with froth before falling in on themselves. In the middle distance was the dark hulk of a castle. Not a castle. A fort. No, that wasn't right either.

Lights shone from the windows and she desperately wanted to go there.

Suddenly, she realized that she had seen this building, at a distance, from frighteningly high. It had looked like a tinker toy, or a child's castle. Now she shuddered at the memory of talons gripping her shoulders, of falling through the air to land on soft ground, winded and frightened.

Movement attracted her eye and she blinked in confusion, trying to focus. There, coming out of the trees by the shore. Her breathing quickened. Amadan! The fire in her brain abated for a moment, chilled by her fear. She looked at the castle again and for the first time saw the archers on the battlement.

Then a keening sound made her raise her gaze and she saw them, the winged ones, flying toward the castle. Her mouth suddenly dry, she looked back at the castle, at the focus of the winged ones' attack.

She took a step toward the castle, only to pull up as the brown man yanked her back.

She had forgotten about him. She looked down into his too-big eyes, wondering why he was there.

"Will's there," she explained patiently. "I have to go to him."

The brown man nodded as if he understood, but kept her firmly in place. He looked intently at her and spoke, but she couldn't make out what he was saying. Then he pointed at the castle and made a wide circling motion with his free hand.

And somewhere deep inside the fever, Moira's military soul recognized a strategy. She nodded.

"Yes," she said. "We'll go around the back way."

And with that, they re-entered the trees.

***

On the torchlit battlement, Fin Bheara's rage lent color to his cheeks and ice to his eyes.

"I would not have thought a son of Kirwan could be so dull-witted." He spat the words at Will.

The king's anger caused the Fey around him to edge back. Grace began to wonder if fifteen feet was enough distance between herself and the storm brewing between Will and Fin Bheara.

The king's anger didn't seem to frighten Will, however. He stood toe-to-toe with Fin Bheara and matched him icy syllable for icy syllable, ignoring the Fey around him as if they weren't there.

"I don't give a damn what you think," he said. "I'm not leaving Soutien to fetch my brother and sister."

At the mention of Soutien, Grace automatically looked past the battlement to the ground below. The waxing moon shed enough pale light to reveal forest and sea. Her stomach lurched as the ground spun up at her and her head reeled with the knowledge of how high she was, how easily she could fall and die. The wind flattened her dress against her body, sending shivers up her arms and scalp.

She closed her eyes briefly, trying to recapture her equilibrium. When she opened them again, she kept her gaze on the stone floor of the battlement, where torchlight cast fitful shadows.

Will and Fin Bheara argued, their voices rumbling like thunder below the thin whistle of the wind. The thirty or so Fey on the parapet remained quiet, half of them keeping an eye on Will, the other half watching the sky.

Ignoring the trembling in her legs, Grace pressed her hands flat against the inner wall of the battlement for support and scanned the dark trees for signs of activity. Amadan's envoy was gone, bearing Fin Bheara's summons. Would Amadan come? Would he bring Moira with him?

Only the winged Unseelie remained, wheeling like vultures over the forest, their dark shapes blotting out the stars. Grace shuddered at the memory of Moira hanging like a puppet between the claws of the winged Unseelie. So high...

Finally, she allowed herself to look away. Over the sound of the wind, Fin Bheara's voice rose and fell in the cadence of anger, but Will's remained even, a testament to the control he still maintained over his need. She glanced in their direction and the wall of Fey shoulders parted momentarily, revealing Will. His chin was low and his shoulders hunched. He was through arguing.

Before he could make his move, one of the winged Fey flew up to Fin Bheara, shouting, "*Kattis! Kattis!*" Grace—and everyone else—turned to follow his pointing finger. She gasped in alarm when she finally made sense of what she was seeing. Dozens of winged Unseelie were flying toward Knockma at a dizzying speed.

As they approached, the air filled with keening cries, raising the hackles on her neck. At a sharp word from Fin Bheara, the archers loosed their arrows, but more winged Unseelie replaced those who fell.

Grace stood like a post, mouth agape, staring at the sky. How could the archers see well enough in the dark to find their targets? Then Will's shout cut through the keening and she tore her gaze away to look at him. He pointed to the forest.

The ground below heaved with shadows. Hordes of Unseelie creatures were swarming out of the forest, heading for Knockma.

Grace willed herself to move, but her feet ignored her. The winged Unseelie were now so close she could see the oily sheen of their brown fur and the glittering of their eyes in the torchlight. Even as she watched, three fell to the ground, pierced by arrows.

It wouldn't be enough, Grace suddenly realized. The Fey on the parapet couldn't keep up. Already the winged ones were too close for effective use of the bow. And soon Amadan's army would be at Knockma's door.

With horrified fascination, she watched the flying horrors approach. Will... Where was Will?

Then a Fey caught her by the arm and pushed her toward the battlement door. She struggled against him, trying to reach Will.

"Will!" she called. He looked past the wall of Fey warriors and immediately tried to push his way through them.

"Hang on, Grace!" he shouted.

Fin Bheara roared a warning and raised his sword high just as

winged Unseelie swooped down in a vee. Only then did Grace understand that they were after Will.

She had time for a frantic "Look out!" before she was through the
parapet door and down the staircase, stumbling after the Fey.

☙ THIRTY-ONE ❧

Soutien took a different route than the one the brown man and Moira had taken, knowing Cathel would follow him. Hopefully, he could delay Cathel long enough for Moira to make it to Knockma.

He took Aidan with him. It was foolish—Aidan was dead and wouldn't care what happened to his remains.

But Moira would.

Less than fifteen minutes after Moira and the little cousin left, he stopped in his tracks, warned by a whisper of sound from the trees. A dozen dé Danann dropped from branches and stepped out from behind trees. Silence descended with them. Soutien recognized most of them from Cathel's aerie camp.

He glanced at Aidan's body, stifling an urge to hold him tighter. Instead, he placed the body gently on the ground and straightened up.

Then came a flurry of movement as Cathel dropped to the ground, his cloak whipping above his head. He landed soundlessly and his cloak settled about his shoulders.

"Amadan is at Knockma," he told Soutien.

Soutien looked at him steadily, trying to read the High Lord's expression, but Cathel only stared back, his face closed. A bullfrog croaked in the distance, and the breeze carried the fecund odor of a marsh. Knockma was close. Another few steps and he would surely hear the sounds of battle.

"Have you come to help the king, or Amadan?" he finally asked the lord.

For the first time, Cathel seemed to notice Aidan's body. His hair gleamed in the silver night as he bent his head in acknowledgement.

"I grieve for your loss."

Soutien believed him. The High Lord was old enough to remember when Fey and humans shared the same time and space. Perhaps he even longed for those days. But that didn't mean he would help Fin Bheara.

"Your sorrow is of little use," said Soutien, surprising himself and raising Cathel's eyebrows. A rustle in the trees told him that the dé Danann were surprised, too. He didn't care. He had no time for games or niceties.

Cathel looked intently at Soutien, then back at Aidan. From the High Lord emanated a smell that was a cross between vinegar and nutmeg. Anxiety, Soutien realized suddenly. Cathel was worried.

"Lord Cathel," he said sharply. "Are you here to help Amadan, or King Fin Bheara?"

Cathel looked at Soutien.

"Neither," he said. "I am here to serve you."

A trembling began in the pit of Soutien's stomach. Only a few nights ago—a lifetime ago—Elin and her kin had sworn allegiance to him. Now the wild cousins were dead.

He fought down an urge to turn and run. Elin and her kin were dead. So were Mack and Aidan. But he had a chance to save Moira, Will, and Grace. Cathel's reasons didn't matter. All that mattered was that he wanted to help.

"Very well," Soutien said abruptly. As if he had given them the order, two dé Danann immediately stepped forward. One removed his cloak and laid it on the ground. At once, Soutien was back in the forest after the goblin attack. There, too, dé Danann had carried the Kirwan dead.

Before they could pick up Aidan and place him on the cloak, Soutien stopped them.

"Leave him." His tone was harsh, but he couldn't help it. Once more, he was betraying Moira.

All eyes were on him. Soutien took a deep breath and looked at Cathel.

"There will be many more dead before this is over. Do you still want to help?"

Cathel nodded. Without another word, they set off.

❧ THIRTY-TWO ❧

THE Fey towing Grace by the arm moved so fast she had to scramble to keep to her feet. Behind them, grim-faced Fey poured in from the battlement doorway, passing them at a run or on the fly on either side of the wide hallway. Light from the sconces glinted off their raised swords. The sounds of battle, muted by the thick stone walls, reached them from the Great Hall, two floors below, and through the battlement door.

The Fey stopped before a door, opened it, and propelled her in. He touched a torch in a wall sconce and it lit up. Then he gave her a terse command, which she interpreted to mean "Stay!" and slammed the door in her face.

Grace immediately opened the door and stuck her head out. The Fey, running toward the staircase at the far end of the hallway, glanced back at her and scowled. She quickly closed the door. No locks, and no enchantments. She would wait until all the Fey were gone, then find her way down to the main floor.

Will would head there. His first thought would be to find Moira, and Grace couldn't let him go alone.

Stepping away from the door, she looked around. A loom almost filled the small room. A half-woven tapestry mounted on its racks seemed to await the weaver's return. Her questing finger revealed bright colors beneath a thick layer of dust. Wicker baskets filled with shuttles and balls of yarn occupied the corners of the room. A small fireplace set in the opposite wall would keep the room toasty warm in winter.

A sudden shriek nearby sent her leaping for the door. She reached it unharmed and looked up. In a recessed window, set high in the wall opposite the door, was a monstrous, furry face. Framed by the window and lit from below by the uncertain light of the wall torch, huge brown eyes glared at her. Then the mouth opened to reveal needle-sharp, inch-long teeth. The creature shrieked its frustration, sending panic skittering down Grace's nerves.

Then she looked again. It was too big to get in.

As if hearing her thought, the creature suddenly left the window. Grace stared at the empty rectangle of dark sky until realization hit her: it was giving up its spot for a smaller creature.

She could slip out the door, but she desperately wanted a weapon. Glancing around the weaving room, she saw what she needed. Gathering her skirt, she reached the fireplace in three running steps. The small stand holding the fire tongs, broom, and poker—presumably made without iron—fell over with a jarring clang as she rummaged frantically for the poker handle. She finally grasped it and whirled to face the window. Still empty.

Backing toward the door, she kept her eyes on the opening. Just as she felt the rough wood of the door at her back, something small and black hurtled through the window opening with a hair-raising shriek.

Grace met it with a shriek of her own. She fumbled for the handle and let herself out, slamming the door just in time. She heard a satisfying thud from the other side.

Heart beating wildly, she looked down the empty hallway. By the shouts and clanging of metal coming from the stairway at the end of the hall, it wouldn't stay empty much longer.

Damn. She had to get down those stairs.

With a deep breath, she clutched the poker in both hands and ran toward the fighting. Before she could make it twenty feet, however, the fighting boiled up the staircase and onto the landing. Fey fell back against goblin swords and Grace fell back with them. The sight of those grinning goblin faces, as much as the wall of stench that preceded them, weakened her knees and her resolve.

She would find another way down.

Fin Bheara's Fey fought back fiercely, but there were too many goblins. It was only a question of time before they overran them.

Grace turned and ran back the way she had come, past the door to the weaving room and up the steps to the battlement door. There she paused. She could no longer hear fighting through the door. It didn't matter. She had to get out to the battlement, find another tower, and try to get down by a different staircase.

She glanced back at the battle inching its way toward her. One tall Fey looked over his shoulder, saw her, and shouted.

Taking that as her cue, Grace opened the door and peered outside. In the flickering light of the abandoned torches, she could see that the battlement was empty. Closing the door behind her she ran along the battlement, one hand grasping the poker, the other trailing along the inside wall. She glanced at the sky often, but it remained empty. Where were all the winged Unseelie?

The wind buffeted her and she cursed the stupid dress that kept trying to trip her. Finally, she let go of the tenuous comfort of the wall and gathered the skirt up in her free hand.

Sounds of fighting reached her from below, from the open Great Hall. She couldn't see into the hall because the inside wall of the battlement on this side of the keep rose above her head. The glow of the torches in the hall limned the edges of the wall. Cries of pain pierced through the ululating cries of the goblins and Grace's heart sank. The Fey were losing.

A movement caught her eye. In the distance, above the forest, a dark shape dove to the ground, wings spread. Following its movements, she inadvertently looked through an embrasure at the ground. Far below, in the intermittent light of a few torches, tall Fey fought goblins at Knockma's door. She stared for a moment, surprised that there were more Fey outside than goblins, almost as if the Fey were trying to get *into* Knockma and the goblins were trying to keep them out.

Beyond the fighting figures, dark humps lay on the ground. After a moment, she recognized them as winged Unseelie, fallen by Fey arrows. There were many of them. Good, she thought.

Then the realization of height hit her, and she dropped to her knees, dizzy and nauseated. The poker clanged to the stone next to her. She closed her eyes and curled her body over her knees, pressing her hands on the rough stone of the battlement. Too high! Even with her eyes closed, she could still see the ground rushing toward her, still feel the wind against her plummeting body.

She lay shuddering for long minutes. The cries of battle reached her from two sides now, from outside the keep and from within the Great Hall. She tried to reason past the terror. The embrasures on the battlement were waist-high and narrow, and the merlons rose above her head. There was no way to accidentally fall. She would have to climb the embrasure, squeeze into the narrow opening, and throw herself off.

Even the brown man's shoes didn't help. Like her, they didn't function well at heights.

With grim determination, she felt along the rough stone of the walkway for the poker. When her fingers found it, she kept her eyes closed and crawled toward the inner wall. The dress got in her way and she cursed it with fervor. When her left shoulder finally butted against the inner wall, she sagged in relief.

Ignoring the trembling in her legs, she forced herself to her feet. She clung to the wall and finally opened her eyes, but kept her gaze on her feet. A wave of dizziness threatened to overwhelm her, but she fought it. The far tower with its staircase wasn't far. She could make it.

A sudden longing for Will's sure strength caught at her and she swallowed a sob. It was her turn to be there for him. She couldn't afford to give in to weakness.

She reached out with both hands for the inner wall of the battlement. The poker bumped the wall, reassuring her.

She could do this.

Risking a glance, she saw that she was almost at the far tower. The door to the tower yawned open, obscuring the battlement on the other side. No sounds escaped from the inner staircase. That was the staircase Will, Fin Bheara, and the other dé Danann must have taken.

Obviously they had made it to the Great Hall—where all the fighting was....

She reached the door and peered cautiously inside the tower. The staircase was dark and empty.

She breathed a heartfelt sigh of relief and edged into the doorway. Turning her back on the battlement lifted the dizziness like a cloak billowing in the wind. Almost there.

Just then, a cry of rage sounded on the battlement and she froze. That had sounded like Moira.

Metal scraped along metal and Grace's hands tensed around the poker. Taking a deep breath, she stepped back onto the battlement, grasped the edge of the door, and pulled it shut. The sounds came from around the corner. Holding the poker firmly in front of her, she edged her way around.

The sea wind whipped at her hair and clothes, riding on the smell of fish and seaweed. The inner wall on this side of the battlement was only waist high and three feet wide. From where she stood, she could look down into the Great Hall, where Fin Bheara's Fey fought goblins in the firelight and cries of anguish and pain rose like dark birds on the air.

This is what hell looks like. She stared at the figures below in fascination. Dizziness swirled through her and she swayed, clutching the low wall for balance.

You can't fall, she told herself. *You're safe.* But her fingers tried to dig holes in the stone wall.

A sudden laugh startled her out of her daze. She looked around, then up. On the low wall, by the far tower, two figures fought with swords. Despite the uncertain light, she could clearly see the one facing her.

Moira.

As she watched, Moira raised her sword and brought it down with a harsh clang against the other woman's casually raised weapon. There was no strength behind the blow.

Something was clearly wrong. Even in the weak glow from the Great Hall, Grace could see that Moira's face was drawn and so pale it seemed to glow, save for two bright spots of red on either cheek.

Her eyes glittered feverishly and her chest heaved with exertion. She raised the sword as if its weight were almost more than she could bear. The movement caused her to reel dangerously close to edge of the wall, and Grace gasped in fear.

The other woman laughed again and Grace dragged her gaze back from the precipice. She knew that voice. And although the woman had her back to Grace, there was no mistaking the white-blonde hair, the elegant stance, the confident grip on the sword.

Oh, hell. It's Ilyane.

She had no idea how either of them had come to be in Knockma, let alone on the deserted battlement. Moira had somehow freed herself or been rescued. Grace looked around hopefully, but except for the three of them, the battlement remained deserted.

Ilyane laughed again, and with a flick of her wrist, left a long, bloody scratch on Moira's arm. Moira raised her sword in a futile attempt to stop her. For the first time, Grace realized that Moira was covered in bloody scratches. The two high spots of color on her cheeks weren't from exertion. Now that she knew what to look for, Grace could see the nicks on either cheek.

Ilyane was playing.

Moira attempted to lunge at Ilyane, but the dé Danann easily deflected her sword, leaving another long scratch on Moira's wrist.

Grace looked back the way she had come. At any moment, the goblins would push Fin Bheara's Fey onto the battlement and any chance she had of helping Moira would be lost.

She had to get up there, while Ilyane was distracted.

A trembling began in the pit of Grace's stomach and traveled outward to her limbs. She would have to climb the wall and make her way to Ilyane without alerting the dé Danann to her presence. And without falling to her death thirty-five feet below.

Grace closed her eyes tightly, shutting out the night, the torchlight, the two women.

I can't do it.

It was too much. She could not climb the wall without falling. She couldn't help Moira. She could barely help herself.

"C'mon, you bitch!" said Moira.

Grace opened her eyes. Backed against the tower wall, Moira held the sword before her in both hands. Even from that distance, Grace could see the effort it took.

"Come and get me if you're so good!"

A reluctant admiration pushed through Grace's fear. Moira was clearly outmatched, but still faced Ilyane with courage.

Without giving herself time to think, Grace placed the poker on top of the wall, being careful not to make noise. Then she heaved herself up to a sitting position, pushed the skirt away from her legs and, using the poker to keep her balance, stood up.

The wind caught in her skirt and hair and she leaned into it, afraid it would blow her over the side.

Ilyane's sword flashed out and left another scratch on Moira's shoulder, drawing a grunt of pain from the woman. Damn! At this rate, Moira would bleed to death before Grace could get close enough to help.

Focus! she told herself sharply as her gaze strayed to the Great Hall. It was hard to keep from looking down when the frenzied ballet of battle caught constantly at the corner of her eye. *Focus*, she breathed.

She dragged her gaze back to Ilyane, as if by ignoring the chasm to her left it would go away. Her insides clutched in fear and she fought the instinct that would have her hugging the ground. She inched closer to the two women, hoping her snail's pace would get her there in time.

Unaware of Grace's presence, Ilyane pranced away from Moira's clumsy sword, taunting her in the Fey tongue.

With an inarticulate cry of rage, Moira lunged at Ilyane, a move that would have pierced the dé Danann's heart had she not whirled away.

And in whirling, she saw Grace.

Ilyane's drew herself up in surprise. She glanced over her shoulder, as if to make sure Moira wasn't sneaking up on her, then turned to Grace again.

She looked at Grace, then looked down into the Great Hall. When she looked at Grace again, her face was full of mirth. Only then did Grace remember that Ilyane had been present when she'd had to climb to Cathel's aerie. She knew about Grace's fear of heights.

Ilyane began laughing, her head back, her shoulders shaking. Without warning, she ran at Grace, startling her into stepping back.

Falling! With a cry of fear, Grace dropped to her knees on the wall, shaking with terror.

Ilyane laughed even harder, pointing at Grace as if she were the butt of a vast joke.

You bitch, thought Grace. She struggled shakily to her feet. Anger percolated past the fear, filling crevices and pushing aside fear. "You bitch," she said.

Ilyane ignored her, still laughing. Behind her, Moira took a step, then another. She raised her sword in trembling hands.

Grace allowed the anger to fill her. For that brief moment, she felt as if she were invincible. She stepped into the moment, raised the poker, and slashed at Ilyane.

Ilyane's eyes widened at the sight of the poker, and for the first time, Grace realized that Ilyane hadn't seen it, hidden as it was by the folds of her dress. The dé Danann stepped back, raising her sword to fend off the poker.

Then, as if suddenly remembering Moira's presence, Ilyane glanced over her shoulder. But it was too late.

Without a word, Moira stabbed the point of her sword into Ilyane's side.

With a grunt of pain, Ilyane jerked away from Moira. The movement brought her too close to the edge of the wall and with a cry of fear, she whirled her arms in an effort to regain her balance. Her sword fell with a clang on the battlement wall. Then Ilyane's struggle took her over the edge to fall to the stony floor of the Great Hall.

❧ THIRTY-THREE ❧

H<small>IS</small> back against the cold stone wall of the Great Hall, Will wielded with growing fury the sword he had picked up from a dead dé Danann. Faced with three Unseelie creatures, he slashed at furry arms and poked at exposed chests. Their blood was black in the flickering light of the torches. For every creature that fell under his sword, another popped up to replace it.

The din of swords scraping against each other merged with the cries of goblins and Fey to create a dull roar in Will's head. Next to him, a chair broke as a goblin threw it against a dé Danann. The dé Danann spun and lunged, skewering the goblin on his sword.

Will absorbed the sounds into the growing dissonance of his thundering heart and singing blood. The need to find Grace and Moira receded further as each new adversary fell under his sword.

It felt light in his hand, the handle just the right size and heft. He saw an opening and lunged, stabbing deeply into a goblin chest. The vermin stiffened, black blood spewing from its mouth, and Will roared his satisfaction.

He looked up at an answering cry and found himself looking into Fin Bheara's eyes. The king's eyes glittered with blood lust and his mouth was split in a fierce grin. His powerful sword arm swung left and right, leaving behind dead Unseelie.

Something inside Will leapt to answer the king's joy. His ancestors had fought like this, when called by the king. Side by side with Fin Bheara.

A dé Danann face swam into Will's view and he automatically raised his sword. He retained just enough reason to pause, recognizing that he was not the enemy.

With a look of contempt, the dé Danann raised his own sword and stabbed at Will.

Almost too late, Will countered. His sword clashed against that of the lighter dé Danann, deflecting his aim. Still, Will was no swordsman, and the dé Danann's thrust left a long gash along Will's thigh.

The pain was like fire stitching along his leg. He bellowed in anger and stepped in close, grabbing the dé Danann's sword arm before he could dance away. He pulled the lighter man sharply toward him. Off balance, the dé Danann stumbled. With a grunt, Will sank his sword into the other's belly.

The dé Danann looked into his eyes, and Will came to his senses. He whirled him around and booted the dé Danann back into the fray.

Nausea swirled through him as he realized what he had almost done.

Killing goblins and other Unseelie creatures was the same as exterminating vermin—he had no compunctions about killing them.

But the dé Danann... A deep sense of shame and guilt swept through him. He had wanted to kill the dé Danann, wanted to see his life blood spilling onto the flagstones of the Great Hall.

Will glanced up. The battle raged on amid cries of pain and triumph. This was no time for guilt.

Now he could see that dé Danann fought dé Danann. Had some in Fin Bheara's army turned against him?

A wave of confusion threatened to overwhelm him. What was he doing here? He wasn't a warrior! He needed to find Moira and Grace and get out of here.

Something small and wiry with huge eyes and bigger teeth leaped at him, and Will ducked. The creature landed on the stone wall of the Great Hall, stunning itself.

Will reclaimed his sword from the floor. He was no swordsman, but the sword was the only protection he had.

At that moment, the doors to the Great Room burst open, slamming back against the walls like a boom of thunder. A dozen dé Danann spilled through the opening, followed by another dozen. And another. Will's heart sank. There was no way...

Then the newcomers threw themselves on the Unseelie creatures. Will scanned faces, wondering how he would know which dé Danann were enemies.

"Will!"

He turned at the sudden shout and saw Soutien by the doors. The man raised a fist clenched around a sword hilt and Will's own arm lifted to return the salute. Was Soutien trying to tell him that he had found Aidan and Moira?

Soutien's eyes glittered in the flickering light. He pointed with his sword at the far end of the Hall, to a closed door behind the throne. Will nodded. Already the Unseelie creatures were falling back against the onslaught of the newcomers. This battle had turned in Fin Bheara's favor.

He had a fleeting thought about other battles, where his camera had recorded death and bravery, foolishness and confusion. There would be no record of this battle, only what imperfect memory could provide.

He looked around again, but there were no goblins or other monsters nearby. Where was Amadan?

Just like a general to send the troops to slaughter while he stayed safely behind.

Then a scream from above silenced the combatants. All eyes turned to the dark sky in time to see a body plummet from the parapet. Will caught a flash of pale hair and stopped breathing.

There was a scuttle of movement as dé Danann and goblin scurried out of the way. The body landed with the sound of a watermelon splitting on pavement.

"No!" The cry of grief filled the silence and a dé Danann pushed through the fighters. Stomach twisting in dread, Will found an intact chair and stood on it.

Was it Grace's hair he had seen?

Over the heads of the assembled, he first saw the kneeling dé

Danann. Even before the dé Danann raised his face to the sky, Will had recognized him.

Cathel.

And then he knew. The fallen one was Ilyane, Cathel's daughter. He forced himself to look down, past Cathel's shoulder, to see the pale hair stained dark with blood, the broken body lying still on the hard flagstones, the open eyes staring at nothing.

As if sensing Will's presence, Cathel looked around. His gaze found Will. Cathel's shocked face brought back with full force Will's initial disbelief at Mac's death.

For the space of a deep breath, Will closed his eyes against the pain.

Then Soutien's voice fell like a knell in the uncertain silence of the Great Hall.

"We have seen enough death this night," he said, his quiet voice carrying to the farthest corners of the hall. "Let us end it now."

From his vantage point on the chair, it seemed to Will as if a great sigh passed through the assembled. Everywhere he looked, shoulders sagged and sword arms drooped. The fight had lost its glory. With their leader dead and Amadan nowhere in sight, Ilyane's dé Danann had neither reason nor the heart to keep fighting.

Then a goblin screamed and launched itself at the nearest Fey. Just like that, the battle resumed.

Will's shoulders sagged in despair. It would go to the bitter end, then. From his vantage point, he could see that it was only a question of time. With the addition of Cathel's dé Danann, the defenders were now more numerous than the attackers. It was only a question of time.

Something small and furry landed on Will's head and he yelped. The hand he reached up to dislodge the creature came back bloody. As he finally freed his hair from the creature's grasp he noticed three goblins making their way toward him. Only then did he remember that Amadan wanted him dead.

Time to remove the goal from sight, he decided. He looked for Fin Bheara and found him at the door Soutien had earlier indicated. The king was watching him, a small smile on his craggy face. When he saw that he had caught Will's eye, he nodded toward the door.

Will nodded his response. He flung the tiny monster at the nearest goblin and jumped off the chair. Just then, a movement caught his eye and he turned to look at the southern tower. There, coming down the tower staircase were Grace and Moira.

Relief made Will reach for the chair back for support. He almost called out to the two women, but stopped himself, not wanting to call attention to them. In a break in the wall of fighters, he saw Moira lean heavily against Grace, her dark head lolling as if she didn't have the strength to hold it up. With a jolt, Will realized they had been on the parapet when Ilyane fell. What had happened?

He searched the crowd for Soutien, hoping the other man was nearer to the two women, but couldn't find him. Without hesitation, Will stepped into the fray and fought his way toward his sister and Grace.

Less than a minute and two goblins later, he reached them. Grace had her back to him and he placed a hand on her shoulder.

She released Moira, whirled on him, and slashed at him with a sword he hadn't known she was carrying. Only his quick step back and her last-minute recognition saved him from a severed hand.

"Will!" Her face was dirty and drawn, the planes of her cheeks sharp with exhaustion and fear. She looked stunned. Was it only an hour since he'd last seen her looking like a princess?

"We were looking for you..." she said.

Will could barely hear her above the din of battle. He glanced around to make sure there were no immediate threats.

"Hold this," he shouted, handing Grace his sword. When she took it, he leaned down and gathered Moira in his arms. Her eyes were closed and he couldn't tell at first if she was breathing. His heart contracted with fear. She weighed practically nothing. He held her close, noting with alarm the heat that emanated from her skin.

"She's sick!" yelled Grace. "We have to get her out of here!"

Will nodded. "This way!" he shouted back, and led the way.

Cathel's dé Danann and Fin Bheara's Seelie were pushing back the Unseelie forces, tumbling them out the door and into the night. Will risked a glance up but nothing came sweeping down from the starry sky. The Fey had killed many of the flying ones before they were forced off the parapets. Still, he had expected the few remaining winged Unseelie to regroup and attack. Maybe their wings were more a hindrance than a help in the Great Hall.

In a moment, they reached the door through which Fin Bheara had disappeared. Grace tucked one sword under her arm and pushed open the door with her left hand, keeping the other sword at the ready.

Will looked over her head. When he saw no immediate danger, he nudged Grace through and followed her in. Only then did he see Fin Bheara sitting in a wide wooden chair in the center of the room. The king lounged in the seat as if he hadn't a care, one huge hand wrapped around a plain metal goblet. And yet his other hand held a large sword flat against the armrest, ready.

Will used one foot to close the door. Immediately the sounds of battle dimmed and a pressure he hadn't known was there lifted from his awareness.

He noted in passing that the room was big, with a fireplace in which burned a fire and a couple of stools set on either side of a chess set. Holding Moira close, he turned to face Fin Bheara.

"She's sick," he said. Now that they were safe, at least for the time being, he tasted fear like bile in his mouth. Not her, too. He couldn't lose her, too.

Fin Bheara rose slowly from his chair. For the first time, Will realized that the chair was on a small platform, like a throne.

"Bring her here," commanded Fin Bheara.

Will was dimly aware of Grace following a step behind, but he kept his attention on the king, hoping. Surely, if Fin Bheara had been able to heal Grace, he would have a way of restoring Moira to health.

He reached the platform and Fin Bheara took Moira from him. She looked like a rag doll in the king's arms and Will struggled against the fear spiking through him. Moira was tough, tougher than any woman he had ever known. No illness would keep her down.

Fin Bheara carried Moira to the chair and set her across it. Her head lolled against the armrest and Will wanted to protest, but Fin Bheara sank to his knees by her side and proceeded to run his hands lightly over her body.

"Her injuries are many but minor," Fin Bheara said finally, rising. "What—"

Before he could complete the question, the door to the study opened again and Soutien entered, followed by Cathel, carrying his daughter. Beyond them, the Great Hall was empty and silent. An occasional muted shout told Will that the fighting was moving farther from Knockma.

"My lord," said Soutien, bowing formally to the king. Straightening, he let his stained sword point at the floor. "Amadan's forces have scattered to the woods. We can thank Lord Cathel. Without his help, things would have gone worse."

Fin Bheara nodded his acceptance of Soutien's report. "And Amadan?"

"No one has seen him, my lord."

Again, Fin Bheara nodded, but this time his gaze was on Cathel. "I thank you, old friend. And I grieve for you," he said softly.

Cathel raised eyes cold with anger. "Your grief comes too late," he said. His face seemed carved from ice. "Had you done your duty when it needed doing, my daughter would be alive to rage at me. All this bloodshed..." He looked down at Ilyane's ashen face, then looked back at Fin Bheara. "All this bloodshed I lay at your feet. Why do you yet live, coward?"

***

Grace caught her breath at the fury slicing through Cathel's words. Fin Bheara's face drained of color. He took a step toward Cathel.

Without thinking, Grace stepped between them.

"Can we put the egos aside and deal with Moira, please?" The harshness of her voice startled her. She hadn't meant to sound so angry, but Cathel and Fin Bheara would come to blows while Moira lay dying. Will glanced at her, gratitude plain on his face.

He looked truly awful. His eyes were haunted and his dark hair was disheveled and stiff with drying blood. It looked even darker against the pallor of his face.

"Moira...?" Soutien said. He looked at Grace, then around the room, only then seeing Moira laid out on the king's chair. He dropped to his knees by her side. His sword fell to the floor with a clang. Just as Fin Bheara had done, he ran his hands over Moira's body. His shoulders sagged.

"What's wrong with her?" asked Will.

Soutien didn't turn. "Goblin blood," he said, his voice so low Grace had to strain to hear it. "In the fight... she bit one... I had hoped..."

Grace turned to look at Fin Bheara and caught the same expression on his and Cathel's faces—sorrow mixed with resignation.

Will saw it, too. "What does that mean?"

There was a long silence. Finally, Cathel spoke.

"It means your sister will die." His lack of inflection highlighted the cruelty of his words. He stooped and gently deposited the body of his daughter on the floor. His back to them, he took a long time arranging her limbs. Finally he straightened and faced them.

"Goblin blood is poison to all," he continued. He looked directly at Will, a hint of pity in his expression. "There is no cure."

"No!" cried Grace, drawing everyone's attention. She stared at Cathel in horror. He had *flirted* with Moira! How could he stand there and blithely announce her impending death? Cathel stared back at her, shame mingling with pity in his eyes.

Soutien stood up and she turned on him. "No!" Her cheeks felt wet. First Mack, now Moira? No, she wouldn't accept it. Her voice rose. "Haven't you done enough? This damned place—"

"There's more," said Soutien brutally, cutting through her outburst. He looked at Will, his expression set as if against a great pain.

"What?" said Will, his voice deadly quiet. The look on his face was hard and unforgiving, as if he knew...

"Aidan is dead," said Soutien. He looked steadily at Will. "Red Cap was about to kill Moira. Aidan saved her life, but died doing it."

Grace felt all the blood leave her face. Dark motes danced before her eyes and the room blurred at the edges of her vision.

Then hard hands pushed her onto a stool and urged her head between her knees. Her cheeks pressed against the stiff fabric of the dress.

"Deep breaths," whispered Fin Bheara in her ear. "Again." After a moment, the darkness receded and Grace sat up. Fin Bheara's hand slid from the back of her neck to her shoulder and remained there.

"I'm all right," she said, looking up at him. Only then did she realize that all the men were arrayed around her, looking down at her in consternation. Even Will.

A sudden fury swept through her. "You bloody fools!" She leapt to her feet and stared at each one with all the contempt in her. "Moira is *dying*—don't just stand there staring at *me*!"

A harsh laugh sounded high above their heads, startling Grace out of her rage. She looked up in time to see a man-like form jump from the top of the study wall.

As if blown apart by a sudden wind, they all moved back to make room for the newcomer. Grace blinked hard, trying to focus on the creature that landed lightly in their midst. Like the brown man, its proportions were inhuman. It was much too wide. Powerful arms and legs, huge hands and feet, a face like an unfinished sculpture... Then the creature turned to face Fin Bheara and Grace shivered in atavistic fear. For a moment, he had almost disappeared, as if receding into the distance.

Silence descended on the room. Fin Bheara stared at the creature, his face old with pain and sorrow. In spite of the creature's size, Fin Bheara had to look down.

Grace glanced at Cathel and Soutien. Both had expressions of near-awe on their faces.

"Amadan-na-Briona," said Fin Bheara slowly, as if the words grieved him. "You have no place here."

Amadan laughed and to Grace's amazement, thunder boomed in his voice. She looked at Will. He stood by Fin Bheara's chair, protecting Moira. He stared at Amadan with such hatred that Grace shivered. Soutien moved to stand by the king.

"My place is everywhere," said Amadan, waving a hand at the room, the sky. Sparks flickered at his fingertips, like static electricity. "Even you know that." He glanced around the room, taking in Soutien and Will, Moira's prone body, Cathel between him and the door, Ilyane. Finally he looked at Grace, a fleeting look that left her reeling. There were galaxies whirling in his dark gaze. A universe of indifference to her.

From him emanated a strange smell, like leaves composting on a forest floor, mingling with the smell of sun-warmed rocks, stagnant water, and wet fur. It was the odor she had encountered on her first night in this place. He had been there. Amadan had watched, hidden, as she and Moira arrived from Kirwan. They had been so vulnerable in those first few moments. Why hadn't he attacked?

Because it wasn't her he had been after. Nor even Moira, despite her Kirwan blood. It was Kirwan's sons he had been after.

Was still after.

"Will!" she shouted, shoving past Fin Bheara to place herself between the last of Kirwan's sons and Amadan-na-Briona. Almost casually, Amadan blew on her and she whirled away, propelled on a gust of wind. She tripped on the stool and sent the chess game flying, but managed to remain on her feet. When she finally turned back, she saw Fin Bheara and Soutien standing shoulder-to-shoulder, facing Amadan. She breathed a small prayer of thanks.

Behind them, Will still stood, still protecting the unconscious Moira. He held a sword in front of him.

A sword wouldn't stop Amadan.

"Enough!" said Fin Bheara, holding out a hand as Amadan advanced. "I forbid this!"

Amadan stopped. He faced Fin Bheara, his gaze full of contempt. "You *forbid* it?" he said. "Who are *you* to forbid me anything?" He took a step toward the king, then another. Soutien's sword rose higher, but Amadan ignored him. "I had no wish to return here, to this time, yet here I am. Here we all are. And here we will now remain until *I* choose to leave! *I* am first among you. You rule because I allow it!"

"You are first among us," agreed Fin Bheara, his stance relaxed. "But you are not of us." He spread his empty hands before him. "Your time is past."

Amadan laughed, but there was no thunder this time, only the sound of icicles falling and breaking. Grace held her breath. A movement caught her eye—Cathel had drawn his sword.

"Give me the boy," said Amadan, and it took Grace a moment to realize he meant Will. "He means nothing to you and you do not wish to die."

It was Fin Bheara's turn to laugh. "Eldest you may be, but even you cannot kill me, Amadan."

But Amadan was shaking his head. "Only Kirwan's eldest son can, this I know." The smile on his face reminded Grace of a fox. "But what point is there to your death now? You have forfeited your ability to join Oonagh." His face suddenly looked as bleak as a windswept cliff. "If you die now, there will be no one, nothing waiting for you. You will be eternally alone."

A shiver of dread raced down Grace's scalp. She hadn't given much thought to what came after death, but to *know* for a certainty that there would be nothing...

Fin Bheara's steady gaze faltered and dropped. For a moment, he seemed smaller. Grace stole a glance at Soutien's face and saw her own anxiety mirrored there. Then Fin Bheara took a deep breath and looked up.

"Such is the fate I chose for myself," he said. "But remember this, Amadan. I will go to my death knowing that I was beloved by Oonagh. You will live on, knowing you were not. Which one of us is to be pitied?"

A low moaning filled the room, so low at first that Grace felt it in her bones rather than heard it. Then, in the space between two breaths, it grew from a low growl to a shrieking, howling wind.

Grace instinctively looked up, pushing the hair away from her face. She blinked, her eyes streaming in the sudden wind. The stars had disappeared. Her hands began to tremble as dread seeped into her. Wind buffeted her, catching in her skirts and whipping her hair into her face.

Amadan faced Fin Bheara. A nimbus of white light surrounded the creature, crackling with energy. Neither man moved. Beyond them, Cathel looked grim. He stood with his sword held in both hands before him, his feet spread as if to brace himself. Wind tugged at his hair and clothes.

Will was staring at her in consternation. She opened her mouth to tell him she was all right, but at that moment, a deluge of rain suddenly drenched the room, shocking a gasp out of her. The torches went out with a faint whiff of pitch.

"Grace!"

She heard Will's cry but before she could answer him, the wind doubled in force. She stumbled back, trapped by her wet, heavy skirts, only to slam up against the cold stone wall of the study. Shouts of anger pierced the terrible noise and she struggled to see in the inky darkness. Something smashed against the wall by her face, showering her in slivers. She cried out as several embedded themselves in her cheek and hand. Something small and hard hit her temple and she staggered. Then a series of small objects peppered her body with blows—the chess pieces, turned into lethal weapons by the wind.

Grace dropped to her knees, the heavy dress cushioning the fall. As she struggled to protect herself against the fury of the wind, she finally realized that Amadan was trying to kill them all. Fin Bheara would survive, but Soutien and Cathel could die. The humans certainly wouldn't survive long under this assault.

Why did Amadan no longer care about Will?

Then a bolt of lightning struck high on the wall of the study. In the stark light, Grace had an instant to see, frozen as in a tableau, Cathel reeling back from a blow by Amadan. Will, face contorted by hatred, was trying to reach Amadan. Only Soutien and Fin Bheara stood perfectly still, Soutien with his hand on Fin Bheara's shoulder, face straining as if with a great effort.

Then the room was plunged in darkness again and part of the wall came tumbling down, showering them with jagged pieces of stones. One struck her on the back and she cried out with pain, but had the presence of mind to clamp her hands over her ears before the boom of thunder that immediately followed could burst her eardrums.

And then the noise stopped. For a moment, Grace thought her hearing had been damaged after all. In the eerie silence, she listened hard, trying to discern any sound at all. The wind had ceased, too, and she took a deep, shuddering breath before struggling to her feet. Only then did she realize the rain had stopped.

The torches suddenly flickered back to life, illuminating a scene right out of one Will's photographs.

Every piece of furniture in the room had been turned into kindling. The marble chess board lay smashed into deadly shards in a pool of water. Part of the wall directly before her had been destroyed, opening up the study even further to the night. Pale starlight shone from a cloudless sky. Over everything hung the smell of ozone.

Reluctantly, Grace looked to see who was still standing. Amadan hovered two feet above the floor, powerful arms wrapped around himself, face contorted in impotent fury, looking down on them. A fine haze shimmered around him, as if a nearly invisible bubble surrounded him. He looked at her, eyes filled with blackness, and she quickly looked away. Fin Bheara stood before him, feet planted firmly on the stone floor of his study, ignoring the nick on his cheek that sent a small stream of blood flowing into his beard. He had one arm around Soutien and was supporting him. Soutien looked exhausted.

He used Soutien's energy, thought Grace in shock.

Will stood less than three feet from Amadan, sword held ready. Grace took one look at his face and swallowed hard. He didn't look anything like the Will she knew.

Cathel lay crumpled on the floor. She couldn't see his face or tell if he was still breathing.

"Let him go," said Will. Grace looked at him in confusion. He was staring at Amadan. "Let him go!"

She took a step toward him. Had he lost his mind? The thought of Aidan hovered close. They had lost Mac and Aidan to this godforsaken place. Was she now going to lose Will to insanity, too?

Then, with a sinking heart, Grace remembered Moira. She looked around, trying to find the woman in the debris. Moira lay partly crumpled on the floor, where the wind had tossed her like a heap of rags. Part of the wall had landed close by. Had anything landed on her? Grace stumbled over and checked for a pulse. There, but too faint.

"Let him go!" said Will, turning to Soutien.

"No," said Soutien, straightening with obvious effort, but not releasing the king. "You can't kill him, Will, no matter how much you want to."

"Let him go!" shouted Will. "He's going to pay!"

"Will!" said Grace sharply, looking up from Moira's ashen face. "Moira needs help!"

Will didn't even look at her. He was staring into Amadan's eyes.

"I cannot hold him much longer," said Fin Bheara, strain evident in his voice. "You must end this now, son of Kirwan."

Will didn't move.

"Will!" said Soutien, reaching out to shake him. Will turned on him, his sword raised, but Soutien didn't flinch. "It's time," he said. "You must kill the king."

Will shook his head, the blood lust slowly receding from his eyes as he absorbed Soutien's words.

"No," he said. He glanced at Amadan and shuddered. "It's *him* I want dead."

"What you want doesn't matter!" shouted Soutien, startling Grace. "If you don't kill Fin Bheara, Amadan will kill us all!"

Will stared for a long moment at Soutien, breathing slowly. Finally, "You can keep him prisoner..."

"It wouldn't change anything," said Soutien roughly. "We would still die. All of us. It would just take longer."

"He is first among us," said Fin Bheara, not taking his eyes off Amadan. "He draws his power from the primal force of the world." His shoulders shook. "I cannot keep him from killing you. I can only hold him back for a short time." His voice took on a new urgency. "You must do it now, Kirwan!"

Grace's heart constricted. She had so hoped Will wouldn't be faced with this. But Fin Bheara was no longer a match for Amadan. His power was caught up in keeping the Fey in this time. Only by drawing strength from Soutien could he keep Amadan prisoner. The very sacrifice that had kept the Fey safe for so long was now killing them.

Only Will could help now.

Grace found herself weeping, but forced herself to say the words. "Do it, Will, or none of us stand a chance." She took a deep breath. "Moira is dying."

The look he gave her filled her with shame, but she held his gaze.

Will stared a moment longer. He looked old, old as pain. Finally, he turned to Fin Bheara.

"I'm sorry," he said, and Grace's heart sank. He wouldn't do it.

Without another word, Will swung the tip of his sword up to the king's chest and with one sure lunge, pierced his heart.

Grace gasped. Soutien's arm shot out in aborted protest. The king staggered back, supported by Soutien, and Will freed the sword in a gush of blood, tearing a cry of pain from Fin Bheara. The king fell to his knees, clasping his bloody chest, body curved around his mortal wound. In spite of herself, Grace screamed in horror.

The king remained on his knees for long seconds, head down, swaying. Soutien stood behind him, helpless in his anguish.

Then, Fin Bheara struggled to his feet. His bloody hands fell away from his chest and he raised his head. His face was red with fury.

At that moment, Amadan dropped to the floor, released from Fin Bheara's constraints. The eldest of the Fey landed lightly on his feet, his laughter ringing through the destroyed room.

☙ THIRTY-FOUR ❧

SOUTIEN took an involuntary step back, unnerved as much by Fin Bheara's anger as by Amadan's laughter. The sword had pierced Fin Bheara's chest. He had seen blood flow from the wound. He couldn't reconcile those facts with the angry king now before him.

"What...?" said Grace, looking bewildered. She held Moira cradled in her arms, like a mother holding a dying child. Beyond grief, Soutien dragged his gaze back to the king. How could he still be standing?

As if sharing the thought, Fin Bheara grasped the neck of his black tunic and ripped the sodden fabric, revealing his powerful chest. One hand wiped at the blood. The flesh he revealed was unmarred.

He turned to Will, eyes hot. "Why am I still alive, Kirwan?"

Pity for Will echoed through Soutien, fleeting yet intense. To have gone through all that anguish, to have gone against his principles, for nothing...

Will stared at Fin Bheara, his face pale. He dropped the sword as if it burned his hand. The clang of its landing cut through Amadan's laughter. Soutien glanced at the elder lord.

"Be quiet," he said softly. To his amazement, Amadan stopped laughing. He scampered over the rubble to the broken wall. With an agility at odds with his proportions, he swiftly climbed the rubble to the top of the wall, where he sat down. Hands clasped around one upraised knee, he stared down at the group, an expectant smile on his face.

As if he's at a show, thought Soutien. What does he know that we don't?

Fin Bheara reached the same conclusion. He abandoned Will to turn his raging face to Amadan. "What have you done?"

At this, Amadan laughed so hard Soutien fully expected him to fall off his perch.

Amadan regained enough composure to grin down at Fin Bheara. His eyes danced with dark stars. "Not my doing, Fin Bheara. Not mine!" And the laughter overtook him once more.

Fin Bheara stared at him for a moment, then looked over his shoulder at Soutien, who shrugged to indicate his confusion. He had no idea what Amadan was about.

His strength was coming back, now that Fin Bheara no longer tapped it to keep Amadan in check. And along with his strength came a relief so huge it filled his chest. Fin Bheara would not die. His lord, who had been father to him as well as liege, would live. Soutien knew he should feel anxiety and seek to understand why Will's thrust hadn't killed the king, but at the moment, he didn't care. Fin Bheara was alive. It was enough.

Will took Moira from Grace and sat down on Fin Bheara's huge chair, cradling his sister. He turned a bewildered expression to Soutien, but it was Grace who spoke.

"What's the matter?" She pulled herself up using the chair and Soutien wondered if she had been hurt in Amadan's attack. "You said we would go home when Will killed the king." Her tone was accusing.

Soutien didn't know what to say. The king's barely checked rage clashed with Amadan's mirth, irritating him and forcing him to clamp down on his impatience.

"I don't understand it, either," he said. "Fin Bheara's immortality belongs to the Kirwan family. He should be dead." The word sent a shiver up his spine.

But Grace had gone pale. She turned a questioning face to Fin Bheara. "To the eldest Kirwan son?"

The king nodded.

"Me, now that Mac and Aidan are dead," said Will. His voice was flat and emotionless.

Grace stared down at him, her expression grave. "Maybe," she finally said, her voice barely audible above the cackling of Amadan's laughter.

Soutien turned to look at Grace, as did Fin Bheara.

Amadan hugged himself in delight. "Human she may be, but not entirely witless!" He laughed even harder.

Will was the first to speak. "What do you mean?"

Grace glanced at Soutien as if for support.

"If Fin Bheara can only die at the hands of the eldest Kirwan son," she said, "and Will tried to kill him but couldn't, that must mean..."

"That he is not the eldest Kirwan son," finished Fin Bheara. He turned to Amadan, sitting smug and satisfied on the wall. "What do you know of this, Fool? Is there another Kirwan?"

At this, Amadan leapt from the wall, unable to contain himself. He cartwheeled among the rubble, springing lightly from hand to foot and laughing with glee.

"An older eldest!" he cried. "Another Kirwan!" He stopped capering atop a pile of rubble and squatted there, looking at Fin Bheara. A huge smile split his face and his eyes seemed to spin in their orbs so that Soutien had to look away.

"Who is the fool now, O King?" asked Amadan softly.

Fin Bheara stared hard at Amadan. Soutien saw the king's muscles bunching in his powerful shoulders and knew that the king had reached the end of his patience.

A whisper of breeze, the tantalizing scent of wild roses, and then...

"My love."

As if pulled by one string, all of them turned toward the sound.

"Oonagh..."

The joy on Fin Bheara's face warred with the pain in his voice. Tension eased out of his shoulders as he looked at his wife.

"Why...?"

Oonagh's smile faded a bit. "I am called here," she said. "I am still tied."

Soutien felt anguish like hot blood running through him. She still wasn't free.

Oonagh stood in the center of the destroyed room, her robe and fair hair shining as if she stood in a shaft of sunlight. Her gaze took in the king's bloody tunic and she quickly looked away, turning to Soutien. Her smile melted the sadness from her face.

"Dear child," she murmured. "How worn you are."

And immediately, Soutien felt better.

"Never so, my lady," he said, and swept her a formal bow. "Your presence revives me."

Her smile deepened. Then, as if drawn, she turned again to Fin Bheara.

"Beloved…"

Fin Bheara's eyes closed as if in ecstasy. Or perhaps, agony. Soutien could feel the struggle in the king as he fought against the urge to reach for his wife.

"I have missed you," whispered Fin Bheara.

"And I, you," she said. Her eyes filled with longing as she looked at her husband standing less than five feet from her.

Soutien looked away, giving them at least that much privacy. Will and Grace looked away, too.

Amadan, however, stared directly at Oonagh, the hunger in his eyes frightening in its intensity.

"Why do you waste your love on such as him?" he asked in a hoarse whisper. "He is weak, more human than Fey."

Oonagh didn't take her eyes off Fin Bheara, as if she needed to sate herself.

"Perhaps that is why I love him."

Amadan rose and clambered down the small rubble hill, dislodging dust and broken stone. The light from the torches lit his face fitfully, lending him a pied look. "He does not deserve this love," he said, coming to a stop before Oonagh. Even he, however, did not try to touch her.

"And why not?" asked Oonagh. She gazed at Amadan with pity, which seemed to incense the elder Fey.

"Because he betrayed you!" he cried, waving a big hand toward Fin Bheara. "He begat a child on another!"

The ghost of an old pain flitted over Oonagh's face, then disappeared.

"What child, Amadan?" she asked softly.

Fin Bheara stepped forward, a storm of emotions on his face. He hadn't known. Soutien felt a familiar distress. Oonagh had never had children of her own. In the early years, he had wondered if she thought less of him because he wasn't her flesh and blood. That insecurity had eventually worn itself out on the constancy of her love, yet here it was again, resurrected by Amadan. And now, a child... Would Fin Bheara still have wanted him if he had known about the child?

Fin Bheara opened his mouth to speak, but Grace broke in before he could.

"What difference does it make?" she said. Two spots of color high on her cheeks betrayed her anger. Was she trying to protect the king? "It's not Fin Bheara's children we care about, it's Kirwan's!"

Amadan only narrowed his eyes and remained silent.

A cold dread began to seep through Soutien, an awareness of impending doom, though he could not say why. Suddenly, Amadan's grinning face was too much to bear.

"Tell us!" he ordered.

The face Amadan turned to him was full of mystery and madness. His gaze threatened to undo Soutien.

"Are you certain you want to know?" he asked softly, his gaze fixed intently on Soutien's.

Soutien found himself speechless before the abyss of Amadan's madness.

"Yes," said Will in the ensuing silence. "Yes, *I* want to know." Moira lay so very still in his arms. Soutien was afraid to look closely, afraid he would discover that her chest no longer moved. His own breathing came quickly.

"Tell us," said Oonagh. Her face was no longer smiling and the look she gave Amadan made his face darken.

"You already know," he told her stiffly. "You were there."

They stared at each other, she with confusion, he with longing and anger.

And then, Oonagh's face paled and she stepped back from Amadan. "No..." she whispered.

"What?" demanded Fin Bheara. He came to stand by Oonagh, his hand reaching out to support her. He stopped before he could touch her and let his hand drop. "What is it?"

Oonagh was staring at Amadan with loathing. He sucked in a breath but held her gaze.

"This you call love?" she whispered.

His wide face scowled. "This I call necessary," he said.

Fin Bheara went to speak but Oonagh raised a quelling hand, gaze still locked on Amadan's.

"Do you remember Gisèle, Lady Kirwan?" she said.

For a moment, Soutien thought she was talking to Amadan, but it was Fin Bheara who responded. The king nodded jerkily, even though Oonagh was not looking at him.

"She sent for me, all those long years ago," whispered Oonagh. Now she turned to look at her husband. "A favor, she said." She clasped her hands together and held them tightly. She was trembling. "She had a child, a beautiful baby. She said it belonged to her maid-servant and that the father was Fey."

Oonagh took a deep breath, and it seemed to Soutien as if the sunlight surrounding her dimmed a little.

"She asked me to find the child a home in the Fey world, for it would not be accepted among humans."

"Why did she turn to you?" asked Fin Bheara harshly.

Oonagh looked at him, and a hint of exasperation slipped into her voice.

"I came to know her, once you started bedding her."

"You... knew?" said Fin Bheara, his voice faint.

"You knew?" repeated Amadan with undisguised shock.

Oonagh ignored Amadan and gave Fin Bheara a small smile. "I knew about all of them, dear one."

"Then, why?" wailed Amadan. His shape shifted and wavered as if moving past a smoky glass. "Why?"

"Because they meant nothing to him and I meant everything."

Grace stared hard at Oonagh, obviously baffled by her reasoning. But Soutien understood. For Fin Bheara, the sun rose and set over Oonagh. She had been his wife for well over seven hundred years.

Oonagh had never expected her lord to remain physically faithful to her. She had valued his love more than his fidelity.

Will cut through the discussion. "Did she lie?"

Oonagh nodded. "I now believe the child was hers."

"But why lie?" asked Grace.

Amadan's shape wavered even more as he began to laugh again. Then, suddenly, he took on Fin Bheara's shape. It was imperfect, of course, but only in small details.

"Because I told her to," said the false Fin Bheara. Then the eyes were Amadan's again. Soutien blinked and Amadan stood before them as himself.

Fin Bheara snorted his contempt, but his face was pale. For the first time in his life, Soutien thought he saw fear in the king's eyes.

Grace shook her head, obviously unnerved. Will glanced at her, then at Soutien. "So what?" he said. "So what if she lied? The child would have died centuries ago—"

"No," said Soutien softly. The dread coalesced into a cold ball in his belly. "Not if he were half-Fey."

Grace looked at him. "You said 'he'."

Soutien turned to Oonagh, but he couldn't find the words. She smiled at him.

"We so wanted children," she said softly. "Even then, our fertility was dropping. To be handed a child, a baby... I persuaded Fin Bheara that all would be well, that the child would be happy, as would we." Now her eyes filled with tears.

Grace stared at Soutien in dawning horror. "You're the baby? You mean Fin Bheara really *is* your father?"

Soutien's world was falling away from him. He couldn't answer, couldn't breathe, could only look at his father. In Fin Bheara's eyes, he saw the same horrible realization.

"Gisèle..." said Fin Bheara.

"...was a Kirwan!" completed Amadan triumphantly. "She had other children, but Soutien was her eldest."

"Oh my God," said Will. He looked at Soutien, but Soutien couldn't face him. Couldn't.

"Listen!" said Grace suddenly. In the first few seconds, the only thing Soutien heard past the pounding of his heart was the hissing of the torches. Then he heard it, a heavy sound, as of huge wings beating air. Instinctively, he looked up.

"Unseelie!" he shouted, even before he saw their dark outlines against the starry sky.

Amadan shrieked an unintelligible order and Soutien finally understood that he had been delaying, stalling until his winged Unseelie could come for him.

Then Amadan turned toward him and Soutien knew that he intended to take him away, intended to keep him alive until he was ready to go back. It was never Will and his brothers that Amadan had wanted. Rage and grief filled Soutien as he saw that Mack and Aidan had died for nothing.

"Soutien," said Oonagh, her voice very near his ear. He turned jerkily toward her, for the first time realizing that he stood within her shaft of sunlight. Oonagh was so close he could have touched her.

"It must be done now, my darling boy," she said softly. She looked past him and, as if drawn by a force beyond his strength to resist, he turned to follow her gaze.

Beyond the sunlight, in the relative gloom of Fin Bheara's study, Will and Grace were looking up at the sky, their faces mirroring dismay and anger. Amadan was staring straight at him, his eyes narrowed in rage, his hand reaching out as if to stop him. A deep silence surrounded them all. Soutien glanced upward, but the winged ones were no closer. Soutien faced his liege.

His father.

Fin Bheara stood within the sunlight of Oonagh's presence. For the first time, Soutien wondered how much of Fin Bheara's control over time had come from Oonagh. Was it only when she left that Fin Bheara began to weaken?

"Soutien." The king looked at Soutien with pity and love. Soutien knew the look. It was the same one he himself had given Will. Soutien wanted desperately to turn away, to reject that look, that duty. Instead, he bowed deeply.

"Father," he said for the first and last time, and in spite of himself, his voice broke over the word.

Fin Bheara smiled at him and Soutien felt a cool, feather-like touch on his cheek. Oonagh's touch. He glanced at her and although tears brimmed in her eyes, she nodded.

Soutien turned to Fin Bheara. The king opened his arms. Soutien stepped into his father's embrace, feeling the solid warmth of him, the strength in his chest and arms, the stability of his legs.

Then Soutien drew his dagger and moved back slightly. He looked into his father's eyes. Gone was the pity. Fin Bheara clasped Soutien's knife hand with both of his. Together, they plunged   Soutien's dagger into his father's heart.

Sound rushed back like a wave crashing to shore. First came Fin Bheara's agonized gasp. On its heels, Amadan shouted, "No!" just as Will cried, "Look out!" At the same time, Soutien heard the wind whistling past the unfurled wings of a winged Unseelie.

Then he pulled the dagger out and Fin Bheara slumped in his arms, dead.

The last thing Soutien heard before they all plummeted into icy darkness was a soft sob and a whispered "Goodbye," but he couldn't tell if it came from Oonagh, or himself.

❧ THIRTY-FIVE ❧

GRACE was cold. And uncomfortable. The hand she raised to brush something off her cheek came away wet.

Her eyes flew open in sudden panic and she looked at her hand, but it was only water. Not blood.

Relieved, she tried to sit up and groaned at the pain in her side. Ignoring it, she propped herself up on the opposite elbow and looked around. Only then did she become aware of the moaning of the wind around her.

She was on a snow-covered knoll. Below her, oak and fir trees marched downhill toward a small vale. The branches of the fir trees were heavy with snow.

No wonder I'm cold, thought Grace.

A dark straight line cut through the trees and with a great sigh of relief, she recognized it as a cutline for power poles.

"Are you all right?"

Startled, Grace looked over her shoulder. Soutien was approaching, his face glowing. It's morning, she thought. The sun is rising.

Only then did she realize that the moaning didn't come from the wind. It came from the dark, huddled shapes all around her.

"Grace?" said Soutien. He knelt by her side but didn't touch her. "Can you get up?"

"I think so," she said.

"We can't stay here," said Soutien. "It's too cold for you."

You're a fine one to talk, she thought, noting his bare chest.

Only then did she become aware that her dress was soaking wet and beginning to freeze on her. She immediately began to shiver.

"Moira..." she said, suddenly remembering. "She's only wearing a T-shirt..." She accepted Soutien's help, but couldn't help a cry of pain when his supporting hand pressed on her cracked rib.

With Soutien's help, she turned around. The huddled shapes were Fey. Some were groaning and starting to get up, but some remained deathly still. Farther down the hill were more shapes, some grotesque. The Unseelie, she thought. Already a few were on their feet, although reeling. Some stumbled and fell, only to get up and continue down the hill.

Past the trees, maybe half a mile away, were farmhouses surrounded by snow-covered fields that glowed in the sunrise. Beyond the houses was another straight line cutting through the fields. A road. Smoke rose from chimneys and a few windows already shone yellow with electric light. Grace looked down again at the Unseelie stumbling for the trees.

"Where are we?" she asked.

"We're back," he said expressionlessly. "All of us."

Automatically, she looked around the knoll. "But where?" It looked familiar, but at the same time, not.

Soutien shrugged as if he didn't care. "A forest, a park. Perhaps Algonquin Park—it is about the right distance from Kirwan."

A sense of unreality flooded through Grace. After all they had been through, after the days they had marched, could they really be so close to home? But Knockma had been by the sea. Had the sea been closer then?

"Where's Will?" she asked, suddenly overwhelmed. "And Moira?"

Soutien nodded and Grace turned around. Will was thirty feet away and standing. His stubbled face looked gaunt and his eyes were sunken and dark. He looked twenty years older. Then he crouched and picked up Moira. Dread robbed Grace of speech and she looked up wordlessly at Soutien.

"She's still alive," he said grimly, "but barely."

"We have to get her to a hospital," whispered Grace. She started toward Will, her feet crunching in the hardened snow, then stopped. She glanced around the knoll, at the Fey slowly picking themselves up and looking around. Then she looked uncertainly at Soutien.

"Fin Bheara?"

Soutien swallowed hard. For a moment, she thought he wouldn't answer. Then, "Gone. As are all who were dead before the transition. Cathel, too, is missing."

In spite of herself, relief flooded through Grace. They wouldn't have to search for Aidan's body. "What about...?" She nodded with her chin at the still figures on the knoll, now limned by sunlight.

Soutien's expression hardened. "Dead. During the transition."

"And Amadan?"

Soutien's face underwent a transformation so sudden that Grace stepped back. She had never seen raw hatred before.

"He lives. Weakened by the transition, but strong enough to escape." He nodded toward the trees that led further into the forest.

She wanted to ask him more questions, but the look on his face stopped her. Besides, Will and Moira needed her and they all had to get out of the cold. Already her feet were beginning to freeze, in spite of the brown man's shoes.

She glanced at Soutien. Naked to the waist, he still didn't look cold. With a shudder, she turned away and stumbled down the hill toward Will and Moira.

Will looked up as she made her halting way toward him. He held Moira clasped to his chest, as if to share his warmth with her. "You're hurt," he said.

Grace shook her head, and a massive shiver convulsed her, tearing a gasp of pain out of her.

It's my dress, she thought. Too wet, too much exposed flesh. Then she looked at Will's T-shirt and at Moira, her skin ruddy with cold. Soon it'll be white, thought Grace. And we'll have to fight frostbite, too.

"We have to get out of here," said Will.

Soutien stepped up to Will and held his arms out expectantly. The two men stared at each other for a long moment. Then Will wordlessly handed Moira to him.

Together, they made their way down the hill, past the disoriented Fey, past the broken bodies of winged Unseelie, down through the forest into the farmland and finally, to the road.

By the time they reached it, the sun was well up. Grace's feet were frozen and her bare legs under the dress were scratched from punching through the icy crust. Will had to help her up the ditch to the side of the road. There, Soutien handed Moira over and turned back to the trees.

"Where are you going?" called Grace, suddenly afraid. The road looked alien and unfamiliar, as if she'd never seen one before. Where would it take her, now that everything had changed?

Soutien stopped and turned around. Sunlight gleamed on his fair hair and Grace was suddenly reminded of Oonagh.

"My people need me," he said. "I'll see you at Kirwan, when I can." He looked down at Moira's still face, then turned away abruptly. Grace watched as he walked toward the edge of the forest. A movement caught her eye and she looked at the trees themselves. There, peeking out from behind an oak tree was a familiar figure, its too-large features scrunched into a too-small face.

Immeasurably cheered, Grace raised a hand to wave at the brown man. At that moment, a pickup truck came around the curve. Seeing the three of them by the side of the road, the driver stopped.

"You folks need a ride?" the woman asked, her seamed face crinkled in concern.

When Grace looked again, the brown man and Soutien were gone.

***

Soutien stood on the shore, arms crossed, and contemplated the lake. Its solitary island rose in the middle, wreathed in mist. In the slanting light of late afternoon, it wouldn't be hard to imagine a ruined keep brooding in silence, waiting.

He came here every day, away from the camp and its despondent Fey. The mile-long trek was half penance, half escape, and the island, despite its peaceful setting, came to represent all his losses, all his failures.

But it was only an island, inhabited by nothing more than shrews and birds.

The sun was setting and it was time to return, yet still he lingered. They would swarm around him, hounding him with their questions and requests, their fears and petty worries.

Of the Fey who survived the crossing, only the wild cousins fared well. They were used to living outdoors and gathering their own food. As brave as Fin Bheara's Seelie had been in battle, they fell to pieces in the wild. Many of them resisted learning from the wild cousins, as if they expected Fin Bheara to come striding through the forest at any moment and rescue them.

But Fin Bheara was dead and Knockma was gone. That life had disappeared forever, and it was time all Fey accepted it.

They hadn't asked to return to this, their old home, but it had been necessary. Just as it was necessary for Soutien to accept his new role. He did not want to be a leader, but he was the Fey's best chance for survival.

Sensing a gaze upon him, Soutien turned. The brown man waited patiently, standing by an oak tree. A small tension loosened inside Soutien. The brown man had missed three of their daily rendezvous. Even knowing how the little man wandered and explored, Soutien had been worried.

"Cousin," he said.

His presence acknowledged, the brown man joined Soutien on the rocky shore. His gaze took in island, water, and sky, searching. Soutien couldn't bear to watch him.

There were so few animals, compared to the place—the time— they had left behind. Soutien tried to see through the brown man's eyes, tried to understand his grief at the state in which he had found his new/old home. But he was numb to the brown man's heartache. There was too much grief already in his heart to take on more.

He tracked a jet flying toward the setting sun. Even here, in the middle of a national park in northern Ontario, it was impossible to escape human technology.

The familiar despair welled up in him. Of the few hundred who had survived the transition, most clung to the camp he had set up in the park. Although by nature a solitary people, the Fey now sought each other out for comfort. And they looked to him for everything— food, shelter, solace.

He closed his eyes against the beauty of the setting sun. He was no Fin Bheara, able to keep his people unified and safe. The thought of his father brought with it the familiar pain and he rode it out, waiting for the edges to dull.

And what of Amadan? What was he up to while Soutien dithered in the woods? Soutien's only hope was that the Unseelie would be as shocked and disoriented by the transition as his Fey. But it had already been a month. The hiatus would surely end soon.

According to the brown man, the Unseelie were already beginning to move into the human settlements. They were only rumors now, but all too soon, the world would realize that they were real.

But for now, it was enough that the brown man was safe.

"It's good to see you again," he said, and was rewarded by a shy grin. "Where did you go?" The brown man's forays were useful, although he had never been gone so long before.

"I found something," said the brown man.

Something in his voice alerted Soutien. "What did you find, little cousin?"

The brown man looked over his shoulder and only then did Soutien see the two figures lurking in the woods. They were downwind and he could get no scent.

"What are you doing here?" he asked, unable to force a smile to his lips.

Grace glanced at Will, then back at him. "We came to see you." Her hair was short, and she was dressed in warm clothes and sturdy hiking boots. Like Will, she carried a full backpack.

Will said nothing. Instead, he examined Soutien from head to toe, then turned to look at the brown man. Soutien found himself studying the young man. Pain emanated from him in waves. Why had the little cousin brought them here?

A possible reason occurred to him and sudden fear spiked through him. "Moira?"

"She's all right," Grace quickly assured him. She came closer. "She's still in the hospital, but the doctors think she'll make a full recovery."

"It was the goblin poison." Will spoke for the first time. Finished with his examination of Soutien, he pulled his backpack off and set in on the ground, as if he had been invited to stay.

"It took them a long time to synthesize an antidote," added Grace, dropping her backpack next to Will's. "We almost lost her once or twice."

Soutien looked inward for the Moira pain. It was still there, twining around the Fin Bheara and Oonagh pain, though now it was tempered with relief. He closed that door and turned his attention to Will and Grace.

"Why are you here?"

The brown man flinched at his tone and made a move as if to step back into the forest. Instead, he crouched, watching attentively.

Grace glanced at the brown man, then at Soutien.

"We were worried about you," she said.

Once, her words would have warmed him. "How did you know where to find me?"

She shrugged, still eyeing him warily. "We've been hiking through the park for a week, looking for you. Fortunately, our friend here found us and led us here." She nodded at the brown man and smiled.

Soutien frowned. He didn't want them here. He had too much to do. They belonged to a different life now.

"Spend the night," he said abruptly, "but you'll have to leave in the morning." He turned away.

"Wait a minute," said Will sharply. Soutien glanced over his shoulder at him. "That's all you have to say?"

Soutien shrugged tiredly. Once he would have tried to ease Will's suffering, tried to point out that he had only done what needed doing. But Soutien had his own share of guilt to bear, his own demons to fight. Will would have to work his way out of the tangled web of guilt by himself.

"Your presence endangers us," he said. "You must leave as soon as possible."

"Actually," said Grace, stepping in before Will could say anything, "that's the other reason we came."

"What do you mean?" asked Soutien. The sun was almost down. He needed to return to camp.

"We need you to come home," said Will.

Soutien's mind went blank. "Home?"

"To Kirwan," said Grace.

Soutien looked at the brown man, who stared back unblinkingly. "Kirwan is not my home."

"It's as much your home as it is mine," said Will gently.

"This isn't the Fey world," said Grace, waving at the trees around them. "And the Fey can't keep their presence here a secret. The world is already becoming aware that the Unseelie are back."

Will nodded. "They're starting to regroup," he said. "Some kids have seen goblins. And the newspapers are reporting that something big is flying around at night." He looked at Soutien gravely. "People are becoming afraid."

Soutien focused his attention like a searchlight on Will. "What of Amadan?"

"We don't know," said Grace. "But you can be sure he's behind these Unseelie appearances. He's up to something."

They were right, of course. Amadan was up to something while Soutien hid in the woods. It was only a matter of time before his Fey were discovered. And then what? More running and hiding? He'd had enough of secrecy. Enough of pretending he was something else, that the Fey did not exist.

Soutien thought it through. The Unseelie were in the cities. Which meant his Fey could also survive in the cities. But how to integrate his Fey back into the human world? Would they be accepted or hunted down? How would they adapt to so much iron in the world?

"It's a great risk," he said finally. "Only a few hundred Fey survived the crossing. And they've lost everything. How can I subject them to this danger?"

Even as he said the words, he knew he had no choice. As dangerous as reintegration would be, it was the only way to ensure their survival.

Even Will could see that.

"You have no choice," said Will. "You are half-Fey and you've lived here for centuries. You're the only one who can help them adapt. And they will have to, Soutien. Sooner or later, they will have to face the new world."

Soutien looked down at the ground. The enormity of what they were asking—what he knew he had to do—dwarfed him. They had no idea how difficult it would be to keep his Fey safe while integrating them into a world that no longer believed in them.

As if guessing his thoughts, Grace placed a hand on his arm. "We'll be with you every step of the way, Soutien."

"You know the O'Rourke resources as well as I do," said Will. "We can do this."

Soutien looked from one human face to the other, noting the tension in both. Their mission had forced them together, but obviously they had not made peace with each other or with the things they had had to do in the Fey world. In Will's eyes, he saw self-loathing. Until he worked it out and forgave himself, Will would never forgive Grace for her role in his attempted murder of Fin Bheara.

As for Grace, an ineffable air of sadness clung to her, in spite of which Soutien thought she was at peace with herself.

Of all of them, Grace was the one who had best come to terms with her decisions and actions. Her sadness obviously stemmed from her affection for Will.

For the first time, Soutien accepted that he was still linked to these two, and to Moira.

He suddenly found himself smiling. Keeping his Fey hidden was no solution to the problems plaguing both races. It was time to reunite them. That had been the point of Fin Bheara's sacrifice. And Oonagh's.

As for Amadan, Soutien would deal with him when the time came.

"We'll take over the grounds," he warned.

"There's over forty acres," said Will with a grin. "And it's a big house."

"Of course," said Grace, giving Soutien a sly smile, "you'll have to put up with Moira."

Soutien felt himself blush and glanced away from her knowing eyes, catching the brown man's shy smile as he rose from his crouch.

Then Soutien turned toward camp, his friends by his side. It was time to get on with it.

THE END

ABOUT THE AUTHOR

After 35 years in the Yukon, Marcelle Dubé now lives in small-town Alberta. She has published 15 mystery and fantasy novels, including two series. Her short stories appear in a number of anthologies and magazines. Her work has been short-listed for the Derringer Award and the Crime Writers of Canada Award of Excellence for Best Crime Short Story, which she won in 2021 and 2024. She is best known for her Mendenhall Mystery series.

Find out more at www.marcellemdube.com.

NOVELS BY MARCELLE DUBÉ

Mendenhall Mystery Series:
The Shoeless Kid
The Tuxedoed Man
The Weeping Woman
The Untethered Woman
The Forsaken Man
The Wronged Woman

A'lle Chronicles Series:
The A'lle Murders
The A'lle Mutation

Standalone:
Ghosts of Morocco
Identity Withheld
Jilimar
Kirwan's Son
Obeah
On Her Trail
Shelter

A Little Strangeness (collection)